Acclaim for

THE KATROSI REVOLUTION

Winner of **The Realm Award 2022**: Fantasy (*Silverblood*)

Finalist for **The Independent Audiobook Awards 2021**:

Young Adult (*Emberhawk*)

Semi-finalist for **The Realm Award 2021**: Reader's Choice (*Emberhawk*)

"A heartfelt fantasy whose tinges of darkness don't threaten the endearing relationship at its core."

— FOREWORD REVIEWS MAGAZINE

"Brilliant fantasy with a unique and complex world of elemental entities, political machinations, and unlikely love."

— LOREHAVEN

"*Emberhawk's* danger grips, the humor lands, and the romance smolders. Foley examines the beauties and hardships of pluralistic societies, and themes of faith, duty, and cultural expectations are skillfully woven into the narrative. Whether you're looking for an entertaining YA fantasy romp or something a little deeper, *Emberhawk* delivers."

— LINDSAY A. FRANKLIN, Carol Award–winning author of *The Story Peddler*

"Jamie Foley's ability to worldbuild opens an easy door for you to step into her creative world. With descriptions so vivid and beautifully written, combined with a fast-paced and exciting plot, you won't want to miss this new offering from Foley."

— BETH WISEMAN, bestselling and award-winning author for HarperCollins Christian Publishing

"An enthralling story about love in a world on the brink of war. Though I suppose I should warn you that her captivating world building, vivid prose, and compelling plot are certain to lead to sleepless nights and antisocial tendencies."

— ELIZABETH NEWSOM, author of The Torvan Trilogy

"*Emberhawk* has all the ingredients of a great book, tied together beautifully: heart-pounding danger, delicious romance, wonderfully complex characters, a fascinating magic system, and an explosive ending. I cannot wait to read the sequel."

— CATHERINE JONES PAYNE, author of *Breakwater*

"Fantasy at its finest! The rich world-building and gorgeous prose pulled me deep into the story, and the fascinating characters and brilliant story kept me turning pages well into the night. *Emberhawk* has it all: tension-filled adventure, a slow-burn romance, and witty characters who will steal your heart and tug your emotions."

— S.D. GRIMM, author of *A Dragon by Any Other Name, Summoner,* and The Children of the Blood Moon trilogy

"*Emberhawk* weaves intrigue, romance, and vivid worldbuilding into a tapestry of a story that readers will marvel at. The unique magic system, dynamic characters, and slow-burn romance create a riveting read that can't be missed!"

— R.J. METCALF, author of The Stones of Terrene series

"Vibrant worldbuilding and rich cultures make *Emberhawk* sing! Add to that a spunky heroine and snarky hero (not to mention that explosive ending) . . . and when can I read Book Two?"

— GILLIAN BRONTE ADAMS, award-winning author of *Of Fire and Ash*

Lotus Fall

Books by Jamie Foley

<u>The Sentinel Trilogy</u>
Book 1: *Sentinel*
Book 2: *Arbiter*
Book 3: *Sage*
Prequel: *Vanguard*

<u>The Busy Mom Guides</u>
The Busy Mom's Guide to Writing
The Busy Mom's Guide to Indie Publishing
The Busy Mom's Guide to Novel Marketing

<u>The Katrosi Revolution</u>
Book 1: *Emberhawk*
Book 2: *Silverblood*
Book 3: *Lotusfall*
Book 4: *Eldersoul*

<u>Short Story Collections</u>
Steampunk Fairy Tales Volume III: The Elves and the Synth-Maker
The Sun Still Rises: Crimson Stain

LOTUS FALL

THE KATROSI REVOLUTION BOOK 3

JAMIE FOLEY

FAYETTE PRESS

To my mother,
who gave me her smile,
her joy in serving others,
her passion for righteousness,
and prayed over me all of my life
that I would become a strong woman of God.

ROYAL PROVINCE
OF
VALINOR
REDFISH
ISLAND
KOOA RIVER
VERIDIAN PLAIN
WAELYN'S
PYRAMID
ODA'E'S
RANCH
ROANOKE
THE
GNARLED
WOOD
SILVERMEAD RIVER
KATROSI FORESTS
RIVER MOSSU
Navarre
to Darkwood
Jadenvive
Tribal Alliance
Territories
CORIANDER'S
CAMP
TRADE ROUTE
LAKE MOSSU
Rainosek
GRANNY ZELLE'S
RETREAT
Sekoiako
EMBERHAWK
SOVEREIGNTY
PHOENIX BAY
Quin Zamar
RIFT OCEAN

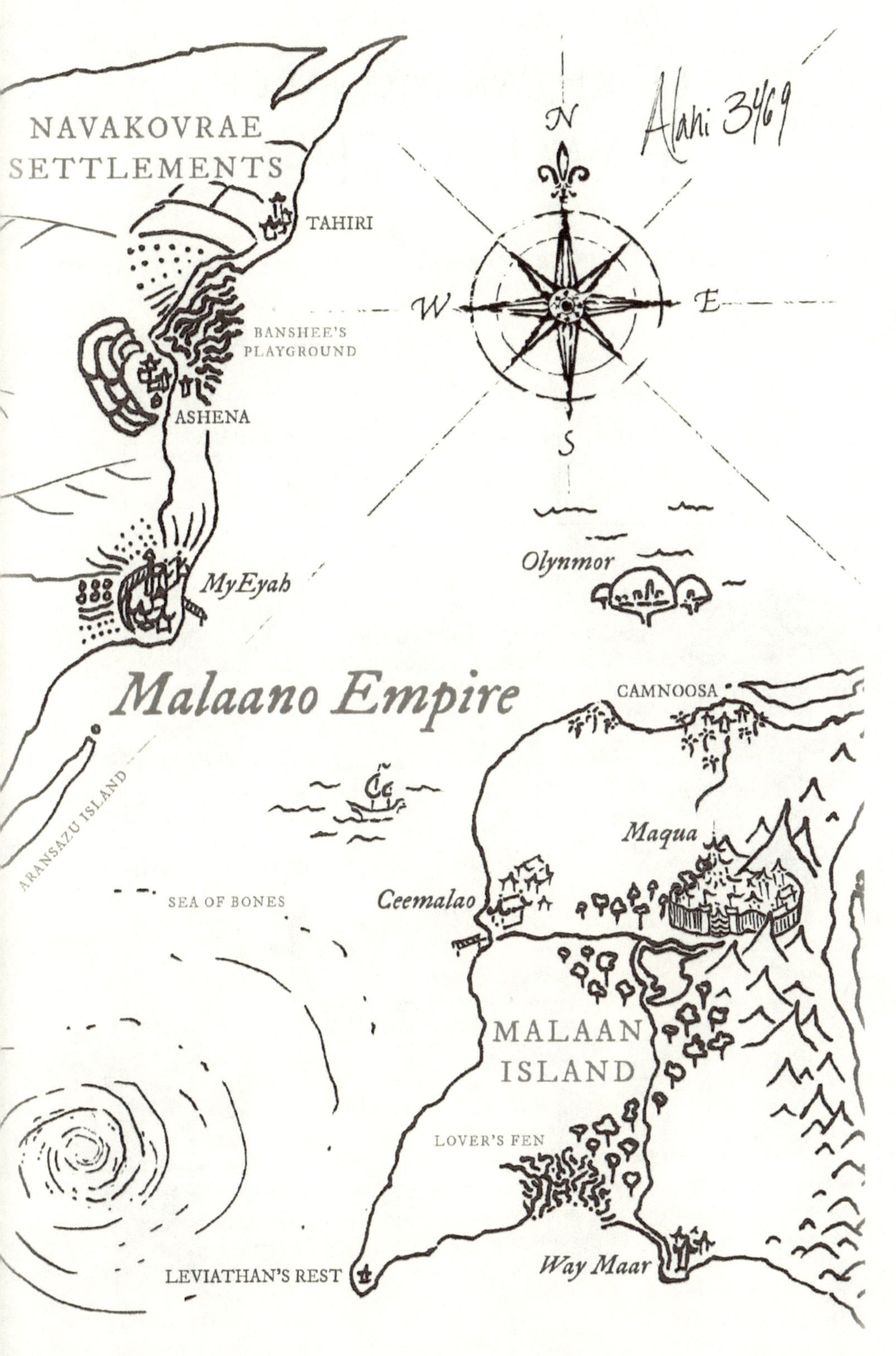

NAVAKOVRAE SETTLEMENTS
TAHIRI
BANSHEE'S PLAYGROUND
ASHENA
MyEyah
Malaano Empire
ARANSAZU ISLAND
SEA OF BONES
LEVIATHAN'S REST
N
W
E
S
Alahi 3469
Olynmor
CAMNOOSA
Maqua
Ceemalao
MALAAN ISLAND
LOVER'S FEN
Way Maar

Emberhawk Monarchy Family Tree

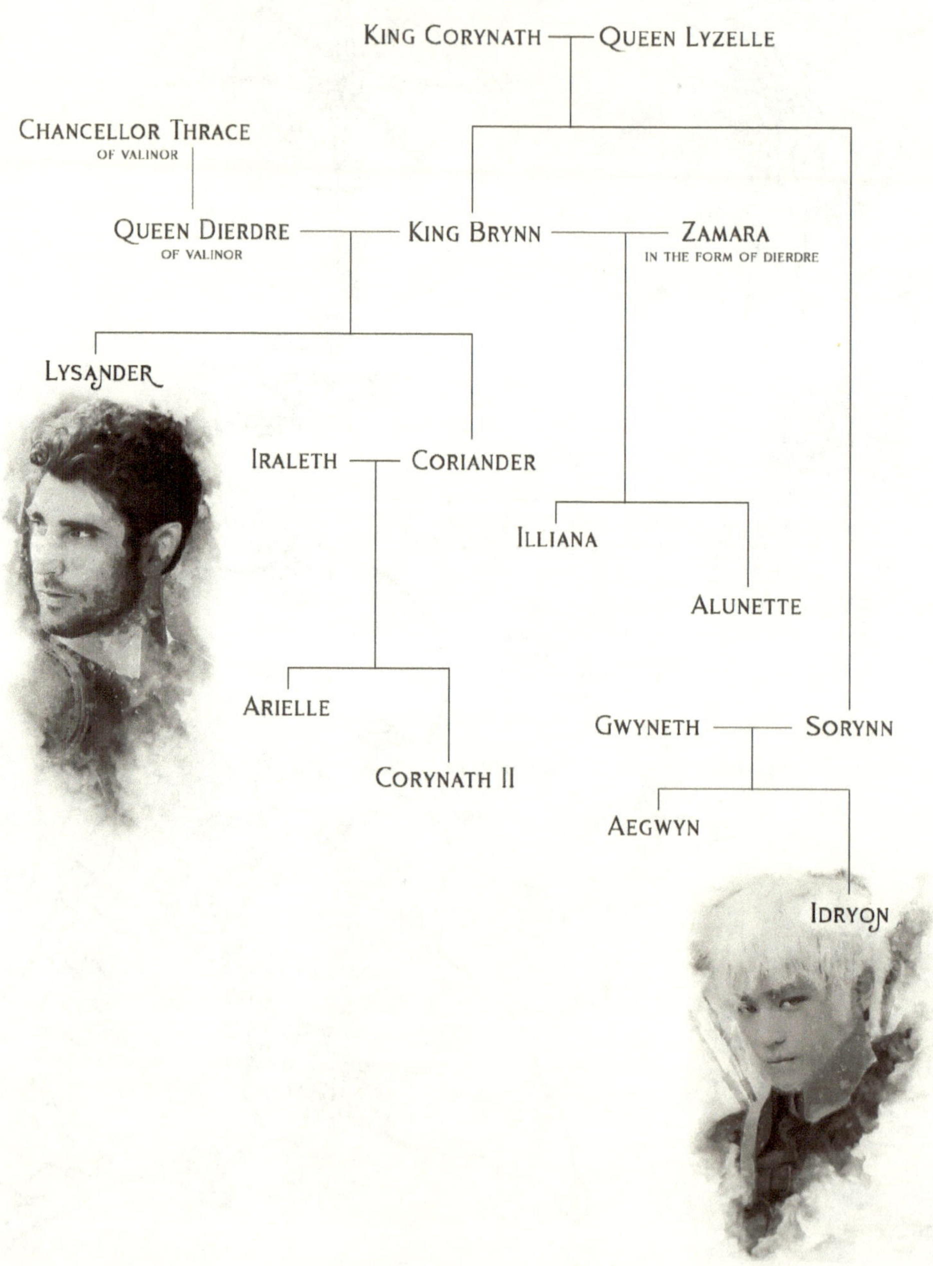

GLOSSARY

AEO — The creator god who formed the physical and spiritual realms and all races therein.

AEO LEYWA AI SHEA — A farewell wish in the Ancient language meaning, 'Aeo be with you and protect you.'

AETHER — A spiritual energy generated by one's soul.

ALANI — The name of the planet on which the story takes place.

AMOS — A semi-mortal shapeshifter who serves as the primary source of power for their element. There is one *amos* for each element.

BALEMBA — A Phoeran word meaning 'butterfly.'

D'HAKKA — A giant tree-scorpion with an appetite for large prey.

ELEMENTALS — Shape-shifting spirits created after angels but before humans, thus their nickname 'second born.' There are one *amos* elemental and seven *trai'yeth* elementals for each of the four elements: Malo (liquid), Terruth (solid), Aris (gas), and Phoera (energy).

RUPERO — Syn-forged coin currency used by the Phoeran tribes.

SYN — The silvery metal in a human's blood that allows them to control their element. Elementals control syn itself as well as their element.

TRACE CAT — An apex predator the size of a lion. They wield the Phoera element to manipulate light, disappearing without a trace.

TRAI'YETH — Shape-shifting lesser elementals who can remove syn from humans and redistribute it. Means 'sealing vessel' in Ancient.

TRIBES — The five tribes that immigrated from Illyria across the Rift Ocean hundreds of years ago: the Katrosi, Emberhawk, Roanoke, Darkwood, and Sekoiako.

XAVI — Like feathered velociraptors with the faces of dragons, xavi are native to the tribal lands and used as mounts by the Malaano Empire.

ZOTH — A frigid region of the spiritual realm occupied by exiled rebel angels, said to be devoid of the creator's light and warmth.

1

VYLIA

Let's go home.

Vylia couldn't breathe. Couldn't think. Couldn't move. The horror would only allow her to stare at Sousuke as he coughed and clung to life.

Blood seeped rhythmically from the wounds in his chest and shoulder. The red stain grew across his armor and dripped into the mud. A Malaano soldier moved, blocking her view.

You look like you're drowning! Poor thing. Lillian's voice slithered through Vylia's mind. *Take my stone. Fill it with your aether. Then the pain will subside, and you can rest.*

Vylia's vision blurred with tears. "Save him," was all she could manage. Could he be saved?

He's already gone, little minnow—

"No," Vylia whispered. "He's still alive. Please!"

Lillian seemed to sigh. *Death is so much more painful for mortals. But if you become my vessel, you will taste immortality.*

Vylia cringed and glared at Sa'alu, who stood still on the muddy road, holding the opalescent Malo stone as if it were a marvel beyond comprehension.

"Please," Vylia called, begging for the Malaano lieutenant to listen to her. "There must be a village somewhere nearby. Bind his wounds and find a healer!"

Sa'alu stared into the depths of the Malo stone, apparently ignoring the bleeding cut in his ankle where Sousuke had stabbed him. He didn't respond.

Be reasonable, my dear. He is beyond saving. But if you let me in, you will want for nothing—especially a man. The false pity in Lillian's voice invoked a violent flare in Vylia's mind.

"You said you were a goddess," Vylia said through her teeth, glaring at Lillian's stone. "What kind of god can't save their own people?"

He's not one of mine. He's a pagan.

Rage pulsed through Vylia. "He's *mine!*"

Oh, come, now. Just because he protected you doesn't mean he loved you.

Vylia's heart lurched. "If he dies, I will never help you. You will never get what you want!"

Sa'alu blinked and turned to look at her. Beyond him, a soldier crouched over Sousuke, though Vylia couldn't tell what he was doing.

Hot tears streamed down her face. She stared up at Sa'alu. "Order your men to take him to a healer immediately," she pleaded. "If you save him, I'll do whatever you want."

A long moment passed, quiet except for Sousuke's labored breathing.

Take my stone and absorb it. Then you will have access to all of my power, and you can save him yourself.

Vylia gritted her teeth. Every second that passed felt like an excruciating eternity. "If he lives, I will do it."

You will willingly become my vessel?

"Yes!" The lie burst from Vylia's lips. Hopefully the devil creature couldn't hear her thoughts or fantasies of casting the water opal into a lava flow and watching it melt into trickles of molten color. She clenched her fists, shuddering with the attempt to control her body and appear genuine. "Stop the bleeding. *Now!*"

Sa'alu's eyes went distant for a long, silent moment. Then he blinked and his gaze seemed to clear, sharpening into a serpentine intellect. "Put pressure on his wounds and bind them," he ordered, turning toward the reptilian xavi that waited to pull the carriage. "Then place him in the carriage and make haste to Sekoiako."

2

BROOKE

Brooke clung to Lysander's waist as he held onto Felix's thick scaled neck. She lay as flat as she could on the wyvern's back, trembling against the frigid whip of the wind on her arms and legs. Lysander's back was her only source of heat—Felix's cold-blooded form offered little protection against the chill.

Had his dragon form always been this cold? When Felix had rescued her from the jungle, clutching her bleeding form within his claws, she'd thought his scales had warmed her with a gentle heat. Or was that just her imagination, since he was a Phoeran elemental?

"How much longer?" Brooke shouted over the wind.

She received no response.

Brooke clenched her chattering teeth together and dared to look down to the landscape below. They were lower now than before.

Gargantuan trees gave way to a lake's shoreline as she watched the forest speed by. Mist floated upward from the gray waters and was sliced by Felix's wing, spinning into whirls behind them. The waters must be Lake Mossu, she guessed, judging by the expansive size of gentle waves that stretched out before them.

Brooke closed her eyes, hoping to stop their watering against the bite of the wind. Anxious thoughts bubbled up within her. How would her people welcome her? With the shame of failure? Understanding felt like too much to hope for. Ulysses's letter had seemed positive, but how much could she really expect from her old rival? Yes, she'd offered him the position of her vice, but she'd assumed that they'd have more time to improve their relationship before anything catastrophic happened.

Like her losing the chiefdom under the worst of circumstances.

Brooke squeezed her eyelids tighter. How she'd longed to stay in Granny Zelle's pyramid, enjoying the solitude and the love of her new husband. The thought of returning to Jadenvive haunted her. It was too soon. She'd rather remain hidden in the jungle. Perhaps indefinitely.

You're shivering. Lysander's thought-voice touched upon her mind.

Warmth blossomed from Lysander's back and wrapped around her like a quilt. More than what naturally emanated from his body. He must be using Phoera for her.

Brooke hugged him tighter and released a slow breath, savoring the heat and closeness. *Thank you.*

I can feel your fear.

Brooke pursed her lips. *I'm not afraid. Just . . . nervous.*

She felt him twist, perhaps to look over his shoulder at her. *You're not alone anymore.*

Brooke breathed in his scent, which mingled with the smell of his leather armor, before the wind could snatch them away. He was a dream come true from a future she hadn't dared to dream. But she'd scarcely had a chance to enjoy it.

We have the rest of our lives to enjoy each other, Lysander said. *Quite a long time, according to my plan.*

Brooke peeked an eye open to see the wind whipping at his dark hair. *Stop reading my thoughts all the time. Can't I have any privacy anymore?*

He turned back and gave her an impish grin from the corner of his eye. *No.*

She felt herself flush, but her retort betrayed her and morphed into a smile. He looked so intimidating while wearing her grandfather's headdress, heavy with wyvern horns and xavi feathers whipping in the wind. It was the height of disrespect for anyone to wear it aside from the late High Chief himself, but how else was Brooke supposed to return it to the Great Hall in Jadenvive while riding on Felix's back? She wasn't about to damage the headdress by stuffing it into a bag after she'd found it displayed like a trophy in Zamara's statue garden of the Emberhawk palace of Quin'Zamar. At least it was Queen Iraleth's garden now, and the palace itself had its former name of Quin'Alor restored.

Brooke wondered how long it would take for Zamara's legacy to be forgotten. Or if some of the Emberhawk people had actually mourned her or her crazed daughter.

She rested her head lightly on Lysander's back. Hopefully the fresh wound in his heart after losing his half-sister would scar over soon. Brooke silently determined to watch him to evaluate what he needed, then support him in every way she could.

He would have made a good king, she thought. Not as a young man, certainly—but now, after he'd learned his lessons. But Brooke supposed everything had turned out fine regardless. Coriander seemed a good man, too, and the type to listen to the advice of his brother. After sufficiently teasing each other first, of course.

Brooke closed her eyes and felt a wayward feather from her own headdress tickle her underarm. Normally she'd have it repaired by a master craftsman after her encounter with the late Darkwood prince, Heron. But she wasn't the chieftess any longer. Her headdress would be retired in the Great Hall as well, beside her grandfather's, ending the line of Stillwind chiefs.

Apprehension and shame smothered her. She took a deep breath and held it. There was no telling how her people would react—if they would believe she'd acted in good faith or not. If she'd intended to flee Jadenvive when they needed her most. If she'd married one of the arsonists involved in burning the city in the Emberhawk attack.

She cringed. Well, what was done was done. She wouldn't apologize for marrying Lysander or saving the Emberhawk people—whom many Katrosi still regarded as enemies. Her actions would likely save lives on both sides in the long run. If that cost was her headdress, her reputation, and her grandfather's legacy, so be it. There was nothing she could do about it now.

"Hey."

Lysander's voice jolted Brooke from swirling dread. She looked up at him as he watched her from the corner of his eye.

"It's going to be okay."

Brooke finally released the breath she'd been holding. *I could be executed if they decide I'm a traitor,* she thought to him.

Lysander's shock blasted through her mind. "There's no chance of that happening."

A small chance.

"No." Lysander shifted uncomfortably, and Brooke was reminded that a slight adjustment in the wrong direction would send them both tumbling to the forest below. Which seemed much closer still, now that she looked.

"But if, by some horrible luck, it did happen," Lysander said, "I would get you out. I seem to have a talent for escaping Katrosi justice."

A laugh escaped her. *So it would seem.*

"We could always live in Quin'Alor. A palace isn't bad for a worst-case scenario." He winked over his shoulder.

Brooke grinned and hugged him from behind. *As long as no one calls me Princess.*

"No promises."

A treetop branch whipped by so closely that it nearly struck Brooke's foot. She jerked back and peered around Lysander, careful to maintain her balance.

"Felix?" she yelled over the wind. Hadn't they just been flying over Lake Mossu? They shouldn't have reached the opposite shore yet.

The wyvern didn't respond.

The trees broke into a sandy beach. Their flight path dipped lower. And lower.

And lower.

"Felix!"

The impact sounded like bones cracking. Brooke was flung off of Felix's back. The world toppled end over end until she was plunged into dark water.

A frigid, wet tomb abruptly enveloped her. Brooke hadn't had the time or awareness to take a full breath. Which way was up?

She haphazardly swam toward the light. Broke the surface. Gasped.

"Brooke!"

She wiped water from her eyes and found Lysander swimming toward her, the horns of his headdress dripping. "Are you all right?"

"Yeah," she sputtered, then nodded as she confirmed her pack still clung to her shoulders along with her spear, which had twisted wildly in its cloth wrapping. "You?"

"Fine." Lysander swam toward the beach. A crumpled body of a dragon lay there, still, after having trailed deep lines through the sand up to the edge of the shoreline. One broken wing floated limp in the water.

Oh, no. Brooke funneled her adrenaline into swimming as fast as she could. She sloshed onto the shore and ran to Felix's side, kicking up sand that stuck to her shins.

The wyvern's form shrank, its scales morphing into orange fur. Soon Felix was a fox again, lying in the crater. His eyes were closed, his breathing ragged.

"Felix, I'm here." Brooke rushed forward and cradled him. "What can I do?"

"Stop . . . Lillian," Felix wheezed. "Don't let her get . . . keystone. If already free, kill . . . her vessel."

Vessel? Brooke took a chunk of silver syn from her pouch and offered it to him. "Here, take this."

The syn lifted and formed thin sheets, and Phoeran script appeared on them like tablets of carved stone. "Deliver these . . . letters," Felix said. "Keep my stone. I can resurrect . . . in seven . . . years. Give my stone to Ryon . . . to be my vessel . . . at that time."

Brooke barely heard him over the panic in her mind. She reached a hand out to his fur. It was cold. "Stay with us!"

"If Lillian is ruling . . . the world . . . when I come . . . back . . ." Felix's voice was so frail that Brooke had to strain to understand him. "I will . . . kill you all."

The green light of Felix's eyes dimmed.

"No." Brooke lifted the fox's limp body and hugged him, willing her own warmth into him. "Please."

The weight in her hands lifted as light blinded her. She wasn't holding a fox anymore. Her hands were coated with a fine silver dust. The sand had turned silver all around them, and the mist glistened with floating shimmers that slowly fell to the earth.

A gleaming emerald was all that remained, lying in her arms.

Tears clouded Brooke's vision. She'd known it would happen. He'd said it would happen. But that didn't make it any easier.

Seven years was too long. That demon, Lillian, would be free by then, if she wasn't already. The Emperor would have conquered the entire continent by then.

She let the tears fall.

Lysander draped his arms around her and held her close. "It's okay. He's not gone forev—"

Brooke waited but Lysander didn't finish. She looked up at him.

He was staring into the tree line. She followed his gaze and realized they must be on a small island in the middle of Lake Mossu, judging by the way the beach curved. But she wasn't aware of any island in Lake Mossu. Was this Lake Mossu at all? The mist was so thick.

Brooke wiped her tears and looked again.

A pair of eyes glowed from the darkness of a rocky cave that loomed above the sand. Serpentine eyes, each one bigger than Brooke's head, fixated on them. But unlike Felix's, these eyes bore long, thin pupils, and a feral hunger.

Her heart seized. *A wild dragon!*

3

KIRALAU

Kira awoke to golden sunlight warming her cheek. She inhaled deeply, and the subtle scent of incense welcomed her into a gentle morning.

Through the mist in her mind, she remembered: she was married.

Married!

Just a few weeks ago, she would have denied that possibility. And yet it felt like so much longer she'd waited for her and Ryon to be together.

Kira turned over, rustling the enormous bed's sheets, looking for Ryon's form among the pillows. But he wasn't sleeping beside her.

She frowned and sat up, gazing around the room. Ryon wasn't sitting at the expansive window that looked down over the colorful marketplace of Quin'Alor—formerly Quin'Zamar—with the docks and ocean to the south, the jungle and mountains disappearing into the misty west. He wasn't at the hardwood writing desk with its quill, ink, and bronze royal seal at the ready. Nor was he eating at the table in the corner, plucking delicacies from the serving tray. There, a melon had been cut into a bird-like sculpture, offering berries and exotic fruits from every crevice. Those delightful chocolate-stuffed pastries and some kind of cured meat were arranged on the side like a work of art.

Was that supposed to be her breakfast? Was this normal for the royal family?

Everything was so beautiful yet so foreign at the same time. Kira had never seen precious stones used to make something as simple as a table before, or the gold-inlaid doorframe, or the mosaic on the floor wherever it was not covered by plush lambskin rugs.

Ryon hadn't batted an eye at any of the decor. And yet she felt something akin to guilt just for sleeping in this room. Others, including the orphaned "root rats," slept in muddy caves. She didn't deserve this luxury any more than they did.

A folded note on the marble nightstand caught Kira's eye. It wasn't sealed, and she was fairly certain it hadn't been there the night before.

She took it and recognized Ryon's handwriting. Phoeran script was scrawled across the page beside inkblots, though it wasn't as sloppy as normal.

Kira groaned. Ryon had mentioned something about wanting to help her become more adept at reading Phoeran. Well, now that she'd married into the Emberhawk royal family, learning their language should probably be at the top of her priority list.

She sat up straight and slowly read:

> *Balemba,*
>
> Sorry for leaving so early. You are so beautiful in your sleep, I just couldn't make myself wake you up. Is that creepy? Well, you're mine now, so deal with it. My admiration of you is *igniciabe.*

Kira didn't recognize that word. She squinted at the letters. *Nici . . .* That portion was in the word for "negotiate." Perhaps *igniciabe* meant non-negotiable?

Her growl was foiled by a treacherous smile.

> Tekkyn regaled me with stories of fish in the ocean that are supposedly as long as boats. Of course it is *lanosh,* but I've never been ocean fishing before, so I thought I'd let him show me the ropes.
>
> He says the fish that are the most *maccipoblado* right now bite early in the morning. We're at Cat's Warf if you want to join. Ask for a palace escort.

I've never had a brother before, so maybe we can avoid killing each other until noon.

Then I'd like to treat you to my favorite street food for lunch. Just me and you.

Ryon

Kira smiled, her loneliness soothed for the moment. It was good that Ryon and Tekkyn were attempting to get along. They'd be wagging their tails one minute and baring their fangs the next. Although that was normal for brothers.

Brothers.

Kira's heart lurched in two opposite directions at once. It hadn't been long since they'd lost Lee. If it was Tekkyn's idea to take Ryon fishing, that was something special. Maybe it was a step on the path to healing.

And Ryon had expressed frustration with hunting since Zamara had damaged his vision. The new lenses Felix had gotten him were growing on Kira, but Ryon complained about them getting in the way of his bow. Perhaps he was interested in learning how to fish as an alternative to provide for his mother, sister, the orphans, and his new wife. But now that Ryon's cousin Coriander was on the throne, surely everyone would be provided for.

They'd been through so much. But now everything seemed bright and hopeful. Peaceful. Perfect.

Kira stretched and reached for her bandana on the nightstand, tying her thick curls back. She moved to the polished bronze mirror that hung from the wall and fixed the butterfly pin Ryon had given her in place.

Something looked warped on her neck. Was the mirror bent? No . . .

Kira frowned as her fingers traced the scar from the burn that Zamara had seared into her neck. It was so ugly. And she would bear it the rest of her life.

But Ryon had married her anyway. The way he looked at Kira made her forget she had the scar at all.

She took a deep breath and tried to exhale her insecurity with it. They had survived. If this was the cost of that miracle, she would take that deal.

Kira turned from the mirror and stared at the quill pin with its brilliant teal xavi feather. She had to write a letter to her mother and grandmother or the dread would eat her alive. She'd gotten married without them in attendance. And she'd married a tribesman, no less, which her mother hadn't been too fond of. Would she ever be forgiven?

She forced herself to cross the expansive room to the writing desk and sit. Opened the inkwell and dipped the quill's nib into the black liquid that smelled like the sea. Took a piece of parchment from the drawer.

In both Phoeran and Malaano languages, she addressed the letter:

> Oda'e of Navarro of the Navakovrae people

He wasn't "Commander" anymore because that title was from the Malaano army, right? And he was certainly branded a traitor now, as the leader of the Navakovrae Resistance.

She didn't know what else to write. It would have to do.

> The Great Hall
> Jadenvive
> Katrosi

Kira grinned as she wrote. Jadenvive was still in Katrosi territory, despite the Empire's best effort.

She blew on the ink, encouraging it to dry before she flipped it over and wrote:

> Dad,
>
> I've taken Ryon's hand in marriage. I'm sure you already heard that the rightful heir is on the Emberhawk throne—Ryon's cousin. We are safe in the palace. Everything is so beautiful and elegant

here. There are many wonderful foods

Kira realized she was blabbering. She swallowed a knot of nervous energy as she struggled to finish phrasing the sentence and form the next.

                                                              and I am
            well provided for. I am so happy!
                 I hope you and Mom approve. I'd love for her
            and Granny to come and visit, and you, of course,
            if the war effort allows.

Her writing felt stiff. She'd never talk to him like this in person. Why had she written that she hoped Oda'e approved of Ryon? He had already approved their *evadir,* and he knew that carried with it the intent to marry.

It was her mother Inowae's reaction she was truly worried about. Thus Kira's decision to write the letter to Oda'e instead. Hopefully he could convince his wife that Ryon was a good catch. Inowae had acted like Ryon was a gift that had fallen from above when he'd first visited the ranch, but Inowae had also been mourning the loss of Lee at that time, and her entire demeanor had been smothered with grief. Kira's mind was constantly going back and forth like a dog's tail on the subject, remembering Inowae's happy reaction to the news that her daughter was finally courting a man, then doubting her memory entirely.

Kira shook her head in an attempt to return her thoughts to the present. Oda'e might be the only one who knew where Kira's mother and grandmother were right now. Surely he'd made them evacuate the ranch after revealing the Navakovrae Resistance. Not only would Oda'e's family be targeted by the Empire, but being on the border was dangerous enough.

A thought suddenly occurred to Kira: Inowae had been pressuring her to get married for years. She'd played matchmaker with every empty-headed boy in Navarro. She'd probably be over the moon that Kira had finally found a husband. A Phoeran husband . . . but one of royal blood. Surely Inowae would think Ryon better than a farm boy with nothing but drought-starved cattle to his name?

Kira closed her eyes and decided to try and think the best of her mother. To direct her thoughts in a more positive direction. There was no use worrying about what her mother and grandmother thought when there was a good chance they would be delighted and proud.

> I love you all. Please be safe. Hope to see you soon.
> Kiralau of Navarro

Oops. She'd always been Kiralau of Navarro, the nearest town. Was she Kiralau of Quin'Alor now? Were they going to live here permanently? She had barely given it any thought yet.

Well, she was Ryon's now, and she'd heard him identify himself as a Katrosi citizen of Jadenvive more than once. Would he want to live there? Surely not until the war was over and it was safe again.

> Kiralau of ~~Navarro~~ ~~Quin'Alor~~ to be determined

Well, that wasn't her best letter. But she wasn't sure that starting over would improve anything.

Kira folded the parchment and inspected the red wax and Emberhawk royal seal—an image of a fiery bird. She knew how the wax cauldron was supposed to work, as a curious girl who'd studied many tribal designs in schematic scrolls, but she couldn't find a match to light the wick and warm the wax for pouring.

Of course the Emberhawk royalty didn't need matches to light fires. They were all silverbloods with the ability to invoke fire on a whim.

Kira pursed her lips in annoyance. Well, she wasn't sure if it was appropriate for her to use the royal seal, anyway.

She plucked fruit from the serving tray and enjoyed the foreign flavors—some more than others. She wished Ryon were there to tell her whether the seeds and skins were safe to eat.

The washroom gleamed with polished stones of many colors, and Kira recalled how to use the running water from her experience in Waelyn's—rather, Zamara's—pyramid in the Gnarled Wood. As Kira washed, she wondered why Zamara had built the pyramid there. It didn't make much sense. But then, Zamara had arguably been insane.

After donning the most modest Emberhawk silk garments she could find in the wardrobe, Kira was finally satisfied with her appearance, though unsure if she'd tied the red sash around her neck properly. At least her scar was covered.

She grabbed her pack, a strange serrated spoon, and half of a yellow citrus fruit drizzled with salt crystals and honey. She opened the heavy chamber door with her shoulder and felt her face contort at the tartness of her first bite of the fruit.

"Oh, good morning, my lady!" a short young woman called from down the hall. Her dress swished as she scurried toward Kira and bowed. "Is there anything I can do for you?"

"Good morning," Kira returned in Phoeran, feeling eased at the girl's excited expression. "What is this fruit called?"

"Pomelo, my lady."

"It's very good," Kira said. It was sticky, though. Maybe not the best choice for a road snack.

Kira dug for her letter in her pack. "Do you know how I could send a letter to Jadenvive?"

"I can take care of that for you, my lady."

"Oh, thank you. And do you know where Cat's Warf is?"

"Yes, my lady. It hosts a popular fishing pier on the eastern beach."

Kira wished she had a map. "Can you tell me how to get there?"

"I'll arrange an escort for you immediately."

4

SOUSUKE

Sousuke awoke to pain. It thrummed with every heartbeat, filling him, seeping from a wound in his chest.

It felt dangerously close to his heart. To his core. Did he have a core?

Regardless, he knew the wound would be fatal. He could feel the weakness in his limbs, the shallow desperation in every breath, the fog clouding his mind. He must have lost a terrible amount of blood.

Sousuke gritted his teeth. He'd known they couldn't escape the carriage once it was surrounded. But he could have used his element to fight them. To save himself.

The idea was almost as revolting as the feel of his open wound. He'd sworn never to use his element. Or *any* element lurking in his blood. Grasping that power would mean acknowledging that he was descended from pure evil. He would rather die.

Focusing through the haze of agony, Sousuke discerned his surroundings. He was lying in an uncomfortable position on the small floor of a carriage, which he assumed to be in motion as it rattled and bumped beneath him. His legs, too long for the tiny space, were folded and flopped to the side. He didn't dare try to move them, though his whole body ached to be repositioned.

A young woman was curled up, asleep on the carriage seat above him. Dark hair fell over the smooth skin of her perfect face.

By the falls, she was beautiful.

Sousuke squeezed his eyes shut. No, Princess Vylia wasn't beautiful. She was off-limits. She was a mission.

A mission he'd failed.

He bit the inside of his lip, creating a new distraction of a different pain. He might have been willing to die as a mortal, rejecting his forefathers as one final act of rebellion. But what had his defiance proved or achieved? Only that he was more stubborn than a mule-bear.

He hadn't realized in that moment that his decision had doomed Vylia as well. Now that he was going to die, she would be alone. Mourning the loss of her last companion in a foreign land. Helpless.

Now her captors would be her only company, and they would bring her to her father to be executed in secret. Her supposed death at the battle of Jadenvive was the emperor's excuse for the invasion of tribal lands. If the people learned that their princess was alive, they might not support her father's vengeful war.

So the Imperials would do anything to kill her secretly, quietly. And the Lotusfall would do anything to save her.

Except, apparently, in his case, use his own power.

Sousuke cursed himself. Dying to prove how much he hated the *trai'yeth* did nothing for Vylia. He had to live. To protect her.

It was already too late, though—he could feel the darkness creeping back into his vision. But if by some miracle the creator allowed him to live, he would use *every* power within himself to escape the Malaano snakes that had captured them. And destroy them.

Even if it meant drawing upon the ancient evil that festered in his veins.

Then Vylia would realize what he truly was. And any hope of a relationship with her would be gone.

But at least she would be alive.

Creator, help me . . . By some miracle, if you let me live, I will never hold back again.

5

BROOKE

Brooke stared into the eyes of the wild dragon, unmoving, as it watched her and Lysander from a cave beyond the mist.

This island wouldn't just be Felix's grave, but the death of all of them.

The reptilian eyes didn't blink. Didn't move. Brooke knew a young dragon could cross the distance before she could react. She waited, not daring to breathe.

Why wasn't it moving?

A second pair of eyes appeared in the darkness. Even larger than the first.

Lysander moved between Brooke and the dragons, obscuring her view of them.

She scrambled to her feet, hastily stuffing Felix's emerald into her soaking pack, and grabbed at her spear. The cloth that held it to her pack was tangled.

A deep, rumbling sound undulated over the sand. Brooke looked up and her heart nearly burst at the sight of an elder dragon towering over Lysander, fixated on him. He gripped a dagger in his hand, as if that could defend them from the beast any more than a blade of grass could.

Brooke's terrified mind couldn't form a prayer. Just a constricted scream of the creator's name.

But the dragon's jaws didn't open, and its serpentine neck didn't lunge. Its massive head tilted as it blinked slowly, still focused on Lysander. Then on her.

Brooke noticed its saddle then. Aged leather straps looping around its muscular wings and thick chest, artfully crafted to avoid its spikes.

Her breath tumbled out as she recognized her grandfather's dragon. The wyvern matriarch who'd disappeared along with High Chief Torvyn. What was her name . . . ? Beryl.

It's okay, Brooke thought to Lysander, though her pulse still pounded through her. *I know her.*

The great beast dipped its head and slowly approached Brooke, slitted eyes peeled, until its nose was within arm's reach. It inhaled, and the strength of its wind sent Brooke's wet braids fluttering toward it.

"Beryl, it's me," Brooke said, bowing low. "Do you remember?"

The dragon lifted its head and a guttural noise rumbled from its nostrils. It mimicked Brooke's bow.

"Yes, we are friends." Brooke felt herself shake with relief. "Have you been hiding here all this time?"

"Do you want to tell me what's going on here?" Lysander murmured.

This is my grandfather's wyvern, Beryl, Brooke thought to him, hardly able to believe her own words. *She must have survived, and . . .* Brooke reached deep into her memories. Was this the secret place where her grandfather would take her as a child to play with the baby dragons? She remembered sand castles and the hatchling that had bitten her finger. *This might be the home of her brood.*

Brooke reached a hand up to the dragon's enormous face. "I missed you! I thought you were dead."

Beryl lowered her head until Brooke could touch the bumpy scales of her nostrils. Her eyes fixated on Lysander and a low growl tumbled from her throat.

No, she wasn't fixated on Lysander, but the headdress he wore. Torvyn's headdress.

Take off the headdress, Brooke thought to her husband. He slowly complied.

"I'm sorry," Brooke whispered.

A memory, much more vivid than her own, pressed upon Brooke's mind. She saw a vision of a boy, running away before tripping and falling face first in the sand, then laughing.

Then another memory of the same boy, now a young man, offering an enormous slab of red meat. *"You deserve it, Ber."*

The same man again with a beard, wearing a chief's headdress. *"How do I look?"*

Another memory—a dark twilight with torches and drums. *"Ready to fight the blood-hawks?"* The man put a hand on her muzzle. *"They are sacrificing children. We have to stop them. But do not eat them—they are our brothers."* The man swung up on her saddle. *"They will return to the light by their choice or our arrows."*

Then his beard was much longer, and he beamed with pride as he held up a little girl with brown hair. *"Meet my granddaughter! Think we can find a playmate?"*

Brooke choked on emotion. This beast recalled her grandfather's face more vividly than she did.

She closed her eyes and allowed tears to fall as she spread her fingers over Beryl's nose. She recalled her last memory of Torvyn—on Beryl's saddle, waving goodbye before flying from Vanya's platform in Jadenvive and soaring over the distant trees.

Beryl made a sound like a whine, high-pitched and mourning.

Brooke leaned in and touched her forehead to the dragon's. "I miss him, too."

"Are you . . . communicating with this dragon?" Lysander whispered.

Dragons can share memories with us, Brooke thought to him as she removed her hand and swiped at a tear. *It's how they are tamed and bonded.*

"Dragons can use aether?" Lysander said, incredulous.

Brooke chuckled at his expression. *Trace cats use Phoera.*

"Yeah, but . . ." Lysander huffed as if to give up, at a loss for words. He cautiously sidestepped around Beryl, examining her flank. "I thought dragons were extinct."

I did, too. Brooke took a steadying breath and smiled up at Beryl as she extended to her full height—easily taller than four men stacked head-to-toe. *I'm so glad she survived . . .* She decided not to try and ask Beryl the memory of whatever fate Torvyn had met. Perhaps another time.

"She must have been wearing this saddle for years," Lysander said, leaning forward and squinting but not daring to touch the aged leather straps and metal rings. "We gotta get this off."

Oh, no. Is it hurting her? Brooke rounded Beryl and ducked under her wing, looking at the worn scales beneath the saddle's joints. But aside from some discoloration of the scales—their dark gleam had dulled and color lightened—Beryl didn't appear to have suffered injury. Brooke marveled at the craftsmanship. Each leather strap and buckle had been placed to compliment the dragon's anatomy.

Brooke reached for a buckle near the base of Beryl's neck. *I might need your help with this. It looks really ti—*

She hiccupped as she noticed a second wyvern sniffing her from behind. An enormous black face hovered just above the sand, nearly her height with its horned head alone. Wide blue eyes shone brilliantly from glinting jet scales.

Brooke knew those eyes. Except now they didn't belong to the hatchling who'd bit her finger and destroyed her sand castle. The young drake before her was nearly as big as his mother.

"Onyx?" she breathed.

The black dragon rumbled a low tone and closed his eyes.

Brooke swallowed her fear and reached out to gently touch the cold scales between his eyes. She recalled one of her earliest memories: watching a dragon egg, as tall as her five-year-old stature, crack and fall apart. Blue eyes blinking sideways within the darkness of the shell.

A memory not her own overcame her mental vision. She saw herself as a girl. *"We did it, Onyx!"* Young Brooke jumped in excitement, then grabbed the viewer's head and rubbed her knuckles between his eyes. *"We're officially bonded now. We're gonna be friends forever!"*

Brooke stumbled a step back as the vivid memory faded, returning her to the island of mist. She blinked down at the hopeful blue dragon eyes and grinned. "Friends forever." She rubbed the same spot, as she'd done countless times as a child, and Onyx purred.

"I understand why you Katrosi won the Sacrificial War," Lysander said, "now that I see your secret weapons."

Brooke couldn't stop smiling. *This is my dragon, Onyx! We bonded at a young age. I thought I'd never see him again.* She leaned close to Onyx's face and sent him the memory of Lysander carrying her into Granny Zelle's pyramid, exhausted and bleeding, and the birth of love she'd felt for him in that moment. "Lysander is mine, okay? My mate."

Onyx focused on Lysander and inhaled. Then he tilted his maw upward and unfurled his wings.

Brooke recognized the threat display and ran between them. "Hey, now! Yes, he's worthy. He is good. Friend." She reached up and ran a hand along his dark wing. "Look at that wingspan! Wow, you've grown. How handsome!"

Onyx sat up straight and trilled proudly, stretching his wings further in an even more exaggerated display.

Lysander shuddered as Brooke cooed more motherly admirations. "This thing is death with wings," he muttered. "I'll remember never to get on your bad side."

Brooke's grin stretched ear to ear as she cuddled into Onyx's neck. "That's right. You're still a good boy, aren't you? You're not wild. You're a good boy."

Onyx's scales rumbled with a contented purr, and childlike joy blossomed inside her.

"Felix must have meant to land here," Lysander said. "I guess you didn't remember how to visit this place, or you would have done so."

Brooke's happiness crashed as she remembered Felix. Then she realized that, although Onyx's glossy scales shone at any opportunity from sunlight peeking through the mist above, the effect was magnified wherever she touched. She looked at her hands. She was still covered in powdery silver syn.

Lysander moved closer to Brooke, slowly, keeping his distance from Onyx's jaws. "I'm sorry. We'll get him back in a few years."

Seven years. Brooke took a shuddering breath as she looked down at herself. She looked like a ghost.

Sorrow bubbled up. But more swiftly, her rational mind sliced through her emotions, shutting them down and putting them in their place to be dealt with later. Or never.

You can use this, right? Brooke cleared her throat, wondering if the syn was now coating her lungs. She looked back at the beach, wounded with a long scar at the crash site, which ended with a crater filled with silver.

"Yeah . . . I shouldn't let it go to waste." Lysander shifted his weight awkwardly. "We will honor Felix's memory by continuing his mission. He was emphatic that we have to recover the keystone and prevent Lillian from using it to free herself from the Malo stone. Right?"

Right. Brooke swallowed firmly, as if to reinforce the seal on her sadness. *The keystone was stolen from the treasury. We have to get to Jadenvive and ask Ulysses for any information they have to track it down.*

"Okay." Lysander glanced about their surroundings. "The only problem is . . . We appear to be stranded on a small island covered with mist, which I don't recall seeing on Ryon's maps." He put his hands on his hips. "We could try to build a raft . . . but which direction would we paddle in? Or we could try the cave." He made a face at the dragons' lair.

Brooke inspected Beryl's saddle, comparing her size and shape to Onyx's body. It had been custom-made for her, but it could work . . .

"What do you think, buddy? Do you know the way to Jadenvive?" Brooke shared a memory of the vertical city with its platforms and bridges suspended within the heights of three giant white-bark trees. She remembered an aerial view from her last dragonflight with her grandfather. Since then, the city walls had expanded around its roots, and the surrounding forest had been cleared more as defensive space from forest fires and d'hakka, allowing more room for newly plowed crop fields, but Onyx should be able to recognize Jadenvive if he'd ever flown over it before.

Onyx gave an affirmative growl.

"Excellent," Brooke said. "Let's see if we can get you saddled up."

6

KIRALAU

By the time Kira found Cat's Warf, she understood why Ryon had said in his letter for her to get an escort from the palace—and why she should have waited for it rather than going off on her own after getting directions. Even though she wore a traditional Emberhawk white dress with flowing red and gold sashes, she still received a few guarded looks. She'd just begun to worry that someone might recognize her from her and Ryon's wedding. What might someone do to the newest member of the Emberhawk royal family, found wandering the streets alone, during a time of political turmoil?

Kira's hand frequented the hilt of her d'hakka stinger dagger, hidden beneath the folds of her dress. She'd much preferred the Katrosi pants and leather split-skirt. So much more practical.

A sigh of relief warmed her lips as she found a sign that read in flowing script:

CAT'S WARF

King Lysander's pride of trace cats

would feast upon coral trout

when they returned annually

to lay their eggs.

Yes, after re-reading it twice, Kira was pretty sure it said, "King Lysander." Perhaps Ryon's cousin's namesake?

Laughter sounded from beyond the sand dunes. Kira dodged the tall grasses with beige tufts until a pier came into view with a small structure for shade, which looked as if the salty ocean winds had been wearing it down for a lifetime. Kira squinted and saw two long, thin poles waving from the end of the pier like antennae.

With a look over her shoulder, Kira picked up her dress and jogged across the sand, leaving her worries behind.

Unfortunately, Ryon and Tekkyn weren't talking as she approached, so she couldn't eavesdrop. The creaking of wooden boards of the pier also made sneaking up on them impossible. Disappointed, Kira approached and admired Ryon's profile instead. Reflected sunlight from the ocean gleamed on his wind-tousled silver hair. Fiery orange eyes turned and landed on Kira, and a bright smile lit his face. "Hey, *balemba*. Where's your escort?"

Kira deliberately dodged his question and wrinkled her nose. "Ugh, what's that smell?"

Tekkyn harrumphed and pulled on his fishing line. "That, my landlocked sister, is the scent of freedom."

Kira found the source of the smell to be a barrel nearby, full of water and long, blue fish. "What do you do with them? Surely people don't eat things that smell so disgusting."

Ryon looked astonished. "Do you really not eat fish?"

"Not much," Tekkyn said. "The ranch is far from any coast . . . We have creek beds and tanks that only fill up when it rains. And the Silvermead River is a bit too close to d'hakka territory for comfort."

Ryon turned to Kira, incredulous. "Have you never eaten fish?"

Kira approached the edge and looked down at the waves, surprised at how high up they were. "I had some in Navarro once. I didn't like the weird flaky texture."

"Okay, change of plans." Ryon reeled in his fishing line. "Fish tacos for lunch. Immediately."

Ocean breeze filled Kira with a new scent, and she gazed over the flat horizon, spotting a ship in the distance. "What's a taco?"

Ryon's expression was somewhere between exasperated and horrified. "Don't worry, my young wife. I shall deliver you from this tacoless existence."

Wife. Kira's heart melted like chocolate cream in the afternoon sun. She couldn't help but smile as Ryon set his fishing pole in a wooden rod holder.

"How nice to have a husband to dote upon me," Kira said. "Tekkyn, are you ever going to get married? Perhaps you could find a nice flounder to wed?"

Tekkyn harrumphed, again. "You've been married for two seconds and you're already flaunting it?"

Kira's grin turned devilish. "You've been teasing me for years. Fun, isn't it?"

Tekkyn remained sitting with his back toward her, facing the sea. "I think I'd rather find a nice bass. I have my eye on one."

"Wait, what?" Kira said. "Who?"

"Y'all have fun," Tekkyn said. "Bring me back a taco."

"Oh, no you don't!" Kira marched forward, trying to get a look at her brother's face. "You tell me who she is right now!"

"Get me that spicy sauce, too," Tekkyn said.

Kira leaned out in front of him. "Is she Malaano? Katrosi? Emberhawk?"

"She likes her privacy."

"You're bluffing. You're a lying fork-tongue."

"Well, yeah, but not about this."

"Tekkyn'ashi, you—"

His deep laugh cut her off. "You get married and suddenly turn into Mom, Frizz?" He reached out to tousle her hair.

Kira jerked back, holding on to the butterfly pin Ryon had given her within the dark curls. "Don't you dare touch my hair! I will destroy you."

Tekkyn grinned. "Love you too. Extra spicy, eh?"

"Get your own taco," Ryon said. "I have a meeting after lunch." He took Kira's hand and began walking down the pier toward the beach.

"I'm headin' back to Navarro today," Tekkyn called after them.

Kira stopped. "Today?"

"Yup. Dad needs me." Tekkyn leaned back, grabbed his wide-brimmed hat with his free hand, and rested it low on his brow. "He's settin' up the Resistance there. It's go time."

Worry creeped into Kira's chest and lodged in her gut. "You be safe, now."

Tekkyn waved. "Y'all behave."

Kira rolled her eyes, then grinned at the feeling of her hand in Ryon's as he gently directed her away from the shore. If being alone with him meant enduring a lunch of fish, it would be worth it.

"So, what do you think?" Ryon asked.

Kira watched her step, feeling the heat of the sun-baked pier through her thin sandals. "Of what?"

"Of the city." He watched her from the corner of his eye as he stepped down onto the sand, offering her support with his hand.

"Oh, it's lovely," Kira said as she stepped down. "I've never seen such beautiful curves in the architecture, or so much glass. And the plants that grow here are so different—I've never seen the majority of them. Like that one!" She pointed to a large bush growing from where the pier met a nearby sand dune, where plumes of flowers erupted from purple to pink to brilliant orange. "I have a lot to learn about the culture, but I love it. Just have to get used to the clothes."

"They look great on you," Ryon said, looking well-dressed himself with a royal sash across his chest.

"Do you think he was lying?" Kira whispered, as if Tekkyn could overhear her over the distant crash of the waves. "Have you noticed him actin' sweet on anyone?"

"'Sweet?'" Ryon looked amused. "No. He hasn't mentioned anyone."

"Ugh. I can't decide if I love him or hate him. He still teases me incessantly, as if we're still kids."

Ryon chuckled. "Sounds like a good brother, yeah?"

Kira almost said Lee wasn't like that. But the younger brother they'd lost in the first battle for Jadenvive had teased her plenty, too. The pang of loss squeezed her heart.

But Lee would surely be happy for her, if he could see her now.

She took a deep breath and released it. "Yeah. Of course I love Tekkyn. But if you tell him I said that, I will retaliate."

Ryon laughed. "I always wanted a brother. I was jealous of Lysander and Coriander growing up, even though the three of us were practically brothers." He gazed toward the morning sun. "So I'm trying not to be awkward with Tekkyn and ruin it. I can't actually call him *brother*, right?"

"I... don't know," Kira said. "Do you think Aegwyn will call me *sister*?"

"Absolutely."

Kira smiled. "I haven't seen her or Gwyneth since the wedding. Are they staying in the palace?"

"Yeah. Poor Aegwyn is shaken up from what Xavier did during the fight with Illiana. Even though it's obvious now he wasn't going to hurt her." Ryon looked down at the black sand in thought, and Kira wondered if that awful man who'd kidnapped Ryon would recover from his injuries. She hoped not. Although she supposed that things had worked out all right.

"If I see her in the palace, I'll see how I can help her," Kira said. She let go of Ryon's hand to take a sandal off and cautiously set her foot on the sand. It wasn't as hot as she'd expected. The grains seemed larger than the sand at the bottom of the Silvermead River. And it didn't stick to her feet as readily.

"Have you never been to a beach before?" Ryon asked.

"Not one with dark sand like this." She dug her toes into the sand and enjoyed the sensation. "I always wanted to go to Aransazu. But it's hard to vacation when you live on a ranch. You can't just leave all the livestock. But once, my mom's cousin's family came and watched our place and we taught them to do all our chores, and we went to the northern coast. We could actually see Valinor in the distance."

Ryon brightened. "Really? You could see the mountains?"

Kira swooned at the way the sun hit his face. "No, the castle on Redfish Island. It sticks out from the cliffs over the coast."

"Wow," Ryon breathed, staring into nothing as he appeared to envision it. "Funny that I've never been there, considering Lysander and Coriander's mother was from there."

"Wait, so there's such a thing as a place that you haven't already been to?"

Ryon snorted. "Yeah, Brooke hasn't had a reason to send me to spy on Valinor yet... Well, I guess she lost her chance."

Kira brushed her foot off, leaning into Ryon for support as she replaced her sandal. "What kind of job do you want now?"

"I dunno. I'm a man of the wilds. But I don't want to be alone so much anymore." He winked at her. "I'm sure Cori could hook me up with some pointless government job. But I couldn't be happy with something like that."

"I'm sure he could figure somethin' that would use your skills," Kira said. "Kings always need spies."

Ryon raised an eyebrow at her. "Who said I was a spy?"

It was Kira's turn to snort. "You're gonna play that game 'til we're fifty, huh?"

"At least seventy-two." Ryon offered her his arm as they crested the sand dune. "I hope Brooke is okay. I wish they would have had a big wedding I could have crashed."

He still thinks about her frequently, Kira thought. She'd felt jealous once, but she didn't feel any threat from the former chieftess. "Do you think of Brooke like an older sister?"

Ryon blinked. "I guess I do. Well, she just married my cousin, so . . ."

"They're an odd couple, huh?"

Ryon chuckled. "I don't think I've ever seen Lysander so happy in my entire life. I wonder what they'll do for their honeymoon." He waggled his eyebrows at her. "I wonder what we'll do for *our* honeymoon."

Kira grinned wide. "You just mentioned Valinor. Mountains and castles! And snow would cut this heat pretty good."

"Yeah, but we have a nice view of Sleeping Panther from my room. And snow isn't all that."

Kira recalled that the nearby flat-topped volcano was named Sleeping Panther. "How is snow not a big deal? Do you get snow here? I would think a jungle like this wouldn't get any snow."

"I can make snow anytime it rains," Ryon said.

"Oh." Kira had forgotten that the Phoera element was the manipulation of energy, so Ryon could make things cold just as well as he could make them hot. She wondered if she'd ever stop being surprised at the diverse abilities of his magic. "You'll have to show me that sometime!"

"Can do." Ryon led her toward a break between the houses that dared closest to the shoreline. "What about the Moon Festival? Have you been since you were little? And it sounds like your dad is in Navarro."

Kira ducked under a creeping vine that spilled out from a window planter. "No, it'd be too dangerous to go back to Malaano territory. I'm worried for Tekkyn." She wondered how dangerous her own ranch was, with its location on the Katrosi border, which was now a battle line. Surely Oda'e had evacuated Inowae and Granny to Navarro. What would become of their cattle? Would the Malaano soldiers butcher them for food?

Balemba, if you only knew how many times I've been in Malaano territory."

"And how many times have you been captured?" Kira shot back.

"Only once. By an exquisite woman with an affinity for chickens."

Kira narrowed her eyes at him. "You were also captured just a few weeks ago by an Emberhawk assassin."

"That wasn't in Malaano territory, so it doesn't count."

Kira sighed. "Seriously, the last thing I want to do is to go back into danger. Ever."

Ryon nodded. "Okay, so maybe we postpone our honeymoon until the war is over so travel will be safer. But in the meantime, I at least want to take some sort of a vacation with you. Navarro is close. And I've heard you speak longingly of the Moon Festival more than once."

Kira shook her head. "It's too dangerous. Just being here in Quin'Zamar is like a vacation to me."

"Quin'Alor," Ryon corrected. "But this could very well be your new home. And it's nothing special."

Kira balked at him. "The palace is literally made of gold!"

Ryon shrugged. "Let me take you to the Moon Festival. Please. While you are forgetting my elemental abilities, don't forget that invisibility is my specialty."

Kira pursed her lips as she considered. Surely Navarro didn't belong to the Malaano Empire—her father would have left it to loyal troops, and he'd just returned there. According to Tekkyn, Oda'e's old barracks there was now the base of operations for the Navakovrae Resistance. And they'd be focused on punching back and driving the Empire all the way back to My'Eyah. Hadn't Tekkyn said they'd been planning the coup for at least a year?

Maybe their ranch was safe after all. A trip home would mean she could see her mother and grandmother. And visit Lee's grave.

Lee had died, and she'd gotten married. It wasn't fair.

Kira's heart squeezed. He should have been the one to survive, not her. She didn't deserve it.

"Hey," Ryon said gently. "We don't have to go if you don't want to."

"No, it'll be okay. We'll just be careful." Kira forced a smile. "I always loved watching the water dancers as a child. If they're holding the festival at all this year, I'd like to go. I'm getting a slice of your childhood here, and there, you can see mine."

Ryon watched her, unsure, as if wondering what her true thoughts were. "All right. We'll be careful. I promise."

The houses opened up into an open square—a bazaar cluttered with vendors and colorful strips of fabric strung across ropes overhead. Scents of grilled meat, bread, and spices filled Kira's nostrils, and suddenly she was hungry again. Drums and some sort of wind instrument cut through the noise of the midday crowd.

Kira felt like she stood out until she saw one other Malaano-heritage person in the crowd. She stood up straight and tried to relax.

"We don't have too much time to eat, so we might have to take our tacos to go." Ryon looked up at the sun, judging its angle.

"Where did you say your meeting was?" Kira asked.

"The throne room," Ryon said. "Wanna meet the king?"

7

VYLIA

Vylia slipped from a dream she was already forgetting. Something about water . . . the element that had abandoned her. Betrayed her.

Muscles in her back tightened in protest as she pushed herself to a sitting position. The carriage's seat was hard and thin beneath her, hardly serving as a bed. For a princess, no less.

But she wasn't really a princess anymore. Her father had betrayed her, too.

Painful memories revived as she stared at the thin curtains covering the carriage's window, squinting at the invading sunlight. This wasn't her carriage. Hers was inlaid with fine silks and cushions and filigree . . .

Sousuke!

He lay on the floor at her feet, his legs bent awkwardly to fit his masculine stature in the small space. His eyes were closed, either in sleep or death. Sloppy, scarlet bandages stretched across his middle and left shoulder.

Vylia choked on a gasp and fumbled to her knees on the floor beside him, careful to avoid landing on his outstretched hand or the bag that contained her coral crown. She called his name. He didn't respond.

How long had she been asleep? She whispered an incomprehensible prayer and pressed her fingers into his neck. Was the beating she felt from his heart or her own frantic pulse?

Vylia moved her hand to Sousuke's nose. Faint, warm breath blew against her fingers.

Thank the heavens! She sighed in relief, then frowned down at him. His bandages needed changing. And whoever had provided his medical care in the first place obviously wasn't a healer, judging by the haphazard way the cloth covered his armor. Why hadn't they removed his armor to treat him properly? Curse them!

The carriage lurched to the side, and Vylia lost her balance. Her shoulder hit the door, but it didn't open. Sousuke didn't react.

Vylia pursed her lips and stood, using the carriage's concave wall for balance. She grabbed the door's handle and pushed. It didn't budge. Neither did the door on the opposite side.

She steeled herself against the soreness in her side and looked at the windows. Too small for a child to crawl out of.

Vylia mentally kicked herself. Even if she could escape now, there was no way she'd be able to carry Sousuke. And no way she'd leave him.

So what could she do?

The sound of the wheels changed, rhythmic and loud, as if they now drove over stone or wood. A bridge, perhaps?

Abruptly they lurched to a stop. Vylia lost her balance and nearly stepped on Sousuke in an effort to catch herself.

Voices muffled through the walls. Sa'alu's voice. But he was speaking Phoeran.

Vylia wished she'd learned the language of the tribes. But why would she, when before this trip, her father scarcely let her out of the palace walls?

Still, she stood and listened, hoping to catch the meaning of at least a single word.

Rupero. Wasn't that the tribal currency?

Jingling, clinking. A brief pause, then a shout. Footsteps approaching.

Vylia tensed and stared at the carriage door as it flung open.

Lieutenant Sa'alu stood there, contempt and exhaustion mixing on his face. His silver plate armor was speckled with mud, the metal-forged lotus on his breast encrusted with grime. Rat-like eyes flicked from Vylia to Sousuke and back again.

"Where are we?" Vylia demanded.

"Sekoiako Village," Sa'alu said in a low tone. "Behave or there will be consequences." He shut the door.

Vylia's heart lifted in relief as she felt the carriage rumble forward again. "Praise Lillian," she breathed, then caught herself. She'd have to break that habit.

She looked down and carefully stepped around Sousuke to get a better look out the window. The forest broke into fields, then a wooden barricade, then strange flat buildings made of sticks, straw, and daub. Half-naked children stopped their game of ball to stare. Their mothers ran to grab them and yank them away from the road.

Vylia stared back. These people reminded her of her own people in the slums of Ceemalao, where she'd snuck away to once and received the harshest punishment of her life. But the Sekoiako people were dotted and striped with intricate designs—even some of the children were tattooed. As the carriage ambled deeper into the heart of the village, Vylia noticed the same type of patterns and symbols on different people. Perhaps they had some significance or meaning? Rank, status, or role?

Fascinated, Vylia committed every detail to memory. Squat, reaching forms of the trees whose trunks were ensorcelled with strips of fabric, and dead trees whose trunks had faces of various animals and human expressions carved into them. Women's hair was frequently pulled into updos, twisted purposefully and decorated with beads. White-spotted furs marked the doors of longhouses, and the air smelled of drying meat from an unseen smokehouse.

The carriage came to a stop near a longhouse on the far edge of the village. When the door opened, Vylia cautiously stepped out, pausing when she realized they were surrounded by no less than two dozen warriors, each with notched spears taller than the men who wielded them. Vylia avoided eye contact as her feet touched the blessed earth, finally free of her moving prison.

Somehow, the presence of the tribal warriors filled her with peace. They greatly outnumbered her captors. Perhaps if they could be notified of the situation, turned against Sa'alu . . . Why had the Sekoiako offered to help Malaano in the first place? Weren't they at war?

Sa'alu's men began pulling Sousuke's limp form from the carriage but were quickly shooed away by scantly clothed tribesmen who handled him with much greater care. They hurried inside the longhouse, and Vylia followed.

A strong hand dropped on her shoulder. "Stay with the carriage," Sa'alu growled.

"No!" Vylia ducked and wrenched free, then scurried to catch up.

For reasons unknown to her, Sa'alu didn't press the matter. Vylia dodged into the longhouse and breathed a prayer of thanks, feeling the comforting brush of soft furs that hung from the doorframe.

Inside, dim light emanated from glowing crystals that hung from the rafters. Vylia stared at them in awe for a moment before reverting her attention to the Sekoiako men gently lowering Sousuke onto a cot near the center of the room. They muttered to each other in Phoeran, and Vylia desperately wished she could understand them.

As the tribesmen dispersed, Vylia knelt next to the cot and frowned at Sousuke. His dark skin had a strangely pallor undertone, and not just from the odd green-blue hue of the crystals. But his chest still rose and fell with breath.

Vylia rested her forehead on his arm, calming in the perceived safety of the tribal village but unable to dislodge the knot of anxiety in her chest. "Stay with me, soldier," she whispered.

"Are you his soulbound?"

Vylia jumped at the closeness of the deep voice. A man and a woman stood across from the cot, she with a sash over her simple robe and he with a necklace of bones and fangs. The woman leaned over Sousuke, pressing her fingers into his temples, neck, and chest while the man stared at Vylia with a piercing expression.

"I, um . . ." Vylia had to recall what he had asked and decipher the words through his thick Phoeran accent. "I'm not sure."

The woman said something in Phoeran, and the man responded in kind. Then he held out a hovering hand over Sousuke's stomach and closed his eyes.

Vylia didn't realize she was clenching every muscle as she waited until they began to burn. She forced herself to relax, one muscle group at a time.

The man's hand still hovered over Sousuke, and Vylia wondered what he was doing. The woman appeared to be a healer, but what was this man supposed to be?

"Yes, she is da heala, and I am da spirit heala. Der is more dan one way to die."

Vylia stared at the man, whose eyes were still closed. Who was he talking to?

The spirit healer opened one eye. "Your thoughts are loud, girl."

Vylia couldn't stop the shocked expression from spreading across her face. "I'm . . . sorry?"

He seemed amused. "Body, mind, heart, spirit. Da death of any means da death of you." He tilted his head toward the woman beside him. "Did ya only tink da body mattered?"

Vylia's tired mind struggled to keep up. She was well aware that a person could die of an ill mind, or of heartbreak. She'd witnessed the death of her father's former self due to the loss of the empress. The man that remained was an evil husk.

"How can someone's spirit die?" she asked.

The spirit healer chuckled. "All of our souls are dead, girl. Since da beginning. Only da creata can fix dat." He finally dropped his hand and focused on her. "Dis man's spirit is burning too bright. Burning out."

Alarm flashed through Vylia. "What does that mean?"

"He hides a dark secret. *Zothari manicus.* A great evil."

One of the tribal women near the door gasped and ran out of the room.

Vylia frowned. "That can't be true. He's a good man."

The spirit healer rested his hands on the cot, closed his eyes once again, and leaned over Sousuke. "He tries to fight darkness with darkness."

Vylia's mind spun. "I don't . . ." Frustration threatened to boil over. "Can you heal his wounds?" She enunciated the words slowly, worrying that these people couldn't heal Sousuke at all.

The man locked her in a piercing brown gaze. "You tell dis man, if he lives, dat darkness can only be fought wit light."

The woman beside him spoke in Phoeran, then turned away and left.

Vylia's heart lurched. "What did she say?"

The spirit healer's frown drew deep. "His body cannot survive dis." He stood up straight. "Creata be wit ya."

"Wait, please!" Vylia ran after the woman, fell to her knees in front of her, and bowed. "Please at least try."

Vylia stared at the healer's unmoving sandaled feet for a long moment before looking up. She saw the truth in the woman's eyes: Sousuke was not long for this world.

8

BROOKE

The drake's back was barely wide enough to support his mother's saddle. Lysander's blade had pierced new holes in the leather straps to cinch the buckles tighter, but still it didn't fit perfectly. Regardless, Brooke was grateful to have a saddle at all, unlike Felix's back.

As much as she already missed the snarky fox, she felt safer on Onyx's back. Somehow her bond with the young dragon hadn't seemed to fade. He would only tolerate Brooke to ride at the front of the saddle, emitting a low hiss whenever Lysander had tried. Now Lysander clung awkwardly to Brooke's waist, eliciting a grin she couldn't suppress.

She scanned the trees as they passed at a high rate of speed. She could only assume they were heading to Jadenvive, as Onyx had insisted through his memories that he'd been there before. An idea that both relieved and concerned Brooke at the same time. How numerous were this wild brood? And if she allowed them to repopulate, would they eventually seek revenge against the Katrosi for hunting the wild dragons? Lysander seemed alarmed at how intelligent the creatures were, and he didn't know the half of it.

"That's Cheyenne!" Brooke called over the rush of the wind through her braids and pointed down at a break in the trees, where rooves broke through the leaves and smoke lazily leaned into the sky.

Then she remembered that her husband's ears had been cut so they were pointed, signifying his lack of hearing. *That's Cheyenne village,* she thought-spoke to him. *We're going the right way.*

This is a lot easier than shouting, yeah? Lysander thought back. *Sorry. I can still understand some things if they're loud enough. And I can read lips.*

His embrace around her waist tightened, and he leaned closer to graze his lips across her cheek. *And I'm getting very familiar with yours.*

Heat flushed through Brooke. *Do you want me to fall off this dragon?*

Lysander chuckled low but only barely receded.

I'll remember and form a habit for thought-speak hopefully sooner rather than later, Brooke thought. *Never apologize for it. It was not your choice, and I love you more despite it.*

Lysander set his forehead on her shoulder. *What did I possibly do to deserve you?*

Brooke reached up and ran her fingers through his slate-colored hair. She squinted at the horizon where she expected Jadenvive to appear. Sure enough, the trees grew even taller and thicker than they already were. Onyx's nose pointed straight toward the ancient trio of the tallest trees in the Katrosi forest.

Relief coursed through her. Onyx had done it! These dragons were blessings from above.

But where would he land? It occurred to Brooke then that they were in war time, and she was riding a dragon. They'd be shot at for sure.

She racked her brain to think of a place they could land on the outskirts of Jadenvive, outside the reach of arrows from the walls and harpoons from the upper fortifications. For a memory she could send to Onyx.

But they were approaching too fast. Onyx broke past the tree line and soared over fields of squash, corn, and beans growing together in tangled spires.

Brooke shot a memory of Cheyenne village to Onyx. The trunk of a massive tree that had died to drought had been cut down there many years ago, and the stump still served as a stage. He could land there!

Onyx returned a memory of Beryl landing near the Crow's Nest of Jadenvive, at the very top of the massive birch tree called Vanya.

"Stubborn reptile!" Brooke pulled back on the reins as they crested into the range of longbows. An arrow whistled through the air to their right.

Lysander pushed her to lean down, closer to Onyx's back, while covering her with his own body.

Can you make us invisible? Brooke thought to him.

"No. He's too big and his wings are moving too fast. Maybe if Ryon were here . . ."

Brooke closed her eyes and gathered her aether, calming herself and summoning the quiet whisper of power from deep within her soul, just as the Elder of Aether had taught her.

Then she amplified her thought-voice and yelled in the direction of Jadenvive's defenses, so that any willing or weak mind would hear: *I am Brooke of Stillwind, and this is my wyvern. We are not hostile. Strength and humility.*

She clung to the saddle and breathed, somehow physically taxed from the effort of sending so much aether. Had it worked?

The sky looked clear, and she heard no whistling of projectiles.

"If my brain had ears, you'd have ruined them, too," Lysander grumbled from behind her. "But you're a genius."

Gargantuan leaves streaked past as Onyx glided closer. Brooke held on for her life as the dragon shifted his rear legs forward and his claws slammed into a shaded wooden platform, built decades ago as a dragon-perch. The only one Brooke hadn't ordered to be torn down like the rest, to make room for the messenger birds, in memory of High Chief Torvyn and the dragon-riders of the past.

"Whoa!" Brooke patted Onyx's neck as he shook his head, apparently uncomfortable with the bit in his mouth. "Great job, boy. That was an amazing first flight." She scanned the platform around them, but no amber masks were in sight.

Lysander shifted behind Brooke, and she glanced back to see him carefully removing Torvyn's headdress and holding it at his side instead. She breathed in relief that no one had seen him wearing it. She should probably remove hers, too, but that would require a bit more effort.

Onyx gave a rumbling growl as he lay down on the platform and lowered his head and neck, allowing Brooke and Lysander to jump off. A memory filled Brooke's mind: a little brown-haired girl, yelling from the viewer's back, *"Yah! Why can't you fly yet? You're bigger than me—you can do it! Yah!"*

Brooke laughed and jogged around to nuzzle Onyx's face. "Look how big you are now! Look how well you fly. What a good boy!" She rubbed the scaled crest between his eyes. Onyx gave a high-pitched trill.

"Strength and humility."

Brooke turned to see two amber masks in full armor coming up the stairs, their spears held casually.

"I answer a summon from Ulysses," she said.

"You are acknowledged in peace." Through the eyeholes in their masks, she could tell the guards were staring wide-eyed at Onyx. "Is this . . . yours?"

"Yes." She patted Onyx's neck. She couldn't claim that he was tame, but he was hers.

A memory from Onyx bled into her mind. Torvyn closed his eyes, and after a moment, Beryl landed on the misty island and lumbered over to him. Then another memory: hearing Brooke's call to the soldiers of Jadenvive, just moments ago, loud in Onyx's mind.

"A moment, please," she asked of the guards and turned back to Onyx. She tried to breathe off the stress now that they were safe. What was the dragon trying to say?

Onyx, Brooke called through the aether. "Can you hear that? Are you saying I can call you when I need you?"

Onyx closed his bright blue eyes, and a burst of yearning slammed into Brooke, nearly staggering her. What a strange sound, or was it a sound at all? It was more like a feeling—something unseen wrapping around her heart and pulling it in a direction. The direction of Onyx.

"You can call me, too, eh? I see." Brooke nodded, and a broken feather of a headdress waved in her peripheral vision. She could find the island with Onyx's direction, if that's where he called from.

"I require fresh meat to refresh my mount," Brooke said to the guards. "A whole goat, please."

Brooke closed her eyes and felt Lysander moving her braids around, carefully unhooking clasps and freeing her of her headdress. For the last time.

She breathed deeply to steady herself and opened her eyes. They were in the room behind the Great Hall's throne room—a meeting place of sorts which displayed trophies, medallions, and cultural treasures. The wall before her was lined with the armor and headdresses of chiefs past.

Careful not to move her head as Lysander worked behind her, Brooke's eyes drifted to High Chief Torvyn's headdress, finally back in its place above his d'hakka chitin armor. Seeing it there after it had been missing so long filled her with a sense of closure. Finding it on display in Zamara's garden had all but answered Brooke's question of what had become of her grandfather. He must have been lost to the war with the Emberhawk, like so many other Katrosi men during that dark time.

It mingled with the sorrow of the sunset of her own time as chief, threatening to spill tears down her cheeks. She knew she couldn't stop them. At least she and Lysander were alone while they waited for Ulysses to summon them into the war room.

"You have so much to be proud of." Lysander's voice sounded restricted.

And so much to be ashamed of, Brooke returned.

"No. You did what you thought was right at every turn."

What I thought *was right. Not what was actually right.* She took a shuddering breath. *Everyone will remember the first female chief as a traitor who fled Jadenvive in its time of need. I'm a failure.*

"Hey. Nobody talks to my wife that way." Lysander stopped his work on her headdress and hugged her from behind. "You were instructed by an Elder to do that. And by the creator. And I'm glad you obeyed. Otherwise we wouldn't be together, because you'd be dead . . . and I probably would be, too." He squeezed her tight. "You had no way of knowing that Jadenvive would be attacked."

Yes, but nobody knew that I was told to leave, and there's not really a way to prove it. Brooke swallowed a lump—it felt like swallowing a hard truth. *Well, the Elder of Aether told his granddaughter before he passed, at least, so I guess that's proof. But the people were still abandoned and hurt regardless.* The tears fell. *I just wish it hadn't ended this way.*

"I know. I'm sorry." Lysander's voice quieted as his arms moved from their embrace and returned to her hair. "I think it's ready."

Brooke's hands rose to her headdress and lifted the weight from her head. She turned it around in her hands, admiring the horns and claws—trophies from the hunts of deadly animals which had proved her worth to be considered for the position of chief. And the cloudy facets of the aether stone, which she now knew to be the fake one. Still, Ulysses would have it removed and placed in his own headdress. Fake crystal or not, it was a symbol of their people.

She wondered where the real one was.

"I'm sure an artisan can repair it," Lysander said. "Or you could go on another hunt . . . ?"

Brooke's thoughts returned to the present, and she examined the blue and green feathers that trailed down the sides and back of her headdress. Several had snapped in her fight against Prince Heron's assault.

I don't want them to be replaced, Brooke said. *These are feathers from the wild xavi whose blood was the sacrifice for my leadership—the proof of my ability to lead. There's no need for more blood to be spilled just for the sake of vanity.*

Lysander was quiet for a long moment. "I think I understand."

Brooke glanced over her shoulder at him and smiled. Yes, their cultural differences would make their relationship more challenging, at least in the beginning of their marriage. But it was a bridge that needed to be built, not just between them, but between their two peoples. A salve of forgiveness over generations of wounds.

A challenge she was excited to face head on, with understanding and patience. Because peace was worth it, and because he was the right person to walk the path with her.

Brooke laid her headdress to rest on the mannequin that had been made with a woman's shape—shorter, smaller, and more curved than the rest, yet placed with the same proud stature, with equality to the masculine figures beside.

She'd keep her leather armor for the time being, though. The war was just beginning.

"The Jade Witch has returned."

Brooke cringed internally at the guard's announcement as she entered the war room. Clearly, some guards treated her with honor, and others saw her as a betrayer.

Ulysses looked up from where he was leaning over the massive table in the center of the room and fixed the guard in a pointed glare. Black streaks of warpaint around his cheekbones and brows accentuated his reprimanding expression. "Respect."

The guard bowed his head. "Sir."

Ulysses straightened and turned to Brooke. Stress seemed to slip from his shoulders as he approached her with a weary smile. "Strength and humility."

"Strength," she returned, then suddenly remembered the tradition to bow to the chief. She did so awkwardly, off-balance with the weight of her headdress now missing. It appeared Ulysses hadn't had time to craft his own headdress—or perhaps he would not until an official election, as he was now serving as interim chief. Brooke couldn't clearly recall the specifics of those rarely used laws.

Ulysses and Lysander nodded at each other. "It's good to see you," Ulysses said to Brooke.

"And you," Brooke said. "It appears that you evacuated the city. A good decision."

"Of course. A tough call, but necessary. Civilians have been relocated to our surrounding villages, with the exception of a few men left to salvage what's left of the autumn harvest, who are willing and able to take up arms if necessary." Ulysses motioned at the guards. "Summon the hand-language signer. Then stand watch outside when you return." The guards bowed and stepped through the thick doorway.

"You brought the aether stone, I presume?" Ulysses asked.

Brooke shifted uncomfortably. "It's in my headdress, which I put next to the others. But unfortunately we've learned that it was the double."

Ulysses frowned. "What do you mean? It's a fake?"

Brooke realized he must not have taken all of the vows of the office yet, and therefore not sworn to protect the keystone or know the secret of its doppelganger. "Many years ago, a false keystone was created to be swapped out when our chiefs went into dangerous situations."

"So the one that was stolen from the treasury was the real one?"

"Yes," Brooke said reluctantly. "I thought I was taking the real one when I left . . . I didn't have enough time to have it switched out. The Elder of Aether told me to leave that same night."

"Mmm." Ulysses scratched the stubble on his jaw. "This sounds like a problem. But unfortunately I'm not very familiar with the artifact. And I'm more concerned with the safety of our people at this time."

Brooke nodded. "But we have reason to believe that the keystone is of utmost importance. Not just to our tribe, but to the human race as a whole."

Ulysses's brows drew together. "Explain."

She glanced at Lysander and sent a thought in his direction. *Should I tell him everything about Felix? And the aether stone, and Lillian?*

Lysander didn't take his eyes off of Ulysses. *Do you trust him?*

I don't know him personally, but he's seemed to do a good job so far . . .

Maybe we should tell him, Lysander said. *We could use his resources.*

Brooke told Ulysses everything she knew, and by the time she finished, the hand-language signer had entered and translated for Lysander.

Ulysses crossed the room and took a seat at the table, apparently pondering her words. "If what you say is true . . . all may already be lost. Especially if the thief is in league with this ancient evil, and uses the keystone to release her."

Brooke nodded, just thankful that he was taking her wild claims of elementals and magic seriously. "Yes. If Lillian is released and reclaims the Malaano Empire, their war effort may increase. Who knows what ancient weapons she may unleash."

"Mmmm." Ulysses seemed to agree.

"So I'd like your blessing to pursue the thief and recover the stone."

Ulysses watched her for a long moment, almost seeming to stare through her. Finally, he said, "You have lost much favor with our people. In addition to your departure just before the Malaano attack, Prince Heron's bodyguard, Long Root, made many dishonorable claims about you. And then you married one of the Emberhawk arsonists from the initial attack."

Brooke winced with each truth he spoke. He didn't speak them with spite, but they felt like accusations regardless.

She swallowed. "I understand. But anything Long Root said was probably a lie."

"Absolutely a lie," Lysander interjected. "And I paid for my crimes according to the Katrosi justice system. Although I tried to stop Zamara and nearly paid with my life."

Ulysses turned his dark gaze to Lysander. "Witnesses confirmed that. However, it takes an open mind to understand and accept all of that. A rarity." He leaned forward, resting his elbows on the table, which was filled with maps and parchment. "I understand your predicament, and I don't say these things to shame you. Only to speak plainly. It may be many years in the future before our people can accept the truth and your decisions, and appreciate your efforts for peace, which are in the best interest of our tribe long-term."

Brooke fought against a rising heat in her chest, like a knot composed of all her guilt and worries. She forced her stiff body to nod. "You speak the truth."

"All this to say that it would be good for you to lay low for a while," Ulysses said. "Perhaps investigating the disappearance of the aether stone is our solution for now. Even if nothing you fear about it is true, it is a sacred artifact and must be returned. You have my blessing and resources at your disposal."

Brooke released a breath of relief. "Thank you. Do you have any leads on the theft?"

"Just one. We believe the culprit could be of Malaano heritage. Possible witness sighting by a civilian. But that report could be biased."

Brooke glanced at Lysander, who raised an eyebrow at her. "I've noticed a lot fewer Malaano-heritage people in the city," she said.

"Oda'e and his forces relocated to Navarro, with only a few remaining here to fortify the city as we recover," Ulysses said. "Navarro is the new base of his Navakovrae Resistance, and they are planning to push the battle line east and drive the empire into the Sea of Bones. We are working closely together. Praise the creator for him and his men."

"Yes," Brooke agreed. "I doubt the thief was among the Resistance, but I'll look into it."

"I'll let the masks know you have full authority in this investigation. If any of them give you trouble, let me know."

Brooke thanked him, and the conversation shifted to the commitments Brooke had made as the former leader of the Katrosi tribe. As they discussed the details, Lysander looked more and more bored until Ryon's name came up.

"He quit?" Ulysses said.

"The job didn't seem to be a good fit for him," Brooke said. "Do you have someone else in mind for your vice?"

"I do. And what of your man, Dimbae, the azure mask?"

"He was severely wounded while we were in the Emberhawk lands, and he is recovering there. Please see that he receives the best benefits we can give upon his return."

"Done." Ulysses proceeded down his list. "Nariellyn has decided to retain her position as the chief's personal healer. Her magic seems very powerful, so I am glad for it."

Brooke felt a pang of longing for her friend at the mention of her name. So, Nari would be Ulysses's healer now. That made sense. But she made a mental note to meet with Nari and catch up as soon as possible.

"And the last on your payroll . . . Kiralau and Tekkyn'ashi of the Navakovrae."

"Oh, yes. You can remove them now that the imperial princess has left Jadenvive. Kiralau was to become Vylia's confidant, and Tekkyn her bodyguard after her entourage was betrayed by one of their own."

Ulysses scribbled notes as she spoke. "They didn't accompany her when she left?"

"No . . . it's a long story," Lysander said. "They are both in Emberhawk lands with Idryon."

"Good." Ulysses struck lines through all three names. "Now, where shall I have your belongings moved to? The Stillwind estate, I presume."

Brooke hesitated. Her parents were gone. Her grandfather was gone. That estate was filled with nothing but memories of loss.

She'd heard that their family home had been damaged in the fire. She hadn't even had the time to assess the damage.

Would her uncle and cousins want her to return? Did they believe the rumors about her? Had they repurposed her old room?

The only true family she'd had recently was the Elder of Aether.

She opened her mouth, but no sound escaped. How many things did she have to move out of the chief's chambers? There was Torvyn's old bear rug, and her spears, and her wardrobe—

"Move everything to Queen Lyzelle's pyramid in the Emberhawk Sovereignty," Lysander said. "I'll cover all expenses."

Brooke blinked at her husband. That . . . would work. For now, at least.

Relief soothed her like a clearing storm. How did Lysander recognize her needs and resolve them before she could finish thinking? The benefits of marriage kept accumulating more than she'd ever thought possible. She'd have to find some way to thank him.

"Consider it done." Ulysses stood and bowed low toward Brooke. "Thank you for your service. Any disrespect toward you will not be tolerated."

Brooke remained still, accepting the gesture of utmost respect.

"Keep me updated," Ulysses said as he returned to standing. "I'll send a messenger hawk to find you when it's safe for you to return to Jadenvive."

Brooke returned his bow. "Thank you, Chief."

9

KIRALAU

Kira looked up at the glass-gold pillars in awe. Gold ribbons and flecks swirled through what appeared to be semi-translucent marble holding the shining roof aloft, but she knew better. This elementally-forged material held great significance to the elemental race.

Was it Felix who had crafted Quin'Alor himself? For what purpose? Had he really meant it to be a grand palace? Or a stronghold for protecting the keystone or other ancient treasures? Or a prison for the stones of vanquished elementals?

"I'll never get used to this," she breathed.

Ryon didn't pause his ascent up the stairs in front of her. "Meh."

"'Meh'? Seriously?" Kira hurried to catch up until the stairs made way for enormous, intricately carved doors. "We get to live in the most gorgeous building on Alani and that's your response?"

"I grew up here, remember?" Ryon lowered his voice. "Not the best memories. Both from childhood and a few weeks ago."

Kira's awe evaporated. How could she forget? Ryon's father and his family had been banished for opposing Lysander and Coriander's father during the Sacrificial War. And subsequently assassinated.

"I'm sorry," was all she could think to say. Of course the most beautiful places in the world could still house the most despicable evils.

She was Ryon's wife now. Supporting him was far more important than any appearance of grandeur she might enjoy.

"Not your fault." Ryon turned and smiled at her. "Would have been a lot worse without you saving me, yeah? It was all blurry, anyway."

Kira barely heard him, infatuated with the way the sunlight played with his silver hair and the depth of affection for her in his fiery gaze. He was so handsome. Somehow even more handsome than when they'd first met. And he was *hers*.

Ryon's smile turned mischievous. "Are you in there, *balemba*?"

She felt her cheeks flush with heat as a screech emitted from the doors as the guards opened them. "We don't have to live here if you're uncomfortable," she said a little too quickly. "Where do you want to live?"

He shrugged. "I might not want to put down roots too deep in any particular place. I get bored, you know."

Kira grinned. "Maybe near some wilds so you can go exploring."

"And hunting." Ryon nodded curtly, then adjusted his lenses. "We wouldn't even have to avoid d'hakka, since they avoid me and you've learned to kill—"

"No d'hakka," Kira interrupted. "Absolutely not."

Ryon chuckled and turned to enter the palace doors, which had finally finished opening.

The entryway was even more grand than the exterior. Hanging braziers from each pillar burned with a mystical blue fire. Kira stayed close to Ryon as they made their way through the heavily-guarded hallways until they reached the throne room. They didn't have to wait long before a guard whose armor reflected a golden sheen waved them in.

Kira's eyes adjusted to new brightness, thanks to a ceiling of windows that allowed sunlight to pour in and dance through hanging crystals positioned to illuminate the throne. A scarlet rug felt plush even through her sandals. She inhaled the smoke of incense, and calm flooded through her apprehension.

"Idryon!" King Coriander called from the golden throne decorated with large red plumes from an ember hawk—an enormous fire-breathing bird that Kira had thought to be legend until she'd seen Zamara transform into one.

Ryon bowed low, and Kira did the same. "Your Highness," Ryon said.

Coriander snorted. "Do former kings address each other this way?"

Ryon cringed. "I've been told I was an illegitimate king for about five seconds."

"Are you recovering from the muddlewort?" Coriander motioned for them to come closer. "Can you recite the alphabet?"

Ryon snickered, mocking Kira's genuine concern. "Phoeran wasn't my best subject in school."

"It's fine; half the people in government jobs probably can't either because Illiana was giving out jobs as favors." Coriander relaxed against the stark white furs within the throne. "I've got a lot of interviews to do. Want a job?"

Ryon laughed. "I . . . don't know yet. I've discovered recently that jobs involving an office aren't my favorite."

Kira was glad to hear his answer, since he'd quit the job as Brooke's vice. That position had fit him like a yoke fit a sheep.

"Hmm. You're the more adventurous type, yeah? Unfortunately I don't need a scout. We aren't on the battle line so long as Navarro and Jadenvive hold. I need to meet the new leader there . . ." Coriander sighed. "Ugh, so much to do."

"Which leader?" Ryon asked. "The new chief, Ulysses, or the Navakovrae Resistance leader, Oda'e?"

"Both."

"I'm familiar with Ulysses, and Oda'e is my father-in-law." Ryon winked at Kira.

Coriander rose from the throne and stepped toward them, trailing a cloak that was entirely too long. Kira froze as the king took her hand and kissed it, narrowly missing her with the gleaming spikes of his crown, which curved upward like talons.

"It's a pleasure to meet you, Kiralau," he said with a warm smile, then tipped his head in Ryon's direction. "You sure you know what you're getting into, marrying him?"

Kira found her voice, but she sounded like a little girl in her own ears. "So far it seems like the best decision I've ever made."

"Adorable." Coriander leaned back and examined them both with a pleased expression. "So, where are you two going to settle down?"

Ryon looked at Kira. "We're not sure yet."

"You're welcome to live here in the palace if you like. I'm cutting the tradition of royal allowances, though, at least until the economy can recover from ending slavery. But of course, if you take a job for me, you'll be paid well."

Ryon's eyes widened. "You're ending slavery?"

Coriander nodded. "I will still allow indentured servitude, but we will need time to recover. Hopefully forging true peace with the Katrosi and joining the Tribal Alliance will buy us time . . . I'm sending some troops to the battle line and praying they can hold the Malaano."

Kira breathed with relief at the trickle of good news as Ryon eyed his cousin and spoke in a low voice. "That's great, but I'm surprised to hear you freed the slaves so soon after being sworn in. Are you concerned about losing the support of the people?"

"Not the wisest move, perhaps, but I refuse to begin my rule on the back of a single unwilling slave." Coriander fluttered his royal cloak in annoyance as it curled around his feet. "Zamara's loyalists are being weeded out as we speak. Let them try and oppose me."

The king turned his attention to Kira. "You, my new cousin, will probably be seen as a political tool, as many of the foreigners in Emberhawk lands—from other tribes and some of Malaano or Valinorian descent—are former slaves. I hope you know that Iraleth and I will never treat you that way, but anything you'd like to do as a member of the royal family to aid in the healing and unifying of our peoples would be encouraged and appreciated."

Kira stood stunned. A purpose for her specifically within the royal family? "I would love to help at the first opportunity," she blurted. "However, I, uh, have no experience being a royal, least of all in a foreign country—" She cut herself off and grasped desperately for better words. "W-well, not that that Emberhawk territory is foreign anymore, if this is my new home, I mean—"

Coriander waved as if that would disperse her discomfort. "You might have noticed that all of us are out of practice living in a palace. I'll ask Iraleth to help you with the . . . uh . . . expectations for ladies of the palace."

She swallowed. "'Lady'?"

"You are Lord Idryon and Lady Kiralau. And if anyone is foolish enough to look down on you, let me know."

Kira looked at Ryon in shock, and he seemed amused. "You didn't know, my lady?"

"Ah!" Coriander snapped his fingers. "I've got it: you would make the perfect ambassador to the Katrosi and Navakovrae for me. No office required. Adventure on the road! Good pay!"

Ryon tilted his head. "I'll think on it. But first we need some time to rest and recover. And honeymoon."

"Yes, of course," Coriander said as Kira's head spun. "Please feel free to stay here in the palace for now. Let's revisit the idea when you're ready."

"First I would need to ensure that Mom and Aegwyn and the orphans are taken care of," Ryon said.

Coriander's brows knitted together. "Did you think I wouldn't take care of Aunt Gwyn? Leave them to me. And the children in her care, too, of course."

"You'll take the orphans in?" Ryon asked.

A disgusted look crossed the king's face. "What kind of man do you think I am? Didn't you want me on the throne?"

Alarm flared through Kira, but Ryon appeared as calm as ever. "Right, I just mean . . . previously they couldn't return to Emberhawk lands because of their affiliation with the Katrosi," Ryon said. "And the Katrosi didn't want to adopt them either because of their Emberhawk blood."

"Well, I'm securing a formal alliance with the Katrosi now," Coriander said. "As ambassador, you could help me get that finalized."

Ryon shifted his weight and hooked his thumbs around his belt. "Perhaps."

Coriander narrowed his eyes. "Don't play coy with me. You're perfect for it, and we both know it."

Ryon just grinned.

The king sighed and glanced over his shoulder at a woman who'd been standing just outside of the throne's focused sunlight. She hurried forward and offered the king a sheet of parchment.

"Ah, yes—thank you, dear. I knew I'd forget something." He read from the parchment. "Xavier is recovering and expected to survive thanks to the Katrosi healer. You might want to pay him a visit since he saved

Aegwyn from Illiana."

"He survived?" Ryon looked as surprised as Kira felt.

"I need to get one of those aether healers for myself," Coriander murmured.

"You!"

They all looked to a side door where an old man with milky eyes and a bent stature entered. He pointed an arthritic finger in their general direction.

"You," the man repeated as he hobbled toward them, feeling his way forward with the help of a cane. "I have seen a vision of you."

Kira stared into the man's pupilless gaze and wondered for a moment if he was an elemental, then decided his pupils were clouded from blindness, not lacking from elemental heritage. But then, what kind of vision did he mean? And who was he talking to?

"He must cross the waters," the old man said.

"I don't recall asking for a prophecy," Coriander said.

"How dare you interrupt the king?" said one of the guards, his voice distorted by his golden helmet as he followed the man, watching Coriander and apparently waiting for orders.

"It is not for you, my king." The old man stopped and leaned on his cane. "I have never received a prophecy like this before. The fate of the world depends on him!"

Kira instinctively took a step behind her husband's back. Did he mean Ryon?

Coriander and Ryon exchanged a look. "Cross what waters?" Ryon asked. "The Sea of Bones?"

A sliver of dread coalesced in Kira's stomach. The Sea of Bones that separated tribal lands from Malaan Island? It was called that for a reason: the countless number of sailors' lives claimed by its constant, violent storms.

"Enough." Coriander pointed toward the side door, and the guard escorted the man out. "I apologize. Still working on removing the shadows from Zamara's reign." He offered Kira a smile, but it felt hollow. "Don't let it trouble you."

Kira forced herself to smile in return but hovered close to Ryon's back.

"Thank you for the offer, Your Highness." Ryon bowed his head to Coriander. "I'll give you my answer when we are rested. I will take my bride on a vacation and return soon."

Coriander nodded. "Fires warm your spirit, brother."

Ryon took Kira's hand and guided her out of the palace with barely concealed haste. Upon exiting, Kira felt like she'd forgotten to breathe that entire time.

"Who was that?" she whispered to Ryon as they descended the palace steps.

"A prophet," Ryon muttered. "Or at least, he thinks he is. They believe the sun is the source of power for the Phoeran element. They stare into the sun, praying to it until they go blind. Then they believe they have received second sight from the sun."

Kira had never heard of such a thing before. She stared at the steps, watching her footing as she considered it. Was there any truth to such a belief?

"But that tradition is not from the creator," Ryon said. "He is just a raving old man, probably trying to keep the old job he had under Zamara."

Kira wondered if the prophet had predicted the downfall of Zamara. She decided not to ask.

10

SOUSUKE

Pain.

In his chest. His back. His shoulder.

His heart?

Sousuke breathed and regretted it. A moan escaped him.

Firelight above him. Blurry. Flickering onto a roof of dried grass. Wooden poles, bending, curving, swaying together in their hatch pattern.

He closed his eyes, but the darkness was no escape from the agony. Where was he?

"Sousuke?" A feminine voice nearby. Something touched his arm. "I'm here."

A young woman sat beside whatever he lay on. Dark skin. Black hair. Indistinct face . . . kind and gentle, maybe . . . worried. Bright hazel irises, like crystals beneath a watery surface.

"Vylia." His voice sounded like a chariot trying to stop suddenly on a rocky road.

"Yes! It's me." She leaned closer and her visage became clearer. "How are you feeling?"

Dead. He felt like death. Even worse than the last time he'd awoken. How long ago had that been?

He couldn't figure out how to form the words. What should he say? She must know already. He could see it in her eyes.

His time in this life was over. But he had nothing to fear—his soul belonged to the creator.

But did it, really?

Yes. But he'd spent his life in anger. Hatred. Defiance.

Why would the creator save someone like him? His soul should be sent to Zoth. But if that was the creator's will, then so be it.

At least he'd wasted his life trying to save others.

"Sousuke?" Vylia whispered.

He still didn't know what to say to her. He observed the area around them, gritting his teeth against the sensation in his shoulder when he moved his neck. This long room might have been a healer's hut, judging by the drying herbs hanging from the rafters, the scent of infused oil wafting from a shelf with folded clean cloths, and his own presence in one of the rows of cots that lined the wall. He didn't recognize the cultural style, but probably a Phoeran tribe, judging by the decorative markings in the woodwork. It wasn't Malaano, at least.

And yet a Malaano soldier stood watching at the far end of the room.

So Vylia was still their prisoner.

What could he do for her before he died? How much time did he have left, exactly? If Lillian took her . . . everything the Lotusfall hoped for would be over. Maybe it already was.

Thinking made his head hurt, in addition to everything else. His skull felt like it was full of grease. He closed his eyes.

"Please, give him something for the pain, at least," Sousuke heard Vylia say.

After a minute of controlling his breathing against the collective agony, Vylia spoke again. "Here, drink this."

He'd learned better than to move his neck again. But Vylia slid her hand under his head and gently lifted. He nearly choked on the foul liquid but forced himself to swallow. He closed his lips tight, suppressing the urge to spit it out before allowing Vylia to administer the rest.

She offered something that tasted like honey next. Bless her.

"There you go," Vylia said softly. "Rest and hopefully you'll feel better in a few minutes."

Sousuke peeked an eye open and allowed himself to admire her. She might not have the fighting acumen of other women in his family, but her nourishing instinct outshone her lack of skills that most women had been taught as girls. Her care for others hadn't needed to be taught or practiced—it was clearly as natural to her as breathing.

It reminded him of his mother, who'd shown him unconditional love even when all reason and logic compelled her not to.

He would use his last breath to save her—if, by the creator's grace, such a thing was possible—by telling her the truth. His reasons for secrecy were no longer valid. Yes, telling her everything would put her in danger, but it was also her last hope. The only thing that was worse than her current predicament would be becoming the victim of an assassin.

No, becoming a slave within her own body, at the mercy of an evil false goddess, would be worse.

"Thank you," Sousuke said, realizing that his pain had lessened and his head was beginning to clear. "Listen. You have to escape. And when you do," he paused for a labored breath, "you have to find the Lotusfall."

Vylia's dark brows furrowed. She leaned closer. "I don't know anything about the Lotusfall except that they are enemies of the imperial monarchy."

At least she hadn't accidentally called him a pagan this time. Sousuke looked beyond her at the Malaano soldier by the far door. Out of earshot.

"We are enemies of tyrants," Sousuke whispered.

Vylia's eyes widened. "So you really are one of them? Then why have you been protecting me, the daughter of a tyrant?"

Sousuke shifted slightly, testing the responsiveness of his hand. "If given the chance to become empress, would you be a tyrant?"

Vylia's face darkened with disgust. "Absolutely not."

Sousuke nodded slightly. "My father sent me on a mission to become one of your guards years ago. I determined that you were not like your father or brother." He chose his words carefully, not speaking his assumptions for why that might be: that she had not been groomed for imperial rule because her older brother was ahead of her in the line of succession.

Something like sadness crossed Vylia's face, but she waited for him to continue.

"So I trained hard to be assigned to your team of bodyguards." Sousuke swallowed, wishing for water but pushing the desire aside. He wouldn't need it soon, anyway. "I'm sorry . . . I failed to protect you."

"You didn't fail. You've already saved me more than once . . . I've lost count." Vylia squeezed his hand. "But you have to stay alive and keep protecting me now. I need you now more than ever."

Sousuke squeezed his eyes shut as longing flooded him. He did his best to keep his face straight. Letting her catch on to his affections earlier would have been unprofessional. To do so now would also be cruel, since fate would not allow them to be together.

Not that it had ever been possible in the first place.

So why had he never been able to control his feelings toward Vylia? Why had he allowed them to put down roots and grow in the first place?

A tear slid down his temple—from the agony that throbbed with every heartbeat, or the hopeless despair, he didn't know.

Because I am weak.

No. That was his evil father speaking. His evil nature.

His true father would understand. Would never speak to him like that.

But he would demand excellence. And Sousuke would deliver to the best of his remaining ability.

"I will do everything in my power . . . to stay with you," Sousuke whispered. "But you have to listen to me. Trust my father. He will hide you from the emperor . . . and his assassins." He paused to catch his breath. "It's too dangerous for me to tell you . . . exactly where the Lotusfall are. But if you go to Way Maar, find the tavern . . . called the Whistling Night. Ask for a drink called a fire in the sky."

Vylia held him in an intense gaze. "What's your father's name?"

"That is too dangerous for you to know . . . until you arrive safely."

A huff of frustration escaped her. "Then what can you tell me? I know next to nothing about them!"

Sousuke glanced at the guard behind her, but he either didn't hear her outburst or didn't care.

How much should he tell her, exactly? As much as possible, he decided. It would give her the best chances. The motivation. And the ability to tell the difference between good and evil.

"Come closer," Sousuke whispered. "I have to start from the beginning.

It's a long story. Okay?"

Vylia nodded, sending a black hair in front of her face, which she hastily pushed away. "I'm listening."

He swallowed, and his throat felt like a chasm in the Kioan desert. "Water?"

Vylia quickly supplied some that had been sitting in a jar nearby, and Sousuke drank slowly but deeply. Through the movements, he confirmed that his pain was even more dulled now. Glorious skies!

"When Aeo created the world, he gave humans great power," Sousuke began under his breath. "Two different powers: the elements and the aether. He hoped that humans would use them for good, but also knew in his great wisdom . . . that many would use magic for evil. So he split the aether into different gifts . . . and gave each human child a talent for only one. But as for the four elements: Phoera of energy, Malo of liquid, Aris of air . . . and . . ."

His throat constricted, and he coughed, sending pain lancing through his chest like branches of lightning.

"T-take a rest," Vylia said. Lines of worry creased her brow as she dabbed at his chin with a damp cloth. It came away with blurry red speckles. "I know the final element: Terruth, of solid materials, like stone."

At least he didn't have to say it.

"Yes," Sousuke said as his breathing steadied. He swallowed the taste of blood. "The elements were split . . . into four human bloodlines. Four *amos*—one for each element—served as the source of elemental power on Alani. And seven *trai'yeth* . . . for each element . . . acted as stewards . . . and policed humans who abused their power."

"This was the original purpose of the gods and lesser gods?" Vylia murmured, staring past him in thought. "Then why do they have domains, such as fertility, warfare, music, luck—"

"Some idiot made all that up." Sousuke suppressed another cough. "Just because humans worship them as gods doesn't mean they truly are."

Vylia looked amused. "I've never heard any of this before, and yet you're so sure of it. You're telling me the entire elemental religion is false, and a continent full of people who believe it are idiots?"

"They are deceived," Sousuke said. "Many of the elementals enjoyed being worshiped and claimed to be gods themselves. Ruled over people. All kinds of wickedness flourished." He looked behind Vylia to the guard again, who still looked bored and hadn't moved. "The Lotusfall is an alliance of the few *trai'yeth* . . . who remain loyal to the creator. We stand against the false gods to free humans of their tyranny."

"'*We?*'" Vylia repeated. "Are you an elemental, soldier?"

"I am quite mortal, I assure you." His wounds were excellent reminders of that. "However . . . nearly every member of the Lotusfall does have elemental heritage. They were originally formed . . . by the children of Lillian and Felix."

Vylia's eyes widened. "You are descended of Lillian?"

Sousuke closed his eyes and took another deep breath in defiance of the pain. "There are other *trai'yeth*—who have been loyal to the creator from the start—who compose our bloodline and lead the Lotusfall today."

Vylia leaned forward and her whisper grew louder with her excitement. "Who? Shayara? Jasper? Arianne?"

Sousuke shook his head. "Too dangerous to say." He wondered if there was any more of that nasty liquid she'd offered before. "The children of Lillian and Felix rose up against their empire, but there was a big problem: evil *trai'yeth* are more powerful than those who are good, and the same is true for *ko'yeth*."

"Human and elemental hybrids," Vylia said.

"Yes." Sousuke opened his eyes again and studied her features, particularly her eyes. The black of her pupils was deep and strong, so she was clearly human. But he wondered if the imperial monarchy had any elemental blood in it as well. Considering how often the power-hungry *trai'yeth* slithered their way into royal palaces in disguise, it wasn't just possible, but probable.

"*Trai'yeth* cannot hold an unlimited amount of syn—elemental power— like the *amos* can. If they absorb a vast quantity, they will have great power, but it will drive them mad. So they tend to hoard vast amounts of syn and lose their minds, inflicting all sorts of deranged evil upon the humans who follow them. Human sacrifice, senseless war, slavery, perversion."

Vylia furrowed her brow. "Humans are capable of great evil as well."

"Yes, but it is easier to overthrow an evil king than an evil elemental," Sousuke said. "The Lotusfall act as an organized unit because it takes several sane *ko'yeth* and *trai'yeth* to match the power of a single unhinged *trai'yeth*."

"I understand," Vylia said quietly. "But then, why are the Lotusfall moving against my father? We are human—"

Sousuke squeezed Vylia's hand, and she stopped talking as the far door opened. Lieutenant Sa'alu stepped in through the light.

His blood boiled at the sight of the man. If only he'd unleashed his element and destroyed him when he'd had the chance!

"Say goodbye, Princess," Sa'alu said as he approached. "We're leaving."

"What?" Vylia turned and balked. "Leaving?"

"We did everything you asked, but he's going to die regardless. No use sitting around and waiting." Sa'alu looked down his nose at Sousuke's bandages. "I'll remind you that we're in enemy territory. You're lucky they agreed to treat him at all. But of course the medicine of savages is nothing but sticks and leaves. Surely you didn't think they could save him."

Tears fell down Vylia's cheeks as Sousuke's anger burned. "You can't just leave him to die alone!" Vylia shouted.

"I can and I will," Sa'alu said. "Say goodbye and get back in the carriage."

Vylia shot to her feet and screamed, "No!"

Sa'alu motioned to the guard, who crossed the room in a few long strides and grabbed Vylia by the arm. She cried out and twisted helplessly in his grip.

Sousuke reached for his sword, and blinding pain seared through him. He couldn't find the hilt. Where was his sword?

The guard dragged Vylia, writhing and yelling, to the back door and out of sight.

Sousuke cursed his wounds and relaxed, calling for the element that he'd forbidden himself from using for years. Did he remember how to use it? Had he ever really learned in the first place?

"What is the meaning of this?" a voice called from the opposite direction in the Phoeran language.

Sousuke's concentration shattered as he turned his head to see a tattooed tribesman appear from the opposite door. In his hand was a flint weapon that looked like a hatchet.

"It is shameful for you to treat a woman this way," the tribesman said in a deep voice.

"Apologies for the noise," Sa'alu said in Phoeran, but with such a thick Malaano accent that Sousuke wondered if the man would be able to understand. "She is mourning the loss of her man here. We must go now. But we leave him in your care, and we thank you." Sa'alu dropped a handful of *rupero*, the tribal currency, on Sousuke's bandaged chest.

The tribesman glared at him. Strode forward and collected the money. Sousuke realized as the weight of the coins lifted that it was payment for his burial.

"Leave our lands. Take your war back to your island." The Phoeran turned and left the way he had come.

A faint smile lifted Sa'alu's face as he watched the man leave. "Well, then." Sa'alu looked down at Sousuke. "Enjoy Zoth." He strode toward the back door.

"What are you going to do with Vylia?" Sousuke demanded. "Collect on the bounty that the emperor put on her?"

Sa'alu paused, his back still turned. "Of course not. A bounty would confirm that she is, in fact, alive."

"There are assassins after her," Sousuke said. "But you have not killed her yet. So what are you planning to do with her?"

Sa'alu glanced back over his shoulder, tired eyes landing on Sousuke. "What point is there in talking to a dead man?"

"To cure your boredom," Sousuke tried.

The lieutenant appeared amused. "I don't have any plans for her, actually."

"Lies. You are the type of man to plan and scheme for years in advance to effectuate your own wealth."

Now Sa'alu looked intrigued. "You are perceptive for your age. Curious. Perhaps now I understand why such a young one was assigned as a royal bodyguard."

"You are evading my questions," Sousuke said. "If you truly have no plans, it won't hurt you to answer."

Sa'alu sighed. "I suppose not." He turned to face Sousuke but kept his distance. He turned his head and yelled, "Get everything ready and let me know when we're ready to depart," then turned back to Sousuke. "One of my companions has an interest in her."

So, Lillian was speaking to him, then. He was keeping Vylia alive on her behalf, and she would do everything in her power to force Vylia to become her vessel.

Because, with a royal vessel in line for the throne, Lillian would have a rightful claim to her millennia-old title of empress.

Sousuke considered his words carefully. "You won't speak to a dead man, but you'll speak to a rock?"

Sa'alu chuckled. "A rock with knowledge of ancient treasures."

Lillian had promised him treasures from her vault, then. "That vault was emptied years ago," he lied. Lillian's vault was locked up so tight that no one had ever been able to enter.

"So, the vault *does* exist," Sa'alu said.

Sousuke mentally kicked himself but kept his face straight. "If you are half as intelligent as you appear, you know Lillian is a liar. She won't give you a feather's weight of her riches, if any remain."

"And how would a pubescent bodyguard know of these things?" Sa'alu took a couple of steps closer, inspecting Sousuke. "You don't appear to be fully Malaano. Your skin is darker, your hair lighter and straighter. A Terruthian half-breed, if I had to guess."

The room suddenly felt hotter. "Tell me what Lillian has planned for Vylia, and I'll share a secret," Sousuke said. He was playing with fire. But he had nothing to lose.

Sa'alu's eyebrows lifted. "All right, then. It seems Lillian seeks a vessel, and Vylia is her first choice."

He already knew that. "What will Lillian do if Vylia refuses?"

"Ah, but it's your turn."

Sousuke reached for something to offer that wouldn't harm his people. "I am not as young as I look."

Sa'alu tilted his head. "Is it your Terruthian side that was an elemental, or your Malaano?"

Alarm flared through Sousuke. This man was dangerous.

Somewhere beyond their room, Vylia's shout pierced the air.

Sousuke gritted his teeth. "Your turn. What will Lillian do if Vylia refuses?" he repeated.

Sa'alu considered for a moment. "I don't know, though it would be foolishness to be rid of such a valuable asset at this time."

Tribesmen burst through the entrance. The one who'd left a few moments ago, plus another on either side. All with weapons drawn.

"Tell us who you are and who your prisoner girl is," the one in the middle said.

Sousuke prayed a wordless, desperate prayer that these men would not let the Malaano escape.

"Prisoner?" Sa'alu said. "What makes you think that?"

The tribesman just stared.

Sa'alu's friendly candor evaporated. "It is beyond your understanding and not your concern."

"We have shown you much grace and understanding, son of water. You are our enemy, yet we allowed you in for the sake of the dying. You owe an explanation."

"The girl is your enemy, and she deserves no mercy." Sa'alu began to leave. "Thank you for your hospitalit—"

"Liar!" Sousuke said in Phoeran. "He lies."

Sa'alu turned on his heel and fled.

The tribesmen burst into a sprint, and Sousuke remained still as they ran around his cot. Five, seven, nine . . . He lost count.

A woman ran in behind them, and Sousuke called out to her. "Wait!"

She fixed him in a brown gaze.

"Please," Sousuke said. "Will you send a letter for me, as my dying wish?"

She seemed to understand, as she pulled parchment and charcoal wrapped in cloth from a fold in her dress.

Sousuke took a steadying breath. It felt like the effects of the foul drink were beginning to wear off. He did his best to concentrate.

"To Rhu Hana of Shallowater . . . in Way Maar, Malaan Island. Sell my belongings to pay for the postage." He had no idea where his belongings were, or if Sa'alu had taken them, but he had nothing else to plausibly offer.

The woman wrote and nodded.

"The kitsune takes the bud . . . and moves for her treasures."

Sousuke closed his eyes and thought of his mother. She'd be devastated to hear of his death in a letter like this. But what else could he say? How could he thank her for all she'd done, for all she'd endured, all she'd sacrificed, in a coded letter?

"The last protector falls . . . and sends all his love. He waits on the shores of kai'lani."

It was the best he could think to do.

The tribal woman finished writing and looked up at him. *"Firma?"*

Sousuke didn't recall the meaning of that Phoeran word, but she was offering him the charcoal and parchment. Oh, perhaps she wanted him to sign his name.

He couldn't seem to grasp the charcoal properly. His signature looked terrible. But it would have to do.

"Then write . . . a second letter, please. Send it to the Katrosi chief immediately. Tell him . . . the Imperial Princess Vylia is here."

The woman's eyes widened. "Princess?"

Sousuke nodded. "She must be rescued from those men . . . at all costs. For the sake of both our peoples."

11

VYLIA

Vylia yelled in rage and terror as the earth flew beneath her feet. The grip on her arm was so tight that she'd lost feeling. The man hauled her as he ran as if hoisting a heavy bag.

Her squirming was of no avail, but at least she could keep yelling through her tears. Then the Sekoiako would hear her and know where to pursue. Surely being taken by the tribesmen—not her own people, whose language she didn't even know—would be preferable to these Malaano brutes with no respect for their own princess.

She would not leave Sousuke to die alone if there was any strength left in her. She'd lost the majority of her entourage, her friends—Uma, Juli, Xi—without getting to say goodbye before the traitor Aoko had murdered them.

Sousuke was the last one she had left. And . . . he was more than just a bodyguard. She didn't know what he was, exactly. But she couldn't let him go.

Vylia struggled in the Malaano soldier's grip and snarled, though, admittedly, it sounded more like an angry kitten. She found a break between the metal plates of armor, slipped her hand under the chain mail between, and dug her nails into the flesh beneath sweaty cloth.

Then she screamed again with all her might, until her voice began to fail.

Something slammed into the side of her head. Pain exploded with visions like fireworks from the White Snow festival in Maqua. Then her vision blackened entirely.

Fear and sorrow eclipsed her last hope as the world slowly returned as a moving blur and a whine in her ears. She felt her body being tousled, like a doll being hastily maneuvered into a sitting position. What was she sitting on? It was moving!

"Hold on," a man's voice commanded.

The thing beneath her jolted forward and Vylia instinctively gripped the man in front of her—his back? She looked down. A scaled beast? Blood streamed from a cut on her head and obscured her vision.

Her tears helped to clear the blood from her eyes. She blinked through the pain and shuddered with uncontrollable sobs. Between her and the beast was a tribal-style saddle made of leather and beads that clattered rhythmically as the animal trotted through the underbrush. Had the Malaano stolen some Sekoiako xavi?

I'm sorry for your loss, little minnow. A voice entered her mind, soothing like water.

Vylia gritted her teeth as she found a target for all of her anguish. "Curse you, Lillian!"

Join with me and you will never taste that sorrow again. Or fear. I will protect you.

"Indeed, I would never feel anything again, because you would carve out my soul and use my body like a geku doll," Vylia said, her voice flickering in and out through her ragged throat.

Oh no, my dear! You would maintain your own will and consciousness, sharper than ever before. You would simply share yourself with me, as I would share my power and vast knowledge with you. I may not even have to inhabit your body, since I am an amos. *It could just be a simple bond. Let's find out together.*

Vylia felt a devious smile curl her lips as a thought occurred to her. "I must need to be willing, because otherwise you would have forced me already."

Silence fell, other than the sound of beasts crunching through the forest. Then a man yelling at another, and someone yelling back.

Lillian's voice emerged again. *It would certainly be more pleasant for both of us if you were willing.*

Vylia found herself laughing, reveling in the only power she had left over anything in her life.

"Never."

A disapproving sound like a clicking tongue reverberated through Vylia's mind. *You called me a liar, but you are a liar yourself. You said you would accept me if I saved that young man.*

Vylia hated her more than anything. More than being called a liar. She didn't care what Lillian thought. She didn't care what the soldier in front of her thought, either, hearing her respond to nothing but the wind.

"I said I would do it if he lived," Vylia said, though of course she wouldn't have unleashed this demon-god upon the world regardless.

If you are not willing, you are worthless to me. I could have Sa'alu end you and leave your body on the road, and no one would know or care.

Vylia wondered how fast they were going. Very fast.

She let go of the soldier and flung herself from the xavi.

The earth came up and slammed into Vylia, wresting the breath from her lungs. She gasped and started from the pain in her shoulder, head, hips.

No! Foolish girl! You cannot escape . . . Lillian's voice faded away.

Vylia determined the direction of Lillian's voice, although it was not physical. She hauled herself up and ran in the opposite direction.

The xavi had broken through the forest, leaving a trail that Vylia followed, limping and wheezing.

Creator god, if you are real, please! Save us!

Thumping pounded behind her. Louder and louder.

No! Vylia screamed as loud as she could. Her voice cracked and failed.

Rough hands grabbed her. Lifted her. The tears returned as she struggled, as helpless as a fish in a bear's mouth.

"You have lost your privileges." She recognized Sa'alu's voice. "I told you there would be consequences."

Something that tasted vile was forced down her throat. She coughed and sputtered. No, the vile taste was blood—the goo tasted like sleep-time tea. Fadeleaf.

Her strength drained and her vision blurred once again, but in a more pleasant way this time. Her pain ebbed.

"Can't take that infernal carriage, anyway," she heard someone say.

"No roads the way we're going."

The image of a map floated to Vylia's mind as sleep beckoned her. But not a map of the tribal lands. One she'd seen affixed to the wall of her father's war room as a child. In the center was an artful depiction of Malaan Island, with frothy waves on its shores and stalwart palaces nestled in its mountains.

Home.

The comfort of sleep beckoned Vylia, but she refused to accept its embrace. Rejected it wholeheartedly.

She fell, numb and writhing, into a dark oblivion.

12

KIRALAU

Kira grunted as she pulled back on the string of her invention, wondering how much tension the bending wood could take. It was meant to be a miniature version of the Katrosi harpoon launchers from Jadenvive—just on her wrist instead, shooting feathered bolts instead of giant javelins. But judging by the amount of modifications and lack of progress, the contraption seemed more likely to maul her arm rather than actually fire anything.

A knock on the door startled Kira into loosing the string, which dry fired with a loud *thwap.* She cringed, sighed, and carefully laid the amalgamation of wood, gears, and leather straps atop her schematics.

"Coming," she called as she ran to the door. On the other side was her new sister-in-law, Aegwyn, beaming at Kira with her hands behind her back. Her resemblance to Ryon was striking, with the same tilt to her eyes, olive skin tone, and something else about her slender face that Kira couldn't identify.

"Hi! Sorry to bother," Aegwyn said.

"No bother." Kira grabbed an oil rag and rubbed a smudge of grease from her elbow. "How're you today?" She stepped aside so the other could enter.

"All right," Aegwyn responded as she came inside. "I ran into Idryon in the hall, and he asked me to help you pack for your trip."

Kira shot her a confused look. "Trip?"

Aegwyn tilted her head. "To the Moon Festival?"

"Oh! Uh . . ." Did Ryon want to leave so quickly? Was it that late in the year already? Yes, now that Kira thought about it, she remembered the corn looking ready for harvest . . . Which would mean cornhusk dolls for the festival.

Kira surveyed the mess her experimenting had made and put her hands on her hips. She'd have to pack it all up again. Or should she leave it here? Why did she need to make a weapon, anyway? The time of conflict had passed. For her and Ryon, at least.

But she wouldn't mind some extra protection on the way to Navarro.

"Well, I guess I'd appreciate your help," Kira said as she knelt to begin organizing components. "I wouldn't really know where to start in gettin' provisions around here."

"Already procured!" Aegwyn sang. She revealed two bags that had been hidden behind her back. "I wasn't sure what you like, so I got a bit of everything. Took a dozen eggs for Ryon and wrapped them well, so hopefully they won't break."

"Thanks," Kira said with a grin. "Was Ryon finished with his meeting with the king, then, if you passed him in the hall?"

"Yes," Aegwyn said with a sparkle in her eye. "He looked really excited about something. He told me to tell you to meet him at the trace cat den."

Kira had never heard of such a place. And what was Ryan so excited about? It was strange enough that the king had summoned Ryon back so soon after they'd already met. "The what?"

"The trace cat den," Aegwyn repeated. "On the first floor, around the side of the fountain, near the stables."

Kira stared at her, wondering what on earth the Emberhawk wanted trace cats for. Surely not as pets. She'd seen the sign about King Lysander's trace cat pride at the beach, but surely that was just an eccentric old king flaunting his wealth.

"For fightin' for sport?" she guessed.

"No, for riding!" Aegwyn said with a laugh.

That was even more bizarre. "I think I've heard someone mention Emberhawk ridin' trace cats before, but I thought that was a joke . . ."

Aegwyn shook her head. "It was commonplace for our forefathers, but Zamara slaughtered the royal pride for their syn. Cori and his rebels were able to sneak in and steal a few of them before the bloodline was completely lost. So there are a few tame trace cats left, and Cori returned them to their den here in the palace. Iraleth is determined to tame new wild cats to interbreed, save the royal bloodline, and restore the tradition."

"Fascinating," Kira mused as she tried to envision such a thing. Then a frightening thought struck her. "Surely Ryon doesn't mean for us to ride trace cats to Navarro . . ."

Aegwyn giggled and sang, "Let's go find out!"

Kira wasn't prepared for how large the royal trace cats were. The one she stared at now, in an enclosure surely not able to contain such a beast, was so much bigger than the wild one she and Lee had killed. And she couldn't even tell if it was male or female.

The beast turned its enormous head and caught her in an intense yellow gaze. Its stripes were much more vivid than the wild cats of the Gnarled Wood, etching its face in a fearsome pattern. Its two saber teeth looked as long as Kira's arm.

Kira broke eye contact and hurried past the enclosure, regretting saying goodbye to Aegwyn. How she wished her sister-in-law were still with her as she anxiously looked for Ryon, feeling more and more like prey with each passing second.

"Ryon?" she called as she passed another pen. The cat in this one had the strangest blue color to its fur.

"Here!" a familiar voice called, and Kira was flooded with relief. She rushed toward Ryon's shout and, finding him *inside* a trace cat enclosure, the relief disappeared. An enormous feline towered over him. Ryon was petting the thing as if it were a sheepdog.

"Hey, *balem*—" Ryon stopped when he saw her expression. "It's okay. This is Klandagi. I've known him since I was a kid."

That didn't make Kira feel any better. She moved to the railing and clutched it like Ryon's life depended on it. "What are you doin' in there?"

Ryon gave Klandagi two solid pats and jogged over to Kira. "It's safe, I promise," Ryon said as he approached.

Words jumbled and lodged in Kira's throat. She couldn't take her eyes off the massive tiger.

"Oh, I'm sorry, I forgot . . . You've had some scary encounters with trace cats, yeah? Don't worry—these are tame."

Kira had a hard time believing that. "Please don't ask me to ride one of those."

Ryon chuckled. "Oh, no. I'd have to train a long time with one. Form a bond of trust and re-learn the saddle and commands and all that. I've been gone too long."

"Then what are you doin' in its enclosure?" Kira said through clenched teeth. She didn't take her eyes off the massive feline, who stared at her with apparent disinterest.

"I, uh . . ." Ryon scratched the back of his neck. "Well, it's a long story. Basically I promised Felix I'd get something for him. And he hid it somewhere in here."

Kira re-played his words in her head, trying to get them to make sense. "Felix hid somethin' in a trace cat enclosure?" How was that elemental rascal still sowing chaos from beyond the grave?

"It was part of my oath to become one of Felix's vessels, a long time ago." Ryon gave her a sheepish look, apparently unaware or unconcerned that he was still inside the lair of a man-eating beast. "He told me that if he ever died, I should go to the fire in the Crow's Nest of Jadenvive and find a small box with an artifact, and to keep it on me for the rest of—" His tanned skin flushed as he stumbled over his words. "But, well, since I know Lysander was one of Felix's vessels, too, we talked, and decided to switch places."

Kira's brows knit together. "Switch places?"

"Since Lysander and Brooke were planning on going back to Jadenvive, he offered to get my box from the Crow's Nest, and I could get his box here."

Kira frowned. "Why would Felix hide ancient artifacts in giant lighthouse fires and trace cat dens?"

"I have no idea," Ryon said. "To protect them, maybe?"

As Kira considered how to voice her displeasure, Ryon spoke again. "But I think I found it already. I just need one more—"

Kira gasped as Klandagi vanished.

"Huh?" Ryon turned around and glanced about the enclosure. "Oh, he does that sometimes."

Kira's gaze darted from shrub to rock to hanging vines, but there was no sign of the trace cat. Her pulse pounded through her ears. "Get out of there," she whispered. All he had to do was climb over the wooden half-wall or gate that separated them. But of course that wouldn't protect them.

"I have to go back real quick. But don't worry."

Klandagi's striped face reappeared not five feet from Kira, enormous yellow eyes still fixated on her as if they'd never strayed.

Panic leaped up and lodged in Kira's throat. Her hand shot for the d'hakka blade on her belt. "Get. Out."

"Dagi, *ona ellwyn.*" Ryon turned and patted Klandagi's mane, and the cat turned its gaze to him. *"Ellwyn."*

Kira didn't recognize that Phoeran, but she didn't care. "Ryon, please . . ."

Ryon turned back to her, further alarming Kira as he exposed his back to the predator. He reached for her hand and moved until he was directly in her line of sight, forcing eye contact. "It's all right," he said gently but firmly. "Trust me."

"I trust you. I don't trust *it.*"

"I'll be right back." Ryon kissed her hand, released it, and turned to walk back into the lion's den.

Kira didn't breathe. Didn't remove her other hand from her dagger. Didn't take her eyes off the beast as it turned to watch Ryon, its tail flicking side to side.

She breathed a curse, then prayed, then felt guilty for cursing and praying at the same time. Her heart slammed into her ribcage as if trying to escape a prison.

Ryon crouched toward the back of the enclosure, where a constructed area with a feeding trough and water bowl met earth and grass. He scratched at something on the ground—whether stone floor or dirt, Kira couldn't tell. She didn't take her eyes off of the carnivore that watched her husband.

Ryon widened his stance and lifted a wide, flat stone with a grunt. Setting it aside, he reached into the earth and retrieved something small and dark.

Dizziness grazed Kira, and she remembered to breathe. She realized her nails were digging into her skin as she clutched her dagger, and she took a deep, shuddering breath and relaxed her grip. She told herself it was okay. Again. And again. But something deep inside her didn't listen.

"This must be it!" Ryon called, holding the object aloft. He then stuffed it in a pocket, replaced the stone, and jogged back to her.

Klandagi flopped to the ground and rolled over, exposing his stomach as Ryon passed. He stretched out wide, flexing paws bigger than Kira's head and exposing claws like curved Malaano fishing knives.

"Aww, fine," Ryon said as he rubbed the cat's belly. "Who's a good one? Who's the biggest, goodest one? Who scared my wife? Who got me in big trouble, huh? Huh?" His pet voice was undeniably adorable, but drowned out by the loudest purring Kira had ever heard.

Kira pursed her lips as Ryon finished doting upon the trace cat and made his way over to her. He leaped over the half-wall instead of going through the gate. "I'm sorry. I completely forgot that these things are scary when they're wild. They avoid me in the forest—they think I'm one of them. Because of the Phoera in my blood, and they're very territorial, yeah?" He kissed her forehead. "I should remember the reason you shot me in the first place is because you thought I was a trace cat."

Kira couldn't stay mad at him as the aftershock of terror gave her the jitters. "It's okay. I tried to control myself, it just . . . I didn't have much control over it." She hated to admit it. Hated not being in control. Shouldn't she have mastery over her own mind?

"We all have fears, *balemba*. I will be better at respecting yours." Ryon reached into his pocket and withdrew a dirt-encrusted object, which Kira could now see was a small chest.

"It's not *mine*. Well, I don't want it. I'll get rid of it," Kira said. "It makes sense that they could be tamed, I guess. I should be able to reason with fear."

"Easier said than done." Ryon turned the box around in his hand and located a tiny mechanism. "Whoa, it's so old. What kind of lock is this?" He picked at the grime.

"Can we . . . do this somewhere else?" Kira said, still all too aware of the trace cat in her peripheral vision.

"Yes, of course." Ryon looked up and started walking toward the nearest exit. "I've never seen anything like this before. Felix didn't say anything about a key, if memory serves."

Kira released a deep breath as they left the beasts and their smells behind. She appreciated the distraction of the ancient treasure. How could something so small be so important?

"Did Felix say what it was?" she asked.

"No, and he wouldn't answer my questions when I asked," Ryon said. "I got the feeling it was something he never wanted to see again. And obviously he wasn't planning on dying. Like a worst-case scenario . . ." He bit his lip as if regretting the words as soon as he'd said them.

"That's not ominous at all," Kira muttered. "Is it something that elementalists could track? Will we have one of Felix's old enemies hunting us down now?"

"No, it can't be tracked. Trust me, it took forever to find, even knowing where it was hidden," Ryon said. "So I assume Aegwyn found you? Are you all packed and ready to go?"

An obvious and sudden change of topic, but Kira decided to allow it. "Yes, she packed us all kinds of food, but I have to grab a few more things." She looked at him sidelong. "Why the rush all of a sudden? And what did the king have to say, after we just met with him?"

"There's an armed caravan leaving the palace later today, heading west to resupply the battle line. I'd like to join them and take advantage of the opportunity," Ryon said. "Strength in numbers, you know. I wouldn't want to run into bandits or anything on the road. We can join them for part of the journey, at least."

That was a relief. Kira was glad to hear that Ryon was taking her concerns about their safety seriously. "Only part of the way?"

"Yes." Ryon elongated the word with a sultry tone. "We're making a stop along the way, just you and me. Then we'll go the rest of the way to Navarro ourselves. The Moon Festival should have started by the time we'll arrive, yeah?"

"Oh, really? A private stop, you say?" Kira grinned. "What're you plottin'? I notice you're avoiding my question about the king."

Ryon's fiery eyes lit with excitement. "It's a surprise."

13

BROOKE

Brooke felt strange without Lysander at her side. They'd only been married for a few weeks. How had she become so attached to him already?

And yet, it felt good to be alone again. Except she hadn't truly been alone for years . . . The invisible azure masks had followed her everywhere.

Maybe they still did.

That familiar concoction of doubt and worry slithered in the back of her mind. Could Ulysses really be trusted? As a former political opponent, he had reason to oppose her in any manner of ways . . .

Brooke banished the thought. Ulysses hadn't given her any reason to worry—recently, at least. She'd been the one to make him her vice. And now, if there were consequences to be paid, well, it was her own doing.

She pulled her hood down further, so much so that it was difficult to see her way along the empty city street through Jadenvive's ground level. Surely no one would recognize her without her headdress and warpaint, but she wouldn't take any chances. Especially in this part of the city. Especially without Lysander.

Where was he right now? Did he miss her, too?

"*Chk*." Brooke made the noise to scold herself. How could he miss her after less than an hour? He was probably shopping for healing herbs, exactly as he'd told her.

She took a deep breath. Why was she worried about everything? Hopefully Lysander was also acquiring ingredients for that calming herbal tea.

Music escaped through the slats of a wooden door before Brooke. It neither stood upright nor lay flat on the ground, but leaned into the base of one of Jadenvive's great trees at an angle. A sign above it bore etched letters: THE ICE BOX.

Brooke took hold of the enormous iron handle and hauled it upward with all her strength. Cold air and sounds of mirth rose up to greet her as she descended the steps.

Drums and deep strings plucked out a familiar song. Right on queue, the voices of dozens of men shouted a refrain and pounded on tables.

Brooke couldn't help but smile as the underground tavern came into view. Previously a massive cellar that had served as one of Jadenvive's storehouses, an unfortunate flooding accident had forced the damaged goods to be evacuated years ago. Now, the Ice Box only held waterproof stock—namely, spirits and brew stored in glass bottles. Hundreds of them lined walls made entirely of ice, upon shelves of ice. Glowing mushrooms were grown in the earth behind them, giving the tavern a glassy ambiance through the elementally maintained ice, making it glow blue like the sun lighting upon a glacier.

There were noticeably fewer bottles since the last time Brooke had visited. Perhaps the Malaano had raided some. Or maybe they'd been distributed to other villages in the evacuation. Or the boisterous Katrosi soldiers crowding every table could provide enough explanation for the shortage.

Brooke spotted a table in the corner and kept her head bowed as she slipped into the chair, glad for her hooded cloak for warmth as much as secrecy. It didn't appear that anyone paid her any heed. She found herself humming the familiar tune about a farmer who fell in love with the daughter of his father's enemy.

"What can I get you?" asked a server who suddenly appeared.

Brooke ordered her favorite meal from memory: chicken bone-broth soup with roasted green peppers and cheese. Unfortunately the kitchen was out of slow-cooked long beans, even though they were in season—the fields must have been consumed by fire, or the harvest taken by the evacuees. But grilled sweet corn on the side would do nicely. Brooke was happy to have whatever she could of the meal she'd ordered countless times, regardless.

She looked around for Nariellyn, who frequented this place, but was so filled with comfort at being here that she wouldn't mind if she couldn't find her friend. If she hadn't attracted any attention so far, maybe she was safe.

After a minute of scanning patrons, Brooke located Nariellyn at the bar. She grinned at the sight of her predictable friend.

"Nari!" Brooke yelled twice, then waved when the healer turned, searching for whoever had called her name. She spotted Brooke and wove through the crowd, still yell-singing the folk song.

"What're you doing back here in the dark?" Nariellyn scolded. "I barely recognized you."

"That's the idea," Brooke said. "I'm not very popular right now."

Nariellyn frowned. "What?"

"Everyone thinks I'm a traitor," Brooke muttered under her breath, unsure if her friend could hear her over the song. "How've you been? I wish we hadn't been separated, but thank you for healing Iraleth."

"Nonsense," Nariellyn said, slamming her mug down on the table for emphasis. "Anyone who thinks you're a traitor doesn't know you."

Brooke shrugged. "Well, I guess nobody knows me then. It's my own fault for marrying a blood-hawk." She patted the seat next to her. "Join me?"

Nariellyn pursed her lips together and furrowed her brow, then stared into nothingness.

"It's fine," Brooke said. "I'll just lie low for a bit."

Nariellyn didn't move.

Brooke frowned. "What's wrong?"

"You are."

Brooke examined her friend. She seemed guarded. Angry.

"It's no big deal," Brooke said.

"Yes, it is," Nariellyn said. "You're wrong, and I'll prove it. Just give me a minute."

What was she up to? Surely she wouldn't do anything stupid . . .

"Don't you dare—"

Brooke reached for her friend and missed as Nariellyn jumped up on the table and yelled at the top of her lungs: "When the blood-hawk attacked, who was the first to charge into their lands?"

The crowd fell quiet as the song ended.

"Who went in without an army, but just a handful of men?" Nariellyn cried. All eyes focused on her.

Brooke's throat clenched shut. She grabbed Nariellyn's ankle and pulled, but the young woman didn't budge.

"Stillwind," said a man in the crowd.

"Who uprooted the daughter of the blood-hawk queen?" Nariellyn demanded.

"Stillwind," said a few.

"And placed our own puppet on their false-god throne?"

"Stillwind!"

Brooke didn't breathe as Nari beat her chest, and somehow her voice got even louder. "Who spared your sons from the blood-hawk's black shores, where the blood of our forefathers spilled and dried?"

"Stillwind!" more men yelled back.

"And who freed us to turn our spears on the devil Malaano and drive the water-dogs from our lands?"

"STILLWIND!" the crowd roared, pounding on the tables.

Heat prickled Brooke's neck and flushed up to her eyes. She would not cry. She would not cry.

Nari looked down at Brooke and gave a devilish grin. "You were saying?"

"I hate you," Brooke whispered. She yanked her friend off the table and climbed up in her place. She pulled her hood off to reveal her face. The men whooped.

"I chose Ulysses!" Brooke yelled. "But I will never stop fighting for you. Together with our allies, we will destroy any invader who dares step foot in the shade of our trees. Strength and humility!"

"STRENGTH!" The table shuddered beneath her feet.

"A round on me!" yelled a man in the crowd. Cheers erupted, and a new song began as Brooke hopped down from the table.

Nari finally took a seat, and a long swig from her drink. Her tankard thumped down on the table, and she seemed mighty pleased with herself.

"Anyway," she said in a sweet voice.

Brooke glared at her friend, her heart on fire. "I can't decide whether I should hit you or thank you."

"Maybe both, but your disguise wasn't working anyway."

Brooke sighed. "Thank you, you insufferable sprite."

Nariellyn sported a huge grin. "No problem. Any time you're feeling delirious again, come back here, and I'll set you straight."

"This was a mistake," Brooke said through her teeth as she smiled at a red-cheeked young man who approached their table offering his gushing adoration. He looked barely old enough to wear soldier's garb, much less have a drink.

By the time Brooke's line of fans neared its end, her meal was delivered, and the server shooed the remaining patrons away so she could eat. Brooke was grateful for the gesture as the smell of the soup calmed her nerves.

"I was afraid of that," Nariellyn said as Brooke savored her first steaming-hot mouthful.

"Hmm?"

Nariellyn's gaze flicked to Brooke's hairline, and she grimaced. "Your hair is all torn up where your headdress used to affix." She dug around in a pocket, then withdrew a brown piece of cloth with white decoration. "Try this."

Brooke gently patted the hair on her forehead, where short whisps escaped her braids. Nariellyn wasn't wrong—the hair had been damaged from the weight of her headdress, which she'd worn daily. Maybe she should care more about her appearance now that she didn't have a handmaiden to tend to her, or war paint for making a political statement every day. It had been exhausting to determine if she should wear the paint of sorrow or jubilation when funerals and births both happened daily.

She admired the swirls and dots along the cloth as she rolled it into a long strip. Something felt . . . strange about it. "Where did you get this?"

"Queen Iraleth," Nariellyn said. "She was so grateful for my healing, and once she was crowned, she gave me a bunch of stuff from Zamara's chambers. Clearing out the former regime, as it were."

Brooke ran her fingers along the cloth, trying to determine why it felt . . . interesting? Different? She couldn't place it. "Zamara liked bandanas?"

"I don't know. What's with the face? You don't like it? It's your color."

Brooke frowned, wishing that her favorite color, dark green, looked better next to her features when she wore it. Brown just seemed . . . boring, but she would take boring over excitement right now.

"No, I like it," Brooke murmured, taking another bite. Then she realized what the strange feeling was. "It feels like aether."

"What?" Nariellyn snatched the cloth back, held it in both hands, and closed her eyes. "What on Alani? What kind of aether gift is this?"

"The Elder of Aether mentioned a rare gift that could weave aether into physical objects," Brooke said, then reached for the grilled corn. "I think he called it the weaver gift."

"Yeah, but what kind of aether has been woven into it?" Nariellyn wondered, holding it up to the light, as if that would reveal the invisible energy.

"I don't know," Brooke said through a mouthful, then remembered her manners and swallowed the deliciously sweet corn. "It can't be dangerous, right?"

"I dunno." Nariellyn said, handing it back. "I can ask . . ." She trailed off.

Sadness encroached on Brooke like a midnight wave. They couldn't ask the Elder of Aether for his wisdom anymore. Was he given a funeral? Did she miss it? Or would they have a mass funeral for everyone who'd been lost in the Malaano attack?

She put the folded bandana across her hairline and tied it behind her head. Surely some of the wisps escaped. "Like this?" She felt silly.

Nariellyn bit her lip as she grinned. *"Aish,* it's too cute! You have to keep it. Your gorgeous new husband will love it without even noticing it."

Brooke enjoyed the feel of the bandana—she'd felt naked without her headdress. This would be a much lighter replacement. She felt around with her fingertips, trying to get an idea of what it looked like. "Jealous?"

"Of course." Nariellyn stole a piece of meat and Brooke smacked at her hand with the spoon. She was too fast. "But I've discovered a new specimen."

Brooke gave her a warning glare over the bowl's edge as she sipped the broth. "Yes, another five seconds have passed, so that makes sense."

Nariellyn narrowed her eyes. "The world is a wonderful place, my friend. There are marvels and beauties all around us to behold." She leaned forward and whispered, "Have you heard anything about Xavier?"

Brooke gave her a deadpan look. "The Emberhawk assassin who poisoned me with dreamthistle?"

"Oh, was that him?" Nariellyn looked away. "I know him as the one who betrayed Illiana and helped get Coriander on the throne. Although he doesn't tell it that way, of course." She grinned and stared off into nothingness again, but this time, there was a dreamy look in her gaze.

This was a little much, even for her. "Very funny."

"What?" Nariellyn seemed to snap out of it. "I'm sorry, obviously he made a bad choice, but he's on our side now! It was thanks to him that our plan of overthrowing Illiana worked, if you think about it."

Surely she wasn't serious. Brooke glared. "Have you ever been poisoned by dreamthistle before?"

Nariellyn cringed. "Look, I'm not going to marry him, okay? I just met him by chance and had to heal him. Healer's creed."

Brooke maintained her deathly stare. "How exactly did this happen?"

"Well, he was seriously injured by Illiana when he refused to kill Aegwyn. Since you'd ordered me to follow Iraleth around to heal her, I was in the palace for the aftermath of the battle, when you and Lysander frolicked off to your secret wedding or whatever. I will never forgive you for that, by the way."

"I didn't think causing a riot would make for a good reception. Don't change the subject."

"Oh my gosh, everything is political with you. Anyway, I healed Xavier and saved his life." Nariellyn seemed proud of herself. "I think he's grateful."

"Stop swooning over an assassin. Seriously?"

Nariellyn frowned. "Didn't you just marry an assassin?"

"*Former* assassin."

"Xavier is also a former assassin." Nariellyn said.

Brooke had lost her appetite. "Really? Did he declare that, or did you?"

"You know what?" Nariellyn sat up straight in her seat. "I can do better."

"You think?"

"Next time I'll let him die, healer's oath or not," Nariellyn declared.

Brooke couldn't tell if she was being serious or facetious. "You're too much trouble for your own—"

"Healer!" a woman screamed as she leaped down the stairs. "Is Nari here? Nari! We need a healer!"

"Time to be a hero." Nariellyn blew Brooke a kiss as she rushed away and followed the woman out of the Ice Box.

Brooke sighed as she watched her friend go. "What a mess," she muttered with reluctant fondness.

She looked back at her food, trying to regain her appetite, and didn't get the chance to enjoy it before a cloaked man slid into the empty seat across the table. "The azure masks said I might find you here."

Brooke's hand itched for the hidden knife sheath in her belt until she recognized Ulysses in plainclothes beneath his hood. Surprised to see him here, she didn't know what to say.

"Keeping a low profile, I see," Ulysses said quietly.

Brooke snorted. "Get to know Nariellyn, and you will understand."

"She may not be a good fit for me after all," Ulysses said with a hint of humor in his voice. "Well, no harm, regardless. It appears you are not as unpopular as I heard from reports. Or perhaps you just have good favor with the troops."

Brooke spoke louder as another song began. "If we were in the upper levels of Jadenvive before the evacuation, I'm sure it would be a different situation."

Ulysses nodded. "Unfortunately, you will need to take your secrecy much more seriously after we finish this conversation, for your own safety."

Brooke examined his expression. "Has something changed since our meeting?"

He nodded again. "Two things. Tumultuous times we live in, yes?"

"Indeed."

Ulysses leaned forward and whispered, and Brooke barely heard him over the music. "The Darkwood have come to claim you and Lysander. Legally, I must arrest you both and turn you over to them for trial, since the crimes you are accused of were committed outside Katrosi forests."

Brooke's breath fled. He couldn't protect her, even though she was here, in their capital city? That meant . . . she would have to go to Darkwood and stand trial . . . for what charges?

Murder, surely. The murder of their prince. Prince Heron, son of King Raven Eye, heir to the Darkwood throne.

She was as good as dead.

"I will turn myself in to them," Brooke forced herself to say in a restrained voice. Maybe the Darkwood would listen to the truth.

"Absolutely not," Ulysses whispered. "You are not to go anywhere near the Darkwood. That is an order. Do you understand?"

Brooke swallowed hard. "Y-yes, Chief. But this is my trouble. I can't let it sour relations between our tribes."

"This is easily resolved, as long as you stay out of their hands," Ulysses said. "Give me your thoughts—your memories of the event. You can do that, right?"

Brooke nodded. Of course . . . it could work. Her memories were a sort of proof, in a way, if the Darkwood would believe them to be genuine.

She looked up and met the chief's gaze. She sensed that he wanted to know the truth, too.

"It's . . . very private," she murmured. "Traumatic."

Ulysses frown deepened. "Are you willing to show me?"

Brooke nodded and centered herself with a steadying breath. "Look at me."

She gathered her aether and touched his mind. Recalled that horrible day. Every painful detail. She remembered it far too well.

Ulysses recoiled, then recovered. Although his face remained still, she felt his emotions turn from shock to disgust to rage as he watched the scene unfold. Grim approval at Lysander's swift blade . . . then back to rage. Even hotter than before.

Brooke ended the mental connection.

Ulysses broke eye contact and cleared his throat. "I . . . I'm sorry."

Feelings of embarrassment and shame conflicted with a strange feeling of . . . relief? Brooke regretted ever doubting this man.

"Do you think the Darkwood will listen?" she asked.

Ulysses nodded without looking at her. "With your permission, I will share these memories with their envoy. I will ensure that King Raven Eye knows that his son wasn't murdered, but was a victim of justice." He watched as a young man offered a hand to a woman and began a sloppy dance. "Heron's blood was on his own hands."

Brooke took a shuddering breath. "Thank you."

Ulysses reached inside his cloak and placed a letter on the table. It bore the mark of the Sekoiako tribe. He slid it over to her.

"A letter from the Sekoiako. They say the imperial princess was there, as a captive. My vice speculates that her captors may be the thieves who took the keystone." Ulysses looked back up at her with a hard umber gaze. "The azure masks will escort you and Lysander out of the city in secrecy immediately. Do not return until I can get this mess with the Darkwood sorted. Stay hidden."

Brooke took the letter and nodded. "Am I to pursue her captors, then? Free her, or . . . ?" Perhaps he meant to take Vylia as his own captive.

"I do not have enough information to make that call," Ulysses whispered. "I trust you to determine what needs to be done and do the right thing. Remember, you have the authority of the Tribal Alliance Council, even though it hasn't assembled yet."

Brooke had been wondering about that, but had barely had time to think about it. She didn't know what the Council was, even in concept. So how could it convey any authority?

Ulysses continued. "Contact me through coded letter and let me know whatever you need. I'll let you know when it's safe to return. With the princess, or the keystone—whatever is possible. What's most important right now is that you stay hidden and away from Jadenvive and the Darkwood. Do you understand?"

Brooke bowed as low as the table would let her. "Yes, Chief."

"We've brought journeycake and supplies for the road. Do you need xavi?"

"No, I have transportation handled." Brooke couldn't help but grin. "But I will take any injured or abandoned livestock off your hands."

14

KIRALAU

"All right, let's make camp here."

Kira was glad to hear Ryon say it after a long day of riding xavi. She wondered if she would ever get used to saddles as the sun dipped below the vine-tangled treetops. She hadn't ridden as many buffalo as her brothers had back at the cattle ranch—her weekly trade trips into Navarro had always been in a well-worn seat in the wagon behind two yoked oxen, on a pillow her grandmother had sewn decades ago. No saddle, and certainly no feeling of soreness from muscles she didn't know she had.

"Where are we?" Kira asked, feeling a little exposed now that it was just the two of them; they'd broken away from the armed convoy from the Emberhawk Sovereignty something like an hour ago. Ryon still hadn't told her why.

Kira reminded herself that she felt safe with him. But her patience regarding his "surprise" was an hourglass nearly empty.

She looked around for any reason Ryon might have chosen this place to make camp. Perhaps it was just because of the little spring that fed a creek into a tiny waterfall that carved its way to the side of a gentle embankment. The trees broke into a small clearing stuffed half-full of joyberry brambles.

Kira directed her xavi to trot toward the bushes, adjusting her riding glove around the reins as she leaned over and squinted at the bushes. Beautiful black globes reflected the sun's last rays. It was too late in the season for a plentiful harvest, but it seemed they could still enjoy a few overripe fruits for dessert, if she didn't mind a few stinging scratches from the thorns or dying her glove purple. A price entirely worth it.

Kira heard crinkling and assumed Ryan was looking at the map again. "No place in particular," he finally answered, "unless you like it."

His statement sounded more like a question. Kira straightened to find him looking back at her with an unreadable expression. Something between hope and bridled excitement danced behind his eyes.

"Unless?" Kira asked. "There are joyberries, an adorable spring with healthy ferns, a nice clearing perfect for making a fire, and those two trees are probably the perfect distance for stringing up your hammock. What's not to like?"

Ryon directed his xavi in a wide arc, examining everything from the scraggly oaks and young birch to the jungle vines that burdened them, the stones that poked out from the bank at the water's edge, to the white-flowering herbs growing across the top of the hill.

"What would you say if I told you this could be ours?"

Kira blinked at him. "What do you mean?"

Ryon looked down at the map again. "I mean, I'm pretty sure this is the land that Cori offered me in our last meeting, if I take that ambassador position."

Kira's mouth fell open. "Is he tryin' to bribe you into taking another job you don't want? I would rather live in a shack on the ranch then have you go into a political career that would make you miserable."

"I would take any job to provide for you and our future little ones." Ryon trotted his xavi closer to her. "But the thing is . . . I think I might be a good fit. I wouldn't be extremely happy about being the Emberhawk ambassador instead of on the Katrosi side of things, but . . ." He sighed. "Things are different now. Cori is on the throne, and I have full faith in him. I don't think I'll ever be proud to be Emberhawk, but I can represent the monarchy, at least. Since Cori ended slavery immediately at great potential cost to himself, I believe he will write a new story for the Emberhawk people, no matter the cost. For the sake of our children, I could aid him in that."

Kira hadn't thought of it that way before, but she felt he was right. As she fell into deep thought, her xavi took a step back and emitted a low rumbling hiss. She led it toward the water. "Brooke isn't the chief anymore, either. I imagine you'd want to work for Coriander more than Ulysses."

"I don't trust Ulysses as much as Brooke does. Well . . . I guess I just don't know him. So you're probably right." Ryon guided his xavi to come alongside Kira's and dismounted, encouraging the reptile to drink from the stream. Ryon raised his hands up to Kira, and she grinned as she leaned into him. He pulled her gently from the saddle and set her feet on the ground.

Kira started to stretch when Ryon brought her closer and kissed her, apparently unable to resist their closeness. She savored the moment, despite the smell of sweat and dust of the road.

Then she pulled back. "You were sayin'?"

"Oh. Right." Ryon cleared his throat and looked around, finding the map he must have dropped. Parchment crinkled as he maneuvered it to show her. "Look—we're here. Halfway between Katrosi and Emberhawk territories, right on the border. Land like this used to be very low in value because it was at the center of the conflict. But because the Emberhawk just joined the Tribal Alliance, it should be safe and the perfect halfway point for us." Ryon watched her face, waiting for her reaction. "In between my two peoples, but still a long distance from yours . . . Would you rather live on your father's ranch? Or a better halfway point, like Jadenvive?"

"We can't move to Jadenvive right now. I heard the city was evacuated. And anywhere near the ranch is way too dangerous. Who knows how long the war will last?" Kira kept her face directed at the map but looked at Ryon through her lashes. "Speaking of danger . . . Where would you be ambassador to, exactly? The Katrosi or Navakovrae?"

"Both. And the Roanoke, too." Ryon's grin was half-genuine, half-goofy-nervousness.

Kira rolled her eyes. "Doin' too much already, I see."

"But I'm kinda excited!" Ryon crouched to meet her at eye-level. "Do you think I could do it?"

"Of course you could do it. You'd be perfect for it." Kira crossed her arms. "But it sounds like you won't be home much. You'll be off killing some poor folks' chickens and stealing their cherry jam while I'd be trying to make a homestead out of this little glen all by myself."

"Nonsense. I have excellent reasons to be home as much as possible." Ryon slid an arm around her waist, and his fiery eyes communicated his intent quite effectively.

Kira never knew it was possible to be so happy.

A small fire crackled by nightfall despite the recent rain. Ryon had used Phoera to dry the fallen branches they'd found, causing Kira to rejoice in her new husband all the more. Never again would fire-tending be so time consuming or tedious, or dependent on the weather.

Kira pulled a pouch-string tight, sealing their remaining smoked pork jerky within. Aegwyn had spared no expense when gathering their rations; Kira had enjoyed holiday meals less extravagant than the collection of road snacks her sister-in-law had gathered, from jomoco gelatin strips to aged cheese to vials of melted chocolate and cream.

Feeling satisfied and ready for sleep under the stars in their hammock, Kira ducked beneath the trail of smoke and returned to the fire. Ryon sat cross-legged there, fiddling with something small in the dim light.

"What's that?" Kira asked, noticing as she sat down that her fingers still weren't entirely rid of the purple joyberry stains, even after she'd given them a thorough cleaning in the spring.

"The chest I found in the trace cat pen." He stuck out his tongue, looking like a mischievous child as he turned the box over and pried at it from a different angle. "I think it's got some sort of ancient lock."

Kira scooted closer to him and examined the box through his fingers. "Is there a keyhole?"

"No, but see?" He indicated a diamond-shaped design that sat along the dirt-encrusted line where the chest was surely meant to be opened. "And the hinges are on the opposite side. So it must be a lock."

"Hmm," Kira mused. "Did Felix tell you anything about it? Its history, or where it came from?"

"He told me nothing. Of course," Ryon muttered. He held the chest in both hands, resting his thumbs on either side of the diamond, and closed his eyes.

Kira remained quiet, watching and waiting for what he would do. Then she heard a sudden pop. "Oh! Was that the fire?"

Ryon's eyes shot open. "No, I felt it." He tried to pry the box open, but it remained shut. "I heated the metal and something moved inside." He turned it over in his hands. "But then, why won't it open . . . ?"

"It's ancient," Kira said. "Maybe it's broken."

Ryon pursed his lips and the lock popped again. Still it didn't open.

He tilted his head, closed his eyes, and breathed deep.

Click!

Ryon tried to open the chest again. The hinges didn't budge.

"Come on," Ryon growled. "Heat works, cold works. I can feel it. So why doesn't it open?"

"Fascinating," Kira mused. "Are there metals or some sort of materials inside expanding or contracting depending on the temperature?"

"Apparently," Ryon muttered. *Pop. Click. Pop. Click.*

"Maybe you have to do 'em both at the same time," Kira said.

Ryon leaned back and groaned. "That's it, isn't it? That's really difficult to do."

Kira inched closer, staring at the mystery hidden behind the lock's intricate craftsmanship. "Maybe that's the point."

Ryon sighed and closed his eyes.

Pop. Click. Pop-click. Pop-click. Clickpop.

"Could we use the heat of the fire to warm it while you focus on the cooling portion?" Kira suggested.

"No, I don't want to risk destroying it." Ryon closed his eyes again.

Kira leaned away as he focused for a minute, popping and clicking intermittently. Two minutes. Five minutes. She lost track of time.

Night fell deeper around them, bringing a chill with it. Kira took her bandana from her hair, allowing her curls to dangle free and encouraged some to hang near her face, hoping to protect her cold-nipped nose from the breeze. She tied the bandana around her neck, happy to hide the burn scar Zamara had granted her. Warmth accumulated quickly. Kira looked forward to the ability to conceal the ugly handprint of the false goddess as the season changed.

Snap!

Ryon startled as the chest cracked open. Kira cheered and huddled close as Ryon pried it fully open. It cracked against the ancient grime.

Inside, the firelight gleamed across an engraved marking on a small object. Perhaps a square coin?

Ryon gently picked it up and laid it in his palm, dropping the chest to allow more light on what looked like a silver cube with a bronze sphere held inside.

"Do you recognize that symbol?" Kira asked.

"No, I—"

The cube disappeared, and Ryon screamed.

Kira jerked back as Ryon gripped his wrist, staring into his right hand as if it'd just been burned. He snarled and hissed breaths.

"What happened?" Kira cried.

"My hand," Ryon said through gritted teeth.

Kira cupped his hand in hers, squinting through the dim light. The strange symbol was now on Ryon's right hand, over the knuckle of the middle finger in his palm.

"It's okay," Ryon breathed. "It doesn't hurt anymore."

"Where did it go?" Kira asked, staring at the symbol and not wanting to believe it had somehow fused with her husband's hand.

Ryon turned his hand over, but all seemed normal except for the mark on his palm—halfway between a scar and brown writing in a script neither of them knew.

"It could be the Ancient language," Ryon muttered, running a finger over the new texture of his skin. "What on Alani?"

Kira titled her head back and roared at the sky. "Felix!"

15

BROOKE

Brooke shuddered against the wind that whipped her braids across her back. She ducked lower toward Onyx's saddle and pulled her new bandana further down her forehead, lest it be snatched away.

The year's first autumn chill. This winter would be brutal.

Lysander's warmth covered her like an old blanket. He held her tight from behind. "Onyx must be cold, too. He's changed colors."

Brooke squinted against a gale as her dragon dipped lower. Lysander was right—Onyx's scales were dark as jet before. Now, he'd lightened to something more like deep bronze, and black diamond-like patterns remained, complementing the curves and joints of his wings, back, and neck. It reminded Brooke of a venomous snake, moving back and forth slowly beneath them while gliding, as a serpent swims through water.

Beautiful, Brooke admired, *but also . . . scary.*

"Like you," Lysander said with a chuckle.

Brooke clicked her tongue in protest but couldn't argue. She'd built her political career on being scary. Even enjoyed the title of "The Jade Witch" at first. She didn't want to make her friends and family afraid of her, though.

Guess I have a lot to learn about Onyx, she thought to Lysander. *I also don't know why he wouldn't eat the heifer we offered. Surely he wouldn't care that she had those nasty burns. Unless her burns were infected, and he could smell it? Or maybe he was still full from the goat?*

"Dragons don't normally prey on livestock," Lysander said.

She broke her gaze upon the swiftly passing treetops to glance over her shoulder at him. *How do you know so much about dragons?*

"My father kept one, and he fed it our worst criminals," he said. "A mountain wyvern. It was a wedding gift—my mother's dowry from my grandfather."

Brooke's mouth fell open. She wasn't familiar with the custom of dowries, but a wyvern sounded like a valuable one. *Your grandfather from Valinor, then?*

"Chancellor Thrace," Lysander confirmed. "Wonder how the old man's doing."

When did you see him last? Brooke asked, turning back around to continue monitoring Onyx's flight path. She wasn't totally certain that the juvenile dragon could actually navigate to Sekoiako Village. But then again, she wasn't familiar with the route from the perspective of the sky, either. And the trees were so tall and underbrush so thick that she couldn't see the ground at all.

"When I was a teenager. Mom and Cori and I used to visit his castle on Redshift Island. Before Zamara murdered and replaced her." Lysander paused and the comforting heat around Brooke abated, and she wished she could see the memories he must be lost in. "The only time I wasn't a brat was there. He was tough as d'hakka chitin, but somehow also jolly, and I respected him."

Brooke wondered what the castle north of the tribal territories was like. She'd heard the Valinorans built towering walls from hewn stone—their lands didn't have many trees. Such a thing was difficult for her to imagine.

Is giving dragons as gifts a normal practice for Valinorians? she asked.

"No!" Lysander laughed. "They normally ride gryphons. The wyvern was just Grandfather showing off. It was funny because, of course, Father had no way of containing a dragon at first, and no idea how to care for it. But it seemed to acquire a taste for criminals. Crime decreased dramatically after that."

I never knew the Emberhawk had a dragon, Brooke muttered through her thoughts.

"Well, no one knew how to form a relationship with it, much less ride it," Lysander said. "We aren't Katrosi, you know. But we tamed trace cats. Almost as impressive."

Onyx's wings shuddered on the wind, and Brooke gripped the saddle harder. She realized she was already clinging with white knuckles that ached as she moved. She tried to convince herself to relax.

Do you have a trace cat of your own? Brooke asked. *Maybe we could ride in to the first Tribal Alliance Council meeting on our respective fearsome beasts.*

"I used to, but I haven't ridden it since I earned Sorrel in the Valinorian gryphon rider trials," Lysander said. "I had to work and train harder than ever before in my life for that. And we bonded immediately. Sorrel's been with me through some very dark times. So she's special."

Brooke recalled his gryphon's golden and white colors as well as her apparent personality. *How long does she need to raise her new hatchlings?*

"Not long. She can leave whenever she wants. Gryphons are monogamous, and the male helps to raise their young."

Brooke enjoyed the mental picture that emerged in her mind of Sorrel and her mate, together in their roost with their ever-chirping hatchlings. It reminded her of former Queen Lyzelle's pyramid. Which reminded her of Lysander's most recent stunt in front of Ulysses.

So, I guess we're going to live with Granny Zelle, since you had all of my belongings moved there, she thought to him, trying to guard her own conflicted and chaotic feelings on the matter. She hadn't had much time to think about their future together, when the present kept going up in flames.

Thinking of flames . . . was that smoke in the distance? Yes, a thick stream twisted into the heavens. They must be close.

"Well, we can live wherever you want. I just thought, for now, it would be best to stay away from the battle line in general. And you don't seem to appreciate the dramatics in Jadenvive."

Agreed. All of your things are at Granny Zelle's pyramid anyway, so at least our stuff will be together. I don't mind at all if that's our home base for now, at least.

"And I'm sure Granny would love to help with any hatchlings of our own."

Brooke's throat tightened. They probably should have talked about children before they'd gotten married. This is why she hadn't wanted to rush into it!

She ordered her words carefully, worried at how he might react. *I'm already past my prime for childbearing years, you know. And honestly, I'm not sure I would make the best mother . . .*

"Pah!" Lysander made an incredulous noise. "'Past your prime.' You have plenty of years left if you want them. And you would be ten times the parent I would be." She felt him move and scratch his slate-colored hair, then return his arm to his grip around her waist. "I would be immune to the screaming and whining and complaining, at least."

She could hear the grin in his voice and grew one of her own. *I've never seen you around children. That might be highly amusing.*

"Hey, now. I helped Ryon out with the orphans sometimes." Lysander paused. "I was terrible at it, of course, and escaped at the earliest opportunity. But I know the basics, at least. Like don't raise a kid in a greenhouse full of toxic plants."

Brooke laughed out loud. *Guess we can't live at Granny Zelle's, then.*

"No, I've removed almost all of the poisonous ones already."

Brooke hadn't known that. But he'd had dirt-covered fingers every day during their stay there, so it was believable. *Almost?* she repeated. *Was that for the sake of future little gardeners, or are you giving up your life of crime?*

"I thought I'd try my hand at an honest living," Lysander said. "Herbalism is the only skill I know, although I've still got a lot to learn. But I thought I could sell healing remedies and teas and whatnot. And, you know, the occasional rat poison. What do you think?"

Onyx dipped lower, barely above the treetops, and Brooke clenched her teeth. She told herself to trust the dragon, who'd been flying for her entire lifetime, and could probably be trusted not to crash into the branches.

Although she'd trusted Felix, too, and he'd crashed into a misty beach.

She remembered their conversation and fumbled for a response. *I think you'd be great at that. Your teas are the best. Is that what you were doing this morning, when you said you were out buying herbs?*

"Yeah, I was shopping for seeds, bulbs, rhizome cuttings, and the like while you were playing celebrity in The Ice Box. Going to try several and see what grows best in the pyramid. And I did a quick favor for Feli—"

Lysander cut off as Onyx suddenly lurched his hind legs forward and spread his wings to their full girth, jerking the saddle beneath them. Brooke adjusted her weight and held her breath as the tree line broke to a collection of longhouses nestled within the forest. She recognized the Sekoiako chief's massive residence made of curved birch wood and the ever-burning bonfire a second before Onyx's clawed feet slammed into the ground, his haunches quavering with the impact.

Brooke cursed and threw up her hands in a gesture to the terrified Sekoiako people now scattering around them, showing that she had no weapon. "Peace! Peace!" It only took moments for them to be surrounded by a ring of spears.

"Really, Onyx?" Brooke growled under her breath as she kept her hands up. The drake turned a brilliant blue eye on her, raising his neck and chin high, as if expecting praise for his swift and safe delivery to the correct location.

"Hold!" A man covered in tattoos stepped through the spears, raising a hand. Brooke recognized the Sekoiako chieftain immediately. Furs covered his shoulders and a trace cat skull hid his eyes with saber-tooth fangs.

"Apologies, Chief," Brooke yelled over the commotion. "I do not yet have full control over my mount. We come in peace."

The chief's face seemed permanently etched in a scowl, like the poles carved with animal faces surrounding the bonfire. "You are welcome here, Chieftess. It is forgiven." His voice was slower than a mudhoof. "I don't tink dere's a big enough place for such a large beast ta land. We repurposed our landing space for da Katrosi of old when dey lost de dragons. It is good ta see one again." He turned, yelled at the men to stand down, and demanded calm from the women and children.

Brooke released a breath she didn't realize she'd been holding. She slid her leg over the saddle and dropped to the earth. "Thank you, Chief. But I am no longer the chieftess of the Katrosi. I come as an ambassador from the new Tribal Alliance Council."

He stared at her with a face of stone for an uncomfortably long moment, his expression unreadable. "Why have you come, Chieftess? You must have received our letta from da water princess' soulbound."

Brooke struggled to compose herself. It was impossible not to be intimidated by this man, and she pondered at his words. Surely Princess Vylia's bodyguard, Sousuke, wasn't her soulbound, or life-long mate, as the Sekoiako implied? She'd detected strong devotion between them before, but not romance. But it wasn't unlikely, either.

Brooke cleared her throat. "Yes, we received a letter stating that the Malaano princess is here. We want to ensure her safety."

"She is not safe," the chief said bluntly. "The Malaano took her. Stole our xavi and escaped. Only her soulbound is still here. Dey left him as he dies."

Brooke's heart tangled and sank like a bird caught in a net. "Sousuke is dead?"

"Last I hear, his spirit still clings. But not much time left." The chief turned and began walking toward a muddy path. "Come. We will see if he yet has da breath of life."

16

SOUSUKE

Any opportunity, Aeo . . . I will take anything you give me. Any way to save her. I won't fail this time.

That was Sousuke's repeating prayer as he floated through dreamspace. Through the wilds he loved as a child, building forts and weapons from sticks. Through the swamps of Lover's Fen, watching for the draconic eyes of snap-jaws floating just above the water. Through the coastal bay of Way Maar, where his father had taught him to sail.

Maybe they weren't dreams. Maybe his life was replaying before him.

Maybe he was already dead.

Sousuke?

A voice pierced the haze. Clear and feminine.

Strange. His hallucinations had been a bit more blurry as of late.

It reminded him of his mother. Of her strength. Of her confident smile. Of her pain.

Guilt sliced through him like a blade. His death might hurt her even more than his birth.

He continued his prayer, forgetting where he'd left off. *If not me, then please . . . Call someone else to save her.*

Who? Vylia?

That voice again . . . Why was she talking to him like that? Could she hear his prayers? She must be an angel.

But her voice sounded familiar. Not intimately so, but he'd heard it once before. In his mind. And in the Great Hall of Jadenvive . . .

Chieftess?

You can call me Brooke, she said. *I'm here to bring you out of the deep dark once again.*

Ah, yes, now he remembered. Her thought-voice had called him out of the long sleep . . . how long ago?

Guess I have some bad sleep habits.

Brooke's laughter echoed through his mind. *The Katrosi received your letter, and I've come to your aid.*

His letter . . . How long had it taken to be delivered, and for her to make the trip from Jadenvive to Sekoiako Village? Or was he in Rainosek? He couldn't remember.

Why hadn't he died yet?

His elemental heritage must be sustaining him . . . or just elongating his suffering.

If only he had some syn, he could connect with his element again. He'd purged himself of the liquid evil long ago, for many reasons. So he could distance himself from that man's wretched power. So he could become invisible to enemy *trai'yeth.* So he could maintain his sanity.

So he could be human.

He would throw it all away for the sake of another chance at life. He would risk it all for Vylia.

Do you have any syn? Sousuke asked Brooke.

No, I'm not an elementalist, she said.

Sousuke cursed himself. Of course not. Even if she had some, it wouldn't save his life. Why had he expected the creator to do anything for him? He didn't deserve a miracle. No one did.

Wait. A long moment passed. *My husband has some.*

He sensed something different then. Another presence. Not human, not mortal like him . . . a semi-mortal. A *trai'yeth.*

Also familiar, but so different from Brooke's soft ethereal presence. Glowing . . . no, flickering, and burning, as he focused on it. Like a surreal green fire.

Felix Kael Tae . . . Yes, it had to be that wretched *trai'yeth.* Why was he here?

Yes, I have Felix's stone here with me, Brooke said, her voice seeming to slow and quiet in his mind.

His stone? Why had she said it like that? *Felix is dead?*

Brooke's presence mourned within him. *He sacrificed himself to save us . . .* She stopped as if considering her words. *Do you know him?*

Sousuke wished he didn't know Felix. Then suddenly, a thought struck him. A wild idea. An impossible idea.

But was it possible with Aeo? Could this be the answer to his prayer?

No, it was madness.

But what if it was his chance?

No, Aeo, no! Anyone but him!

What? Brooke asked. *I'm having trouble following your thoughts . . . You could possibly resurrect Felix? How? He said seven years would have to pass before he could come back to life.*

That's correct, Sousuke said. *How long ago did he die?*

Just a few days ago.

Sousuke almost laughed, if such a thing were possible in this strange space between life and death. *Impossible.*

Brooke's presence seemed to become more prominent in his mind. *If it were impossible, why did you think it?*

The reason why naturally became apparent in his thoughts, and Sousuke hastily sought to cover it somehow, lest she uncover the truth. But how could he hide something within his own mind?

Because I'm desperate. It was just a passing, foolish thought, he told her.

But there was a reason you thought it might work, Brooke pressed. *What was it?*

It's none of your business.

Brooke's presence held back and grew in strength at the same time. Mounting. Analyzing. Calculating.

Fear lanced through Sousuke. What was she doing? What was she capable of?

What is your relationship with Felix? Brooke's voice was calmer now. Cleaner. Like a surgeon's blade.

Sousuke bristled. *Get out.*

Was he your friend?

Revulsion billowed up on its own, and Brooke's presence seemed to shift, as if examining his brain from a different angle. *Definitely not,* she surmised. *Then, were you enemies?*

Get out! Sousuke delved into his anger and smothered the space with it.

Interesting, Brooke mused. *Not a friend, but also not an enemy. Rivals? No, I'm able to connect with your mind, so you have aether, and therefore human blood. So you can't possibly be powerful enough to rival a* trai'yeth. *Comrades, then, perhaps?*

Sousuke sensed a hesitation within her presence and struck out at it. *Whatever you're doing is wrong, and you know it.*

Brooke's presence recoiled. *It's for the greater good, if you could resurrect Felix. The fate of both of our peoples are at stake, unless you like the idea of war and bloodshed and tyranny. Just tell me how to bring Felix back, and I'll leave.*

You can't, Sousuke snapped.

She inspected him—what she could actually perceive, he had no idea. But after a moment, Brooke said, *But* you *can.*

No, it's impossible, he insisted, his patience past its limit.

What is your relationship with Felix Kael Tae?

Sousuke's memories responded on their own, innocently, like dogs answering their master's call. He grasped at them, and might as well have been grasping at smoke.

You are related to him, Brooke breathed. *You are descended from Felix. One of his grandchildren.* Surprise emanated from her presence. *From his time with Lillian. You bear the blood of both* trai'yeth *and* amos!

Sousuke cringed. *It doesn't matter. A hundred generations past. Get out of my head, witch!*

Brooke seemed to smile. And he hated her for it.

Felix and Lillian aren't your only elemental heritage. Your father was a first generation trai'yeth, *and your mother was the daughter of Felix, Lillian, and many other* trai'yeth *in the Lotusfall bloodline. You are more elemental than you are human.*

Rage ignited and exploded within him. *GET OUT!*

I meant no offense. I see what you were thinking now—you could possibly become a vessel to Felix before the time of his true resurrection, because of your relation to him, and your strong concentration of elemental blood.

A violent urge blossomed in Sousuke's mind. If only he could expel her. Forcefully.

It was a stupid idea, he thought slowly and deliberately, doing his best to control the evil desire, lest she detect it. *It's never been done before. So leave me be and let me die.*

Brooke seemed like she was analyzing him again. *I can tell that was a lie. It has been done before. Or at least, you heard an old legend.*

Sousuke realized her weakness: she had morals. He could wield them like a weapon against her. *Since you can read my thoughts, you know this is foolishness,* he said. *You are torturing a man on his deathbed.*

I heard you praying, Brooke said. *This is no coincidence. It could be the answer to your prayer. It could save your life!*

I wouldn't become Felix's vessel to save my life, Sousuke growled. *He is one of the most evil—*

Would you do it to save Vylia's life?

Sousuke stopped short.

He considered. Weighed the options and possibilities.

Hated every one of them.

Except . . . that one. The faint possibility that Felix might actually be repentant, as he claimed. Maybe Sousuke could finally know for certain if Felix was reformed. Worthy of the trust his father granted.

Highly unlikely.

Creator, help me.

The green fire drew nearer, somehow. Reluctantly, Sousuke gathered his aether. He'd never been skilled in its use, but here, in this strange space between realms, it surrounded him like a living mist. He directed it toward the dormant emerald glow.

Blinding light pierced him. Enveloped him. Imbued him.

17

KIRALAU

How could a river feel like home? Kira didn't know, only the sight of the Silvermead River and its mossy stone bridge filled her with a sense of peace. The clear waters of its wide flow knew nothing of war, only the never-ending passage of time.

Ryon led them past the boathouse, whose docks sent ships brimming with supplies up and down the wide canal. Kira admired the white billowing sails of a riverboat drifting lazily south, its cargo bound for Sekoiako or perhaps a settlement on the southern coast.

Her tired muscles begged for relief, sensing that their destination was so close. But she couldn't help but grin as her gaze followed the river north, envisioning its banks nearest the land her family had called home for generations.

Ryon glanced back at her with a questioning look as they approached the bridge. She nodded and directed her xavi closer to Ryon's as they entered the busy stream of carts, wagons, and passerby traveling to and from Jadenvive and Navarro.

"Wares for the journey!" cried a young boy alongside his closely guarded crates on the bridge's end. "Pemmican, hardtack, Phoera-dried fruit!" Another yelled from the opposite side of the bridge. "Rope, jacks, axels and tongues!"

Ryon joined the line on the bridge leading to the tollhouse and pulled the reins until his xavi champed at the bit and stopped. Ryon leaned forward to offer it a foul-smelling snack from his saddlebag, and the color of the beast's scales seemed to enhance as it swallowed and flicked its tongue.

Kira wrinkled her nose and allowed Ryon to feed her xavi too, not wanting to touch the smoked fish or whatever it was. She patted her xavi's neck and murmured praise into its crown of feathers as she scanned the walls and fortifications that protected Navarro from the tribal lands. She couldn't help but think the fortifications should be relocated to the eastern side of the city in light of recent events.

But she didn't see any streamers on the lamp posts or floral decorations on the gate. "Will the Moon Festival be held at all?" she wondered under her breath.

"Well, Oda'e controls Navarro now," Ryon said. "Would he cancel it?"

Kira chewed on the inside of her lip. "It's technically a Malaano holiday. We might be tryin' to avoid anything associated with Malaan right now . . ."

Ryon frowned and twisted back in his saddle to examine her. "Didn't you say it was a favorite part of your childhood? Would that be true for all Navakovrae people?"

"Yeah . . ." Kira mused.

"Then it has become a part of your own culture," Ryon said. "I hope you won't throw away your own traditions just because they have Malaano roots."

Kira shifted uneasily in her saddle. "But the Empire is evil, and its history is full of all sorts of evil. I don't want to celebrate any of that."

"You could say the same of any nation if you go back far enough in history," Ryon said. "We have to root out evil wherever we find it, and forgive when righteousness eventually wins."

Kira looked up and admired the wisdom that shone from deep within his fiery gaze. "Sounds like you've put a lot of thought into this."

Ryon smirked. "I've had a few years to marinate."

Kira returned his smile. "I'm so happy that the Emberhawk have a new beginning."

"Me too," Ryon said. "Now it's the Empire's turn." He clicked his tongue and directed his xavi forward as the line lumbered across the bridge.

Kira followed and gazed over the railing to the listless current. She sent up a prayer of thanks to the creator for her new husband and wondered if anyone was listening to her prayers.

Yes, she decided. She would have faith, regardless of the lack of solid proof. Not because everything in her life had somehow worked out for good, or their victories, or all of the recent joy, or because she just wanted something to blindly hope in.

Was it the gentle feeling deep inside, like a whisper to her soul? Was it the circumstances, or answered prayers? No—not all of her prayers had been answered in a positive way. Lee was gone. She would give up everything to have him back if she could.

Maybe she didn't have to be able to explain it. Maybe she didn't have to know exactly how all of the pieces fit together, like one of her inventions. Maybe it was something outside the bounds of science and math and logic. Maybe the true god was from a different realm entirely, and only brushed against the physical plane like an ethereal breeze, felt and heard only by those who waited and listened for it.

Kira inhaled and released a deep breath as she blinked back from her thoughts, returning to the bridge over the Silvermead River. Yes, choosing the creator as her god was her decision. And she didn't know how or why, but it felt right. And no one could take that from her.

It would be nice to have some sort of evidence, though . . .

"Are there any old writings or anything I could read to learn more about the creator?"

Ryon whipped back around, his face brightening with surprise and something akin to excitement. "Yes, of course—the ancient scriptures. I'm not sure if they'd be in the library here in Navarro, but definitely in Jadenvive."

Kira nodded. "I'd like to take a look sometime."

"I have a lot of it memorized, too." Ryon grew a mischievous grin. "Be careful. Following an unapproved god can cause trouble."

"'Unapproved'?" Kira wrinkled her nose. It was true—of her people, at least. Even her own family prayed to Lillian. She'd have to share with them all that she'd discovered. "If Aeo is the one true god, I will believe in him regardless."

Ryon raised an eyebrow at her. "I knew you were a troublemaker."

"Ha!" Kira's xavi hissed at a passing cart, and she pulled the reins to redirect its attention. "You're one to talk!"

Ryon blew her a kiss.

As the line progressed, Kira began to miss the shade of the forest as the sun beat down. Finally, it was their turn to pull up alongside the open window in the side of the tollhouse.

"Welcome to Navarro. The toll is—"

Kira's heart lurched at the sound of a familiar voice. The most familiar voice. The one she'd known even from inside the womb.

She squinted into the darkness and found her mother's hazel eyes, dark skin, and black hair whose curls rejected any form of control.

"Kiralau?"

"Mom!"

Her mother, Inowae, nearly came through the window. Kira pulled her xavi up close and almost fell out of the saddle in her effort to give Inowae an awkward half-hug. "What are you doing here?"

Inowae held her in the embrace entirely too long. "My baby girl," she whispered. "Oh, how good it is to see you again!" She pulled back and drank in the sight of her daughter, making Kira self-conscious not only of her appearance, but also those behind her in line.

"Take over for me?" Inowae said to someone behind her, then disappeared into the tollhouse.

A moment later, Inowae appeared on the opposite side of the gate, motioned for the guard to open it, and waved them through. Kira hurriedly urged her xavi forward.

"Uh . . ." The rupero in Ryon's coin purse jingled. "How much is the toll . . . ?"

Kira barely glimpsed the city beyond the gate as worries tumbled through her head in a tangled mess. Her mother *did* approve of Ryon even though he was a tribesman, right? Her mother was no stranger to prejudice. Had Inowae received the letter that Kira had sent to Oda'e? She'd gotten married in a foreign land without her mother in attendance. Exactly how much trouble was she in? Her insides coiled like a threatened snake.

"This way." Inowae coaxed Kira's xavi to an alley on the side of the road with a firm grip on the reins. She held her arms up to Kira with a huge smile, as if Kira were still a toddler wanting a toss into the air.

Kira awkwardly dismounted to the simultaneous relief and disapproval of her muscles, and Inowae immediately embraced her. "I was worried you'd never even like a boy, and suddenly you're married!"

"Yes, I . . . I'm so sorry. We can have a second wedding. And I can show you the palace!" Kira floundered. "W-would you like to travel there?"

"Of course." Inowae released her and turned to Ryon as he dismounted. She flung her arms wide. "Do your people hug, Idryon?"

Ryon smiled and hugged her. "They do now." Then he pulled back and bowed. "My mother and sister would love to meet you."

"It would be my pleasure," Inowae said, and Kira noticed that she looked older than she remembered, but somehow seemed more healthy at the same time. Her skin wasn't as pale as it had been in Kira's memory, and she seemed to have more energy. The tribal medicine for her cloud sickness must be working!

"I lost a son and gained another in a matter of weeks," Inowae said. "Lillian be praised."

Kira cringed but decided to focus on the relief she felt at her mother's apparent approval and new health. "What are you doin' at the tollhouse?" she asked.

"Makin' myself useful." Inowae raised an eyebrow at Kira. "You might recall I worked here as a girl, until a certain country boy whisked me away."

Ah, now Kira remembered. "Dad and Granny must be nearby, then."

Inowae nodded. "Granny's makin' stew for the troops day in and day out, and she fits there like a saddle on a steed. Your father's in the barracks as always, 'cept he's no longer takin' orders from the Emperor." Inowae glistened with pride. "He's incredibly busy, but he'll make time for you. And y'all can stay with me and Granny in the barracks, too. Of course the ranch ain't safe now, but your father has secured livin' arrangements for us here."

Kira nodded her thanks. "I'm glad y'all are safe. But who's carin' for our cattle and chickens? And it's time to prune the cherry trees . . ."

"The ranch hands are still working, and we're paying them extra in lieu of the meals we normally provided. Thank Lillian for the rain—we won't need to buy so much hay now, at least. And as for the cherries, well . . . We'll just have to see how well they produce without pruning this year. It's just not a risk we can take, nor a service we can afford." Inowae sighed, swatted a wayward curl from her forehead, and rested her hands on her hips. "The house'll be a mess by now already, I'm sure. But we're blessed to have this place to stay for now. The inn's full of refugees from other homesteads on the border."

Kira noticed a difference in how her mother spoke to her. Inowae's tone had gone from the regular scolding and ordering to somehow more acknowledging, or almost respectful, as if she was talking to another woman rather than a child. It felt so . . . validating.

She pulled herself back to the alleyway between two stone buildings and patted her restless xavi, then forced herself to focus on Inowae's actual words and formulate a response. "Yes, we are blessed. I'm sure the trees will be fine. Creator willing, this war won't last long."

A puzzled look passed Inowae's face for only a moment before she turned to Ryon. "A word of advice, if I may."

Kira's throat squeezed in anticipation as Ryon said, "Please."

Inowae stepped closer to him and dropped the volume of her voice. "The sheriff's part of the Navakovrae Resistance, but the Malaano loyalists have been targeting tribesmen with acts of detestable violence. Best to lie low 'til things calm down."

Ryon frowned. "Not to worry. You might have heard that I can make myself scarce."

Inowae's eyes narrowed. "As long as you don't disappear on my Kiralau."

Ryon laughed. "Never."

Kira felt her cheeks flush as the corner of Inowae's lip tilted upward.

"Mom . . ." Kira's voice lowered as she took her mother's arm and gently pulled her away from Ryon. "I know how you feel about the tribesmen. But Ryon is a good man, I swear it. I never would have married him if I weren't sure. I hope you . . ."

Inowae waved a hand until Kira trailed off. "I was wrong. Your father wasn't tellin' me everything about the tribes or the Malaano—it would've been unsafe to do so. Once the Resistance revealed itself and it became clear to me who our real enemy was, I set myself straight."

Kira's face must have looked like she'd just seen a buffalo the size of a mountain trot by. Words failed her, unable to penetrate through the shock. Her mother, admitting she was wrong? And so quickly and clearly? It must be a sign of the end of days.

"Listen." Inowae took Kira by the shoulders and looked at her closely with eyes full of love. "I could tell your Idryon was a good man—and good for *you*—from his first visit after we lost Lee. I just couldn't express my joy then through the grief. But the money he provided to cover the loss of the barn was far more than we needed." Her grin spread wide. "I'm sorry I was so frustrated that it took you so long to find a man. But now I know why: the gods had someone special in store for you, and he was worth the wait. A prince, no less!" Inowae leaned in and kissed her forehead. "Now, how long do I have to wait for grandchildren?"

Kira reeled from the barrage of surprising statements. "W-well, he's not a prince, exactly . . ."

Inowae looked over Kira's shoulder at Ryon with an adoring gaze as he leaned out of the alley, his head swiveling to take in the sights of the bustling city. "I heard he was the king for a breath or two!" she said in the loudest whisper Kira had ever heard.

"Mom!" Kira blocked her view of Ryon, catching her eye contact once again. "That's not why I chose him." She centered herself and selected her words carefully. "I need to know that you won't treat him differently because of his heritage. Will you love him just the same as you would a Malaano son-in-law?"

"Of course. Maybe more," Inowae chuckled. "Our people have made our own culture here, more influenced by the tribes than the islanders. We are more than neighbors. They welcomed us, and their ways are a part of ours. Remember, your brother's name is Tekkyn—we named him after your father's best friend growin' up. A tribesman." She returned Kira's serious expression with a genuine one. "I'm sorry for bein' so harsh on you about the tribal scrolls and your inventions. I'm glad you learned from them. Truth be told, our gardens and orchards wouldn't have survived the drought as well as they did without their irrigation schmi . . . schemay . . . Whatever it was."

"Schematics." The apology was a salve to Kira's soul. "Thank you." She grabbed her mother's petite frame in a hug. "I love you, Mom."

"I love you too, baby." Inowae hugged her back with more strength than Kira remembered her having. "Speaking of Tekkyn, he was just here. He said he was going to the cobbler's to get the sole of his boot repaired. Go and say hi!" Inowae moved to the alley's opening and gestured down the street, indicating one building and then another. "You can stable your xavi at the barracks. Just tell the stable boy who your father is. I have to get back to work, but you must join us tonight for dinner!" Her mother's embrace was warm. "Welcome home."

18

SOUSUKE

Sousuke gasped for breath as he shot awake, returning to the physical realm with a jolt of pain. Then, an awareness of all sorts of pain, from throbbing ache in his wounds to discomfort from lying in the same spot for too long. He squeezed his eyes shut.

The light brightened inside him, slowly at first, like a sunrise behind tall mountains. Then suddenly, an intense ray manifested between the peaks.

It softened and a small orb coalesced from it, like a spirit born of starlight. The star turned green, like a gleam through a facet of an emerald. Sousuke felt warmth as it flickered and swelled. The orb morphed and grew features—a head with pointed ears, four limbs, and three tails.

Sousuke opened his eyes but the spirit was still there—present in his hazy vision as well as his mind. It seemed to be floating in the Sekoiako healing hut, just above his own body as he rested on some sort of cot.

He blinked as the form sharpened into something like a dog with too many tails. No . . . a fox.

The light dimmed and condensed inside the spirit, where its heart might be. As it floated down to rest on Sousuke's body—something he couldn't feel, although his eyes swore it was true—pinpricks of light escaped the fox's coat.

Green eyes opened, then closed again as it yawned. It blinked and focused on Sousuke.

"Thank you, mortal," the spirit said. "I am Felix Kael Tae."

Sousuke stared speechless, both from awe and crippling agony and weakness.

"Are you okay?" asked that infernal woman, Brooke, at his bedside.

She glanced up at another man beside her with pale skin. "The stone disappeared!"

"You're not Ryon. For what reason have you woken me?" the spirit called Felix asked, examining Sousuke as if guarded.

Sousuke couldn't tell if Felix's voice was in his head or his ears. Should he respond with thoughts, or try to speak? It seemed Felix hadn't recognized him yet.

The spirit-fox seemed to stand up on Sousuke's belly as it looked around the room. "Why can't I get out . . . ?"

Get out? Sousuke asked within his thoughts. Much easier than speaking. His throat was dry as wastelands in a drought.

"I can't get out of your body. It's like I'm trapped . . . inside your soul . . . Why does it feel like an elemental core?" Felix's fiery gaze fixed on Brooke and the man beside her. "Lysander. And . . . Brooke," he muttered, as if straining to recall their names. "They haven't aged?"

Sousuke leaned his head back to rest on the cot and reeled from waves of pain that echoed with every breath. He clenched his jaw and realized he had no strength to do so. But he wouldn't let a whimper escape—people were watching him.

Felix focused on him. "What year is it?"

Sousuke nearly didn't answer. Everything dimmed and blurred within the agony. What did any of this matter?

"Three thousand . . . four hundred . . . sixty-nine," he managed.

"What?" Brooke leaned closer, then said to her companion called Lysander, "He asked for syn earlier. Maybe that would help?" She made some strange gestures with her hands.

"That's impossible," Felix said. His eyes narrowed. "What have you done?"

It wasn't my desire, trust me, Sousuke said, hoping the spirit could hear his thoughts. *It was the creator's doing.*

"Blasphemy," Felix spat. He lowered his head, and his illusory fur seemed to stand on end, bristling with light. "*You.* I knew you felt familiar. The son of the demon."

Sousuke's jaw clenched. "You . . . are a demon . . . yourself."

The spirit bared its glowing fangs. "Yes, I remember you now. Rhu Sousuke. You are only alive because of the grace of your mother, the *ko'kai.*"

How dare he mention his mother? But the compliment about Rhu Hana's grace was certainly true, and *ko'kai* wasn't an insult. Sousuke had only read that term in the history scrolls. *Fire in the sky,* it meant in the Ancient language—a term for those trapped between the earth and the spirit realm. Not truly human or elemental.

The term is ko'yeth. *You'd know that if you were actually one of us,* Sousuke thought.

"I thought you were calling yourselves the Lotusfall now," Felix shot back. "Just because you change your name all the time doesn't mean I'm not one of your patriarchs."

"*Ch.*" Sousuke was certain now that Brooke and Lysander couldn't see the spirit, not only because they never reacted to it, but because the pale-skinned man held a waterskin obliviously through the fox's side.

"Syn brew. We'll have to help him drink it," Lysander said in a deep voice. "He's too weak, and he's speaking gibberish. It would be a waste . . ."

"Yes, thank kai'lani he has some syn!" Felix's voice garbled Brooke's response. He pawed at the waterskin, but his claws passed harmlessly through it. "You don't have a speck of syn in you. No wonder you're dying!"

Sousuke closed his eyes, but it just made the pain worse. *That is on purpose, to prevent me from turning into a monster like you.*

Lysander slid an arm under Sousuke's shoulders and gently lifted, and a cry ripped from Sousuke as agony tumbled across his chest. "Sorry," Brooke said as she lifted the waterskin to his parched lips. "You asked for this earlier. Will it help?"

Sousuke forced himself to drink whatever she offered. It tasted like stale water and metal with a hint of festival spices. It slid slowly down his dry throat, and he coughed and sputtered. He felt so weak—it took an enormous effort just to swallow.

"Having syn doesn't make you a monster any more than having a sword makes you a murderer." Felix looked like he was concentrating, staring hard into nothingness across the room. "Why can't we separate . . . ? If I'm going to be stuck in your head for seven years, I will find a way to kill you."

So it's just you that makes you a monster, Sousuke thought as he lay back down, relieved that the painful task was over.

Felix's gaze snapped to him. "Doesn't that make you a monster from both your father *and* your mother, then, dear grandson?"

Bleed you and all your tails, Felix. Sousuke controlled his breathing as the syn brew descended. It felt like rain on parched ground. Suddenly he wasn't so weak. Surely that was a figment of his imagination. But as a long moment passed, Sousuke felt his pain slipping away with each new second.

Had he just needed syn in order to heal this entire time?

"Such a pleasant child," Felix muttered. "If you could stay still and refrain from insulting me for a moment, I will determine exactly how much trouble you are in." He remained still aside from his flicking tail for a time, during which Brooke was distantly asking if Sousuke was all right.

Sousuke grew more restless and revitalized with each passing second. *You really expect me to be pleasant with you? You, the tyrant who incinerated two hundred and fifty protestors at the palace in Maqua and let their charred bodies crumble for three days to make an example to anyone else who would dare question your reign.*

Felix blinked several times. "It wasn't that many. And they were starting a riot."

Sousuke scoffed. *You, Lillian's lapdog who hunted down rival* trai'yeth *she perceived as threats, then hid their stones so they could never be found and resurrected again.*

The fox's ears turned back and flattened against his lowered head. "I dug them up again later and brought them back to found the *ko'kai—* your Lotusfall or whatever. Many of them forgave me millennia ago, but I guess that's too much to ask of you."

Lillian caused year-long droughts on lands that you coveted, then you started wildfires, decimating entire nations, which you then conquered mercilessly for your empire. They call it the first apocalypse. Arisia, Keil Egro, Tuumichi, Parosh Netah, Terresuth, Elyon. Your incursion into Terruthian lands was so horrific that Coytuu had to literally cut off a chunk of the continent to escape and save the surviv—

"All right, all right." Felix's ethereal shoulders sagged. "Fine, you can hate me. But by all means, forget that I'm also the one who stopped Lillian, and she killed me for it. I've spent the past couple of millennia working to—"

The Lotusfall never forget, Sousuke growled. *It was the creator himself who had to step in and imprison Lillian, not you.*

"It's not enough," Felix suddenly declared, straightening and perking his ears up. "Even if we had a mountain of syn, I couldn't save you."

Sousuke's accusations derailed as his newfound hope crashed down. Even Felix couldn't save him? Or maybe he just didn't want to after Sousuke's history lesson. Surely that was it. Why would Aeo work a miracle like this to no avail?

"So, speaking of my tails . . . we're going to need them." Felix crouched, raising his three golden-tipped tails up in the air. They passed through a hanging bundle of herbs that dangled from a rack on the ceiling with no effect on it. "Your body is too badly damaged, so we'll have to switch to mine."

Sousuke blinked. *What? No. I can't transform. I have human blood.*

"You're more elemental than human," Felix said. "Are you telling me you've never transformed before?"

Sousuke struggled to focus, so great was the relief from the syn brew. He still felt pain, but compared to just minutes ago, he was alive again.

You're trying to manipulate me. Sousuke managed to form thoughts through the overwhelming positive sensation. *You just want control. If we switch to your form, you think you'll be able to command my body.*

"All right, we'll switch to your elemental form, then. What's your true form?"

Sousuke moved his hand. Clenched his fist. Renewed strength flowed through him.

He tempered his elation. This power was more dangerous than fire.

He should only use as much syn as he absolutely needed. Lest he fall into the trap that so many *trai'yeth* did: addiction to power that would eventually, yet surely, drive him mad.

"Human," Sousuke said.

"What?" Brooke asked. "Did it work? You look like you're feeling better."

"Your human body is dying," the spirit-fox said. "What's your innate elemental form?"

"I said I'm human," Sousuke said, ignoring Brooke as he tried to sit up. He immediately abandoned that idea. Apparently the syn wasn't *that* powerful.

"I know your pedigree, boy. You can't lie to me. You're a wolf, aren't you?"

Sousuke glared at Felix. "None of your business." He tried moving his legs and found them responsive, too.

That syn was amazing. What if he just needed more of it? Just until he recovered, of course. Then he'd be rid of it.

"Would you rather die?" Felix snapped.

"Look, it's been years. I can't—"

"We'll do my true form, then," Felix said.

"No." Sousuke refused to be transformed into the visage of one of the most evil beings in the cosmos, whose many-tailed likeness was carved into motifs and mosaics and vases in museums across the world, displaying dire warnings to any future generations who might make an elemental their god.

"Sousuke?" Brooke leaned into his field of vision. "What's going on?"

"I'm fine," he said to Brooke, then turned back to the spirit. "Do your normal fox form, or anything else."

"I'd have to collect samples from animals again, or go to one of my stashes, and there's no time. I'm not interested in dying again." Felix sat and closed his eyes, and a deep, rumbling, terrible sensation began in Sousuke's gut and spread to his knees, his chest, his elbows.

Sousuke squeezed his eyes shut and resisted with all his might, but the feeling only accelerated and strengthened. Nausea washed over him. "No . . . stop!"

"What's happening?" Brooke cried, but Lysander held her back, his brows knit together in a scrutinizing expression.

"I'm not thrilled about it, either," Felix grumbled. "But it's the only way. I'm going to save you ungrateful mortals whether you like it or not."

Sousuke cried out as a new kind of pain rippled through him. He writhed and twisted and . . . *changed.*

His skin prickled as fur sprouted. His face stretched outward to form a snout, his canines elongating and sharpening. His joints popped and his bones compacted. His clothes and bandages loosened and sloughed away as his body shrank.

His scream warped into a howl.

As soon as it had begun, it was over. And the pain was gone.

Sousuke looked down at himself, shaking and panting. But his panting didn't sound human.

His arms were covered in fur. Dark and spotted with tiny flecks of gold and silver, which seemed to move of their own accord, like stars traveling across his coat. Copper paws instead of hands. Shadows moving like an aura around him like a viridescent nebula.

He was no longer himself. He was a dark kumiho.

The true form of Felix Kael Tae, the one who'd brought about the first apocalypse.

19

BROOKE

Brooke stared in shock as Sousuke muttered and argued with nothingness, as if he were talking to a ghost, then transformed into a mythical creature she'd only ever heard legends of: a three-tailed fox with a coat of black, silver, and bronze. Its flaming green eyes blinked as if out of focus as it slowly stood on the cot and shook off the bandages and clothes draped over its back.

"Well," it said in a different voice. "It seems that worked." It pushed its front paws forward and arched its back in a stretch. Impossible shadows seemed to hover around the fox like a dark mist.

Lysander placed an arm between Brooke and the creature, and she stood and backed away. "Sousuke?" she whispered.

"Felix, actually," the fox said. His viridescent eyes focused on her. "Hello again. How long has it been since I died? Did you send my letters?"

Brooke just stared at him as joy and disbelief mingled and rendered her speechless. "I . . . y-yes, I delivered them to the postmaster in Jadenvive. But it's only been a few days." She wanted to hug him. But he seemed . . . untouchable. And he would hate it. Which made her just want to do it more.

"Where is Sousuke?" Brooke asked cautiously.

"Oh, he's still in here. Unfortunately," Felix said. "Shut up, Sousuke."

Brooke grabbed his strange, tiny body and squeezed it tight.

"Hey, watch it, woman!"

His fur was impossibly soft. Brooke nuzzled his fuzzy little mane. "I didn't think I could miss such a nasty creature so much."

An adorable growl rumbled through Felix, and she released him to swipe at moisture in her lashes.

"All right, get a hold of yourself," Felix said. "Have you located Lillian? Or the keystone—the aether stone? Please tell me she hasn't been released."

"The keystone was stolen from the Katrosi treasury in Jadenvive, if you recall," Brooke said. "Vylia and Sousuke were also waylaid and captured. We think both crimes might have been committed by the same person, who then left Sousuke here to die."

Felix remained still for a moment, yet the surreal flecks in his coat continued moving like the slow swirling of distant galaxies. "Sousuke says both the theft and kidnapping were done by a Malaano lieutenant named Sa'alu and his men."

Brooke uttered a curse under her breath. "I knew he was trouble. I issued an order for his head weeks ago. It seems my azure masks failed to take care of it."

Felix continued to stand as a statue for another few seconds, then murmured, "Sa'alu has Lillian, and she's going for her vault. At least she hasn't been released yet . . . There's still hope." He bared white fangs, then turned to Lysander. "Did you fulfill your oath upon my death, Oathbreaker?"

Brooke looked up at Lysander and reiterated the question in a thought to him. Lysander glanced at her for a second before nodding to Felix. He reached into his pack and withdrew a small chest with a grimy old lock.

Brooke opened her mouth to question, but Felix interrupted her by jumping off the cot. "There's no time to waste. We have to collect my three other vessels and beat Lillian to Ashena. *Now.*"

Brooke's mind whirled. "Wait, what?" She pointed at the chest. "What is this?"

"It's one portion of a four-part cypher needed for opening the vault door," Felix explained in haste. "We have to break in and steal the dreamcatcher before Lillian can reclaim it. Where's Ryon?"

"Hang on one second," Brooke said. "What's a dreamcatcher?"

Felix gave a frustrated sigh. "A relic of the Illyrian people—your people, before you sailed to this continent. Before you were separate tribes, even.

It's infused with the most rare aether—shut up, Sousuke!—a human aether gift called 'sage.' It allows someone to see the future, or at least, many future possibilities. The dreamcatcher is woven with aether from a very powerful ancient sage. With it, Lillian could see exactly how to reclaim her empire and re-establish total dominance. I guarantee that's why she's heading to her vault. We have to take it before she gets the chance."

Brooke reeled with the onslaught of information. "So you want to take us . . . and Ryon . . . and race to Ashena on the east coast, break into a vault, and steal this artifact before Sa'alu and Lillian can get their hands on it?"

"North of Ashena, actually," Felix said. "To Banshee's Playground."

20

KIRALAU

Kira didn't enjoy the smell of the stables but was grateful for the pampering of her faithful xavi. The expression of surprise and admiration from the stable boy when she said her father was Oda'e was an amusing sight. Kira had lived her entire life in anonymity; to suddenly go from ranch girl to a privileged member of a royal family and daughter of the revolutionary leader would take some adjusting.

And Ryon also carried her pack for her, offering her shoulders relief from their journey. How had her life improved so drastically, so quickly? Kira pushed up on her tiptoes to give Ryon a kiss on the cheek as thanks, and his return smile warmed her.

They stepped out onto the street, and Kira relished the familiar sight. Shops lined either side of the street with large signs atop their fronts in both Malaano and Phoeran languages. The Navarro Mercantile, the haberdashery, Aunt Halu'a's Bakery, the Buckhorn Saloon, and the grocer. Colorful streamers tied with hanging ribbons stretched from roof to roof, and laughing children ran past with cornhusk dolls and miniature wooden swords and shields.

The only thing different from Kira's memory was cherry-red graffiti on the side of the saloon. It read: LOYALTY with a lotus symbol whose paint drips had dried like spilled blood.

Kira frowned but was distracted by Ryon pointing to a confectionery. "Best honey drops there," he said. "That's where I get 'em—and orders from Brooke when I was still a scout."

Kira admired how cute the little candy store was—so small it would be easy to miss, even with the hand-painted sign out front advertising all kinds of festival treats. "Is it run by a Katrosi?"

Ryon nodded. "She makes this popped corn for the festival that's covered in this sweet stuff. It's *unbelievable*. Have you ever had it before?"

"Of course." Kira took his hand and squeezed it. "Maybe our childhoods do have something in common, then."

Ryon grinned. "Sometimes she even has chocolate popped corn, too. Although I'm not sure if the Emberhawk were still trading cocoa during all the turmoil . . . If so, maybe I could afford it since we didn't have to pay the toll. Want some?"

Kira enjoyed her husband's childlike excitement as much as the tantalizing scent of popped corn on the breeze. "I don't think I can resist. But can we find Tekkyn first? I don't want to miss him."

"Of course, *balemba*." Ryon pointed a finger at the confectionery. "I'll be back for you."

Kira couldn't recall exactly where the cobbler's storefront was until they'd strolled down the busy street where Inowae had indicated. She spotted it on the right, tugged at Ryon's hand, and opened the creaky door.

The smell of leather greeted her along with a wall with shelves full of footwear, from boots to moccasins to sandals to d'hakka-silk slippers. Kira only spotted two figures as she waited for her eyes to adjust from the bright midday sun: a man behind the counter and her brother looking over his shoulder at her beneath his wide-brimmed hat. He looked so much more like her big brother in his cowboy getup rather than Imperial armor.

"Hey, Frizz!" Tekkyn turned and grabbed Kira in an enormous hug.

Kira couldn't help but notice she was being pressed into all sorts of pouches and equipment on his bandoleer and belt. Something that jingled like *rupero* in one bag, his aged flint and steel firestriker, Lee's lasso, and several knife sheaths on first glance.

"Looks like you're saddled up to make tracks," Kira observed.

"Yeah, I'm on my way out," Tekkyn said. "Don't let me interrupt your time at the festival. Seems a bit bigger this year."

Concern whispered in the back of Kira's mind. "Where are you going?"

"Not quite sure yet." Tekkyn turned back to the cobbler, took his tall boots from the counter, and slid several coins over the counter. "Thank you, sir." He kept a hand on the counter for balance as he slipped the boots on. "East, probably. Hunting."

"Hunting? Since when were you a hunter? You've been a fisherman since you could toddle."

"Yup," Tekkyn grunted with the effort of sliding his foot into the heel of the boot, then examined and admired the craftsmanship. "But when I'm fishin', I can't stop thinkin' 'bout Lee."

Kira's chest sank. At least she had Ryon to distract her from the grief. Tekkyn had always been more of a lone wolf.

"Need to get away from it all," Tekkyn continued. "Gotta find a way to make it sit right in my head, ya know? To honor him."

Kira nodded and her voice softened. "Yeah. Well, just don't get into any trouble, now."

Tekkyn tipped his hat as he affixed his spurs.

Ryon spoke from behind Kira. "East, huh? How far east?"

There was something off in his tone. Kira turned to give Ryon a quizzical look.

Tekkyn side-eyed Ryon. "Not sure."

"But you are sure of more than you're letting on," Ryon said.

Tekkyn strode forward and pushed through the door, holding it open for them to follow. "Also thought I'd grab some jerky at the smokehouse. And it looks like a storm's brewin' in the south, so I might head out pretty quick to get ahead of that. That enough detail?"

Ryon glanced at Kira as they moved back out into the street, squinting against the sun. "Would whatever *it* is be upsetting to Kira? Or she might try to stop you? Maybe something you're ashamed of?"

"What's going on?" Kira demanded, looking from one of them to the other. "Tekkyn, are you hidin' somethin'?"

Tekkyn sighed and rubbed his forehead. "All right, fine." He looked at the festival goers who flowed around them and lowered his deep voice even further. "I'm goin' after Sa'alu. Won't be able to sleep well 'til he's dead."

Kira's throat clenched as if Zamara were choking her again. "You . . . you think he killed Lee?"

"It was a Malaano blade," Tekkyn said under his breath. "Regardless of whether it was Sa'alu or one of his men, he's to blame for supplying the Emberhawk for the attack. Lee's gone because of him."

Kira bit the inside of her lip. "So you're gonna run after Sa'alu, outnumbered at least five to one, and try to assassinate him? Really?"

"Not assassination. Justice."

"Vigilante justice!" Kira exclaimed, and a nearby child with a colorful honey-pop turned to her with eyes as wide as the second moon. She smiled and wiggled her fingers as he passed by, tugged by his mother's hand.

Tekkyn glared at Kira until she lowered her voice to a furious whisper. "Tekkyn, really. How are you even going to find Sa'alu? Do Mom and Dad know about this?"

"I have a way of trackin' him," Tekkyn said. "Assumin' he's the one who took the princess. And I'm fairly certain of that."

Kira's maelstrom of thoughts and emotions slowed. "You have a way to track Vylia, then? How?"

Tekkyn's jaw muscles flexed as he looked away.

"Tekkyn'ashi, I swear by the Silvermead, if you don't tell me—"

"It's not my secret to tell."

Kira stomped her foot. "I was hired to protect the princess, too, if you recall! If it has to do with her safety, I need to know!"

"*Hush!* You're yippin' louder than a pack of coyotes." Tekkyn looked around them again and growled in frustration. "Fine, I guess it can't hurt. If you can keep a secret for once in your life."

Kira's heart lurched with anticipation, and she nodded vigorously.

"Vylia's four bodyguards each had an artifact for keepin' tabs on her. Sousuke said it was attuned to the living coral in her crown." Tekkyn pulled something from a bone-latch pouch on his belt. It looked like a sort of compass, its arrow made of blue coral. It spun for a moment, then lazily pointed east.

Ryon leaned in for a closer look. "Sousuke gave this to you?"

Tekkyn nodded. "The Katrosi had taken three of these from the fallen bodyguards and stashed them in the treasury. And—"

"Sousuke stole them from the treasury when we went in to get the keystone?" Kira rushed.

"Can't call it stealin' since they're the princess's property," Tekkyn said. "I must've gained Sousuke's trust when we protected them during the Malaano invasion. He gave one to me before they set out for Sekoiako, since I was the new bodyguard." He gazed down at the compass. "I'd wager the whole ranch it was Sa'alu who waylaid them. I'll end him even if it ends me."

Dread coiled in Kira's stomach. "If you're that serious about bringing him to justice, you can't seriously think of doing this alone."

Tekkyn met her gaze with his own stone-cold blue. "You don't need to worry 'bout me."

The way he said it left her without retort.

"*Aeo leywa ai shea,*" Ryon said, offering a hand to his brother-in-law. Tekkyn shook it.

"W-we're not going with him?" Kira asked Ryon incredulously.

"He won't allow his sister in danger again," Ryon murmured. "Nor will I."

"Darn straight." Tekkyn reached out and rustled Kira's hair before she could jerk away, curse him. Then he moved to untie his xavi from a post in front of the cobbler's. "Stay safe, Frizz. Word is that the emperor is here in Navakovrae lands."

Kira's already whirling mind spun even faster. "What? I thought the emperor never left Malaan Island!"

"My source is good. There have been sightings of the royal palanquin. We both know that wouldn't be the lost princess."

Kira resisted throwing her hands up and making a scene. "It could be the Imperial crown prince!"

Tekkyn shrugged. "I haven't seen it myself, so I can't say. Y'all just be cautious if you're haunting these parts." He launched himself into the saddle of his xavi with practiced ease. "I'd recommend headin' back to the Emberhawk Sovereignty if I were you, *Lady* Frizz."

Kira cringed. Somehow, that was even worse.

She swallowed and realized her throat was dry. What could she possibly say to stop him? Nothing came to mind. Once her brother set his mind to something, he was like a bull.

Tekkyn tipped his hat to Ryon. "Keep her safe."

At Ryon's nod, Tekkyn kicked his heels into the xavi's sides. The animal launched into a gallop, weaving through the crowd with perfected agility. Within seconds, he was gone.

Kira snorted out her frustration. "Idiot is going to get himself killed!" She clenched her fists and cursed the headstrong nature everyone in her family seemed to have inherited. "He thinks he's so cool."

Ryon shrugged. "Well . . ."

"Don't say it." Kira turned on him. "You didn't even try to stop him! You all but encouraged him!"

Ryon raised his hands. "Hey, we both know he's gonna do whatever he wants."

"He's going to get himself killed!" Kira repeated, words failing her as the feeling of helplessness overwhelmed her.

"Hey, it's okay." Ryon moved closer and lowered his voice, offering a hug if she wanted to slip into it. "This probably isn't the first time he's done something like this. He knows what he's doing."

Kira's mouth opened, hung there, and shut again. In truth, she had no idea what Tekkyn had been up to the past few years, since he was drafted. And apparently working undercover for their father to manipulate the Navakovrae Resistance into being. Arming himself with all kinds of intelligence, both foreign and domestic.

She closed her eyes and dropped her head into Ryon's chest as the crowd moseyed around them. "Do you think he'll be okay?" she asked, her words muffled through his tunic.

Ryon was quiet for a long moment as he wrapped his arms around her. "I think there are a handful of people who could pull it off, and Tekkyn is one of them."

"I can't lose another brother," Kira whispered.

"Try to put your faith in the creator. Our prayers are powerful." Ryon kissed her hair. "I know it's hard. But perhaps some chocolate-drizzled popped corn could provide a distraction?"

Kira took a long, deep breath and released it slowly. "Perhaps."

Kira watched waterdancers spin and twirl to the music, streams of floating water twisting with their movements in a shimmering spectacle. Glowing mushrooms illuminated the flows in green and blue as they circled in seamless rings above Navarro's center fountain, then shattered into thousands of shining droplets, creating a breathtaking display of mastered magic.

The water spun into the shape of a lotus, then twirled up into the darkening sky to form a long dragon that spat streams of water onto the squealing and laughing children in the crowd.

Kira shared a loving look with Ryon and couldn't possibly have been happier in that moment. It was as if the war wasn't happening. Prejudice didn't exist as children of both local ethnicities played in the water and taunted the water dragon for more.

"I can see why this is such a special memory for you," Ryon said. "We'll have to bring our kids here every year."

Kira's heart swelled. "How many kids do you want?"

"How many is too many?" Ryon waggled his eyebrows.

Kira laughed and adjusted the laurel in her hair, ensuring that the butterfly clip he'd given her was still in its place next to the festive flowers. "We'd be limited by the amount of chaos, surely."

"I've been living in an orphanage for years. Chaos is the natural state of my—"

"You would choose savages over your own kin?" someone yelled.

Kira turned to find a young man throwing handfuls of small, white objects into the air. He ran into the center of the spectacle, around the fountain, crashing through the water dragon. The waterdancers staggered away from him, their magical creation splashing down and drenching the crowd.

"Loyalty!" the young man yelled, throwing handfuls of white clutter that floated slowly to the ground. "Remember our ancestors! The empire protects—"

Two guards tackled him to the ground.

Shouts of alarm sent children running back to their parents. Kira clutched her blue d'hakka dagger as the guards restrained him.

"Traitors!" the loyalist screamed as the guards dragged him away.

Kira slowly released the hilt of her weapon, trying to slow her rapid pulse. Were there others, or was he the only one? Would they target tribespeople like Inowae had warned?

"Hey, it's okay." Ryon laid a gentle hand on her wrist. "They got him."

Kira's gaze darted around the crowd, looking for any more potential aggressors. The waterdancers apologized, and the water began lifting up from people's clothing, leaving dry cloth and the muddied road into dry dust.

"Thankfully our snacks didn't get wet. We're fine," Ryon said. "*Balemba?*"

The water dragon began its flight through the sky once again. But Kira's spirit couldn't recover so quickly.

She moved closer, trying to determine what the young man had been throwing in the air. They littered the ground like white pieces of parchment.

Lotus petals.

"Look, I can disappear. And our popped corn can disappear twice as fast." Ryon vanished, and so did an enormous amount of the chocolate-covered treats.

Kira hardly noticed as she stared at the petals. As the drums and handheld rattlers resumed their beat, she realized that the joy and harmony of this place were a façade.

She would not feel safe starting a family until this war was over.

21

SOUSUKE

Sousuke felt Felix curl up between Lysander and Brooke as they rode on a dragon's back. Surely Sousuke would have found it exhilarating if he didn't feel like he'd taken a back-seat in a carriage where someone else was driving his own body. A strange mystical fox body.

Everything about the situation felt foreign. Perhaps he'd died back in the Sekoiako village, and this was just a hallucination or an afterlife dream. That might make more sense.

All he could do now was be dragged along and think. And wonder. And seethe.

Why did it have to be Felix? His great-great-great—how many greats?—grandfather. Who wasn't so great.

There was only one person in the world he hated more than Felix and Lillian: another tyrant of old. The only reason Felix was up a notch was because he was supposedly reformed. And his adoptive father, Tameru, trusted Felix. Finding halfway-decent first-generation *trai'yeth* seemed nearly impossible, so Tameru must have lowered his standards.

Sousuke wasn't so forgiving, nor forgetful. Lysander and Brooke must have no idea about the true nature of the sarcastic fluffy vulpine they apparently thought of as a friend. Had they not read the histories?

Well, many cultures had their own version of history, and some were butchered beyond recognition. Still, Felix was a tyrant to the Malaano, a conqueror of Terruthians and Arisians, and a traitor to Phoerans and the creator himself.

Loathing boiled up inside Sousuke and eked from him like a poisonous fog. He would live in defiance of the evil from every branch of his heritage.

Lands above and below. Felix's voice echoed through Sousuke's mind. *Haven't I done enough to prove to you that I've changed?*

Sousuke growled, then wondered if that had been his doing or Felix's stupid fox form. *Prove to me? You haven't so much as glanced at me my entire life, then you prance over expecting all the honor and glory of a patriarch while you steal my body and prevent me from saving my—*

You're welcome for saving your life, Felix thought. *I've been overseas preventing the next global war on Tameru's orders. You must not trust him, either.*

I trust Father with my life! Preventing global war, eh? Fantastic job.

Felix took a deep breath in through his nostrils, and Sousuke distantly felt the frigid sting of air from clouds that wisped over Onyx's wings. *Look. You hate me. I get it. I deserve it—rather, I did deserve it. But I repented and committed myself to good over a millennia ago, and I have paid the price—*

Whose good? Sousuke demanded. *Your own "good."*

The creator's "good." I follow his orders now. Felix leaned out of Lysander's grip to peek down at the ground far below. Endless treetops were visible only when the clouds permitted, splashing the ground with the colors of autumn. *I don't need your understanding or forgiveness. What concerns me is that you seem to think the same of me and your father. Zeph is far more dangerous. More than you can fathom.*

My father is Tameru. Don't insinuate otherwise again.

All right, fine, I get it, Felix thought. *What I'm trying to insinuate is that we both hate Zeph. I don't know what he's up to, but it can't be good—he is a terrible threat. In pursuing my vessels, we will go near his territory. If you'll work with me instead of against me, we might have a shot at taking him out. Since you're his so—I mean, you have, uh, inherited a large portion of his power—you could use it against him.*

Sousuke's anger reduced from a boil to a simmer. It was a good point . . . One he hadn't considered yet. As much as he despised Felix, Zeph was infinitely worse. The one who'd assaulted his mother.

A shot at justice . . . At avenging his mother's pain, defending his father's honor, proving to all of the Lotusfall once and for all where Sousuke stood, despite what he looked like . . . *who* he looked like . . . It was too good to pass up.

Tameru had forbidden Sousuke from pursuing revenge. He'd said that what Zeph had meant for evil, the creator had meant for good, and given him another son.

Sousuke pushed that conflicted memory from his mind. Eliminating Zeph, their fiercest and most cunning enemy, would be a good thing not just for their family, not just for the Lotusfall, but for all of the Malaano and Phoeran people, whether they knew it or not.

If that meant getting along with Felix, well, he'd have to change his attitude immediately.

It would be worth it.

Sousuke made a concerted effort to reforge his anger and douse it in calm. The calm Vylia had said she loved, and made her feel safe around him.

He considered his words carefully. *You truly think we could defeat Zeph?*

Possibly, Felix said. *I think we've both been granted this second life for a reason.*

The rising hope was invigorating. *All right. After I've rescued Vylia, we can track him down.* It wasn't like Sousuke would still be employed as Vylia's bodyguard after he escorted her to the Lotusfall headquarters in Lover's Fen. He could leave her there safely and—

I'm going to secure the dreamcatcher from Lillian's vault first, Felix thought. *Sorry, but your princess is surely Lillian's vessel by now. Her first move will be for the dreamcatcher. We're probably already too late. I just meant to think ahead about working together if we run into Zeph along the way, since we will be skirting his territory, and I expect he can sense you.*

Sousuke cringed. Yes, he knew all too well that Zeph could sense him. He thrust those terrifying recollections aside.

Vylia would never become Lillian's vessel, Sousuke thought. *She has to be willing, right?*

Yeah, Felix slowly replied. *But no mortal can resist Lillian's charms.*

Just because you *couldn't resist her doesn't mean it's impossible,* Sousuke snapped. *Vylia may seem fragile, but she is more dedicated than anyone to doing what is right.*

Felix snorted. *She was raised by that godless emperor. How could she know what is right?*

She was raised by the priestesses after her mother died, Sousuke thought back. *She is different.*

The priestesses of Lill—a laugh echoed through his mind as Felix cut himself off. *Oh, now I understand. Didn't take you for a lover-boy.*

Sousuke felt warmth rising despite the wind chill. *I don't care what you think. I will save her. Your control is fading; I can sense it. As soon as you lose your grip on my body, I will go to find her and take care of Lillian myself. And then you'll be the prisoner inside my mind, and you'll see how it feels.*

The fox went rigid. *You misunderstand. I'll be happy to help you save the princess and deal with Lillian after we've secured the dreamcatcher.*

So Felix didn't deny it. Sousuke must be right. He'd regain control soon.

Victory would taste so sweet.

I don't think I trust you with the dreamcatcher, Sousuke said, trying to be mature and prevent gloating from infiltrating his thought-voice. *You just want it for yourself.*

That's not true, Felix thought.

I can tell you're lying. You know I'm inside your head, right? Must be a foreign feeling for an elemental.

Indeed. Felix sighed. *I don't want the dreamcatcher for myself. I'll only use it if the need is truly dire. But that would prevent Lillian from using it, too, as it can probably only be used once more to see the future before its power is depleted. And it would give us an advantage, so I will admit it's tempting.*

Wouldn't it already be worthless after not being used in a millennia? Sousuke mused. *The future-seeing magic has surely long-since faded. Vylia, on the other hand, still has a chance. If we rescue her and recapture the Malo stone, we can put Lillian back on her glass-gold pedestal in Maqua and prevent any chance of her escape.*

I seriously doubt Lillian hasn't found a way to escape yet with the keystone and her chosen vessel both in hand, Felix thought. *What idiot priestess removed the Malo stone from that glass-gold prison I made?*

I heard it was the emperor himself who gave the order, Sousuke thought.

Whatever. It doesn't matter now. Felix snorted and wrinkled his snout against the wind. *How could you find Lillian, anyway? Can you sense the amos like we* trai'yeth *can?*

No, Sousuke thought, *but remember that compass I asked you to take from my belongings?*

Begged, you mean? Felix shifted his weight, adjusting the fitted leather backpack the Sekoiako had given Brooke on his behalf, originally designed for their war-dogs. *Yeah, I got the blasted thing. This cursed pack makes me feel like a pet.*

It's attuned to the coral in Vylia's crown. It will lead me to her, Sousuke thought. *You know, if we are going to face Zeph, we should acquire some more syn.* The power it would grant . . . he'd only keep it temporarily. To defeat Zeph. And he didn't want to ever experience dying like that again. Keeping a healthy amount of syn would ensure he healed faster, and lessen mortal pain.

He wouldn't start to lose his mind with just a bit more. Right?

Felix snuggled back into Lysander's arm. *Perhaps . . . We're so low on syn I can't feel anything. But not too much more, or Zeph will sense us that much more easily.*

Zeph's territory is northern Malaan Island, Sousuke thought. *He can't sense me from that far away.*

Also the northeastern Navakovrae lands. My'Eyah, Tahiri, and Ashena.

Well, that's wrong, Sousuke thought, *but even if you're right, all the more reason to get more syn now in case we run into him.*

No, we need to stay hidden until our foremost goals are accomplished, Felix thought. *Both of us being together is like a lighthouse already.*

Frustration pricked Sousuke. *Do you want to fight Zeph or not?*

If only they could separate somehow . . . Sousuke tried to envision himself separating from Felix. Expelling the *trai'yeth* from his core. Their two souls tearing apart.

Good luck, Felix said. *At this point, there are only two things I can think of that would separate us. And neither are anywhere within reach.*

What are they? Sosuke demanded.

An artifact so ancient I haven't laid eyes on it since around the Serran Wars. I'm not sure it still exists, and I have no idea where it could be.

What is it?

A sword called Division, Felix said. *A blade that cuts so deep, it is said to divide between soul and spirit.*

Sousuke wouldn't mind having a new sword. *Could it be in Lillian's vault?*

No, Felix said. *It's not.*

And the other option?

Seven years.

Sousuke drooped. *I'm never making a deal with the creator ever again.*

Heh! You don't know what's good for you. Felix thought. *I want to fight Zeph on our terms. And win. Such a thing will require us to be shrewd.* Felix turned his head and squinted, attuning their vision to a town in the distance that could only be Navarro, judging by the architecture and the river that snaked nearby—the Silvermead. *Now, I seem to remember you promised to play nice if I got your silly compass before we left Sekoiako.*

Sousuke struggled to reel in his annoyance. He would play nice. Because he could feel Felix's control of their body slipping by the hour.

His time would come.

Soon.

22

BROOKE

Brooke pulled up and left on Onyx's reins, and he turned his horned head to look back at her with a slitted eye. She leaned forward and pointed to a clearing she'd found among the treetops.

"Can you land there?" Brooke yelled over the wind, attempting to send Onyx a newly-formed memory. The last thing she wanted was for the dragon to land in the middle of another village and terrify every possible citizen.

Onyx focused where she directed and dove into a steep descent, causing Lysander to clench and hold her tighter from behind. Felix—or perhaps it was Sousuke—gave a sound halfway between a fox's yip and a dog's annoyed growl.

"Easy!" Brooke called, tugging on the reins in a vain attempt to slow the young drake. Onyx swooped in as if nothing was on his back besides his own scales, and his clawed feet slammed into the earth, sending a shock up through thick legs and nearly tossing everyone from the saddle.

"Aish," Brooke muttered as she jumped down into thick grasses that were much more difficult to see now—the darkness was heavier beneath the leaves of the forest that blocked the newborn moon's light. She moved to Onyx's face as he folded his wings and champed at the bit. "Could you be a bit softer on the landings? You'll be the death of us." Lysander more than her, apparently, as he seemed both nervous and eager to dismount.

A memory hit her mind, sudden and strong: a large fish, swimming fast beneath green waters until the memory-holder plunged its face through the waves and caught the fish between its fangs.

"Oh, wow, okay!" Brooke recoiled as Onyx fantasized about the crunch of bones and cold scales in his teeth. "Fish. You want fish. I should have known that lake wyverns eat fish, not goats!" She rubbed the black scales of Onyx's nose. "Okay, I'll buy you some fish in Navarro. I'll bring back as many as I can carry. I promise."

Onyx rumbled a sound like deep clicks in response as he flopped down sideways on the grass.

"We survived," Lysander said from across the clearing. He must have escaped the saddle and made plenty of distance between himself and the dragon as fast as possible.

Brooke chuckled as she crossed to him. *I'll have to see if there are any dragon-trainers left in Jadenvive from grandfather's generation,* she thought to him. *Or we can look for a scroll that teaches how to encourage softer landings.*

Lysander stretched and glared at Onyx. "Not sure he's trainable."

I'm going to write a letter updating Ulysses, so I'll ask him. I'll send it in Navarro.

"Ulysses," Lysander grunted. "I don't trust him. And I doubt he'll have any time or desire to run your dragon errands."

He owes me. I'm the one who made him my vice . . . Twenty-five, thirty-five . . . forty-two rupero, Brooke counted as she searched through her coinpurse. *Anything I can buy for you in town, besides dinner? What are you craving?*

Lysander frowned at her. "Am I not going with you?"

Brooke glanced between him and the dark fox, whose eyes and moving spots on his coat glowed even more vibrantly in the dim light. Felix was mumbling to himself again. Fighting with himself. The fact that he'd seemingly stolen Sousuke's body was unnerving to Brooke on many levels, but she understood so little of whatever had happened that she had no idea how to judge the situation. Best to just observe for now.

I was hoping to locate Ryon quickly without drawing much attention, Brooke thought. Then aloud, she said, "Felix, you're sure Ryon's here, right?"

The fox nodded in the direction of Navarro. "It's either Ryon or another Phoeran silverblood with the exact amount of syn I left him with."

Brooke made sure to face Lysander even as she spoke to Felix, hoping he would be able to read her lips as she spoke. "Any idea where he is specifically inside the town?"

"There's a festival of water-worshippers by the fountain," Felix said. "I sense he's in that area."

"Excellent." Brooke shuddered against a chilled breeze and reached into her pack for a leather jacket. "I'll be right back."

"Wait, what?" Felix said. "You expect me to stay here with your feral winged pet?"

"Can you transform into a trace cat kitten? Or something normal or harmless?" Brooke asked.

Felix remained still and quiet for a long moment. "That . . . would be risky right now. Doubtful."

"Then stay here and baby-sit the dragon." Brooke adjusted her pack, tossing her braids out of the way, and secured her spear.

Felix snarled. "All right, but if you find a library, I'm going in."

Brooke furrowed her brows and examined the dark fox, but a Katrosi mask would have been easier to read. "Why do you need a library?"

He swatted at a bush that Onyx had apparently crushed, shaking a burr from his paw. "I might not remember *everything* about the vault. I don't remember anything dangerous about it, but I want to make sure, so we can be well prepared."

Brooke stared at him. "And you think the secrets of Lillian's vault would be in a scroll in the Navarro public library?"

"Not the secrets, of course. But some of the pagan legends have held up over time. Just a refresher would be nice."

Brooke couldn't conjure a response.

"It's been over a thousand years, okay?" Felix grumbled. "I can let you run headfirst into danger if you prefer."

"What's he saying?" Lysander asked. "The look on your face says we're going to our deaths."

That's entirely possible. Brooke let out a long sigh. *Felix wants to go to a library in Navarro to refresh his memory of Lillian's vault. If I find a library there, would you please stay here and watch Onyx? I'll explain everything when I return.*

She turned to Felix. "Do you need any food, Memory Loss? You can't eat my *rupero* or any syn. We need the money fo—"

"Why can't I go?" Lysander pouted behind her.

Brooke paused, then turned around to kiss Lysander on the cheek. *You're half Valinorian, my love. And taller than everyone in town. You'd stand out. I can get in and out faster if we don't draw unnecessary attention. I'm the only one among us who could pass for a local. No one will recognize me without my warpaint or headdress.*

Lysander grew an enormous frown. He slipped an arm around her waist, forcefully pulled her close, and returned her peck with a proper kiss. *Fine. You'd better bring me back some festival sweets.*

Brooke resisted a smile and the desire to remain close to him, but the smile won out. *Of course I will.*

Be safe.

Brooke's legs ached as she spotted the straight lines of buildings through the trees. Maybe they could stop and rest for the night—her body was by no means accustomed to riding in a dragon saddle any more.

She doubted Felix would give them any rest, though. The *trai'yeth* acted like the world depended on them accomplishing their mission as fast as possible. Perhaps it did. But they wouldn't do the world any good if they arrived at Lillian's vault sleepless and starving.

Brooke broke through the tree line and was hit with scents of caramel and smoke from fireworks as they blossomed in the sky overhead. She took a moment to enjoy the colorful bursts, thankful that Navarro didn't have walls on this side. Something Oda'e would probably want to construct as soon as possible. Perhaps they'd already begun construction, and Brooke just couldn't see it in the darkness.

Braziers lit a fountain that somehow boasted both water and tongues of fire at its top. People danced, laughed, and drank around it, forming an intimidatingly large crowd of mostly Navakovrae people, but also many tribesmen. There was no war here.

Brooke smiled at the display of peace, but unease threw her off balance. She hadn't been to Navarro in so long, and what she knew of the Moon Festival was only from scrolls. She struggled to remember as much about the Malaano holiday as she could. Elemental dances with water, cornhusk dolls for children, flowers in women's hair. Sweets and fireworks. That was it, right? Looked like it.

Brooke took a deep breath and stepped into the light to join the crowd, trying to look like she knew where she was going. She reminded herself that no one would recognize her without her headdress and paints on. Right?

She plastered a smile on and scanned the revelers for silver hair like Ryon's. No, that wasn't him. That girl kind of looked like Kira, but she didn't wear a bandana in her hair like Kira always did. That tribesman was far too large to be Ryon.

Brooke rounded the fountain and let her gaze flick to the road with shops on either side. Would a grocer still be open at this hour? How many supplies would they need for the journey? Brooke had never been to the east coast before. How long would it take by dragonflight? Could Onyx even carry all of them?

"*Osoi!*"

It took Brooke a moment to realize the old Malaano-heritage man in front of her was speaking to her directly. She blinked away from her thoughts and broadened her smile. "*Hanakao umi,*" she returned, giving a standard greeting in the Malaano language before turning away.

The old man took her arm, and Brooke caught the scent of fruity rice-wine on his white beard. "Where is your laurel?" His smile appeared genuine as he offered her a round headpiece adorned with white blossoms and flowing ribbons.

It had been impossible not to notice that nearly every woman in this crowd had flowers of some sort in her hair. Maybe having some would make her look less strange—she was the only one carrying a backpack and spear.

"Thank you," Brooke took his offering and placed the flower-crown on her head, pleased with how comfortably it settled. She grinned and bowed to the old man.

When she straightened back up from her bow, a few in the crowd shouted in delighted surprise, starting a rippling cheer throughout the crowd. The old man grinned back as the crowd formed a hollow around them.

Then he began to dance.

Horror dawned on Brooke as she felt dozens of pairs of eyes on her. The old man's movements were jolting and erratic, but he was unashamed as he approached her and danced around her in circles as the crowd cheered.

Sweat trickled down Brooke's spine as she stood frozen without a clue of what to do. The only dance she knew well was her spear kata. How could she get out of this?

A dark hand emerged from the crowd and gripped her forearm. Brooke jumped and found Kira's face to her right. Behind her, Ryon was doubled over in laughter.

The blessed girl pulled Brooke behind her and took the flower-crown from her head. "She's married!" Kira yelled, handing the crown back to the man. "So are you, Tomo'i."

The old man cackled until an old woman emerged from the crowd, hollering and swinging at his head with her own flowers, whose petals burst through the air like the fireworks overhead. The crowd laughed and booed as they dispersed.

Brooke let out a breath she didn't know she'd been holding. "Thank you," she said to Kira, then glared at Ryon, who was still laughing uncontrollably.

"What are you doing here?" Kira asked. She looked Brooke up and down. "You look like you've been travelling."

Brooke wondered if that translated to her looking dirty or smelling dirty. Probably both.

"Felix needs Ryon. Urgently," Brooke said. "Assuming he doesn't keel over from laughter first."

Ryon wiped tears away, tried to say something, and failed as he saw

Brooke's face and doubled over once again.

"Felix is still alive?" Kira's blue eyes widened. "I thought he was mortally wounded. Is he with you?"

"Nearby—it's a long story. He wants to meet at library. Is it still open at this hour?"

"The place of knowledge is always open," Kira said. "This way."

23

VYLIA

Vylia had never been so badly in need of cleaning in her entire life. As she lay half-asleep on a threadbare military-issue sleep mat, with her ankles bound together, she fantasized about a warm bath. Soothing salts. Fragrant oils. Her personal servants at the palace, whom she missed as dear family.

But she didn't miss them as much as Uma. Or Juli.

Or Sousuke.

Her tired eyes somehow conjured more tears. She let them fall, motionless. If she mourned any longer, her heart would give out. So she built walls around it. Walls of cold anger and patient justice.

These men, her captors . . . She'd never known such evil creatures could exist. They would have betrayed their own grandmother for a handful of coins and not displayed any remorse.

She would see them pay for their crimes or die in the attempt.

"I need to relieve myself," she said to one of the two Malaano soldiers in sight, who exchanged glances with each other.

"Don't go too far," one of them said.

Vylia wondered if she could even conjure the energy to stand. They'd kept her sedated as much as possible with fadeleaf, and she didn't know if she'd ever really feel awake again.

"You're not going to untie my feet?"

"So you can try and run off again?"

Vylia took a deep breath. She'd been treated like a fragile goddess her entire life. But she wouldn't treat animals the way they regarded her now.

She struggled to rise and hobbled into the forest.

Something cold patted her head. Then her arm. Vylia looked up to see low, gray clouds through the leaves. Rain played a quiet beat on the surrounding greenery.

Colors and shapes that didn't match the organic patterns caught her eye above the treetops. Towers—no, castle spires.

Fear jolted through her. The palace in Maqua? Would they welcome her or execute her?

No . . . There were no mountains here. The flora was foreign. And the air was too heavy.

My'Eyah. The port city's castle had been built with the same tall, boastful architecture, like a younger sibling of the Maqua palace. It was the Malaano Empire's foothold on the continent of Kooa, after all. Where they'd sent settlers on mighty ships, many generations ago. With negotiations, trades, and peace with the natives.

Now, it was more like a chokehold. The strangled throat through which the Empire sent more and more troops by way of the Sea of Bones.

Vylia turned back to the two soldiers at the campfire as the rain increased. "Where are Sa'alu and the others?"

"In town," came the response, "for food and supplies, and only the highest quality fadeleaf, I'm sure."

Vylia's back hurt when turning at that angle. She faced forward and hobbled further away, wondering how far she could go before they would protest. But no shouts or footsteps followed her when she found herself a comfortable distance away.

The temptation to run crept up again. But if her escape attempts hadn't been successful the first several times, she certainly had no shot now, when she was more bruised, sore, and weak than ever before.

She remembered a time when her father would not have hesitated to deliver the death penalty to any man daring to inflict a fraction of the suffering she now endured. Dreamily, a memory of a picnic with her family surfaced—her mother, father, older brother, and cousins. She must have been six or seven. Before the war. Before her mother's death. They'd had a bountiful harvest that year. Sweet summer melons. Dragonfly kites with their long tales tangling in the wind. Happiness and . . . love.

Her tears fell with the rain. It poured down harder and harder, but with no wind, it didn't seem violent. More like the sky had pity on her and was offering a shower. Hopefully this would clean her clothes somewhat . . . she'd never cleaned her own clothes before, so she didn't know. Hopefully the clothes in her pack could get washed, too. And the coral in her crown probably needed some water. Unless it had been broken in their travels. Damaged at least, surely, without Juli's attentive care.

Maybe Vylia should throw her crown in the campfire. Then it couldn't be used to identify her.

She looked up to the sky and blinked against the rain. *Creator god . . . Are you real? Do I have to go to your shrine or a holy place or priests to pray to you?* Tears ran from sore eyes, indistinguishable from the rain. *Are you only the god of the Phoeran people? Am I your enemy, because I worshiped Lillian? Or because I am the daughter of your enemy?*

She closed her eyes and let the water flow over her. She could feel it flying, crashing, merging, flowing.

Would you help me, Creator, if I serve you? Vylia didn't know what to say. She was desperate. What did she have to lose? No one was coming to save her now. Only assassins coming to put her out of her misery. *Do you have a bounty on me, too? Or do you even exist?*

I PAID YOUR RANSOM.

Vylia gasped and her eyes flew open. She could hear the storm, the thunder. But she hadn't heard that audibly. Nor had she heard it in her mind, like Lillian's voice.

It had been in her heart. Or her soul.

Or had she heard it at all?

God?

There was no response.

The rain chilled her to her bones, but a small warmth grew deeper. Quieter. Like a candle's flame. It felt . . . so . . . comforting, somehow.

What was this strange feeling? Surely it wasn't peace. Not in her situation.

But she felt it nevertheless. Relief? Gladness? Whatever it was, it was real.

Raindrops defied gravity. Lifted up in thousands of droplets. Slowly spun and swirled around her in a breathtaking display, like stars made of glass glinting against a dark night.

Vylia smiled. *If that was an offer . . . I accept.*

She raised her hands in worship, but not like the priestesses had taught her—not the formal ocean or moon or tide rituals. It came from a deep place that was unbridled and genuine and overflowing with something she'd never felt before. Something like joy. Or maybe it was true joy she was feeling for the first time.

I choose you.

She didn't understand it. Only knew that she didn't feel quite so alone anymore.

STOP!

Water splashed to the ground. Vylia whirled around at the sound of Lillian's voice.

But what she saw behind her wasn't Sa'alu with Lillian's stone, but a thin man crouched in the brush. Startled, she staggered back, tripped over her ankle bindings, and landed in fresh mud.

The man held one finger to his lips and his other hand out, empty, palm toward her in an innocent gesture. *"Paz! Unami sego. Nao greet."*

Vylia stared at him, her heart racing. He was speaking Phoeran, but she knew scarcely little of that language. She understood from his body language, though, that he was trying to communicate that he meant her no harm.

She had seen his tattoos before, on many Sekoiako warriors. "Sekoiako?" she asked.

He nodded vigorously. Then pointed at her. "Navakovrae."

Vylia knew the meaning of that word. Even though she was definitely not a Navakovrae settler, she nodded. "Friends from the east. Yes. Friend."

She looked back in the direction of the campfire. The Malaano soldiers were far enough away not to be within earshot.

Where had Lillian's voice come from? Had Sa'alu left her stone at the campfire? Was she aware of Vylia from this distance?

"Kino." The man pointed in the direction of the Malaano soldiers. *"Mal."*

Vylia had no idea what he was saying. But was she correct in assuming that this man had tracked them all the way from the Sekoiako village?

"Can you help me?" Vylia stretched her legs out toward him and pointed at the bindings, which had rendered purplish bruises on the surrounding skin. "Please."

The tribesman produced a stone knife made of chipped flint. He approached slowly and sawed at the rope, careful not to touch her.

"I was right yet again."

Vylia twitched and the Sekoiako man whirled, brandishing his knife as Sa'alu stepped out from behind a tree. "Too bad you're not a Katrosi. I might never have known we were being followed."

The tribesman whooped and charged at Sa'alu, who pulled a sword and cut the man down in a single downward strike while dodging to the side, like one might fell a charging beast.

Vylia screamed.

Another Malaano soldier crunched through the underbrush behind her, taking both arms and hauling her back to her feet.

Sa'alu whistled and the two men from the camp came running. "Bind that wound and tie him up. If he survives, we'll bring him with us."

The men groaned. "*Another* captive?"

"Lillian says we need a Phoeran to enter the vault." Sa'alu tilted his blade downward, letting it collect some raindrops and using them to wet a handkerchief to clean the blood from steel. "How kind of the gods to provide one so conveniently."

A sob of combined rage and sorrow wracked Vylia. She let out a cry and didn't care how tiny and weak it sounded. "You value riches over human life! How can you live with yourself?" she wailed. "Just kill me then and take my father's money!"

"Lillian's bounty is higher than the emperor's," Sa'alu said as he sheathed his sword, "so you'll live for a little longer. Come along, now. North to Ashena we go."

24

KIRALAU

When Brooke returned with Felix, Kira wasn't sure it truly was the Phoeran god of luck. He didn't look like a fox anymore. He looked like a mutated black coyote, draped over Brooke's shoulders like a dead carcass with fireflies stuck in his coat. And hadn't Illiana inflicted a mortal wound, which Felix said would surely kill him after the battle at Quin'Alor?

But it must have been the same insufferable *trai'yeth*, because the rude and condescending manner in which he'd barely answered Kira's questions sounded just like the Felix she'd come to know.

It was a good thing Felix was playing dead as they moved through the crowd, because the sight tempered Kira's anger enough that she wasn't as tempted to send him back to whatever grave he'd crawled out of. He was trying to ruin her new perfect life. Felix would *not* get away with it.

"Many of the Navakovrae are dressed as tribesmen," Brooke noted as they passed the candy maker's shop.

Kira was aware of Ryon watching her, and his confusion. She didn't share his joy at learning that Felix was somehow alive. She avoided her husband's questioning gaze as she answered Brooke.

"We want to set ourselves apart from the Malaano. And to us, the native peoples of this land represent independence and freedom. We're on your side." Kira gave Brooke a thin smile, hoping it appeared genuine despite her lack of feelings at the present moment. "I hope that's not offensive to you."

"Not at all," Brooke said as she stroked Felix's tails, which draped from her shoulder alongside her braids. "It's quite the compliment. And it will help avoid confusion on the battle line."

Kira knew how grateful the Tribal Alliance was for the Navakovrae Resistance. The amount of soldiers in Navarro of both ethnicities gave her a sense of security and hope that, with their combined numbers, their armies might actually have a chance against the Empire.

As they neared the library, Ryon spoke up. "Where's Lysander?"

"Keeping an eye on my dragon in the forest," Brooke said.

Kira turned her head to examine Brooke's face, searching for her meaning, but the Katrosi warrior woman looked stoic and serious, as usual. "You have a dragon?" Kira asked.

Brooke grinned and nodded. "His name is Onyx."

Ryon gasped. "You found him? He's alive?"

"Yes," Brooke said with more excitement than Kira had ever seen her express. "Beryl too!"

Ryon lit up like a child on the morning of the Festival of the Gifted King. "Are you serious? Where?"

"In a cave on an island shrouded by mist somewhere in the middle of Lake Mossu. Don't you dare tell a soul."

"Lands above and below!" Ryon was practically bouncing. "Can I see him? Please? Please, please?"

Brooke's brown eyes sparkled. "Would you like a ride?"

Ryon's eyes bulged out of his head as Felix peaked a glowing green eye open. "Are we there yet? It's not like the world is at stake or anything."

Even Ryon's giddiness could not deter Kira from her foul mood. Was Felix's situation so dire that it had to interrupt her honeymoon? To plunge them into danger yet again, just as they were planning to break ground on their own homestead and start a new family? What could possibly be so important that he could expect her to sacrifice all of that?

She controlled her breathing. Once they were hidden from prying eyes, she would inform Felix of her thoughts on the matter. And she wouldn't hold back.

The library sat tucked between the grocer and the haberdasher, looking much more intimidating in the night's deep shadows. But Kira was no stranger to long nights spent amid its pages, as she had opted to take the additional two years of higher education that the Navarro school house had to offer. Despite her mother's protests that tinkering would not lead her to either a husband or a specialized vocation—she would have had to live in My'Eyah or one of the large imperial cities on Malaan Island for that.

Kira had dreamed about that once or twice. But family was more important to her. And no one would threaten the new life-path the creator had granted her with Ryon. Least of all an uncaring racist rodent like Felix.

The scent of paper filled Kira's lungs and warmed her heart as they entered the library. A rotund man in a robe shuffled toward them from the back of the ink shelves. "Welcome—oh, Kiralau! Welcome back. What knowledge do you seek today?"

"Hello again," she said with a bow. "Are either of the private rooms available?"

"Yes, yes," he said, turning and gesturing to a door on the side, between the encyclopedias and scripture scrolls.

Felix's lips seemed to move slightly near Brooke's ear, and she said, "We seek knowledge of Lillian's vault."

The man's brows rose. "The vault of the goddess?"

Brooke nodded.

He tapped his chin. "We don't have much more than a mention or two on that. But I'll bring what we have. One moment."

Kira opened the door to the familiar private room that she'd used for study countless times. It was barely large enough to fit all of them, with nothing more than a table and a single chair inside.

When everyone was inside and the door shut, Felix's eyes were still closed. Kira poked his limp body. "What have you done to my husband?" she whispered, pointing at Ryon's hand. "You get this thing out of him immediately!"

Felix's bright green eyes opened and fixed her in an ethereal stare. "I can't."

Kira's face scrunched into a snarl. "I don't believe you. You've done nothing but keep secrets and manipulate us this entire time!"

With Brooke's help, Felix disentangled himself from her shoulders, braids, and the feathers and beads woven into her braids. "Well, I'm about to lay out everything I know of the vault for you, because you have all earned that level of trust. It's hard to trust a mortal, you know. And pointless to explain things. You expire so quickly." He hopped down onto the table. "As far as Ryon's hand goes, that's one of a four-part cypher that acts as a key to open the vault. It took me quite a long time to gather all four from the oceans where Lillian had scattered them. I hid them and took one vessel for each, then told them not to retrieve them unless I died. Then the instruction was to collect them and protect them until I could be resurrected."

Kira's blood ran hot as she glared at the dark fox. "But you didn't tell your vessels not to touch the cyphers, lest they fuse with their hands, with apparently no way to remove them?"

"I placed them in locked chests. It's not my fault Ryon opened his." Felix's strange eyes didn't betray his emotions, or lack thereof. "Regardless, my plan was that when I resurrected, I could track down my former vessels like I am now, and depending on how much time had passed, I could either take the chests from their descendants, or the cyphers from their bones."

First Kira felt horrified shock, then pure rage. The overwhelming urge to strike Felix was one of the most difficult feelings she'd ever had to suppress.

"*Balemba*," Ryon whispered, placing a hand on her side. "It's—"

"You will not be desecrating my husband's grave," Kira said through clenched teeth. "Remove this cursed thing from his hand. *Now.*"

"I don't know of a way to do that," Felix said. "Unless I cut his hand off."

Kira grabbed two fistfuls of Felix's fur and threw him across the room. He hit the wall with a thud.

Brooke exclaimed a wordless protest as Felix regained his footing. Ryon slid between him and Kira, facing Felix with a ready stance.

"What? We already knew she was violent," Felix said in a disinterested tone. "She killed Zamara. She can throw me around all she wants."

Ryon turned to Kira, taking her by the shoulders. "*Balemba.*" He brought his face close to hers, forcing eye contact. "You need to calm down."

Kira exhaled a hot breath. She didn't consider herself a violent person, but her anger was blinding. "It's his fault," she whispered. "If he'd just told you not to touch the blasted thing, we could have just handed him the chest and avoided being dragged along on this ridiculous quest of grand larceny!"

"Everything all right in there?" asked a voice from outside the door.

"Um, yes, I tripped," Brooke called. "Sorry!" She gave Kira a look of scolding and moved toward the door.

Ryon's expression changed into something Kira had never seen him direct at her before. Disappointment, and a look of near confusion, as if he didn't know her.

Shame fell like a blanket, smothering her fire with malaise. The sudden distance between them nauseated her.

They'd only known each other for a few fortnights. Would he regret marrying her?

A treacherous tear escaped and slid down Kira's cheek. She clenched her teeth and fists. "Felix interrupted our honeymoon," she whispered, "and now he's going to take you away from me. I can't lose you again. I sacrificed everything for you. For us. And I don't want to go into danger again. I lost Lee and now Tekkyn is gone, too. We just found the perfect life. And now we're just going to throw it all away because a stupid fox says so? And we should be joining my mom for dinner right about now!"

The words spilled out in a jumbled rush, but Ryon listened intently to every word. His olive complexion turned pensive, then to a forced peace.

"You're right," he whispered back. "Go have dinner with your fam—*our* family. I'll be along as soon as I can. Where did your mother say we should meet—"

"No!" Kira furiously wiped at her tears. "I'm not leaving you. Not now, not ever."

Ryon watched Brooke accept an armful of scrolls through the barely open door and thank the librarian. Ryon didn't respond.

"Felix can't ask us to lay down our lives for the world," Kira continued fervently, though still keeping her voice low. "We're not soldiers. And we've already given so much! Why doesn't the world save us for a change?"

"It has. Many times." Ryon kept his eyes on Brooke as she shut the door and laid the scrolls on the small table. "Your parents brought you into this world. Your mother and grandmother raised you. Your father provided for you. Lee saved you from a trace cat. Tekkyn helped you rescue me. Yesha of the Roanoke helped us in the Gnarled Wood . . . Mayla and Gael and the other orphans gave me distraction and joy and purpose when we lost my father. Aegwyn also helped save me from Illiana. Even Xavier watched over me in captivity and made sure I wouldn't have brain damage from the muddlewort—"

"Okay, all right," Kira interrupted. "I didn't mean the world isn't worth saving. I just meant, why do *we* have to save it? *Again*?"

Ryon finally met her gaze again, his eyes smoldering like embers. "I know you're not a soldier. But I am. And I will do everything in my power to make this world better, and safer, filled with as much good as possible. There is evil that seeks to take control and gain power over us. It will make this world full of misery and spread evil like a cancer. So wherever evil is, it must be defied, outsmarted, outmaneuvered, and crushed, and sent back to whatever hell spawned it."

Kira's mouth felt dry. The words had poured out of him with such conviction, such determination, that she was left speechless for a long moment. How could she possibly argue with him? How much time had he spent thinking about this?

"Yes," she admitted. "But it's not your responsibility."

"It wasn't my father's, either," Ryon said, his countenance rigid as jasper. "He died facing a tyrant, for the sake of doing what was right, and for a better future for our family. And by betraying my uncle, King Brynn, to the Katrosi, he ended the Sacrificial War and the murder of innocents for the syn in their blood. His defiance against evil bought us a better life in Katrosi, but also brought about immeasurable good for countless others over the course of time." His eyes darkened. "And if the Katrosi elders ever become tyrants, I swear by the stars, I'll fight them, too."

Kira's heart swelled so much it felt like it might choke her. Pride for her husband and fear for him warred within. "Your father was a good man. I wish I could have met him. But you are not going to die like he did," she said firmly. "I won't allow it."

"I'm not planning on it," Ryon said. "But if that's what it takes to secure a better life for you and our future children, I will do it in a heartbeat."

"If you die, I will die." Kira gripped his arms as she stared up at him, needing him to understand the truth of her words.

Ryon gazed down at her with something unreadable churning in his mind. "You should stay here in Navarro with your family. I will help Felix stop Lillian, then I'll come back to you."

Kira huffed a laugh. "What am I going to do here without you? Nothing but worry until you get back."

"You could get a job in the barracks. Support the troops."

"No." Kira shook her head firmly. "I'm going with you, wherever you go."

"Well . . ." Ryon sighed and pulled Kira into a tight embrace, propping his chin up over her curls. "I can see that trying to argue with you about it would be like arguing with a tree."

"A very big, old, strong tree," Kira muffled into his tunic. "With really deep roots."

"And lots of fluffy leaves." Ryon toyed with her curls.

Kira pulled back and narrowed her eyes at him. Technically her curls were his, too, now. But if he called her *Frizz*, so help her . . .

Ryon grinned and straightened the butterfly pin he'd given her. "Everything is going to be okay."

Oh, how she wanted to believe him. But as resignation settled over Kira's heart, so did the ominous weight of dread.

"I'm sorry," she breathed, so Ryon could hear but hopefully Felix couldn't. "I don't . . . know what came over me."

"It's okay, it was just Felix." Ryon smirked. "But let's refrain from throwing anything else across the room in the future, yeah?"

Shame flooded her in a warm torrent. "I'm so sorry. I won't throw anything ever again. I've never really done that before . . . It's not who I am. I don't . . . feel like myself. I don't understand." She wished she were an insect who might be able to slip through the floorboards and disappear. "I'm sorry."

Ryon's eyes narrowed for a second before he pulled her into a hug. "It's okay, *balemba*. We all have those moments sometimes, and we learn for next time." He squeezed her tight. "I love you. And I'm not going anywhere."

"All right, that'll have to do. Lillian designed the vault to only be accessible by her most loyal followers—those who knew her and everything about her by heart." Felix stood atop a charcoal drawing on the small table as Kira, Ryon, and Brooke gathered around. Ryon had sketched blueprints of Lillian's vault at Felix's direction, and smudges marked where his memory was unclear.

Kira's pulse beat with anticipation. She was grateful to focus on facts and details rather than the storm inside her mind.

A dark paw landed on what looked to be the only entrance and exit. "The first test: generosity. The one who wants to open the vault must give an artifact that will power all of the vault's internal mechanisms and open the front door."

Kira frowned. "The four cyphers?" She looked at the marking on Ryon's knuckle. Was there some kind of power inside?

"Yes, those are also needed to get inside and face the trials."

"Trials?" Brooke murmured.

Felix nodded. "There are three trials inside the vault, which guard the treasure room where the dreamcatcher is. Well, four, if you count the test of generosity outside. But I already have a battery, and any Phoeran elementalist can charge it, so don't worry about that."

Kira looked around the room, finding Brooke and Ryon to appear just as confused as she felt. "What's a battery?"

"It's a device that holds Phoeran energy. They were very common in the ancient world, until the elements were split and humans didn't work together to make technology anymore." Felix paused, his gaze unfocusing for a moment before he shook his head and spoke again. "I hid a battery inside a lonely rock formation in Banshee's Playground last time I was there. With any luck, it's still here. Mortals avoid that place because of all the spirits. Otherwise, I'd bet there's one in the catacombs under the old castle in Ashena. All kinds of old stuff just dumped down there."

Ryon went rigid. "Catacombs? Spirits?"

"Ghosts," Felix said. "The name 'Banshee's Playground' didn't give you a clue?"

"That's a Malaano word," Brooke said. "I thought it meant . . ."

Ryon's face drained of color as Kira's mouth dropped open. "Are you saying . . . ghosts are real?" she squeaked.

Brooke let out a nervous laugh. "You've never encountered one?"

"We're wasting time!" Felix pawed at what looked like the first room past the entrance. "One of the trials is divinity, because Lillian was a narcissist who played god. What was she the god of?"

"Fertility," Kira murmured. "The Malo element. She made crops grow with her divine water, and brought the rain."

"Water," Felix emphasized. "She built her palace in Maqua, into the side of the mountain that she declared 'holy.' What's her most holy place?"

"Beresai Falls," Kira said. "The highest waterfall which flows—"

"Very good," Felix interrupted. "Maybe it's good to have a heretic on the team after all. Now—"

"Hey!"

"The divinity trial is a water puzzle. There's a maze inside the walls that a Malo elementalist has to guide water through, to a representation of Beresai Falls."

Everyone looked at each other, landing on Kira. "I . . . I'm not a wavesinger," she meeped. "I can't control the Malo element at all."

"If only we had Vylia," Brooke murmured.

"I've already sent a letter asking for help," Felix said, turning to Brooke. "You gave my letters to the postmaster in Navarro, right?"

Brooke nodded. "You were on my shoulders when I did so . . ."

"I couldn't see 'cause I was playing dead!"

"To whom?" Kira asked. "No more secrets. Who did you ask for help from?"

Felix sighed. "An old friend. He's a *malo syn trai'yeth.* The leader of the Lotusfall."

Kira furrowed her brow as she pieced the Ancient language words together: a lesser elemental of water. She exchanged glances between Brooke and Ryon. "We don't know anyone in the Lotusfall, do we? Or even what that is?"

Felix made a face like he smelled something foul. "We're wasting time." After a long, awkward pause, he sighed again and said, "Sousuke is Lotusfall. Do you know him?"

"Not really," Kira said at the same time that Brooke said, "Yes."

Felix turned his vivid green gaze on Brooke. "My friend is Tameru, Sousuke's father. Sousuke wants me to tell you all that Tameru is trustworthy and that the Lotusfall are our strongest allies if we hope to rescue the princess or oppose Lillian or overthrow the emperor—all of our goals are aligned."

Brooke nodded. "So, is Sousuke inside your head somehow? Or is this *your* body? Or—"

"Elementals are spirits. We have no true body, only a unique form of a mystical animal of some sort. Now, another trial is—"

"So you're holding Sousuke hostage in his own body?"

"We don't have time!" Felix snapped. "The only reason I'm briefing you here is because it would be impossible to discuss a map on a dragon's back in the sky. Every minute we waste is another minute Lillian gets closer to escaping, getting the dreamcatcher, and foreseeing how to quickly reclaim her imperial throne. The last time that happened, only the one true god himself could remove her from power. So everyone be quiet and listen up!"

Kira pursed her lips as everyone fell silent.

"The next trial is fertility." Felix used his nose to nudge one of the scrolls which the librarian had brought. Ryon unrolled it and spread it open for him. "You have to choose the crops or whatever Lillian would grow for her people and place it in the right order or something according to the correct harvest season." He nodded at the Malaano writing. "Plants, seaweed, fish, roe, seeds, whatever. We should take this scroll with us."

"I can check it out," Kira said. She just wouldn't mention to the librarian that they'd be taking it on a journey across the continent.

"And finally, thanks to this other scroll, I'm reminded of another of Lillian's aspects that she declared about herself: beauty. She was obsessed with appearances." Felix's voice deepened and his fur fluffed, as if it were cold in the room. Then he cleared his throat. "That last trial needs a Phoeran who can manipulate light. I'll take care of it."

Kira watched Felix closely, but had no idea if the body language of an elemental fox was the same as any other animal she knew. She couldn't tell if he was hiding something—perhaps just his own private memories. Kira decided not to pry and get yelled at again.

"And beyond the third trial is the dreamcatcher?" Brooke asked.

"Yes. So we have everything we need except the last two cyphers," Felix said. "Next, we go to Valinor to get the third from my vessel on Redfish Island. The fourth is with the Lotusfall. I've already asked for Tameru to bring her with him."

Kira tilted her head. "'Her?'"

"The dreamcatcher is only one of many treasures in the vault. There is more syn and ancient weapons and relics than you can—" Felix stopped mid-sentence again, but no one had interrupted him. "Sousuke says that Lillian promised someone named Sa'alu the vault's treasures in exchange for serving her."

Fire churned in Kira's gut and spread heat throughout her body at the mention of the name of the man who'd killed her brother.

She looked at Ryon, whose face darkened. He met her gaze and nodded.

By stopping Sa'alu, they would avenge Lee and everyone who'd been killed or had their lives destroyed or displaced in the attack on Jadenvive. By stopping Sa'alu, they'd cut the head off of the snake that was Lillian. Because without a servant, there would be no hands to do her bidding.

And by stopping Sa'alu, they would save Vylia. And by saving the imperial princess, perhaps her influence could help to turn the tide of war.

Determination solidified in Kira's chest. This wasn't her choice—it had been forced upon her. But it was her choice now to run and hide or to fight back.

Maybe she wasn't a soldier, but she had always been a fighter.

25

BROOKE

A vision of a d'hakka attack assaulted Brooke's mind. She reeled back to dodge the poisoned tail in the memory, jerking Onyx's reins, and he growled in protest.

"Again?" Brooke yelled as she returned to her true body, surrounded by mist as Onyx flew through clouds that kept getting colder and colder as they fell deeper into the night's embrace.

Lysander held her waist tighter from behind her back. "What happened?"

Onyx keeps showing me awful memories of him being attacked by d'hakka, Brooke thought to Lysander. *I tried to tell him I'm sorry that happened to him, but he keeps showing it to me over and over. I think he's mad at me, but what for? He was acting like he was hungry, so I gave him as many fish as I could carry from Navarro, but he's still acting upset. Maybe we're flying too much? Or is carrying four people and a fox too much weight? If so, why doesn't just show me a memory to tell me that? Or . . . is he calling me a d'hakka?*

Lysander laughed in her ear, and she felt him relax against her. "Did you think taming a wild dragon would be easy?"

Onyx isn't wild! she protested. *He's descended from civilized dragons, and he was raised among humans. Trained from the egg!*

"Until he was . . . how many years old?"

Brooke frowned and hunched back over the saddlehorn in a defense against the dark wind that whipped around them. *Onyx hatched the same year I was born. And I was about seventeen when my grandfather disappeared and we lost contact with Beryl's brood.*

"So in dragon years, he's about . . . two years old?" Lysander said.

Brooke snorted. *That explains the tantrums.*

Lysander chuckled, and Brooke enjoyed his warmth on her back. But something about him felt . . . off. They'd already addressed how he hadn't enjoyed being left behind in the woods near Navarro, but she'd hopefully made it up to him with festival treats and by sharing her memories with him. Was there something else?

Brooke gathered her aether and tentatively touched his mind. But feeling emotions and hearing thoughts were two different aether gifts, and she was only skilled in the latter.

Is everything okay? Brooke asked him in a cautious thought.

Lysander grunted. "Is it that obvious?"

No. I just pay attention to my husband. She turned her head over her shoulder to smile up at him.

He adjusted his arms around her stomach. "It's been a long time since I've been to Valinor," he said in a low tone. "My grandfather, the chancellor, rules over Redfish Island and the coastal counties from the castle there. And my cousin, Thrace . . . he's . . . intense. I just don't know how they will receive me after all of the Zamara business."

Brooke frowned. The chancellor had sent his daughter, Deirdre, for a marriage alliance with the Emberhawk's King Brynn, only for her to be murdered and replaced by an elemental shape-shifter. Deirdre hadn't lived long enough to watch Lysander mature or Coriander become king. How often had the former queen missed her home? Did she even have a loving relationship with King Brynn?

Wait a moment, Brooke thought. *You have a cousin named Thrace? I thought your grandfather was Thrace.*

"Family name," Lysander said. "Grandfather is Thrace XIII. My cousin is Thrace XIV, named after him."

Brooke's mind spun. What ridiculous tradition was this? Wasn't the entire point of naming something to be able to identify it?

Should she have met these foreigners before she married Lysander? This was why the Katrosi had the tradition of evadir.

Lysander laughed, and Brooke assumed he'd heard her thoughts. "I'm named after kings of the past, you know. They just refer to each other by their titles. Chancellor and Wing Comman—"

Onyx lurched under them. His wings folded in, and his nose pointed downward into a steep dive. Immediately the misty clouds vanished, giving way to stars in the night sky and the rapidly approaching dark forest below.

Brooke pulled back on the reins as Kira cried out behind her. Lysander clutched tightly to Brooke as she leaned back against the dive, desperately calling out with her thoughts to Onyx. What memory could she send him?

The dragon ignored her.

The Gnarled Wood reached up at them as if with clawed fingers. Patches of scraggly branches streaked by and snapped as Brooke's panic grew. She strained against the reins with all of her might, but Onyx was undeterred.

They slammed down in impact with the earth, flattening Brooke against Onyx's neck and sending the saddlehorn jutting upward into her gut, knocking the breath from her lungs.

Brooke gasped, but no air came. She willed her mind to focus despite it. This wasn't her first experience with no wind.

Onyx had landed in the middle of some kind of ruins. Stone pillars were lashed together with purple lines and bundles. Threads, Brooke realized as her lungs recovered and her vision cleared. Silk.

D'hakka silk.

Black orbs gleamed in the darkness. Dozens of them. Surrounding them.

Click click clicklicklicklick!

Kira screamed as fire erupted from Onyx's gullet, blinding Brooke against the darkness. Flames billowed from his fangs and lashed out in a stream of blue, yellow, and orange, consuming one screeching d'hakka, then another, and another, and another. Tree-scorpions scattered in every direction like they'd crushed a mother spider.

Brooke could only hold on as Onyx swiveled like a turret and torched the largest d'hakka nest she'd ever seen.

Then, when the only remaining movement was the dancing of flames, Onyx stomped over to a burning d'hakka corpse and bit into it with massive jaws. After a few sickening crunches, he swallowed and moved to his next twitching, smoldering prey.

"Brooke!" Ryon called from behind her, his voice higher pitched than normal. "This wasn't on the brochure!"

"We have to keep going," Felix insisted.

Brooke pulled her sleeping mat out of her pack. "Trust me, a burned-out d'hakka nest is the last place I want to sleep."

"Then don't," Felix said. "Every minute you humans waste sleeping is another minute closer to Empress Lillian."

"It's not just humans." Brooke motioned toward Onyx, who had curled up in the crater where he'd landed, after scratching up a bowl of soft dirt in the earth. Brooke was certain that the lake wyvern's belly was bigger after she'd lost count of how many d'hakka he'd eaten. "Onyx needs rest. And flying at night wasn't the best idea in the first place."

Felix let out a low growl and trotted away.

The sound of snoring whistled from Onyx's direction, and Brooke smiled. She couldn't be angry at the dragon for meeting his own needs when she'd been ignorant to them. Onyx had tried to tell her what he'd wanted. And now that Brooke understood, she'd never forget. Thankfully, it seemed Onyx had accepted her apology.

Kiralau, on the other hand, might need some convincing to climb into the wyvern's saddle again come daybreak. The girl was obviously shaken. But then again, they all were.

As they worked to create a campsite, Brooke glanced up at clumps of charred silk that hung from a ruined stone archway. Humans had hunted wild dragons to near extinction, to eliminate the threat they posed, for poaching, and for bragging rights. Had anyone realized that without the wyverns, the d'hakka population would grow out of control?

An engraving in the ancient stone caught Brooke's eye, and she dropped her bundled quilt to move closer. Squinting, she brushed away dead vines that barely clung to the rock.

The pattern etched into the stone was the same as the colorful design woven into her quilt. A traditional Katrosi marking.

Brooke's jaw fell slack. Most Katrosi buildings were constructed from wood. Only foundations and walls on the ground level of Jadenvive were made of stone, and many of the smaller Katrosi villages had no stonework at all.

How long ago had this structure been built? When had it been abandoned? Was this the original location of Jadenvive, before it had retreated to be rebuilt high in the trees?

"What is it?" A twig cracked behind Brooke as Lysander came alongside.

I think . . . this used to be a Katrosi settlement, Brooke mused, her gaze trailing the pattern until it faded to erosion. *We lost it to the d'hakka.*

"This whole forest is infested with d'hakka, right?" Lysander asked. "The original invaders, before the Malaano crossed the sea."

Yes, Brooke thought. *Previous generations killed off the wild dragons, not realizing the d'hakka were the bigger threat.*

Lysander glanced over at the sleeping Onyx. "Think he can clean up this whole forest himself?"

Brooke chuckled. *We need to find a mate for him. A new brood of drakes could burn this collection of kindling to the ground and fertilize new growth. The Katrosi could reclaim this land!*

"Well, let's focus on the current mission first. One step at a time." Lysander grinned and gave her a side hug, admiring the ancient etchings beside her.

"I don't have time for this."

Brooke looked behind her to find Felix shrugging out of his Sekoiako war-dog pack and dropping it to the ground. He dipped his head and transformed.

Lysander and Brooke instinctively took a step back as Felix's form ballooned outward into a serpentine form darker than the night. Wings sprouted upward and stretched until Felix was Onyx's twin, aside from the saddle.

"I'm going to Valinor," Felix said. "Stay here. I'll come back for you, and you'd better be ready to go when I return."

With that, he beat his wings and disappeared over the silhouetted treetops, blotting out the northern stars.

26

SOUSUKE

Sousuke enjoyed being a wyvern. Flying had been a terrifying sensation at first, but Felix did it with such practiced ease that it seemed safe and natural. In his own body. Which was so wrong to be anything other than human.

At least this draconic body felt a lot more powerful than Felix's strange fox-like true form. Powerful, and satisfying. Well worth the frigid wind billowing his wings, chilling his cold blood. But this dragon's core was liquid fire, pulsing like the glow of embers inside his gullet.

Sousuke would have to try out some spitfire when he got the chance.

But Felix still clung to control, though only by a thread of d'hakka silk, as Sousuke could feel him growing weak in spirit. The *trai'yeth's* impatience and desperation mingled with Sousuke's own, tangling inside the ethereal space that occupied both of their minds.

Felix's thoughts had grown quiet—at least, his targeted thoughts toward Sousuke—as they flew northward to Valinor until the sun broke over the waters of the northern sea at dawn. Sousuke tried to keep his thoughts to himself as well, deciding not to distract or pester Felix as distant heights appeared on the horizon over the sea. Sousuke appreciated Felix's attempts at peace enough to grant the relative silence, and he could feel Felix's appreciation as much as he enjoyed it himself.

Perhaps they could be allies after all. At least until it was Sousuke's turn to take control.

The dark island loomed larger, treetops and tall spires illuminated by rays of the rising sun. Bright sand and forest to the left, cliffs and castle to the right. A town staggered down the castle's hillside and melded into fields and livestock pens with sheep and pigs.

Sousuke hadn't realized how small Redfish Island was compared to the sprawling town—barely large enough for a dragon to land in the patch of woods unnoticed by the town watch. Felix flew in low and landed gracefully just before the morning light could fully brighten the landscape.

The wind's crisp bite held a floral scent mixed with the salt of the sea. Sousuke marveled at the strange trees with leaves like needles as Felix pondered, unmoving.

How will you meet your vessel? Sousuke asked. *Go tromping up to the castle gates as a dragon?*

Yeah . . . that won't go over well, Felix mused. *We only have 3 options right now as far as forms go: dragon, kumiho, or your naked butt.*

Sousuke felt a prick of annoyance that Felix had left his clothing, armor, sword, and equipment with the Sekoiako, only bringing the compass attuned to Vylia's crown. And Souskue had to beg for just that. And then Felix had left it in the war-dog pack with Brooke and the others.

So . . . your kumiho form, then? I wonder how people would react to an evil dark fox trotting down the street.

I have a better idea. Felix transformed from wyvern into kumiho, and Sousuke hated the unnatural feeling of it. He would never get used to it.

Felix trotted into the forest and lay down beneath a tree with crumbling bark. He rested his chin and tails on the ground and remained still.

What now? Sousuke asked.

Now we wait.

Sousuke waited five minutes. Ten minutes. Twenty?

What are you waiting for?

A predator, Felix thought. *The light flecks on my coat look like fireflies.*

Sousuke considered the idea. *But don't fireflies come out at night?*

Felix didn't answer.

Sousuke's annoyance grew until an abrupt pain pierced his side. Felix jerked around and clamped down on a bird that had swooped down to take a bite out of them. But as soon as he'd bitten, Felix released his jaw, and the bird squawked and flew away. Felix was left with a mouthful of feathers.

He spat some out, then swallowed one.

Sousuke gagged at the sensation. *Why are you—ugh!*

Felix chuckled, an amusing cackle from the fox's throat. *The creator put his plans for each kind within their body. All I need is a piece near my core to be able to take its form. Claws, scales—wait, you don't know this already?*

Well, yeah, but I never transform. Disgusting.

Tameru didn't teach you how?

When I was a child, he forced me to learn, but I—ach!

Felix transformed again, this time into the form of a nightjar. Vibrant patterns of red and black were accented with a stark white pennant feather that stretched from the middle of the wing far back behind the bird, like twin flowing ribbons. Suddenly Sousuke could see their surroundings—especially everything in the distance—much more clearly.

Give me a warning next time you do that, Sousuke grumbled.

Get used to it, kit.

Felix took off in a flurry of leaves, dodging through the tree limbs until breaking free of the forest and soaring toward the settlement. The sea to the right became scattered with fishing boats heading out toward the ocean. Or perhaps that larger one was a whaling vessel—they looked so different from Malaano ships. And the roofs of the town were made of overlapping red tiles, and the walls of gray stone. Even the lighthouse was an entirely different design from the one at Ceemalao's harbor.

Sousuke yearned to fly closer and study the architecture. Were those arrow slits? Would these walls withstand a seige better? What about the enormous cliff the castle sat on? It looked like the castle had its own harbor carved into the rock below, because one ship with white square sails disappeared beneath the castle.

Felix flew toward the castle, but turned just before its enormous stone walls to swoop down to a tall house with a steep roof speckled with snow.

Sousuke hadn't seen snow since last winter in Maqua. Was it that late in the season already, or were they just that far away from Alani's warm middle?

Felix landed on the open railing of a balcony with swaying purple curtains. "Thrace!"

Sousuke cringed. It was so early! At least Felix was annoying to everyone equally.

"Thrace!"

Shuffling and a grunt sounded through the curtains. Whispering.

A disturbingly tall shirtless man appeared with a sword. His black glare unnerved Sousuke as he stared into the nightjar's ethereal green gaze.

"*Hontar*, Felix?" the man growled. "*Fro rushe burbin neeshga.*"

Felix responded in the same foreign tongue, Arisian. Sousuke's vocabulary consisted of about ten words.

And yet . . . he could somehow glean understanding through Felix's interpretation. The man was angry that Felix had woken his wife.

The conversation carried on, and Sousuke gleaned only two bits of information: this was the man Felix had called for—Thrace—and for some reason, Felix was asking to go to a museum . . . ? Surely Sousuke had misunderstood that.

Thrace turned to go back inside with a huff and tossed the curtain away from him. Felix swooped in behind, far too fast for Sousuke, and landed on a lampstand beside a luxuriously large four-post bed that had curtains of its own.

A pale-skinned woman in a night dress clasped her hands and spoke excitedly to Felix. Sousuke thought she might be very ill for a moment before realizing that pale skin was somehow natural to her. Thrace was pale, too, but this woman might as well be a ghost.

Felix conversed with the pair until Thrace's negativity appeared to lose to his wife's enthusiasm. They dressed, and Thrace kept his sword, though sheathed, as the woman lit an oil lamp and led the way down stairs and into the street.

Sousuke couldn't contain his discomfort any longer. The talking died down as the couple turned toward the closed castle gate and waited for its creaking hinges to make the metal cross-work rise.

Where are we going? Sousuke asked Felix. *Who are these people?*

Thrace is my vessel. We're going to—

How can an Arisian be a vessel for a Phoeran elemental?

He has some Phoeran blood. The Valinorians and Emberhawk have given their children in marriage alliances more than once.

Maybe that was why Thrace wasn't quite as pale as his wife, Sousuke mused. But he was as tall as any Valinorian giant. A lot like that guy who was with Brooke at the Sekoiako village. Lysander?

Finally the castle gate rose high enough for them to pass beneath, and after they did so, it crept back down but still landed in its place with a sound like a gong. Sousuke would have felt trapped, but for their winged form that sat contentedly on Thrace's shoulder, which was armored with a strange leather pauldron. Everything about this place was strange.

Beyond the castle's courtyard stood a door guarded by four men, who stepped aside after exchanging a few brief words with Thrace. A grand entry hall with purple carpets, then a hallway with hanging braziers, a room with white floral arrangements, another hall. Sousuke didn't see any windows, only tapestries. He committed every twist and turn to memory in case escape became necessary.

Finally they stopped in a showroom behind a locked door. Shelves upon shelves of fragile treasures of every kind gleamed in the light of the wall-torches that Thrace lit. Gems and glass, sword and shield, crowns and scepters, heads of dragons and mountain beasts Sousuke had only heard rumors of. Testaments to the might of the Royal Province of Valinor, whose reaches stretched north, far beyond Redfish Island.

Thrace's wife hurried through yet another locked door, behind which was a much smaller, less decorated room with hundreds of labeled drawers. She set about opening this one and that, removing claws, feathers, scales, and furs, and setting them neatly on a broad table.

One of your stashes is a museum? Sousuke balked.

Don't you breathe a word of it to any living soul.

The woman searched though one ornate chest as Thrace hoisted a silver bar from another. More words were exchanged, and they set about scraping small amounts from each of the animal samples.

Sousuke eyed one claw as large as a man's foot. *What did each of these belong to?*

That's for me to know and you to wonder, Felix said. *Now, let's not forget to ask for some clothes and armor for you. And what kind of weapon do you wield? Aside from your anger, I mean.*

Sousuke took a steadying breath, then realized the nightjar had sighed in tandem. No wonder Felix was playing nice—his time in control of their shared body was running short.

27

KIRALAU

Kira refused to spend one more minute in a charred d'hakka nest. Sleep had been nothing more than a wink in there, and now that the sun's first rays were peeking through the forest, she'd given up on any attempt at rest.

But they couldn't leave for the east coast yet, because Felix hadn't yet returned.

"I'm going to change clothes," she declared, taking a fresh Katrosi split-skirt and spare tunic from her pack.

Ryon glanced sideways at her but didn't stop his work of fletching new arrows by the campfire. Unlike her, he was always up early.

"Okay," he said. "Want some venison jerky for breakfast? Or pemmican?"

"No, thanks." Kira already missed the luxurious foods of Quin'Alor. She stood abruptly and marched into the forest. She didn't hear Ryon follow, and she didn't look back.

First he'd summoned her to the trace cat stables, and now they'd camped in the biggest d'hakka nest she'd ever seen. She'd nearly been killed by both apex predators of the Gnarled Wood. Ryon knew she had a deadly fear of them. Was he that forgetful, or did he not care? Why was Brooke in charge? She wasn't the chief or Ryon's boss anymore.

Kira reached a far enough distance from the campsite, where she could no longer hear the *shick* of Ryon's blade over the birdsong, nor see the smoke from their fire through the leaf-stripped trees. The remaining undisturbed leaves were beginning to change color with the season, noticeable beside the occasional purple webs of d'hakka silk. She would have jumped at the risk of collecting and selling that silk in the market not so long ago, and yet it felt like a lifetime ago.

She changed clothes and tried to logic through her emotions. It wasn't Ryon's fault that Felix had hidden the cypher in the trace cat stables. And it wasn't Ryon's fault that Onyx had decided to make a feast out of that nightmare nest. But he could have insisted that they make camp far away from the burned-out ruins with their strange acrid smell. He could have at least acknowledged her feelings. Didn't he know? He should know. Without her having to tell him.

Kira finished changing and enjoyed the swishing of the split-skirt. It would do nicely for dragon-riding.

She held the bundle of dirty clothes at her side and looked back in the direction of camp. She wasn't ready to go back. So she stood there for a long moment with internal debate.

The forbidden wood was an eerie but familiar solace of its own. A lone walk in the woods wouldn't hurt anything, now that all of the local d'hakka were dead. And it wasn't like she needed to hurry back. They were just waiting for Felix, anyway.

Perhaps she could find a spring or some source of fresh water. That would be a boon—she could wash their clothes and replenish their waterskins.

Kira looked up at the sky and decided to wander north. That way, she might see Onyx's elemental double returning from Valinor overhead and know it was time to return to camp.

She dropped her bundle of dirty clothes and headed northward.

Clean air filled her lungs, free of smoke and char. Leaves crunched underfoot. Kira lifted her face to the youngest rays of sun that managed to slip through the branches and enjoyed the subtle warmth.

Suddenly, everything was better. The knot of tension in her chest unraveled just enough for her mind to release its spiral of worry. Freedom was like a salve.

What should they build first on their new land on the Emberhawk/Katrosi border? Perhaps a small, simple cabin to live in as they constructed a larger, permanent home. The cabin could become a guest house later. Which crops should they plant first? Her favorite tubers, onions, and garlic, to be sure, if they could establish a garden fast enough for the fall growing season. Oh, and orange sweetroots. Would her family's cherry trees flourish there? Wait—could she grow the crops from Navakovrae lands in that tribal forest at all? They'd have to cut down a few trees to have enough sunlight to grow crops, for sure. Wood they could use to construct a lovely little grow-house!

Autumn flowers rose up to greet Kira like tiny pink stars pushing up through the leaves. To her right, so many congregated between the trees it looked like the earth had changed color entirely. Like the forest itself was fighting for its life against the d'hakka incursion.

Kira smiled at the sight and listened for the trickling of water nearby. She heard nothing. No water, and no birds sang anymore. No insects, either.

Her smile vanished. Something wasn't right.

She crouched and continued forward, looking up at the sky. No storm clouds. No wind. No movement.

Kira looked all around her, in every direction. Everything was silent and still.

Her hand went for her blue d'hakka stinger blade out of instinct. Something must be causing this . . . She pressed onward, determined to discover whatever it was.

A sound in the distance, like a thump. Low and dull. Then another. To the north.

Kira wished her footfalls didn't crunch the leaves so loudly as she followed the rhythmic thumping. Then more sounds, and more the further she went. Clanking. Voices. Collective noise, like a village.

What village was in the middle of the Gnarled Wood?

Kira spotted colors and movement through the tree trunks ahead. She slowed her pace and ducked lower to the ground, sneaking forward with every sense on its highest alert.

The voices were masculine, the slow thumping louder now, but still distant somehow. Underground?

Light flashed through the forest. Glaring off of silver armor and a glass pyramid. Blue flags.

The white lotus.

Alarm jolted through Kira as recognition hit her. This was Waelyn's pyramid—Zamara's pyramid. Where she'd first met Lysander. Where they had grown the sunburst flowers, whose vivid blossoms had fanned the flames of arson against Jadenvive. Where Ryon had succumbed to infection from the arrow-wound she'd put in his shoulder.

Why were the Malaano here?

They knew that Zamara's Emberhawk and the Malaano—Sa'alu's unit via orders from the imperial chain of command—had been in league for the surprise attack on the Katrosi capital. But now Kira didn't see any Emberhawk. Malaano soldiers had cleared out a wide swath before the pyramid, and only trampled grass and stumps remained. A perimeter of guards encircled the encampment as far as she could see.

Kira's mind spun as she struggled to make sense of it. What was that thumping noise? What did they want with this place?

She ducked low and moved to a tree trunk. Peered around it. She needed a different angle.

Warning blared through her mind as she tried to control her breathing. She knew she should turn back. *Now.*

But if she could just figure out what was going on here . . . That information could be crucial. She'd never understood why Zamara had chosen this location for a pyramid in the first place, so far from Emberhawk territory. It didn't make sense.

Whatever it was, it must be nefarious.

Kira didn't see or hear any guards nearby—not near enough to detect her, at least. She crept from tree to tree, encircling the Malaano encampment until she could see more of the tall structures of wood and rope and metal in the center of the clearing.

Mechanisms of some sort . . . a giant wheel . . . What was that? An enormous awl?

Kira mentally flipped through the hundreds of mechanical schematics she'd studied, invented both by Phoeran and Malaano peoples, from the Navarro library. She watched the wheel turn, the gears move, the men work. A thick, carved tree trunk, with arms bound by chains and ropes, rose up slowly and slammed into the earth, further down than she could see. *Thump . . . thump . . . thump.*

Piles of stones, sorted into different colors, sat to the side. First brown, then washed by robed men who manipulated quivering blobs of water that floated in the air. Another pile of rocks was black like coal. Large chunks were broken by men with pickaxes. The final pile, much smaller than the others, gleamed a brighter silver than any of the guard's armor.

A mining operation. What were they extracting?

Kira's gut twisted as a potential answer presented itself: syn. They were mining syn directly from the earth.

A loud sound from her right made her jump. A trumpet, perhaps?

The men stopped working and saluted as a commotion drew all attention. Kira dashed to another tree for a better look.

A white palanquin with blue accents and billowing flags came to a stop, barely visible through the crowd. A man stepped out as the palanquin lowered. He disappeared among the dozens of men for a moment, then Kira caught sight of him again as he took stairs to stand atop the palanquin, using it like a stage as he spoke to the suddenly hushed crowd.

Kira couldn't make out his words. She squinted but couldn't make out any smaller details aside from the man's billowing cloak. And the fact that his armor looked different from the guards'. Clearly he was a higher rank. But would a high-ranking officer take a palanquin? Not Oda'e when he'd served the Malaano, and not any other military man that Kira had seen in Navarro during her childhood.

Only royals, or maybe something very close to a royal, would ride in a palanquin. Could this man be the prince—the heir to the imperial throne? Surely the emperor wouldn't be—

"What are you doing all the way out here?"

Kira jumped and whirled. A Malaano soldier watched her with a humored expression, his posture relaxed, and yet one hand rested on his sword's scabbard.

Her mouth opened, yet no words formed as her heart slammed as hard as the mining equipment. She clutched the hilt of her dagger.

"Does not look like a spy," came another voice. Another man stepped out from behind a tree. His skin was lighter than hers, his islander accent thick. "Tribal garb, though. A local rebel."

"I . . . My father has a ranch on the border," Kira rushed as her mouth finally cooperated. "I'm just looking for food."

"This far into the wood?" The first soldier stepped toward her. "You're a long way from the border, girl."

Kira ran.

Undergrowth crashed behind her. A hand grabbed her hair and yanked backward. She sprawled across dropped leaves and yelled, clawing at the grip on her hair.

An impact and a grunt sounded behind her. Warm liquid splashed across her arm. The hand released her hair, and Kira scrambled away, drew her dagger, and turned.

One of the Malaano soldiers crashed to the ground in a heap of armor and blood. Kira barely perceived a man in leather armor and a Katrosi pale mask before he turned on the other.

The second soldier didn't have time to raise his sword before life left him.

Kira's rescuer pierced both fallen soldiers once more with his blade, then lifted his mask and spat on the one who'd grabbed her hair.

Ryon looked at her with a face of stone before lowering his mask again. Sheathing his bloodied blade. Picking her up in his arms and running south.

"I'm sorry," Kira choked on sobs that erupted from her shuddering body as she clung to him. "Thank you. I'm so sorry."

"Did you think . . . I would let my wife . . . go alone in these woods?" Ryon breathed heavily. "I didn't allow that . . . even when you . . . were my enemy."

"I'm sorry! I won't ever do it again." Kira squeezed her eyes shut, letting tears fall and trying not to think about the cooling liquid on her arm as she held tight to her husband's shoulders. Nausea rattled through her, and she begged her body to control itself. "W-was that the same pyramid we were at before?"

"Yes," Ryon huffed, "and the emperor himself."

28

SOUSUKE

For the first time, Sousuke was glad when Felix transformed as they crossed the waters back into the tribal territories. The wyvern form felt much more comfortable and safe than the nightjar.

This direction is south, isn't it? Why aren't you flying east? Sousuke asked. *You said Lillian's vault is in Banshee's Playground.*

I need to give this piece of the cypher to the humans, Felix said. *All four pieces are required to enter the vault. And you need to get your compass before heading east as well, yes?*

Sousuke sighed internally. *So that's why you left the war-dog pack with them? To force me to return to them and give them that little chest?*

In case I lost control of this body before I made it back, yes.

Sousuke had to give Felix credit for planning ahead. But every second he would waste on this stupid errand was more time that Vylia suffered. He needed that compass so he could locate Vylia, wherever Sa'alu had taken her. He prayed that she still had her coral crown with her in her pack, though she hadn't worn it since Jadenvive. Hopefully she would remember the compasses. They'd made a point of not discussing it for safety reasons.

Okay, fine, Sousuke thought. *So, where is the fourth cypher? My sister is one of your vessels, right? Does she have it?*

Yes.

So you're going all the way to Lover's Fen to get the final cypher from her?

Yes.

There's no time for that, Sousuke mused. *Sa'alu and Lillian will reach the vault before you could even find a ship. Surely you couldn't fly all the way across the Sea of Bones . . . ?*

Felix didn't respond, so Sousuke continued, *Does Lillian need the cyphers, too? Or could she open the vault herself somehow without them?*

I don't know, but anything is possible. Anything can be eroded with water, and of course she knows the inner workings of the lock. We designed it ourselves. Felix's anxiety was tangible, infectious. *I've decided to give you control earlier than necessary. Don't let me down.*

Sousuke gasped as the crisp, clean smell of night was enhanced a hundredfold. His sight seemed clearer, his focus sharper. He reeled from the sudden sensations.

The feeling of piloting his own body again felt like freedom. Except it wasn't his own body.

And he didn't know how to pilot it.

He was gliding . . . falling.

Sousuke choked on panic and flapped his wings. It had been so long since he'd learned to fly. Too long!

"Hey, whoa!"

A spirit fox sat on his shoulder, as if that made any sense. Its fur was unaffected by the wind.

"No, stop—you're flapping your wings too hard," Felix said. "Just glide and adjust your tail. No, not like that!"

But he'd already lost control, and they were going down.

Sousuke flared his wings as far as they could stretch and braced for landing. He landed hard on the ground on all fours, the shock traveling up his limbs with more vivid sensation than he'd felt since he'd revived Felix.

Pain lanced through his right wing. He must have hit a tree on the way down—that broken one, surely. His wing also looked broken.

Sousuke hissed through the feeling and closed his eyes. He imagined his human form, desperately recalling his own visage in his mind's eye. His mother's bright eyes. Straight, short blonde hair. Brown skin. The physique he'd trained hard for. The scar on his left side from a previous encounter with Zeph.

"What are you—hey, wait! Stay in this form and learn to control it!"

"I don't have time to learn to fly right now." Sousuke found the feeling of speaking with a reptilian tongue through draconic fangs unsettling.

"You will make up for the time spent learning when you can fly," Felix said.

"Judging by the time you spent flying so far, I'd wager we're almost back to Brooke, and she has a dragon I can ride on."

Sousuke concentrated. Did he even remember how to transform?

"Yes, you can," Felix said after a long moment. "Even being out of the water for years, you never forget how to swim. It's as natural to you as—"

"Shut up, Felix."

A warm feeling started in his core and spread to his limbs. He shrank, and the pain in his wing—no, his arm—vanished. Transforming felt so much less disjointed now that he was in control.

He opened his eyes. Lifted his hand. A *human* hand.

Sousuke couldn't remember the last time he'd smiled so wide. Finally, he could use the miracle the creator had woven for him. Finally, he could go after Vylia!

But first, he needed some clothes.

The bag Felix had packed in Valinor. Where was it?

"You dropped it when I gave you control." Felix's voice carried a twinge of snark.

Sousuke cursed and backtracked. Found the pack stuck high in tree branches. Too high. He stared at it.

"Would be nice if you were still a wyvern, huh?"

"You're not helping."

"Why don't you just throw a rock up there like any good Terruthian boy would do?"

"I'm not Terruthian," Sousuke growled. That was just the human form Zeph had chosen, and probably stolen off some admittedly handsome Terruthian man, after he'd murdered him. Probably.

"Do you wield the Terruth element or not?"

"Never by choice." Sousuke sighed. Well, if he'd had enough syn and chosen to use the power of earth when they'd been waylaid by Sa'alu and his men in the carriage, maybe he wouldn't have nearly died, and he'd still be with Vylia right now. So maybe he should reacquaint himself with it, regardless of where he'd inherited it from.

He took a deep breath—one sigh wasn't enough. Neither were two. He closed his eyes.

The earth lay solid beneath his feet. And rocks beyond. Limestone, granite, hazy clay, and sandy loam, all running over and under and beside each other in layers. Roots—millions of them—cut and dug and twisted between them like black snakes, void of his senses.

It was surprising how sharply the Terruth element returned to him after all this time. Perhaps he shouldn't be surprised; Tameru had found him a teacher when he was young and trained him for years. He'd hated every minute of it. All of the other Lotusfall children trained in either Malo or Phoera. And a few of them never let him forget it.

"Don't get distracted," Felix said. "This is *your* power, not Zeph's. You have to let it go, or it will torture you for your entire life. Hinder everything you want to do. You already nearly died because—"

"I know!" Sousuke snapped. "I'm trying, okay? What do you want me to do? I will *never* forgive him. I will kill him."

"And *then* you will be able to live with yourself for the great crime of being born?"

Sousuke clenched his jaw. He'd had this argument before, many times. With Tameru. Maybe Felix really was his grandfather after all.

He blew out a breath. "No, I'll never be able to live with myself. And I'll never fit in. But I'll kill him anyway. And then maybe I can find something like peace." He glared at the stupid bag. It moved slightly with the branches as they swayed on the breeze. Still stuck.

"Or you could find peace and *then* kill him."

"Heh." Sousuke couldn't stop a smirk. "Maybe. After I save Vylia."

The spirit-fox trotted up and sat beside Sousuke's feet, curling his three dark tails around himself. "Show me how strong you are. You're going to need to live up to your full potential to survive a fight with Zeph."

Sousuke looked down at the kumiho. "Or you could teach me Phoera . . . ?"

"Nope."

Sousuke frowned. "How do you know I can't use your element? Did you try using mine when you were in control?"

"No. Couldn't use mine, either."

"What?"

Felix scratched his ethereal ear. "I can't use Phoera. Maybe it's because I'm stuck in a *terru syn ko'yeth* body, so my Phoeran element doesn't work."

Sousuke balked at him. "When did you figure this out? You said you'd help me kill him!"

"When we were in Valinor. I was planning on just using invisibility to get into the castle. Had to improvise."

An ominous feeling lodged deep in Sousuke's core. How was this possible? A first-generation elemental *trai'yeth* without elemental powers?

"Look, I don't know. I've never heard of a situation like this before. Maybe you shouldn't have broken the laws of nature to resurrect me before my time."

Sousuke rubbed his eyes. "We're not going to make it, are we?"

"Probably not," Felix pointed his nose up at the bag. "Unless you really are the prodigy Tameru says you are."

A flare of frustration burned through Sousuke. He reached down into the granite layer and willed it forth. A slice of speckled stone shot up through the earth and hewed through the offending branch, leaving it splintered as the bag crashed to the ground in a flurry of leaves.

Felix jumped to his feet. "Was that your first time in . . . how long?"

"Too long," Sousuke admitted as he went to untangle the pack, hoping the clothing inside wasn't damaged. He wouldn't say it out loud, but that had felt good. Really good.

"Lands above and below," Felix murmured. "Why on Alani did Tameru put you on guard duty?"

"Because I requested it." Sousuke's voice was muffled through the beige tunic Felix had procured from Valinor. It was too large. But the boots looked to be a good size, at least. "It turned out to be the most important position when the emperor decided to use Vylia as a pawn and tried to have her killed as an excuse for declaring war on the tribes."

Being a royal bodyguard also got Sousuke away from home. But he decided not to mention that.

Felix whistled low. "I know all you see is your differences, but this power could be very useful—hey, you dropped that."

Sousuke scooped up a gleaming brooch with a metal clasp that had tumbled out of the bag. He admired the translucent shield with foreign symbols and golden filigree. "What is this?"

"It's a glass-gold family crest that I took from the Valinorian museum," Felix said. "It could be useful for hindering Lill—"

Sousuke stuffed the brooch back in the bag and withdrew a too-long leather strip. He glanced at Felix while he tried to figure out how to loop and tie the weird Valinorian belt. "What?"

The spirit remained perfectly still apart from the dark mist that swirled around him—even the golden flecks in his coat didn't move.

Sousuke stopped fiddling with the belt. "What?"

"Something is coming." Felix snapped his gaze behind them. To the east. "Terruth."

Sousuke's pulse hiccupped. He watched the trees where Felix stared, but saw nothing.

"You don't mean—"

"He's already here."

The decaying leaves beneath Sousuke's feet began to shift, as if a thousand insects below were carrying them away. He leapt back, but his boots never left the ground—they were sinking. Stuck.

Sousuke reached out with his element. The dirt was no longer dirt. It was sand. Quicksand.

He cursed and willed it to solidify, but sand wasn't just a single solid—it was thousands of them. Millions.

He sank lower. Faster.

Sousuke lurched forward, grasping toward the nearest tree for purchase. Leaves and earth there were swallowed up as well. The tree groaned and leaned.

"There!" Felix cried.

"Felix Kael Tae."

The voice was slow. Deliberate. Familiar.

Fire and ice crashed inside Sousuke's veins as a lifetime of rage battled crippling fear. It was *him*. The monster who'd hurt his mother and ruined his life.

Two orbs glowing red appeared from the trees. The enormous face of a direwolf followed. Too large to walk through the underbrush, branches and vines bowed and cracked around it. It stepped closer until its mangy gray and brown coat became visible, along with claws as long as Sousuke's fingers.

"Why did you kill my men?" the wolf asked.

Sousuke stopped moving to slow his sinking. The fire in his veins won out and urged him to kill. Had Felix brought a sword from Valinor?

"Easy," Felix warned.

"What men?" Sousuke asked, wondering if Zeph could hear Felix.

The direwolf approached until Sousuke could smell its musty coat. Its eyes shone like blood-red coals.

"How do you have my son's form?" Zeph growled. "Did you kill him?"

"No. I am Rhu Sousuke," he replied through gritted teeth, "but I am not your son."

The red eyes narrowed. "I sense you both clearly. Explain. Did you kill Felix? No . . ."

Sousuke's mouth opened, but he didn't know what to say.

"Don't tell him about our situation," Felix said. "He'd delight in experimenting and ultimately killing me."

Then what do I do? Sousuke thought, hoping Felix could hear him.

"Tell him you killed me, and he's just sensing my stone."

Sousuke grimaced as the quicksand rose to his stomach. The pressure was enough to suffocate—this wasn't anything like the natural quicksand of the Malaano lowlands.

"I killed Felix," Sousuke said. "What you sense is just his stone."

"Then give me his stone," the wolf said.

Sousuke's mouth snaps shut. *Now what?*

Felix backed away. "I . . ."

"It's in my pouch that your quicksand just ate," Sousuke claimed.

Zeph slowly circled him. Sniffed.

Sousuke's hair stood on end as Zeph slunk behind him. *I'm going to die. He won't let me live this time, because he's obviously not on good terms with Felix. I would rather have died in the healing hut!*

Zeph completed his circle and sat. Several small chunks of earth floated upward, stopping before the wolf. They all turned and spun, compacting in mid-air. Then numbers appeared on each of its many sides.

Earth in the shape of a square bolted up from the ground and flattened, smoothing into a level surface. The first chunks dropped and rolled, coming to a stop with a number Sousuke couldn't see resting upright.

The wolf grinned far too widely, showing an alarming amount of teeth. "The dice say a lying fox will die today."

"I—I'm not Felix!"

The wolf watched as Sousuke began to sink faster. Suddenly the quicksand was up to his neck.

"Transform into your innate elemental form!" Felix yelled, his spirit trotting back and forth at the edge of the quicksand. "Your form is unique to only you. It will prove to Zeph that it's really you."

Sousuke stretched his neck up as high as he could and took a deep breath just before warm sludge and darkness overcame him.

He *never* took his innate form. It looked too much like Zeph's.

His eyelids scrunched shut, and yet he could still feel himself sinking lower. And lower.

But he wouldn't let his own stubbornness kill him again.

He remembered his animal form. The first successful transformation he'd achieved as a child. The pride that had so quickly rotted into shame.

Not a wolf, he'd decided. A wolfhound. A sheepdog, raised and trained for protecting its flock. Against the wolves.

It came back to him with little effort. He grew canines and claws, fur and a tail. His new tunic tore against his expanding chest and shifting shoulders.

The air inside his lungs grew stale. Began to burn.

Could Zeph sense his new form through the quicksand around him? Would he not release him? Or had he finally tired of Sousuke and didn't mind killing him, regardless? Perhaps his association with Felix was enough to warrant being murdered.

Sousuke! Felix's voice almost sounded genuinely concerned.

Fine. He would just have to save himself, then.

Sousuke felt the hazy shifting sands around him—too difficult to control without practice. But below, beside, all around him, were solid layers. He gravitated to a patch that felt the strongest: ironstone. He summoned it to him and felt it push through the quicksand below his feet. It lifted him upward until light and air returned.

He snorted and panted as the quicksand slid and sloughed away in clumps, still sticking to his coat and tattered clothes in a mess. The ironstone slab came to rest at ground level, and Sousuke opened his eyes to glare at the direwolf that watched, motionless.

"So, you really are my progeny," Zeph said. "Then where is Felix? I know he's here." He blew out of his black, wet nose. "His scent is disgustingly strong."

"I am descended from Felix," Sousuke said. "That could explain—"

"You are descended from *me.*" A low growl rumbled from the wolf's throat. "I bred you from Felix and Lillian's line of *ko'yeth* with purpose. But that does not explain why I sense his presence."

Sousuke's vision lit with rage. So his mother's suffering wasn't just for Zeph's sick pleasure or a way to attack Tameru. Rhu Hana had been targeted as one of the world's strongest *ko'yeth*. To produce a strong heir.

Dizzying revulsion and murderous intent clashed inside him. He knew he wasn't strong enough to face Zeph in combat and emerge the victor. But he didn't care.

"What are you doing here?" Zeph demanded. "Is the princess nearby?"

Alarm blasted through Sousuke's body, redirecting his thoughts. "No."

"Where is she?"

Relax, Felix whispered.

"I don't know where she is." Sousuke ducked out of the torn Valinorian tunic, thankfully removing heavy clumps of sand with it. "I was separated from her when I was mortally wounded in Sekoiako."

Zeph stared at him with glowing red eyes for an uncomfortably long silence. "Clearly it was not a *mortal* wound, then."

Tell him the truth about absorbing my stone, Felix thought to him. *He's very curious by nature. Then he may not kill us.*

Sousuke's pulse pounded through him. His wolfhound form was full of energy, eager to fight. It took every mite of control to focus on responding verbally. If this wolf killed him here, no one would be left to save Vylia.

"It *was* a mortal wound," Sousuke said. "But someone offered me Felix's stone—he'd recently died. I was able to absorb his power in order to save my life. But Felix wasn't ready to be resurrected, so he still resides within me, and I have control."

The wolf's lips curled back into a range of expressions. Sousuke interpreted them as first disbelief, then disgust, then confusion, and finally anger.

Uh oh.

"That's impossible," Zeph growled low.

"Agreed," Sousuke said. "But I think you can tell that I speak the truth."

Zeph muttered obscenities—something about a "fox-rat." He looked back down at his makeshift table and dice. The dice lifted, dropped, and rolled. "Do not listen to a word Felix says. He is a fox—a manipulator and a masterful liar. He will say anything to twist a situation to get whatever he wants."

Sousuke scoffed. "And you're *not* a liar?"

"No, I find it distasteful. I've never lied to you."

Sousuke rifled through his worst memories of encountering this nightmare previously. It might actually be true . . . He couldn't recall Zeph ever having a lie sandwiched between his threats and proposals and jackal laughter.

"I am your blood, only one generation away, unlike Felix. I will not only spare you, I will help you."

Sousuke lowered his head. "Wow, that sounds really different from you nearly killing me about eight seconds ago."

"If I wanted you dead, you'd be dead," Zeph said flatly. "But eternal life would be even more boring without you."

Sousuke glared. "So I'm just entertainment?"

"Naturally." Zeph's wolfish smile emerged again. "You will answer the question of nature versus nurture. Will you become like me, or the ones who raised you?"

Anger burned hot enough to send the hairs on Sousuke's back and shoulders on end. "I can answer that," he said. "I will never be like you."

"Clearly. You are much more angry and hateful than me. You must get that from Felix." Zeph raised his head until his full direwolf height—including two very straight and tall ears—was easily double the average height of a man. "Now, I sense you are partially lying about the princess's location. And yet she is not with you. Aren't you supposed to be guarding her? I wonder how this can be explained. Perhaps you don't know where she is presently, but you have a method of tracking her down?"

Sousuke's muscles clenched tight. How could Zeph possibly know all of that? In particular, how did he know Sousuke was one of Vylia's guards? Had he spotted them traveling together on their way to Jadenvive?

Wait. Why was Zeph here in the Katrosi forests—or in tribal lands at all? He was far outside his territory of northern Malaan Island.

Zeph's laugh was full and rough. "Every thought of yours is sprawled across your face. Adorable." He grinned wide. "Join me whenever you come to your senses. You are growing stronger and wiser each time I see you. You know I have more power, in every conceivable form, than you can fathom. And I desire you as an heir."

Sousuke bore his fangs and snarled. "I'd rather die."

"That can be arranged, if you prefer." Zeph turned, and his dice, table, and quicksand morphed into stone that appeared as natural as the surrounding forest. "Wait for me here, and I will return shortly with a solution for you."

He dashed into the forest and was gone.

Sousuke stared after Zeph, dumbfounded. The spirit-fox came to stand beside him, also staring. Both of their minds echoed with the same astonished thought.

"What is he doing?" Sousuke murmured.

"I don't know," Felix said slowly. "I'm not really a liar, you know. I may lie sometimes, but not in a bad way."

Sousuke assumed his human form and tightened his belt. Thank the creator that his pants were still in good enough shape to wear, though questionable and covered in gooey sand. "You are bad in many ways," he grunted.

"But not evil!" Felix protested.

Sousuke breathed a prayer of thanks to the creator, turned to the south, and ran toward the burned-out d'hakka nest.

29

BROOKE

$\mathbf{B}$rooke loved mornings. The perfect temperature, the soft light of the waking sky, and the smell of Ryon cooking over last night's rekindled fire. The chicken eggs, rox-seed bread, and fruit preserves they'd purchased in Navarro—though overpriced—were already being put to good use. Although Ryon had complained no less than three times already that they didn't have any cherry jam from Oda'e's ranch.

"Could you keep your maddeningly jovial thoughts to yourself?" Lysander turned over on his sleep mat in a huff, violently tugging his too-small quilt up to his shoulder.

Brooke grinned and descended on him, curling his straight, dark hair between her fingers. *Someone doesn't like mornings, hmm? A shame. Mornings are the best part of the day-ay!* she sang.

The sound that came out of him sounded more like a trace cat than a man.

Can I make you some tea? Brooke offered. *They're clearly labeled, right? Please tell me you don't keep the poison next to the yarrow.*

Lysander grunted and pointed at a fur-lined pack that he always kept close. Brooke opened it and found his bandoleer full of vials carefully wrapped in patched-together rabbit skins.

"Brooke's Energizing Brew," she read. *Did you make this just for me?*

"It was necessary," Lysander muttered. "No one drinks as much yaupon tea as you."

Hey, leading the tribe required a lot of energy. How else was I supposed to get everything done?

"Have you tried sleeping?"

Brooke scoffed as she found two small cups and set them gently next to the fire. *I can't tell if you're just being grumpy or if something is wrong.*

He didn't answer for a long moment. "I guess I can't hide anything from you." He sighed, pushed his quilt aside in a huff, and sat up. His hair stuck in every direction, and he smoothed it with an agitated swipe. "It's nothing *wrong*, really. I'm just a bit disappointed."

Brooke turned to face him. "In what?"

Lysander watched her lips, then the fire. "I guess I was looking forward to going to Valinor, and I didn't realize it until . . . well . . . We're not going now, are we?"

Brooke frowned. "We can still go and see your family there." She took her waterskin and poured into the two cups.

"No, Felix needs us in the vault."

"Can't you just give Felix your cypher chest thing?" Ryon said from the other side of the fire. "It's not like it's stuck in your hand like mine."

Brooke repeated Ryon's words in thoughts to Lysander's mind, because it didn't seem that he was aware that his cousin was speaking to him.

Lysander glanced between them and landed on Brooke. "Don't you want to go to the vault?"

"I mean, is there a reason for us to go?" Brooke gently pushed the cups closer to the embers. "'Banshee's Playground' doesn't sound like fun for anyone except the banshees."

"You're leaving us?"

Brooke found Kira walking up behind her with firewood. Her expression, stance, and tone communicated a lot more than her words did.

Brooke grimaced. This conversation was already getting out of hand like a political meeting in the Great Hall, where every member of the public had already drawn their own conclusions and ruffled their own feathers before she'd actually said anything. She was tempted to use thought-speak to calm Kira's emotions.

Instead, she chose her words carefully. "It's not like that, of course. We're just thinking of going to see Lysander's family in Valinor. We were looking forward to going."

"Didn't Ulysses tell you to retrieve the real aether stone?" Lysander asked.

"The one that we suspect Sa'alu stole? And he's probably heading for the vault."

"We don't know any of that for certain," Brooke said. "The only orders Ulysses gave me were to stay away from the Darkwood and Jadenvive, for now. If Ryon runs into the aether stone, he can retrieve it. Right, Ryon?"

Ryon took a bite of eggs and reacted like he'd taken a bite of lava, huffing and flailing and nodding through a molten mouthful. "Sure."

Kira smacked him.

"Ow!" Ryon cried. "What?"

Lysander narrowed his dark eyes at Brooke. "You're not one to shirk responsibility."

Brooke shrugged. "I never committed to this. And I'm good at delegating."

"You can't delegate our safety!" Kira dumped her armful of firewood like punctuation to her protest.

This girl was way too emotional, especially recently. Was she always like this? Or maybe Brooke hadn't gotten to know her well enough in the first place, and these were her true colors?

Brooke gathered her aether and sent a whisper of peace toward Kira. "We're not expecting any combat, are we? Felix said he didn't remember anything dangerous about the vault. I assume it's been empty and unguarded for centuries, since the cyphers act as the guards, right?"

"You don't think traveling through enemy territory during a war is dangerous?" Kira balked. Then she blinked and scrunched her nose. "Are you using witch-magic on me?"

Ryon reached for Kira's arm, pulled her closer, and whispered to her.

Brooke breathed through her own rising emotions. This was not a battle she wanted to fight. So she blew out her frustration in a breath.

Lysasnder watched her for a long minute, then murmured, "You think this whole quest is a fool's errand."

Brooke scooted closer to Lysander as Ryon and Kira whispered furiously back and forth. *Look, I'm just saying, the intel on this mission is really shoddy,* she thought to him. *There are a lot of assumptions and trust being placed in a half-dead, body-snatching fox.*

Lysander tilted his head. "True."

Brooke leaned toward the fire and rotated the cups, careful not to burn herself. *I've been thinking . . . Is it possible that your grandfather could equip us with some troops to make up for the loss of the Darkwood in the Tribal Alliance? Because surely they've dropped out after Red Heron . . .*

Lysander's face darkened.

Brooke quickly continued. *The Emberhawk Sovereignty has an alliance with Valinor, right?*

Again, he was silent for an uncomfortably long moment. "Technically, yes. It's possible." He sighed. "Why is it always politics with you?"

Brooke grinned. *Well, you and I are both supposed to be on the Tribal Alliance council, yes? Then technically I'm still a politician, and so are you now.*

Lysander cringed. "Does the council even exist yet? Shouldn't we get sworn in or meet with the other tribal representatives or something?"

I don't think all of the representatives from other tribes have been selected yet. But if Valinor sent us reinforcements, it could save hundreds or even thousands of lives, and turn the war in our favor.

Yet again, he fell silent. Brooke would have to get used to that. Finally, Lysander said, "It won't be easy."

Would it be worth the risk?

"Yes."

Then let's go.

Kira abruptly stood and stormed into the forest. Ryon sighed and scratched the back of his neck.

"I'm sorry," Brooke said over the crackling of the fire. "If you want us to stay, we will. But we'd like to ask Valinor for aid in the war effort."

"No worries," Ryon said, though his voice sounded more tired than before. "It's a good idea. You can go. Felix will be with us."

"Of course Felix will keep you safe." Brooke looked in the direction Kira had entered the tree line. "Will she be okay, though?"

"Yeah, she just . . . didn't want to be here in the first place," Ryon said quietly.

Brooke nodded. "We'd love to have a honeymoon, too." She smirked at Lysander.

He grabbed her and pulled her close. *Why can't we do both?*

Brooke felt her face flush and hoped it was already reddened from the heat of the fire. "We'll petition the Chancellor quickly and hurry to rejoin you, Ryon."

"Do whatever you think is best." Ryon tossed a fresh log Kira had brought onto the fire. "If I find the aether stone, I'll let you know."

The quiet that followed was much more awkward than Lysander's habitual pondering.

Brooke internally squirmed. She watched Lysander test the water temperature, adjust the cup's distance from the embers, and sniff the dried leaves before adding them. Finally, she said, "If you want me to stay, I will. We can go to Valinor after the vault."

"It's fine," Ryon said without looking at her. "Kira's worried for no reason. She forgets I can go invisible and sneak past anything, and she doesn't know how many times you sent me into foreign territory."

"She will learn to trust you," Brooke said. "Give her some time. We've all been through a lot recently."

Ryon nodded. "Her whole life changed pretty fast, yeah?"

Brooke nodded back and adjusted the bandana Nariellyn had given her, which rested above her forehead in a much more comfortable fashion than her headdress had. Perhaps Kira wouldn't be so worried about safety if she could break her habit of getting herself into trouble. Or maybe she just cared a lot more about Ryon's safety than her own.

Or maybe Kira's emotional issues stemmed from something else entirely . . . She was a newlywed, after all. How many weeks had they been married?

Brooke decided not to voice her thoughts aloud.

Ryon pointed his fire-poker stick at Lysander and signed with his free hand. "That pyramid. The one we were at before that's now crawling with royal Imperial guards." His stick pointed north. "Did you know it was over a natural syn deposit? There's now a huge mining operation there."

Lysander patiently studied his movements. "Yeah, that's why Zamara had us build that pyramid there, out in the middle of nowhere. We just didn't have the equipment to excavate anything, so while we waited for the Malaano to deliver it, Zamara launched the attack on Jadenvive to distract from what we were doing there."

"So that's what Zamara wanted this whole time." Ryon cut a slice of bread with his knife and tried to toast it in the fire by balancing it on two sticks, quickly gave up, and toasted it in his own palm. "I wonder how much syn is down there."

"From the way Zamara was acting, I'd say an unbelievably enormous amount," Lysander said.

"Worth going to war over?" Brooke murmured. "But why would the Emperor want syn? He's human, right?"

"He must be," Ryon said. "His daughter looks human enough." He peered in the direction Kira had gone, then scanned the surrounding forest.

Brooke stared blankly into the fire as she wondered. "Perhaps he has elementals in his employ, and the syn is a means to compensate them?"

Lysander huffed a dark laugh. "Elementals working for humans. That's hilarious."

Brooke sensed that she'd overstepped, remembered Lysander's past under Zamara's thumb, and quickly hand-signed an apology. "I'm sorry, love. I'm obviously not as familiar with elementals as you are."

"The Emperor could be a *trai'yeth* who took a human wife," Lysander mused. "Or an elemental half-blood himself."

"He's not immortal, though, yeah?" Ryon said.

"He's not immortal."

Brooke jumped from Kira's voice suddenly behind her.

"My father said he only came to power around the time I was born," Kira continued, "when the former emperor died of illness."

Brooke turned to more easily see the girl. "Kiralau, I hope you know that I would never abandon you or Ryon if I thought you were in danger. Ryon is one of my best spies—or was—"

"Oh, you don't say?" Kira raised her eyebrows at Ryon. "A spy, huh?"

"Only on Middays," Ryon said quickly. "On Duskdays I was a scout. On Moondays, a professional hipball player. Every other day, a soldier. Brooke wanted me to be an assassin too, but I refused."

Kira stared as Brooke stifled a laugh. "How much of that is true?" Kira demanded. "It smells like a spoonful of deceit on rice."

Brooke's laugh escaped. "Whatever he is, I can assure you that he is highly capable. He was one of my best."

"I know." Kira stepped closer and sat beside Brooke near the fire, but didn't look at her. "I'm sorry. I'm just . . . a little frazzled right now."

Relief and discomfort combined, but Brooke held onto the positive. "I understand. No apology needed."

"It makes sense for you to go to Valinor and ask for help," Kira said quietly. "I hope you are successful."

"Thank you."

Quiet fell on them, aside from the morning birds singing and fire popping. Brooke hated the awkwardness. She should say something else. But what?

A sudden idea occurred to her. "I, uh, noticed you wear a bandana."

"My mother's." Kira's fingers brushed across the cloth tied gently around her neck, not fully covering a scar. "It reminds me of home."

Brooke untied the bandana from behind her neck and held it out to Kira. "Nariellyn gave this to me, but I want you to have it."

Kira admired it with wide eyes, but didn't make any move to take it. "The pattern is beautiful."

"Queen Iraleth found it in Zamara's quarters and gave it to Nari as thanks for healing her. It's woven with some kind of aether—I can't tell which."

Kira's awe turned to doubt. "Is it . . . dangerous?"

"I don't think so." Brooke pressed it closer to Kira. "I've been wearing it for days. Take it as a trophy for your victory over Zamara."

A slow smile grew over Kira's full lips. "Thank you." She bowed her head as she took it. "Zamara gave me this scar . . . so now she can decorate it." She replaced the bandana on her neck with Brooke's and posed. "How does it look?"

Ryon whistled through the flames. "You're gorgeous, *balemba*." He winked. "Breakfast is ready!"

30

KIRALAU

Kira couldn't believe Brooke and Lysander were abandoning them. Of all people, she'd thought they were trustworthy. When was splitting up a group ever a wise decision?

Had she overreacted? She didn't know, and she didn't want to consider it, and she surely wasn't going to ask anyone their opinion. Her blood was still pumping hot.

So she'd smiled and accepted Brooke's gift. As if a strip of cloth could make up for planning to leave them stranded in a foreign country during wartime.

It was nice to have a trophy from Zamara, though. She wondered how the bandana's color would complement her dark hair if she tied it above her forehead to hold her curls at bay.

After eating in silence and simmering for a few hours, Kira wanted peace. She'd had anything but peace recently. And she was tired.

Maybe the first step was to stop side-eyeing the Jade Witch who danced her spear kata on the opposite side of the clearing.

Kira opened her pack and shuffled through the scrolls she'd taken from the Navarro library. She pulled out three scripture scrolls and wondered which one to start with. They were all written in Ancient or Phoeran, but in a version of the language that seemed to pre-date the paper they'd been written on—copied, surely. Would she even be able to read them?

She opened one and quickly determined the answer was highly doubtful.

"Ryon?"

He looked up at her, put down the arrow fletching he'd been smoothing, grinned, and jogged over.

Her heart filled with reciprocated love for her husband. She should do something for him. A gift, perhaps. Later.

"Oh, the scriptures!" A new excitement lit Ryon's face. "Want me to read one for you?"

"Are there any that I can read myself?" Kira asked.

"Yes, the more recent ones are in Phoeran." Ryon sat cross-legged beside her and inspected each scroll.

"Recent?" Kira had thought scriptures would be very old.

"Yes, the modern ones are about a thousand years old. The Ancient ones chronicle the beginning of the world—about three and a half thousand years ago."

Kira's eyes bulged. "Oh. Why are they split like that?"

"Because there was a gap in time between the creation of the world, and the time when Aeo split the elements and languages, and the Serran Wars, to the more present time when he sent his son to Illyria to be the sacrifice that took away the punishment for our evildoing."

Kira took this all in with piqued curiosity. "Illyria—the ancestor nation of the tribes, right? Which is why they're written in old Phoeran?"

"Exactly," Ryon separated the scrolls respectfully across Kira's bedding, careful not to let any dirt or leaves touch them. "You need to work on reading Phoeran, so this will be great practice. But I'll read this Ancient one for you."

Kira balked as he unfurled the scroll. "You can read Ancient?"

"A bit. I'm a professional soldier-scout-hipball-player-spy. It's my job to know languages."

Kira snorted a laugh and leaned back on crunchy grass and leaves, tucking her legs in close. She listened as Ryon read:

> "He who dwells in the secret place of the Most
> High shall abide under the shadow of the Almighty.
> I will say of Aeo, 'He is my refuge and my fortress;
> my God, in whom I trust.'"

"Wait—what does that mean?" Kira interrupted. "Where is the secret place?"

"I don't know," Ryon said. "It's probably not a physical place, yeah?"

"What about the shadow? Is it a good shadow?"

"How about you let me read?" Ryon elbowed her and smirked.

"Okay, fine."

"Surely he shall deliver you from the snare of the fowler and from the perilous pestilence.

He shall cover you with his feathers, and under his wings you shall take refuge; his truth shall be your shield and buckler.

You shall not be afraid of the terror by night, nor of the arrow that flies by day.

A thousand may fall at your side, and ten thousand at your right hand; but it shall not come near you.

Only with your eyes shall you look and see the recompense of the wicked."

"What does that word mean? Recompense."

"I don't know. I think it's like a payment. Like, the judgment their evil deeds have earned."

"Oh, okay."

"Because you have made Aeo your dwelling place, no evil shall befall you, nor shall any plague come near your tent;

For he shall give his angels charge over you, to keep you in all your ways. The lion and the serpent you shall trample underfoot.

Because he has set his love upon me, therefore I will deliver him; I will set him on high, because he has known my name.

When he calls upon me, and I will answer him; I will be with him in trouble; I will deliver him and honor him.

With long life I will satisfy him and show him my salvation."

"The salvation from his son's sacrifice?" Kira murmured. "But you said that happened more recently, and this was written a long time ago."

"It was Aeo's plan all along." Ryon carefully rolled the scroll and fastened its clasp.

"Ohhhh." Kira adjusted her sitting position, leaning forward and watching the glint of the fire reflect in Ryon's lenses. She glanced sidelong at Brooke, who had finished her kata and was now chatting with Lysander across the clearing. "So, all you have to do is follow Aeo and your life will be perfect?"

"Not at all," Ryon said. "But he does protect us and promise to be with us, and to forgive us for our evils and make us his own."

"Wow." Kira stared at the scrolls, suddenly feeling intimidated. "I have a lot to learn about this religion."

"It's more like a relationship between you and the creator," Ryon said. "You can just pray and talk to him any time. And he will give you his peace, which goes beyond all understanding, so that you can be calm even in the worst trouble."

Kira leaned back on her palms. "That sounds really nice." But it didn't sound real. "Have you ever felt that?"

"Yeah, many times." Ryon's orange eyes gazed into the forest, seemingly seeing past the trees. "Once when I was tied up in your barn."

Kira grimaced. "You felt peace when you were being tortured by my brother?"

"I felt many things. But Aeo gave me a level head so I could think straight to escape. And he sent your brother to release me in exchange for a promise to protect his family." Ryon's eyebrows bounced. "That all worked out pretty well, yeah?"

Kira smacked him playfully and laughed. "I guess it's pretty miraculous that we're alive and well right now. For the most part."

"You're absolutely right." Ryon stood, then leaned down to kiss her on the forehead.

She beamed up at him. "Read me another one?"

"Read it yourself."

Kira groaned. "But it's old Phoeran; it's like extra hard."

"You've got this, *balemba*," Ryon said as he walked back toward his piles of fletching equipment: feathers, sticks, arrowheads, a hatchet, scraper, and a few other things Kira couldn't identify. He sure had made a lot of arrows, though.

"Which one do I start with?" Kira called after him.

"The one with the blue seal."

Kira was halfway through her struggle with the foreign script when they were alerted to rustling approaching from the north. Brooke shouted and aimed her spear at a dirty, shirtless Sousuke as he emerged through the trees.

Kira leaped up from her studies. "Felix?"

"Kind of," Sousuke answered in a tired voice. "I'm in control now."

"Sousuke, then?" Brooke asked.

"Yes. Felix can still hear you, but he can only respond by annoying me inside my own head. If anyone knows how I can get him out, that would be great." Sousuke continued forward and stopped before the fire, swaying a bit. "Water, please."

Lysander handed him a waterskin, watching him warily. "What happened to you? You can have my spare tunic."

"No, thanks. My last one was ruined when I had to transform. Yours would probably meet the same fate." Sousuke took a long drink, possibly downing the entire thing. Finally he stopped to breathe. "But thanks anyway."

Lysander took the waterskin back. "Then you're just going to run around shirtless? You'll get burned by the sun."

Kira must have heard him wrong. Brooke moved her fingers to make signs and said quietly, "My love, I think you are the only one here who can easily get burned by the sun."

"Oh." Lysander looked as confused and awkward as Kira felt. "None of you can get sunburned? My father got burned once when he stayed out too long, and I don't think there are many trees where we are going to the east."

Kira tried to hide her laughter as Brooke's hand signals became more frantic. Sousuke's skin was darker than any of theirs. Perhaps he was the first Terruthian Lysander had ever met. Kira could count on one hand the number of travelers from the southern continent she'd seen as they'd passed through Navarro.

"I can transform if needed, but thanks." Sousuke held out a small chest to Ryon, much like the one they really shouldn't have opened. "We retrieved the third cypher. Do you have my pack that Felix left here?"

"Yes, it was right here . . ." Kira searched for the pack and found it as Ryon handed Sousuke some bread and offered to cook some fresh eggs.

"No, thank you. But I will take some bread," Sousuke said. "I have to get going as soon as possible."

Kira paused halfway through hefting Felix's pack. "You're leaving, too?"

"I'm going after the princess." Sousuke took the seed bread Ryon offered and slumped beside the fire.

Kira blinked. "But Felix was going to the vault with us."

"I'm in charge now."

Kira's mouth fell open as emotions crashed inside her. "Then . . . how . . . will we get to the vault, with Brooke taking her dragon to Valinor and Felix as your hostage?"

Sousuke gave a heartless, barking laugh. "Felix took my body against my will and has held *me* hostage all this time. You have no idea what that felt like."

Kira frowned through pursed lips. "All right, but then, without Felix able to take dragon form and let us ride on his back, how will we get to Banshee's Playground? We left our xavi at the stables in Navarro."

Sousuke tore into the bread. He didn't answer.

"You said you could transform," Ryon said. "Isn't Lillian going to her vault as well? So we may have different goals, but the same location. And of course we want to help Vylia, too."

"I don't know how to fly," Sousuke said through a mouthful of bread.

Kira and Ryon exchanged glances. What now?

"My pack, please," Sousuke said.

Kira looked down at the Sekoiako war-dog pack in her hand. Maybe she could use it as leverage to get what they needed.

Or maybe, without a means of transportation, they could just turn around and go home.

Sousuke stopped eating and watched her with sharp green eyes. Unmoving, he looked like a sculpture carved by a master craftsman. He radiated intimidation, but not threat. Barely.

"Please," he repeated.

Unnerved, Kira handed him the pack.

"Thank you," Sousuke said stiffly. He opened it and retrieved something like a compass. A strange coral piece moved slowly back and forth beneath glass, then steadied while pointing east. Kira recognized it by the identical compass Tekkyn had shown her in Navarro.

"Shut up, Felix," Sousuke growled.

"What's he saying?" Brooke asked.

Sousuke sighed and took another bite of bread. Chewed. Swallowed.

"He's begging me to take you. Because he handed me control over early, he can take control of my body back and fly us east."

Kira crept closer, examining his compass. "Is that . . . pointing to Vylia?"

Sousuke continued eating instead of answering. He didn't look at Kira.

Rude. Did he know Tekkyn was her brother? Weren't they friends?

"Listen," Brooke said. "You don't know me, but I know you. I've gazed into your mind twice now. I know our values and goals are aligned, and I consider you an ally."

Sousuke didn't respond.

"When you rescue Vylia," Brooke continued, "tell her that you both will always find refuge in the Katrosi forests."

"Thank you," Sousuke grunted.

Brooke crouched by the fire, her leather split skirt rustling across the leaves. "I seek the aether stone—the same man who took Vylia may have stolen it as well. It's a powerful relic, and a treasure of my people. It looks like a quartz gem, about the size of a man's fist."

Sousuke didn't look at her. "If Sa'alu has it, I will return it to you."

"Thank you," Brooke said.

Kira found the tension distasteful. What was it between these two? Did Sousuke not trust them, after all they'd done for him and Vylia?

Or maybe Felix had aggravated him so much that he had no grace to accommodate anyone right now. Or maybe Felix had damaged his mind with their surreal merger.

Sousuke let out a deep breath and reached into his pack. He retrieved a third compass, identical to the first two Kira had seen. "This is attuned to the living coral in Vylia's crown. By the mercy of kai'lani, she still carries it with her." He handed it to Brooke. "Use it to find me and Vylia, and I will give you the relic. Never give this to anyone else. If you do, I will neither forgive nor trust you ever again."

Brooke bowed and thanked him as she took it. "Your trust is well placed."

"You must have really trusted my brother Tekkyn to give him one, then," Kira said. "How many of those do you have?"

Sousuke glanced up at her, his gaze seemingly more relaxed than before. "There are four total—one for each of Vylia's bodyguards. Hiro and I still have ours. Xi was murdered by Aoko, and I gave his compass to Tekkyn'ashi when he became Vylia's bodyguard in Jadenvive. I killed the traitor, Aoko, and this one was his."

Kira wondered where the fourth bodyguard, Hiro, was. But she was unsure of how to phrase that question.

"Will you take us to the vault, then?" Ryon asked.

Sousuke finished his last bite and stood. "Felix retrieved my equipment for me from the Sekoiako, so I will do this favor for him. But please understand that Vy's safety is my top priority."

"We understand." Ryon snapped his fingers, and the campfire snuffed out in an instant. "Let's go."

Kira's spirit clenched as she watched Brooke and Lysander quickly pack their things. Unfortunately, she had to admit to herself that she would miss them.

She bowed to Brooke. *"Aeo leywa ai shea,"* she said, hoping she was remembering the correct pronunciation for the Ancient farewell.

Brooke stopped what she was doing, smiled, and grabbed Kira in a hug, the feathers in her braids tickling Kira's arms. *"Aeo leywa ai shea, my friend."*

31

VYLIA

Vylia dreamed that she was back at the Imperial Academy, but she'd forgotten that it was test day, and she was wearing her layered blue dress uniform on the wrong day of the week. Then suddenly she was playing mah jongg with two bamboo bears, but they disagreed on the rules and became irate. Sousuke appeared and separated them without a single word. And he loved her back.

For once, Vylia didn't want to wake up. Thoughts of Sousuke weren't saturated with grief in the dreamscape.

Since he'd believed in the creator god, and now Vylia had chosen him as her god as well, did that mean they would both go to the same afterlife?

She'd find out soon, because something she'd heard the soldiers say in her half-sleep made her think that they'd finally arrived in Banshee's Playground. She didn't know why Lillian was still keeping her alive, but once she got whatever she wanted at the vault, surely she'd be done with Vylia. At least then, when she was dead, she could get some sleep.

Banshee's Playground was a bog, right? It smelled like a swamp. Decaying plants and stagnant water and blood bugs.

The xavi kept spooking and making strange whimpering noises. Their too-thick legs were sinking into the mud. Was it mud? It was more like goo. Slimy and green and lukewarm.

The men left the xavi behind and walked, grumbling. But Vylia was too tired to walk—she wasn't entirely certain that she was awake—so they carried her. It was very uncomfortable for her midsection, since the stinky oaf folded her in half over the shoulder and hauled her like a sack of rice.

Mangrove trees formed a green mass, their roots tangling and blurring together just above the water. Schools of tiny fish glimmered under the surface, mesmerizing Vylia as she watched them twirl and scatter at the soldiers' splashes.

"She's waking up," the soldier who carried her yelled.

Vylia groaned. If he would just be quiet and still, she could fall back asleep.

"No more fadeleaf," someone else yelled back. "Lillian wants her awake."

Good morning, little minnow, rang a voice through Vylia's head.

Vylia groaned again, too tired to form a response. Lillian was the worst.

If you'll accept me, you can sleep as much as you want.

"Yeah . . . because . . . I would be your puppet . . . doll . . . toy," Vylia muttered.

No, beloved. Lillian said. *You would have whatever you want. We are arriving at my vault now, full of treasures. We will be more powerful than any man has ever been, and live in luxury. What do you want, my darling?*

"Sousuke," Vylia slurred.

We can get you a new one, Lillian said.

Confusion made Vylia's head hurt, rivaling the other irritating injuries that also kept her awake. A new Sousuke?

"The worst," Vylia mumbled.

A sigh flitted through her mind. *Last chance, Princess. Channel your aether into my stone and join with me. Or, when I come into my power, I will choose another.*

"Choose that bullfrog. He sounds . . . like you." Vylia cackled at her own joke. It was so unladylike! Uma would scold her. She laughed more.

"A lonely rock formation. This must be it," said a different voice. "We stop here and dig."

Vylia was set upon a rock. Craggly and hard, but warmed by the sun, and stationary. The men splashed and dug for so long that Vylia fell back into sweet slumber.

"I found the battery!"

Vylia jolted awake at the annoying yell. One of the men held a strange metal object aloft, which gleamed silver wherever it was not coated in algae.

The other men ran over to see the discovery. One of them seemed to fall into a pit of goo, flailing and grasping for purchase. He hollered something about feeling nothing beneath his feet. Then he fell through the goo entirely.

Vylia must have still been dreaming, because it sounded like he was screaming and falling underneath the earth. Then she heard a distant, sickening crunch and clatter. Then nothing.

She cringed. A bad dream.

Vylia curled into a tighter ball, feeling colder than before. Night must be approaching.

The men placed the strange thing the called a "battery" into a hole in the rock formation that Vylia lay on. Nothing happened. The men argued.

They dragged the captive tribesman forward. Vylia had nearly forgotten about the Sekoiako who'd tried to rescue her. He hadn't been in her dreams.

"Charge it," Sa'alu demanded. "Put Phoeran energy into it." He said many other harsh words in a language Vylia didn't know.

She must have fallen back asleep, because suddenly the sky was darker. A grinding noise and a great shuddering within the rock she slept on shook her awake. But surely she was still in the dreamscape, because it looked like stairs appeared in a vacuous slush, descending into the earth with a waterfall of liquid and green slime. It didn't make sense, but Vylia didn't have enough energy to move and get a better look.

The grinding stopped, and Sa'alu removed the battery from the rock. He gestured at his men, and before Vylia could realize what was happening or protest, they threw the Sekoiako man into the gooey membrane that the ill-fated soldier had fallen through before. Likewise, the captive could not escape, and he slipped through the surface of the swamp and fell to what sounded like a decisive end.

Vylia squeezed her eyes shut as the horrifying sounds replayed in her mind. Would she be next? Maybe she should reconsider Lillian's offer.

"Sir, the stairs are so slippery . . . If I try to carry her down here, I'll likely lose my footing."

"I'm not losing another man," came Sa'alu's smoothly formal voice.

"Stay here and stand guard. Let her sleep for now."

Vylia didn't want to sleep anymore, just to defy him. But the taste of fadeleaf was still strong in her mouth. What if they'd given her far too much these last several days, and she never woke again?

She didn't worry long, because the croaking frogs, chirping insects, and singing birds soon lulled her back into darkness.

Vylia dreamed of ghosts.

Of highly skilled men who'd spent years constructing Lillian's vault underground. Who were promised riches but never allowed to return to the surface, burying the secrets of the vault with them.

Of unsuspecting travelers and hunters who'd fallen through the bog's trap to their deaths.

Of the Sekoiako man brave and foolish enough to try and rescue her, only to accomplish nothing except furthering the goals of his killers.

But Sousuke wasn't among the ghosts.

Curious.

32

SOUSUKE

Sousuke, I can't . . . maintain control anymore, Felix's voice echoed through his head with a tinge of desperation. *It was a good idea, but I can't anymore. I feel like . . .*

Like you're going to pass out? Sousuke braced for the jolt back into his own body in wyvern form as they coasted through the sky above the trade route between Navarro and My'Eyah. *Have you never fallen asleep before?*

No! Is that what it feels like? It's horrible! Felix pumped their wings once, trying to maintain the glide. *I've taught you all I can about flying. Now you just have to do it yourself. Don't drop these humans, okay? They are important.*

You land, then, Sousuke said. *My landing would be too risky.*

Can't you just keep flying?

Too dangerous. Let me get on the ground and gain some confidence before I carry two souls on my back.

Felix put them into a gentle dive, blinking in and out, but managed a soft landing in a harvested cornfield that had been halfway cut down. Then Sousuke felt control of his body return with a shock of feeling from every sense. But one sensation either carried over from Felix or was his own, just as strong: he was exhausted.

"Why are we landing?" Ryon asked as he jumped down, scanning the fields of corn, hay, tobacco, cotton, and another crop Sousuke didn't recognize. "And why so far south? Banshee's Playground is north of My'Eyah."

"Felix—" Sousuke cleared his throat, adjusting to the strange feeling of the wyvern's mouth once again. "Felix is too weak to maintain control of my body anymore, and I need to practice flying before we risk your lives."

"Much appreciated," Kira said as she hopped down with Ryon's help.

"We landed south of the travel route to stay away from Zeph's territory as much as possible," Sousuke said.

"What's a Zeph?" Kira lifted her foot with a disgusted look. These fields must have been well-fertilized, judging by the smell.

"My . . ." Sousuke stopped himself. How best to describe Zeph? "An enemy."

Ryon was watching him, waiting, and clearly dissatisfied with the lack of information.

"My enemy, not yours. Let's keep it that way." Sousuke turned and stomped toward the taller stalks of corn that hadn't been cut down yet, raising his wings above them. "I need some privacy to change. We could camp here for the night."

It's not even dark yet! Felix protested.

"Okay!" Kira yelled.

"It will be soon enough," Sousuke told Felix, "and we have to make camp before then." Sufficiently far away from Kira and Ryon, Sousuke changed back to human form and donned clothing, relishing the feeling of freedom and control once again.

What are you doing? Stay in dragon form and practice flying!

"You know that sleep thing you're so unfamiliar with? Well, I might not have to sleep as often as humans, but I do need it. And we haven't slept since you took me as a vessel."

Sleep is for mortals! You need to practice, and you can do it while they sleep. You fly like a boulder.

"I *am* mortal. Deal with it," Sousuke grunted as he pulled on his boots. "I probably don't need very much flight practice, but I won't do Vylia any good if I show up sleep-crazed."

Felix fell silent, and Sousuke rubbed his eyes. With another entity residing in his mind, he'd never felt so close to someone else. It was extremely uncomfortable.

He decided he should keep his distance from Ryon and Kira. In case Zeph found them again.

Definitely a good idea, Felix said. *Give them everything of value, just in case.*

"They have all the cyphers and the glass-gold brooch," Sousuke said. He didn't know or trust them enough to give him his compass.

He raised his voice and yelled, "I'm going to camp over here by the windmill in case Zeph shows up! If he does, stay back and stay hidden! He would kill you without a second thought!"

"Understood," Ryon yelled back. "Need any food?"

"No," Sousuke returned. That bread had been more filling than he'd anticipated. He might have enjoyed an ear of roasted sweet corn, but unfortunately the stalks around him had already been harvested. He wondered which direction the owner's house was, and if they had noticed a young dragon landing in their field. If so, they'd find out soon enough.

Thanks for bringing them, Felix thought.

"Thanks for bringing my compass and the new equipment from Valinor. The debt is repaid." Sousuke pulled out his bedding and wondered if he should make a fire. No. Too tired.

He lay down and prayed the bugs in this region wouldn't be too bad. The smell of manure fertilizer was bad enough—a smell that was familiar to his childhood but not his more recent years in the palace of Maqua. Regardless, it would probably only take him a few minutes of stillness and quiet to fall asleep.

But something nagged incessantly at the back of his mind. No, two things—one of them being Felix's tangible anxiety about experiencing whatever *sleep* was.

"Do you think Zeph will find us again?" Sousuke whispered.

Undoubtedly, Felix responded. *It's just a matter of time.*

"How much time?"

I don't know. We've done everything we can.

Sousuke laced his fingers together over his chest and closed his eyes. "Why did he just leave like that?"

I think, maybe . . . he will try to separate us somehow.

Sousuke opened his eyes and stared up at purple-gray clouds. "Can he? That would be great."

If you want me dead. He would kill me the instant we were separated.

Sousuke frowned. "Or you might die again just from being separated, since you're technically supposed to be dead."

Technically.

"Interesting," said a familiar voice.

Sousuke jumped up so fast his vision spun. A handsome man clothed in silver watched him through the corn stalks with an eerily wide grin. A red-eyed man.

Sousuke reached for his sword. But his scabbard wasn't there. Neither was his sword. Why had Felix only gotten him clothes from Valinor and not a blasted sword?

"Who were you talking to? Felix, inside your own head? So odd," the man said. He sounded like Zeph. But he didn't look like Zeph's normal human form. But he looked familiar nonetheless. Or was Sousuke so tired he was imagining things?

"I brought a gift for you, as promised." Zeph held out an ornate scabbard and sword. "You seemed to be reaching for a weapon, so, here you go."

Sousuke's jaw dropped open. Surely it was a trick. Of course it was a trick. But Zeph just stood there, holding his offering out, if only Sousuke were foolish enough to step forward and take it.

"What is it?" Sousuke demanded.

"It's an ancient spirit-blade called Division," Zeph said. "So sharp, it can cut between soul and spirit. It should free you from Felix."

That's it! Felix cried. *He's had it this entire time? Or who did he kill for it?*

Zeph pulled the handle from the scabbard, but nothing came out—no sound or steel. It was an empty hilt with no blade.

Sousuke just stared. "Is this a joke?"

"No," Zeph chuckled. "Like I said, it's a spirit-blade. Just because you can't see it doesn't mean it's not there. If it pierces your core, it will solve your problem, but it shouldn't kill you."

Sousuke's mouth went dry. *"Shouldn't?"*

"Shouldn't," Zeph repeated. "Just one of the many treasures in my stashes, which you would have access to as my heir."

Disgust washed over Sousuke. "So you think I'm going to just take your word and stab myself with an invisible blade that *shouldn't* kill me?"

"Do you have any other options? Or do you enjoy having a rat in your head?"

Sousuke awkwardly adjusted his stance, since his tensed muscles were beginning to cramp. "No, thanks."

"My grace cannot be denied," Zeph said simply. "No pup of mine will be deceived by Felix's lies any longer. Surely he has fed you all kinds of nonsense and poison about me."

"Unnecessary," Sousuke growled. "You did that yourself."

"Aww," Zeph gave a false frown. "Well, it's going to happen one way or another. Would you like to do it, or me?"

Sousuke's heart beat like a war drum and his mind raced. What could he do to get out of this?

You could offer him an oath, Felix said. *He wants your loyalty.*

Anger and revulsion hit Sousuke. *How could you possibly suggest that? If I made an oath to be loyal to him, it would kill me immediately!*

Your mortal blood could keep you alive, Felix said. *Didn't you make an oath to serve the emperor and protect the princess? Those oaths haven't killed you yet.*

Sousuke's mind reached wildly for the details of the Three Fractures deadly to any *trai'yeth:* a broken core, a broken heart, or a broken oath. They were why it was so risky for Tameru to have married his mother, Rhu Hana. *Ko'yeth* lived much longer than the average human, but whenever Hana did pass away, Tameru's life would be in danger from a broken heart.

It was rare for an elemental to die in that way, though. Many wisely didn't give their hearts away to mortals. Fewer still made any kind of oath.

I never directly broke my oath to the emperor. And I still uphold my oath to protect Vylia. Why on Alani would I risk it by giving Zeph an oath? Are you insane?

Because Zeph will find Vylia's compass in your belongings, Felix thought. *And he was asking about her whereabouts. If he's smart enough to realize what it is—and he is—he will track her down.*

"How funny!" Zeph exclaimed. "Watching you have a conversation inside your own head like that. You look like you're out of your mind! Let's solve that problem, shall we?" He took a step forward, brandishing Division's hilt.

Sousuke reached down with his senses into the earth. The easiest type of stone for him to manipulate was igneous, but he could find none. The layer of marble far below would have to do.

He grasped it, molded it into a spear, and sent it careening upward through the earth, directly at Zeph.

It burst up through the ground and slammed into Zeph, sending him flying back into the vegetation.

Sousuke's instinct was to run, but he knew it was pointless. Had he hit Zeph's core? Was he a pile of silver dust and a blood-red gem on the other side of those swaying corn stalks?

He was afraid to look.

Something flew out of the green, too fast to see clearly. Sousuke dodged right and something slashed across his left arm, eliciting pain and blood. He ran backwards into the stalks, stopped, and crouched.

He'd botched his only chance. Should he have been faster? Stronger? Did Zeph's silvery syn clothing function like armor?

Hiding was pointless. Zeph could sense him.

The corn rustled, and dozens of spikes crashed through dashed leaves, hurtling toward Sousuke. He ducked and brought up a wall of stone that immediately cracked against every other impact. Sousuke willed the wall to stay together and prayed.

The crashing stopped, and a wind picked up. No, not wind . . . swirling sand. A sandstorm. Scratching and biting and piercing. He couldn't see, couldn't hear.

Sousuke slammed his fists into the earth, creating a small crater and bringing the dirt up like a dome around him. But working with earth was so much more difficult than stone, especially this earth—fertile and full of living matter that he couldn't manipulate. Sousuke spat out sand and reinforced his dome with sedimentary rock from below.

The rock hesitated before heeding his call. Sousuke commanded it again and sensed something else below him.

Zeph.

Sousuke punched the ground, sending compacted rails of stone through the layers, down toward Zeph. One, two, three, four, until his knuckles were raw.

Silence.

Something shot upward. Then another, just slow enough that Sousuke could sense it: a formation of rock as tall and wide as three men. And several others, rocketing past him and upward.

Sousuke removed just enough of his shield so he could see them launch so high into the sky he could barely make them out. Then they slowed, turned downward, and plummeted back toward the field.

His shield wouldn't be strong enough. Where to run? Above Zeph. Only there would be safe.

No. He refused to run to Zeph for safety.

He strengthened his shield as much as he could anyway, pulling layer upon layer of marble up from the depths. *Felix, a little help would be great right about now!*

Boom. Booboom. BOOM.

The earth shook, then *cracked.*

Pain. Darkness. Dancing lights.

Sousuke! A familiar voice broke through the strange warbling of sounds in his ears. A glowing fox, like a ghost, yipping at him from the rubble. *You're not dead yet. Snap out of it! Move!*

The ground opened up beneath him, and he fell. Down, down, through a black hole with no bottom in sight.

Sousuke fought to orient himself and commanded a shelf to jut out and catch him. He landed hard enough to make his teeth rattle and ankles riot.

He hissed through the pain and blocked it out. Where was that evil spawn of the abyss?

There. Sousuke sensed Zeph nearby. Gathered all of his strength. Roared as he ordered the earth to collapse inward on Zeph and crush him.

A quake rumbled, sending debris clattering down around Sousuke. He panted. Waited.

Stone came at him from all sides. Conforming to his body and constricting.

Sousuke pushed back at the betrayal from the earth. It wasn't under his command anymore. It grinded and crushed him like herbs between a mortar and pestle.

His full strength wasn't enough to reverse it. Not nearly.

Snap.

Blinding pain in his chest stole his focus. He couldn't breathe. Couldn't—

Snap.

He screamed.

Sousuke! Felix's voice melded desperation with rage. *Just give him what he wants! Let him kill me. I will come back in seven years and destroy him!*

He sensed motion. Upward. Light. Agony.

"Well, that was moderately exciting. You'd fail out of the best Terruthian school, to be sure, but considering you have hardly any syn at all, I'd say it's a passing grade."

Every breath was torture. He tasted blood. Was he dying?

"Oh, hold still. I'll fix it."

Something clenched his side. *Crack.*

Sousuke cried out again, but the pain somehow wasn't as bad anymore. He gripped the debris on the ground around him and struggled for breath.

"Now, just a quick surgery."

Sousuke opened his eyes to Zeph holding Division's hilt over him.

"Wait!" he croaked, holding a hand out. "I—I'll negotiate."

Zeph tilted his head. His familiar face . . . Where did he know that face from?

"A bit late for negotiations, pup."

Sousuke coughed and spat out blood. "Hear me out."

It's okay. I've died before, and I'll be back.

Shut up, Felix. We need you! I won't let him take you!

Zeph chuckled. "Are you afraid to die, my boy? I do hear it's dreadful. Not that I would know, since I'm the only elemental who has never died." His grin was wide and white. "You cannot fathom the treasures I have amassed."

Sousuke hissed breaths through the pain. "If you spare . . . Vylia and Felix, I will give . . . you what you want."

Zeph's bright red eyes widened. "Oh? So you *do* know where the princess is."

Sousuke felt like he would vomit. "I have . . . a way. Swear to me you will never harm her in . . . any way, and I will swear an oath to you."

Zeph made a sound of interest. "But you have already sworn an oath to me."

Sousuke glared at him. "What? Are you mad?"

Zeph's grin stretched from ear to ear. His silver garments morphed and changed, gleaming in the sunlight, until he wore the garb of the emperor of the Malaano Empire.

"Recognize me now?"

Sousuke's pulse halted. How could he be the emperor? *How?*

"Liar," Sousuke croaked. "You are a deceiver just like . . . every other face-shifting elemental!"

Zeph laughed. "Let's find Vylia together and ask her then, shall we?" A chunk of earth moved of its own accord, lifting Sousuke's pack within Zeph's reach. "I assume your method of tracking her is one of the compasses. Ah, yes, here it is." He admired the coral artifact in the sunlight. "Now, where are the others, I wonder? And were you the one to suspect Aoko and ruin my plan? Please, regale me with the tale of how she survived. Sa'alu's report was ever so lacking in detail, and he's not responding any longer."

Sousuke gritted his teeth. This creature was the definition of evil. Did this mean . . . Vylia was his daughter?

That would mean . . . No.

No!

"Oh dear, I can see this is a lot for you to take in." Zeph dropped the compass and squatted next to Sousuke. Small pieces of stone rose up from the earth. Melded in the *trai'yeth's* hand. Rolled on a suddenly flattened ground and clattered with numbers Sousuke couldn't make out. "Hmm. Very well. I will hear your proposal."

So much pain. Sousuke clenched his eyes shut and said, "If you call off your assassins . . . and swear an oath never to hurt Vylia or Felix . . . I will make an oath to become your heir."

"One thing at a time, now." Zeph straightened and rested a hand inside his imperial robes. "Concerning Vylia: letting her live would put me in a very bad position. Everyone thinks she's dead, you see, and that she was killed in Jadenvive. The tribesmen murdered her in their savage, backwards tree-city. So my people are angry enough to allow me the time and resources I need to win a quick war."

Sousuke glared at him. "All so you can have that syn mine . . . in the Katrosi woods?"

"Oh, you scarcely understand, pup. That is the largest natural deposit of syn I've ever beheld. And I've been to every corner of the earth." Zeph turned his gaze north, as if he could sense it even now. "With that much syn, I could hire or control every *trai'yeth* on the planet. And now I don't even have to share the riches with Zamara. Do I have Felix to thank for that?"

Sousuke refused to say anything about Kira or Ryon. Thank the creator they were staying back. Surely they'd seen or heard or felt something.

"None of this is Vylia's fault," Sousuke said. "She never did anything to . . . deserve this. Just let me . . . take her from Sa'alu, and I will keep her . . . out of the public eye until your . . . selfish war is over."

"Hmm. Well, that blasted Hiro has been running around, starting rumors that Vylia's alive, anyway . . ." Zeph snapped his fingers. "Better idea! You can marry her."

Sousuke blinked. Surely he hadn't heard that right. "But if you're her father . . . that means she's my sister—"

"No, no, no. I killed the royal couple and replaced him when Vylia was about eight years old. If she didn't notice a change in her 'father,' she's really quite dull." Zeph sounded bored. "You see, Malaan was nostalgic for me, and Zamara chose to replace the Emberhawk queen at the same time. The Katrosi don't have a royal family, and their chief doesn't really have much power—their elder council of seven men does. So it would have been bothersome and difficult for only Zamara and I to infiltrate and take control, so we decided to simply eliminate them, since the syn deposit was on their land and they were too vapid to utilize it, anyway."

Sousuke's mind spun. "So all of this death and destruction . . . was just because you and Zamara . . . wanted more syn?"

Zeph waved his hand. "Yes, yes, you're so morally righteous. Except you're not. Because you're mine now." His red eyes flashed as he grinned. "You will be my heir, and you will marry Vylia. Then I can introduce you as a hero to the people, with a lovely story of how you saved her that the people will adore. And you will both live in my palace and serve me. And I will lavish pleasantries and wonders upon you for the rest of your days."

Sousuke tried to breathe through the pain, but breathing only brought more pain. "I can't . . . marry her. I don't even know if she . . . favors me."

"No deal, then." Zeph stood. "Ending her is better for me, anyway."

Sousuke grabbed Zeph's silvery pant leg. "Swear to me first . . . you'll never harm her."

Zeph laughed. "Who has the power here, pup?"

Sousuke swallowed congealed blood and choked on it. "I swear an oath . . . to marry Princess Vylia of Maqua." His head swam.

"Very good. Now swear you will obey my every command."

"No. I will never be your puppet."

"Swear that you will be my heir."

Moisture clouded Sousuke's vision. "I swear an oath to be . . . your heir."

Zeph smiled wide. "Swear you will never speak of anything I just told you or reveal any of my secrets."

"Swear to me you will never . . . harm Vylia or Felix."

Zeph straightened. "I swear an oath never to harm Princess Vylia of Maqua in any conceivable way, and that I will recall my assassination order."

Relief coursed through Sousuke. "And Felix."

"Oh, no. Felix was never a part of this negotiation."

Sousuke pulled at his pant leg. "Then you would risk killing me after I swore to you, just to separate me from Felix? Let him—"

"Division won't kill you. I've already altered my plans drastically on your behalf. Felix is non-negotiable."

I told you, Felix thought. *Don't worry about me. Make him swear to protect Vylia. 'Not harming' isn't good enough.*

Sousuke groaned. "Swear you will protect Vylia."

Zeph pursed his lips. "Swear you will never reveal any of my secrets or the locations of my stashes, and I will show you your inheritance."

"Then you will swear to protect her?"

"Yes, I will, because she is to continue our bloodline."

Sousuke turned to his side in a lash of pain and vomited. His vision winked in and out.

"Oh, come now, it's not that bad. Isn't this what you wanted? Surely you want her."

God, help me!

Sousuke spat and panted. "I swear . . . I will never . . . share your secrets or . . . the location of your . . . stashes."

"I swear an oath to protect Princess Vylia of Maqua from all harm." Zeph patted Sousuke's shoulder. "There, there. Everything will be okay now."

Sousuke didn't have the strength to pull away from Zeph's touch. He felt broken. In every way.

God, help me . . .

He should have spat in Zeph's face and died with honor.

"Now, my dear son." Zeph rolled Sousuke on to his back. "Hold still."

A sword pierced his chest.

His heart faltered. He couldn't breathe. Couldn't move. Couldn't think. Only shock, and agony, and the sky ripping open. It wasn't blue anymore. It was pink.

You are my *child, and a child of Aeo.* Felix's voice, from far away. *Don't let him break you.*

Felix . . . I'm so sorry . . .

I will avenge you.

His soul was torn in twain.

33

KIRALAU

"It's been quiet for a long time now. He's either dead or he really needs our help! Let me go to him now or I will lose all respect for you!" Kira fought against Ryon's grip.

Ryon's face was solemn as he released her. "All right. Carefully—slowly! And quietly."

The cornfield was destroyed. Massive rifts had torn it asunder, like the world's smallest and most catastrophic earthquake.

Kira leaped over piles of upended corn and slid down fertilized embankments. She zig-zagged between fragments of multicolored stone and chunks of marble. "Sousuke!"

Ryon cursed behind her. "Quietly!"

Dread sloshed in Kira's gut as she climbed and jumped and ran. Where was he?

There. The body of a young man lay still on the ground, covered in dirt and strands of cornsilk and torn leaves and blood.

Tears stung Kira's eyes. Surely he was dead.

She ran to him anyway.

"Kira," Ryon warned in a gentle voice.

"Sousuke!" Kira knelt at his side and covered her mouth in horror. A terrible bruise stretched from his ribs like wicked fingers. Blood from his mouth dried across his cheek, and a strange scar had somehow appeared over his heart.

Ryon searched for a pulse. Then breath. "He's alive," he announced with a sigh of relief.

"By the tails," Kira whispered. She yelled up at Ryon, "Why didn't you let me help him?"

Ryon surveyed the land around them and wiped his blood-smeared fingers on the bottom of his cloak. "I did what he told me to do. And it was the right decision."

"I've killed a god before!" Kira snarled. She looked back down at Sousuke. He was in such bad shape, and she wasn't a healer. But she had to do *something*, or he wouldn't stay alive for much longer.

Which injury to give attention to first? What was that weird scar on his chest? What kind of monster had done this?

Kira hesitantly reached out to touch his shoulder. "Sous—"

Green eyes shot open, and Sousuke gasped. Coughed. Moaned.

"We're here," Ryon said as he moved closer while Kira staggered back. "I assume this was Zeph?"

Sousuke stared into the sky and breathed with painful effort. He blinked rapidly, his gaze darting around before closing in a grimace. "It's okay. He's gone." His voice cracked as badly the earth around them.

Kira waited for an agonizing minute before Sousuke spoke again. "Glad he didn't . . . find you." He squinted at the sky, and his eyes seemed to focus.

"Who is Zeph?" Kira demanded. "That's the same name as one of the seven *terru'syn trai'yeth*. The wolf. Is that him? But why would he be here, in Navakovrae lands? And why would he do this to you?"

"He is the emperor," Sousuke croaked. His eyes misted with tears. "He took . . . Felix."

Kira's mouth fell open. "What?"

"Privacy, please. I can heal . . . myself."

Ryon and Kira turned around, trying to process what had been said. Sousuke's mind must be broken as well for him to make such claims.

A warped howl like a wounded dog sounded behind them, making Kira jump. But then it sounded like a human's labored breathing once again.

They cautiously turned back around. Sousuke was on all fours, staring into the dirt. Grime and blood still covered him, but the bruising on his ribs was gone. He shook as he pushed himself up to kneeling and looked down at his chest. The scar over his heart was still there. He touched it gingerly.

"How did he take Felix?" Kira asked quietly. "Where did he take him?"

"With a blade." Sousuke's voice warbled. He looked beside him, where an empty hilt and five silver bars glistened in a neat pile on a strangely flat portion of dirt.

Sousuke grabbed one of the silver bars and bellowed in rage as he threw it across the field and out of sight.

Kira and Ryon exchanged a worried glance. Kira knew from experience that when an elemental died, their syn didn't arrange itself into an orderly formation like that. And she didn't see Felix's emerald anywhere, so he must not have died here.

Had Zeph left the syn bars as a gift for Sousuke, after he'd nearly killed him? And why did that hilt have no blade? None of this made sense.

She spotted Sousuke's pack on the ground. An ornate compass lay on its side next to it. She lifted it and watched the coral arrow lazily point east . . . by northeast.

"At least your compass isn't broken," Kira said.

Sousuke fell to his knees. Buried his face in his hands. Shook with sobs. And wept.

Kira's heart shattered for this man she barely knew. What on Alani had happened?

Ryon took her by the shoulders and gently led her back toward their camp. "Let's give him some time," he murmured, "and make some warm stew."

Night had fallen by the time that Kira's stew became aromatic. She'd found several cobs overlooked by the harvesters and was delighted to find they were supple sweet corn, not the varieties grown for popping or grinding into flour. If only she had some cream and her favorite dark green peppers to roast, it would have been quite delicious. But rehydrated jerky, dried onions, and spices would have to do.

The earth rumbled, and Kira feared the hot stew would slosh, but the quakes were much more gentle than before. Rows of corn fell gently in waves on top of one another, one swath at a time, until she could see Sousuke in the moonlight, slowly moving an arm back and forth. The field was flat once again, and the rest of the empty cornstalks brought down for mulch in preparation for the winter season.

Kira smiled at the sight. She'd felt terribly for the poor farmers who owned this field—and been grateful that they apparently weren't aware of the calamity that had happened earlier that day—but now it seemed they might never be the wiser, and Sousuke had even completed a portion of their labor for them.

Ryon stood as Sousuke approached their fire, his pack slung over his back. They called out echoed greetings.

"Would you like some stew?" Kira offered as Sousuke sat beside them. "It's not the best, but it's pretty good for a meal on the trail. I wish I had some dairy. But at least the corn is fresh."

She was babbling. She mentally kicked herself for it.

"Yes, please." Sousuke pulled a blanket from his pack and wrapped it around his shoulders.

Kira ladled three steaming bowls from the small pot and handed them out.

They ate in silence. After a few minutes, Kira couldn't take it any longer. "I hope we can find some water to clean this pot out when we're done. I'd hate to use our waterskins."

Ryon nodded and swallowed a mouthful of stew.

"Aren't you glad we brought this pot now? But I'll admit you were right about not bringin' the cast-iron one. This one's heavy enough to haul around as it is."

Ryon just nodded again.

Kira gave both men deadpan looks. "So . . . it will be good to get some rest. But then what are we going to do tomorrow?"

Sousuke set his empty bowl down. "Thank you for the food. It was good."

Kira brightened. "You're welcome! Would you like some more?"

"Yes, please."

Kira snatched his bowl and refilled it. Maybe she was a decent cook after all, considering the circumstances. Would Granny be proud?

"What did Zeph do to Felix?" Ryon asked quietly.

"I don't know." Sousuke stared into the flames, and Kira noticed a strange glint in his eyes. They looked somehow like a more vivid green than before. She couldn't decide if they were eerie or enchanting.

Wait. Did that mean he'd absorbed those syn bars? After he'd thrown one across the field?

Discomfort squirmed though Kira as Sousuke continued. "I was certain Zeph would kill him. But I saw no evidence of that when I woke. When he stabbed me with Division, I lost consciousness . . . so I don't know what happened or where Zeph went." Sousuke's hand rested on a sword hilt and scabbard on his belt. The design was simple yet elegant, but Kira couldn't identify the style of which people group might have crafted it.

"Is Zeph really the emperor?" Kira asked quietly.

"Yes," Sousuke said, and for the next several minutes, he told them even more unbelievable things. About Zeph's coordination with Zamara and their motivations and plots.

Kira could scarcely take it all in. And yet . . . none of her own experiences contradicted anything he'd said. Could it really all be true? Everything that had happened was just because of two conniving *trai'yeth?*

Maybe they really were some kind of gods, if their whims had such enormous impacts on mankind.

"We can't continue to the vault without Felix," Ryon said. "We only have three out of four cyphers to open the vault door."

"I know Felix's last vessel," Sousuke said. "It's my younger sister, and there's a chance she is coming here."

Ryon perked up. "Really?"

Sousuke swallowed another mouthful. "I sent a letter from Sekoiako to the Lotusfall, thinking I was going to die back there. I told Father that Lillian had taken Vylia and was heading to her vault. I guarantee he will send men there to intercept them as soon as he receives the letter. It all depends on the speed of delivery and the weather on the Sea of Bones."

"Both the Katrosi and the Sekoiako use messenger hawks," Ryon said. "Very swift."

Sousuke nodded. "And it is the calm season for passage through the sea, which is why the Empire is attacking now."

"So the Lotusfall know that Lillian's vault is in Banshee's Playground?" Kira asked as she scraped the bottom of the stew-pot.

"Yes, because Felix was Lotusfall, and he helped to build Lillian's vault. But no one has entered it for millennia. It was, ironically, the safest place to hide her treasures from the world. Like the dreamcatcher—in the wrong hands, it would be as disastrous as it was the first time it was under Lillian's control."

Kira hadn't known that Felix had helped to construct Lillian's vault. Why would he have done such a thing?

"So your father commands the Lotusfall?" Ryon asked. "What are the odds that he would bring your sister, and that she would bring her cypher?"

"Yes, my father, Tameru, leads the Lotusfall. And yes, it's possible. Alunette wants to grow up faster than Father wants her to. She would beg to go with him if he's going. He's protective of her, but Mother has allowed her training even though she's young—she's very intelligent. Though it's been a long time since I've been home, so I'm only speculating."

"That is very good speculation," Kira mused. Although it meant they wouldn't be going home after all. But maybe they still had a chance of saving the world. Assuming Felix had been right about everything.

"Alunette?" Ryon said.

Sousuke nodded and set his once-again-empty bowl down.

"Funny. I had a cousin with the same name."

Sousuke looked at him. Narrowed his eyes. "Are you Emberhawk?"

Kira watched her husband's face as his mind worked. "By blood only," Ryon said.

"But not the royal family," Sousuke said.

"Yes."

Sousuke's too-green eyes widened. "Then she could be your cousin."

Kira gave an incredulous laugh. "How?"

Sousuke pulled the blanket tighter around himself. "Alunette was the youngest daughter of King Brynn and Queen Dierdre—"

"Zamara," Ryon corrected. "Alunette was born of Zamara. She was

Illiana's younger sister, and the half-sister of Lysander and Coriander, who were born of the true Queen Dierdre."

Sousuke nodded. "Right. But Alunette didn't take after Zamara like Illiana did. Zamara kept her in a prison cell like a misbehaving pet. So Felix took pity on her and brought her to the Lotusfall, a family of *ko'yeth*, who desire to do what is right, so she could be with her own kind. Father and Mother adopted her, and she's been my younger sister for years."

Ryon looked like he'd seen a ghost. "She went missing years ago . . . We all thought she was dead." His face darkened. "Felix kidnapped her and never told us?"

"For her safety, surely," Sousuke said. "From what I hear of Zamara, she would not have been very happy to learn what had happened."

Ryon stared blankly into the stars on the horizon as Kira wondered what he was thinking. What other surprises did Sousuke have hidden in those surreal glowing eyes?

Sousuke's voice lowered. "It was one of the few good decisions Felix ever made. Alunette was not the first *ko'yeth* born of an evil *trai'yeth* whom my father adopted. Without him, I might have . . ."

Still, Ryon didn't speak, nor look at either of them. Then, finally, he said, "I'm glad."

"We need to accomplish Felix's mission." Sousuke cleared his throat. "I will go with you to the vault, if you'll have me."

Kira eyed him sidelong. "But you were adamant about rescuing Vylia."

"I will rescue Vylia. But she is not in as much danger now as she was before."

Kira stared at Sousuke. "What? How?"

"Zeph will protect her now."

Another shocker. "Why?"

Sousuke nudged the dirt with his boot. "Because we had a conversation."

Kira narrowed her eyes at him. "Whose side are you on?"

"The creator's. And Felix's. And my family's. And Vylia's. And yours." Sousuke turned his bright green eyes on her. "If you are also for all of the above."

"I am," Kira said. "Though I've yet to meet your family." But apparently some of Sousuke's family was actually Ryon's family? Her head hurt.

"All right, then." Ryon seemed to have returned to them. "We'll set out for the vault at first light and pray that Alunette brings the fourth cypher." He turned to Kira. "If that's what you want, *balemba.*"

Kira slouched. "As long as we don't cross any waters."

Although, they'd already crossed over the Silvermead River, and nothing bad had happened. Maybe that blind prophet in King Coriander's court was just a crazy old man, after all.

34

BROOKE

Onyx wouldn't wake up.

Brooke was growing concerned. Ryon, Kiralau, and the unnerving Felix/Sousuke combination had already left that morning. Lysander and Brooke had finished packing up and readied themselves for the trip to Valinor an hour ago. Surely a generous meal of flame-broiled d'hakka shouldn't put a dragon to sleep for so many hours. But then again, she was no dragon expert.

"What if I just give him a swift kick in the gut?" Lysander grumbled.

I'd rather you not be his next meal. Brooke tried patting Onyx's horned face and speaking gently to him once more to no avail. She huffed and walked around to his back as he lay on his side on the ground, wondering what to try next. What would her grandfather do? Something aromatic, perhaps?

A glint caught her eye under Onyx's wing—something shinier than his matte black scales, and green. No, not just one—several orbs, each as big as her fist.

Brooke moved closer and inspected them. They had little legs! Like enormous ticks, stuck under Onyx's wings, between his softer scales.

Disgusted, she jerked back. *Lysander, I found . . .*

She trailed off when she saw her husband staring at something behind her and slowly pulling out his blowgun and a poison dart.

Brooke turned and startled at the sight. A muscled, lean man emerged from the wood, covered in black paint that left parts of his chest and arms bare in the shape of bones. The upper half of a skull served as his mask, with many dark-green and white-speckled feathers protruding tall and long from it. He bore a hook-sword in each hand and approached casually.

A Darkwood elite.

"Brooke of House Stillwind of Jadenvive. Lysander of Quin'Alor. By the order of King Raven Eye, you are both to be brought to Darkwood for trial for the murder of Prince Red Heron."

Lysander slowly loaded the dart into his blowgun.

Brooke's chilled bones thawed enough for her to move once again. She put her hand on Lysander's weapon, lowering it and stepping between the two men.

"We will come peacefully and stand trial," she said.

Ulysses ordered you to avoid the Darkwood at all costs! Lysander's voice boomed through her head. *And it may be just this one. I can take care of him right now.*

No violence. Brooke pointed at the ticks on Onyx's back. "Did you do this to my wyvern?"

The elite stopped his advance. "Yes, but if you cooperate, we will remove them, and he will recover soon after we depart. Dragons do not get along well with our mounts."

Brooke's pulse quickened as a shadow appeared from the woods behind him. Then another. And another. Darkwood elites—each one riding an enormous d'hakka with saddle and reins. Their normally shiny carapaces were instead a matte gray, and their stingers rigged with some kind of leather contraption.

They were surrounded. Twelve in total.

She'd never seen anything so terrifying.

"Drop your weapons," said the first elite, "and you will not be harmed."

Lysander cursed. "I'm the one who killed Heron," he yelled. "Take me and let her go."

"The king ordered for you both to come with us," the elite said. "Drop your weapon."

It's okay, Brooke said. *I can show my memories directly to the king, and he will know it was self-defense, not murder.*

No king would ever excuse the killing of his heir, regardless!

We have no choice! Brooke thought back. *They will take us, with or without d'hakka stings.*

Lyssander cursed again and dropped his blowgun. His bandoleer. His shortsword. His knives. And Brooke's spear and knives clattered to the ground as well.

"On your knees. Lift your hands."

Brooke reluctantly obeyed. Her skin crawled as elites approached them from behind and bound them. She closed her eyes as they hauled her toward one of the nightmarish beasts.

It was worth it, she decided. To have married Lysander instead of Red Heron, and to have been rescued from his clutches. A few blissful weeks with Lysander were better than a lifetime of misery with Red Heron.

That is what she told herself, again and again, as they lashed her to the saddle and bolted west for Darkwood.

35

VYLIA

Vylia's dreams of ghosts waned, thankfully, and waking felt more genuine than it had in . . . how long had it been?

She shuddered at the quickly fading memories of lingering spirits. It had just been dreams, she told herself. Bad dreams. Not real ghosts, of course. Their claims against Felix couldn't be true. He was the patron elemental of the Katrosi—she'd heard rumor that he'd been the lake wyvern she saw fighting the great ember hawk during the attack.

Pain in the shoulder Vylia lay on roused her more quickly and clearly. She pushed herself upright and looked around. How had she ever fallen asleep on a rock with no pillow or blanket?

The air was heavy with moisture and thick with unpleasant scents she couldn't identify. Wait—was that her own odor? She sniffed her own dress and regretted it. Never before in her life . . .

Stagnant water surrounded the rocky outcropping she sat on, patchy with algae and the occasional droopy herb or spiky grass, but mostly as flat as the distant ocean. In the opposite direction, far to the west, appeared to be the mangrove from blurry memory. To the southwest, short angles, brown hues, and smoke—a town or village of some sort. My'Eyah? No, the grand port town featured castle spires of greater heights.

What was its name? Vylia couldn't remember. To her, its name was Freedom.

"Good morning, Your Highness."

Vylia turned to find one of the Malaano soldiers smirking at her from a campfire set on a sort of small island where the earth bulged up above the water. Several packs surrounded the compact camp, but this man squatting in his smudged silver plate armor was the only human in sight aside from her.

Behind him, green-slicked stone steps descended into the earth and disappeared into darkness.

"Make us some food," the soldier ordered.

Vylia stared blankly at him for a moment. Didn't he know she was a princess? She knew as much about cooking as he likely knew about child-rearing.

Still, she could try. If he gave her something in return.

"My ankles are bound," she said, scooting to the rock's edge and swinging her feet off the side.

The guard sat there with an annoyed frown for several heartbeats. Then he looked in the direction of the town. "Are you going to make me go running after you to Ashena?"

Ashena. Right.

"I can't run through this bog," Vylia said. "And you could see me all the way there, anyway."

The guard stood with a rumbling grunt. Vylia's pulse sped as he approached, but he only untied the thick knot between her ankles without making eye contact and returned to his seat. "These embers are all we've got left. No more dry wood around here. You'll have to make do."

Vylia rubbed her feet and frowned at the indentions in her skin. But when she jumped to the muddy island, her ankles felt strong. She was quite well-rested, at least.

She studied a pile of sticks near the fire. Clearly they were water-logged and would do more harm to the fire than good.

Vylia looked again at the steps. Sa'alu, the other two men, and Lillian must be down there. Was Lillian's vault down there? Why would it be in such a nasty place? And not on Malaan Island? And wouldn't it be flooded?

Well, depending on how far down it went, the Malo stone could be quite a distance away . . . Lillian's power over her element might be diminished.

Vylia reached out toward the wood pile and sensed the water within.

She closed her eyes and willed the moisture up . . . out . . . and into the water that surrounded them.

"Hey!" The guard leaped to his feet and staggered away from the wood.

Vylia opened her eyes and grinned at the new, lighter color of the sticks. After Lillian had been blocking her power for so long, it felt so good to reconnect to her element.

The soldier stared at her in a ready stance, as if she were an unknown and potentially dangerous creature that had suddenly appeared.

Still smiling, Vylia pretended to ignore him as she collected a few sticks, placed them on the embers, and blew small flames to life. "What kind of food do we have?"

With jerky movements, and without turning his back to her, the man moved to one of the packs and tossed it to her.

"Thank you," Vylia said sweetly.

He sat back down with a huff, further away from the fire than he'd been sitting before.

Vylia unfurled the pack and looked at the provisions, but her mind's eye only saw escape possibilities. He was afraid of her. And he was just one man. If she could somehow take him out quietly, the others down below might not hear, and she could slosh her way to Ashena before anyone realized she was gone.

Was she capable of killing another human being? No. But she could just put him to sleep somehow. Fadeleaf!

But there wasn't any of the succulent beneath her tongue anymore—Lillian had ordered they stop drugging her for some reason. Probably so she could try begging again. Thank the creator that Lillian apparently needed a *willing* host. Which meant she would never be released.

Vylia took great solace in that fact. No one would ever know that the world would be saved by only one girl's defiance against evil.

She glanced sidelong at the other packs. Which one of them contained the fresh fadeleaf they'd acquired at My'Eyah? Maybe she could make a stew and spike it. But her stomach rumbled . . . She should grab a bowl for herself before secretly filling the pot with fadeleaf. Would he be able to taste it? Or if he got a potent mouthful, would it matter?

First, she needed him to stop watching her.

"I'll make a stew," Vylia said. "But we're going to need more wood—preferably some larger logs. Could you gather some, please? I can remove the water to make them usable."

"There aren't any trees around here, so no logs. Only driftwood." The soldier stood and searched the still water. Then he stomped around, his back to the fire, and stared in the direction of the distant mangrove trees in silent contemplation.

Faster than Vylia's eyes could follow, a rope lashed out from a bush and grabbed the man from behind with a loop. It cinched tight and pulled backward, yanking the soldier off-balance and sending him crashing into the fire.

He stared up at the sky for a moment, then he must have registered the embers heating his metal armor, and he screamed.

Vylia jumped back as the man writhed, but the lasso had slipped tight between his armor plates and clamped his arms to his sides.

Her eyes followed the rope to the man who held it, who rose from a nearby shrub and approached as swiftly as the mud would allow.

Tekkyn'ashi!

The Malaano soldier finally managed to roll onto his side and continued his momentum, rolling and splashing into the water like a flaming log.

Tekkyn'ashi gathered and coiled his lasso as he stood over the soldier and stood on the back of his head, keeping the thrashing man underwater.

Vylia stared in a sickening mix of horror and joy as the Malaano's desperate writhing slowed.

"Look away, Your Highness."

Vylia bowed her head and closed her eyes, squeezing new tears out to flow down her cheeks. She was saved! How had she forgotten about Tekkyn'ashi? Maybe she'd never really believed that he'd genuinely joined her royal guard. She'd assumed he was just a temporary assignment while she was in Katrosi. And he wasn't even Katrosi. His Navakovrae people had just started a revolution against her father.

Maybe he was here for her bounty.

She hugged herself and shook, then covered her ears, trying to drown out the sounds of splashing . . . and sloshing . . . and silence.

"If my methods seem cruel, please understand these men murdered my baby brother," Tekkyn'ashi said. Vylia opened her eyes to see him untangling his rope from the fresh corpse and looping it into a series of large circles. "And many other atrocities I can't mention in polite company."

Vylia cleared her throat. Was she polite company? She was certain she didn't look or smell like polite company right now.

"I fully understand, Tekkyn'ashi." She tried to make her voice sound more tranquil and in control than she felt. "Are you . . . here for . . . ?"

He glanced over his shoulder with a quizzical look. "Well, I ain't here for the view."

"What about my bounty?" Her fingertips tingled with the resonance of the plentiful water surrounding her. Her life may have been utterly ruined, but she would fight for it anyway.

"I accepted a job as your bodyguard." Tekkyn'ashi's eyes focused on the downward steps nearby. "No one's collectin' any bounties today."

"But . . ." Vylia's relief clashed with logic. She hadn't met many trustworthy people recently. "I have no way of paying you."

"I'll be honest," Tekkyn'ashi said, his Navakovrae drawl growing low and dark. "I have an ulterior motive." He inspected a burn mark on his rope. "No payment required."

Vylia's gaze dipped to the corpse floating in the water, and she quickly looked away. "H-how did you find me?"

Tekkyn'ashi affixed his lasso to his belt and produced a compass—one of the four her bodyguards each carried. "Sousuke gave me this."

Seeing the familiar artifact filled Vylia with comfort. Those compasses were associated with the men who had watched over and protected her for her entire life. They represented safety.

And if Sousuke had given Tekkyn'ashi one, there must have been some desperation involved, but also a nominal level of trust.

Vylia decided to allow herself to trust him. What other hope did she have?

"Blessings upon you, Tekkyn'ashi." Her voice warbled. "I had all but given up hope. Sousuke . . ."

Tekkyn'ashi watched her quietly for a long moment. "I'm sorry." His tone sounded genuine, yet calloused. Like death followed him as closely as his shadow. "Call me Tekkyn."

A male voice drifted up from the deep. Then footsteps.

Vylia's throat closed. "They must have heard," she whispered.

Tekkyn headed back to the shrub that he'd somehow managed to hide behind. "Can you lie?"

She stood, wondering with rising panic if he meant for her to follow. "I was trained in speechcraft from birth."

"Perfect." Tekkyn continued his stride but turned back and pointed at her with an enrapturing blue gaze. "I'm not leavin' you. You're safe now."

Vylia nodded and clasped her hands together to stop their shaking. She stared at the steps and predicted the coming conversation. Put on a look of horror. It wasn't difficult when she saw the dead man's charred body floating in the haunted bog.

The footsteps grew louder until another Malaano soldier emerged. Not Sa'alu.

"What happened?" he demanded. His gaze followed hers to his fallen comrade and his countenance lit with rage. "What did you do?"

"He slipped on the mud and fell into the fire! He rolled into the water to put the flames out, but he stopped moving, and I'm not strong enough to pull him out of the water. Please, help!"

The man rushed to the body and tugged at the armor plates, splashing dirty water as he slipped and grunted.

The noise covered the soft whirling sound of Tekkyn's lasso. It lashed out, just as before, surrounding the man and pulling his arms tight against his torso as he looked down in bewilderment.

The soldier whirled around and saw Tekkyn coming for him. He snarled and reached for his sword. Couldn't pull it out because of the rope.

Tekkyn yanked the lasso backward, testing the man's balance before suddenly releasing the rope. He drew his own sword and dispatched the second man with frightening ease.

"We've only got a few seconds, now. Can you run?"

"I think so," Vylia managed.

"Make for Ashena as fast as you can." Tekkyn pointed south at the distant rooftops and smoke plumes.

Vylia forced her stiff body to retrieve her pack. "What about you? There are two men left, and Lilli—"

"I'll make sure they don't come after you."

"But Lillian can—"

"Go!"

Vylia ran, sloshing through the bog, and got one shoe stuck in the mud. Would it be faster to take deliberate steps rather than trying to run? She left her shoe and pushed through the water. *Creator, help us!*

A familiar smooth masculine voice sounded behind her. She dared to look over her shoulder.

Sa'alu and his last man had finished ascending the stairs. Their swords were drawn, and they moved to Tekkyn's either side to flank him.

Movement caught Vylia's attention to the west. She stared in disbelief as she tripped on something slippery below the water.

A black dragon with two people on its back. It couldn't be a dragon, but it was. A young wyvern, not unlike the one she'd seen in the battle in the skies over Jadenvive.

And it was heading straight for them.

36

KIRALAU

"Straight ahead," Ryon said.

Kira wished she could get a look at the magical compass in Ryon's hand, but she didn't dare shift her tentative position behind him on the dragon's bare back to get a better view. She squinted ahead.

A rock formation underlined with green and brown stood above the grass-pocked bog, and close by, the earth crested above the waters to form a small island topped with a dying fire. Three human figures stood atop it.

"There!" Kira cried. "Is that them?"

"Another one," came Sousuke's voice that rumbled up through his scales. "In the water, to the right."

Kira strained her vision to its furthest distance as they rapidly approached. All three on the island were men . . . Two of them armored . . . All three dark-skinned . . .

Her heart leaped into her throat as she recognized her older brother. "That's Tekkyn!"

The other two were flanking him, one one either side. That silver armor and dirty blue-and-white tabards were Malaano.

Kira clutched Ryon's waist even tighter. "They're surrounding him!"

Sousuke dipped low—so low that the claws of his back feet skidded across the surface of the water and kicked up white fans behind them. "Jump off."

"What? Why?" Kira cried. "It doesn't look very deep!"

"So I can kill them without killing you," Sousuke said.

Ryon glanced over his shoulder at her, a question in his fiery eyes.

A reinforcement consisting of a dragon was the best that Tekkyn could hope for. So Kira braced herself and nodded.

Then let go.

Brown, lukewarm water enveloped her. Her back hit something soft, and her tunic stuck to it. Kira flailed and tore free, righting herself only to get her feet stuck in the mud instead. Her head broke the surface and she gasped for air, wiping her eyes and snorting the repugnant water from her nose and shaking it from her hair.

Ryon wasn't far ahead, flinging algae from his arm as his eyes locked on hers. "You okay?"

"Yeah!" Kira looked just in time to see the wyvern cruise in a tight turn around the island, focused on a Malaano soldier that pointed a sword at him. Flame erupted from Sousuke's throat in a torrent, consuming the man first in white, then blue, then golden fire.

The man's agonized cry dug into Kira like poison. He didn't even make it to the water to douse himself before doubling over and illuminating the island in a sickly glow.

"Last time I'm flying on a dragon," Ryon remarked as he gathered arrows floating around him as Kira sloshed closer.

She barely heard Ryon, her gaze fixed on Tekkyn and . . . that was Lieutenant Sa'alu. She recognized him from the brawl in Het'saya.

Their swords clashed.

Then streams of water lifted slowly all around them like rising snakes.

Kira's breath hitched. She'd seen water move unnaturally like that before in only two places: the water dancers at the Moon Festival, and Lillian in the Katrosi treasury.

She bit her lip to prevent herself from screaming her brother's name and distracting him from defending against Sa'alu's quick sword strikes. She slipped on something slimy beneath the water and staggered.

Sousuke circled back and breathed fire at Sa'alu. Water shot up in a column, hitting the dragon's jaw and dousing his flame in an explosion of steam. Sousuke emitted a gurgling roar, flapped his wings, and flew in a wide arc, water streaming from his horns.

"Stop," Ryon called.

Kira's bones creaked as she forced herself to halt, but she couldn't tear her eyes from her brother's battle.

Ryon handed her his bow and water-logged quiver. "Don't shoot me again," he said as he continued forward and drew his shortsword.

Kira wondered if the bow would be damaged by the water but pushed the thought aside as she nocked an arrow. The fletching was slicked flat, which would surely compromise her accuracy. She cursed and tried to fluff the three rows of feathers back to their needed positions.

As Sousuke rounded closer once again, another enormous stream of water shot into the sky, knocking him off course and clinging to him in a gravity-defying blob. White and blue fire lit up the water in a flash, but didn't penetrate the globe of water that concentrated on the dragon's head. He fell and crashed into the water, creating waves spotted with plant matter.

Tekkyn landed a hit on Sa'alu, and Kira's heart soared. But it didn't seem to have any effect. She aimed her arrow only to be staggered by the dragon's wave. Sousuke thrashed, but no matter which way he stretched, the orb of water clung to his face. The only thing that escaped was the bubbles that floated to the top of the orb and vanished.

Kira stared in terror. Lillian was drowning him, even above the surface of the water. And Tekkyn would be next.

She startled as someone ran up on her right, arms outstretched toward the unnatural water. Princess Vylia!

The water came away from the orb in sheets, then abruptly burst and showered back down into the bog. The wyvern wheezed and gulped in air with yowling gasps.

Metal clanged and a man grunted. Kira righted her attention to the island as Ryon sloshed closer. Tekkyn's leg was drenched in blood.

No!

Kira aimed at Sa'alu as her vision blurred with tears. She couldn't get a clean shot . . . not without high risk of hitting Tekkyn. He and Sa'alu were locked in close combat, fueled by rage. And now Ryon was in the way, too.

A shadow raised behind her. Kira looked over her shoulder to behold a tsunami heading straight for Vylia.

Kira tried to run aside the wave's breadth, but it was too wide. It hit her like a charging buffalo, tossing her into a green and brown maelstrom. She lost hold of Ryon's bow and arrows as the water flipped her over and over.

Finally the spinning stopped, and she perceived light through the waters above. The surface wasn't far. She broke through, coughed, and inhaled deep breaths that smelled of rot.

She turned just in time to see Ryon's shortsword slice into Sa'alu's side. The lieutenant faltered, and Tekkyn cut him down.

Kira was flooded with relief as the two men left standing were her husband and her brother. Shuddering, she wiped water from her eyes and trudged toward them. *Thank you, god!*

But something was missing. No, two things: Vylia and the wyvern. Kira looked around but couldn't find them anywhere. Even when, filled with dread, she searched the bog waters for floating bodies. The only unmoving bodies were those of Malaano soldiers.

"Vy!" Kira cried.

There was no response.

Confused, she searched the horizon again—then realized that she couldn't see *under* the water.

Lillian! She must have pulled them under and was drowning them!

Kiralau. A silky voice entered her mind. *How lovely it is to see you again.*

Kira dashed to the island as fast as the mud beneath the water would allow.

I seem to be in need of a new sponsor. And how lucky for you—my vault of treasures is within reach. Claim my mirror, and you will be immediately rewarded.

Kira did her best to ignore the voice. She quickly surmised that Tekkyn was only bleeding from his thigh, but he was still standing. She shoved Ryon aside and dug into Sa'alu's pockets.

But you will never claim my riches without me. You don't have all four cyphers, do you? Lillian's voice had a tense edge to it. *Is that why you've come? To steal?*

Streams of water rose all around them. Dozens of them.

This is your last chance. Take the aether stone in one hand and the Malo stone in the other, and become my vessel. Do it or I will KILL YOU like I killed Vylia.

The voice crested into a cacophonous boom, wrenching Kira's mind. "The glass-gold brooch from Sous—" She stopped when Ryon handed her the Valinorian brooch.

The water-snakes shot at them from every side.

YOU WILL SUFFER!

Kira slammed the brooch into the side of Sa'alu's belt pouch.

The ribbons of water shattered and splashed into them with harmless droplets and mist.

No one moved. No voices. No birds. No insects. Nothing.

The three only breathed and scanned their surroundings.

There was no splashing in the waters. No ripples. No bubbles. Just a sound like a waterfall, but Kira hardly registered it.

Kira carefully opened Sa'alu's belt pouch. Inside was a magnificent opal, flat and smooth and as large as her palm. Trembling, she pulled it out and held the glass-gold brooch closely to it.

"Good job, y'all," Tekkyn said. He backed away and sat down with a grunt. "I'd have been fish bait."

"Can . . . Can you untie my mom's bandana?" Kira asked Ryon, then turned on her brother with equal parts frustration and hesitant relief. "I told you this would be dangerous!"

"Keep the reins, Frizz. It all worked out."

"No, it didn't! Vylia . . . and . . ." Kira tried to examine Tekkyn's wound out of the corner of her eye while holding still enough for Ryon to untie her bandana. "How deep is that? Are you hurt anywhere else?"

"No. It'll heal," Tekkyn said in a tight voice as he pulled a pouch from his belt. "Dang it. Everythin's wet."

Unrestrained, Kira's hair lifted as Ryon handed her the bandana. She wrapped the Malo stone and brooch up together like a lunch she used to pack for trapping in the Gnarled Wood. Ensured it was tightly and securely fastened. Stuffed it in her pants pocket.

She stood and searched again, desperately, for any sign of the princess. "Where are Vylia and Sousuke?"

"Sousuke?" Tekkyn asked.

"The wyvern," Ryon said as he pulled a cloudy faceted gem from

Sa'alu's corpse. It resembled white quartz. The aether stone.

Ryon handed it to Kira, who stashed it in her opposite pocket.

Tekkyn looked perplexed as Ryon pointed to a wide, dark hole in the surface of the water that Kira somehow hadn't noticed before. No—it hadn't been there before. That spot had used to be a strange slimy circle of a different shade of green than the surrounding algae. Stairs encircled the outer edge, spiraling downward.

Kira's heart clenched. She jogged closer, but not close enough for the current to catch her—water poured into the inky blackness of the hole from every side in a circular waterfall. She couldn't see the bottom.

"Vylia!"

37

VYLIA

Vylia awoke to the sound of crashing water. She was surrounded by darkness, and yet directly in front of her—no, above her?—was a circle of light. Water rushed toward her from the edges of the circle.

She squinted and moved—whatever was beneath her was jagged and unsteady—and hissed at pain in her back. It felt like she'd pulled a muscle or strained something.

A clatter sounded at her feet. Vylia grimaced and pushed up to sitting, looked to the side, and came face-to-face with a skull.

She was lying on a pile of bones and bodies.

Vylia yelped and scrambled away, sliding down a slope of rattling bones and frayed clothing and . . . that one smelled like the worst rot imaginable. Her back rioted at the movement, but she put as much distance between herself and that nightmare as she could stand.

"We're alive!" a male voice yelled from behind her. "Everything okay up there?"

"Yes!" came a relieved female voice from beyond the cascading waters. "Sa'alu is dead and Lillian is subdued!"

Vylia was utterly confused. That sounded like good news, but where was she? And the bodies . . . there were so many. She felt like she might vomit, but there was nothing in her stomach but acid.

Then, quieter and closer: "Your Highness, it's all right. You're safe now."

It was familiar. But it couldn't be Sousuke. He was dead.

Vylia turned to see a pair of glowing green eyes, like a scavenging creature of the night. She jumped back and winced at the pain in her back as her eyes adjusted to the darkness.

It *was* Sousuke. His demon-eyed ghost.

"It's okay." Sousuke lowered himself and offered an empty hand. "It's me."

Vylia dared not touch the specter and be sucked into a deeper layer of hell. "Your eyes . . ."

Sousuke closed his eyes and bowed his head, scoffing at himself. "I'm sorry. I needed . . . to take some power to . . . Well, I forgot it would change my eyes."

He made no sense. But his hand looked solid. Real.

Vylia reached out a shaking hand and touched his palm. Rougher and darker and bigger than hers. Warm. And gently closing around fingers.

"I thought the creator god would save us." Vylia's voice cracked. "Take us to the good afterlife in kai'lani. But this place must be Zoth."

"No, no. We're alive." Sousuke released her hand and dared to open his viridescent eyes again. Vylia didn't find them so disturbing anymore as they beheld her with compassion and . . . what else was that in his gaze? Expressions other than a serious one were foreign on his chiseled face.

"We can't be alive," Vylia whispered, her gaze pulled back to the pile of death. "I watched you die, and . . . Where are we? How did you get here?"

"Do you remember the big wave?" Sousuke asked. "I tried to catch you, and we broke through some sort of membrane above. We landed here. Are you hurt?" He sidestepped to block her view of the bones and bodies with his bare chest—wait, where was his armor? And those pants were too small and stained with bog water. What on Alani was all of this?

She tore her gaze from his physique, a strange heat blossoming inside her. She knew that each of her bodyguards were always in peak condition, but she'd never imagined the toned muscles hidden beneath his imperial armor. He was dangerously attractive.

Too bad he was insane. And how did he get here?

But something snapped inside her at that moment. He was *real.* And he was *alive.*

Vylia crashed into Sousuke, hugging tight and crying into his chest, not caring about the impropriety. "I'm so sorry I left you," she sobbed.

"Is it really you?"

"Yes, I just . . . haven't been entirely truthful with you, Your Highness." He wasn't hugging her back.

She pulled away and narrowed her eyes at him. "You are to call me Vy."

"Your Vyness."

Her glare broke into a smile. "You can't be Rhu Sousuke. I've never heard him tell a joke."

Sousuke smiled back, and Vylia wondered if she'd ever seen it before. It brightened and warmed her.

"I'll admit to being happy to be rid of Sa'alu and to find you alive," Sousuke said. "But are you well?"

Vylia decided not to mask her face as the pain in her back grew worse by the second, and she couldn't seem to find a posture to relieve it. "I think . . . I landed . . . poorly." She reached out to the ground and began to lower herself, though it was quickly flooding with the downpour from above.

Sousuke opened his arms. "May I?"

"Please," she managed.

Sousuke lifted her as if she were weightless. He moved to a stone staircase Vylia hadn't noticed before, which curved up and around the pit they were in, spiraling to the waterfall above. He slowly sat on the bottom stairs above the rising water level and cradled her in his arms.

She adjusted until the pain subsided, and relaxed into him. "Thank you." Her voice choked with emotion. "I can scarcely believe it. I was certain you wouldn't survive."

"Me, too." Sousuke leaned back and craned his neck to look at the hole to the sky above. "Are you coming down?" he yelled to the people above.

After a moment of quiet, Kira called back, "Tryin' to figure what to do with the bodies."

"Throw them down here and I'll bury them," Sousuke said.

Vylia stared at him, confused. Did he have a shovel somewhere? "Excuse me. You owe me an explanation."

Sousuke looked down at her with wide eyes. "I would use my element. Won't take long."

"No, no. I mean—wait. You're an elementalist?"

"Yes . . . I—"

"No." Vylia held up a finger. "No more distractions. What did you mean about House Rhu being a royal house?"

Sousuke blinked at her. "What?"

"When we were waylaid by Sa'alu in the carriage, you asked me who I would want to marry if I renounced my crown. And I said anyone not in a royal house. Then you asked if House Rhu was a royal house. Why?"

She felt him stiffen, and his eyes landed anywhere except on her. Slowly, he said, "House Rhu is a front for the Lotusfall. It's not a true royal house like the others."

"You're dodging my question. *You* are of House Rhu. So you were implying with your question that you were interested in my hand for marriage. Unless you want to set me up with a cousin of yours?"

"No . . . I . . ."

"Do you fancy me, soldier?"

Sousuke closed his eyes. Swallowed. "Of course I do."

Her heart soared. Every kind of pain dulled as air fled her lungs. "Truly?" she whispered.

Still, he didn't look at her. "I would die for you without a second thought."

Vylia frowned. "Any of my guards would."

"No—" Sousuke sighed. "I'm not supposed to favor you. It's inappropriate and foolish on many levels. Nothing can come of it. But I . . . can't stop. I didn't realize when it started . . ." He hung his head. "I've never had so much trouble controlling myself. I'm sorry. You have every right to dismiss or punish me, Your Highness."

Watching him flounder was one of the most adorable displays Vylia had ever seen. Her most stoic guard was so smitten he couldn't control his emotions—when all his other feelings were strictly in line? She could not have possibly been more joyful in that moment.

Vylia knew it would hurt to move, but she didn't care. She stretched up and kissed him on the cheek. "I believe I favor you, too."

His lips tugged upward, but his gaze narrowed. "I knew it."

An offended noise escaped her. "Excuse me?"

"Your diplomatic training only goes so far when it comes to your affections, Your Highness. You're easier to read than a painted sign."

Vylia's jaw dropped open. She scrambled for a comeback. "Well . . . you just . . . Maybe I don't like you as much as I'd thought!"

Sousuke chuckled. "If you want a relationship with a commoner, you need to get used to not always being treated like royalty."

She puffed her lips out and crossed her arms. "Well, I might not be royalty anymore anyway. But if you want a relationship with me, you should *always* treat me like a princess."

"You will always be my princess." Sousuke kissed her forehead, making her heart stumble. "But right now, we both smell like wild hogs."

"How dare you!" Vylia exclaimed, though unable to control a burst of laughter. She smacked his shoulder. "Have a shower, then!" She flung her hand up toward the cascading water and sent a stream directly into Sousuke's face.

He laughed through the downpour and turned his face toward the onslaught. "Much appreciated," he gurgled.

Vylia snorted but couldn't stop smiling. "Unbelievable."

38

BROOKE

Brooke hadn't realized she could possibly hate d'hakka any more than she already did. The ride from the woods north of Navarro to Darkwood proved her wrong.

Their captors directed their mounts through the forest with dizzying speed, spidery legs moving in a flurry through branches and somehow avoided crashing into them. Brooke couldn't close her eyes or the movement made her feel sick.

What the Katrosi saw as a nightmarish, man-eating plague that needed to be exterminated, the Darkwood saw as an intelligent creature whose presence was perennial. The d'hakka served them now, their tamed mounts territorially keeping the wild ones at bay.

Brooke would rather let Onyx hunt and eat every last one of them.

The forest grew darker as they went lower. Each tree looked as tall and thick as Vanya, but not pruned and trained like the Katrosi forest. The Darkwood was a tight cluster of savage wilds.

Instead of sun-kissed fields bearing crops, these enormous trees were laden with vines bearing fruits and fungus of every color sprouting from the bark, changing with elevation. Below, the forest floor was covered in purple foliage.

How are you? Lysander's voice was tense as it touched her mind. *This ride is rough. But I think we're almost there. Tonight I'll find a way to sneak us out of this hellscape.*

I'm all right, Brooke lied, forgetting the aether would reveal it to him. The way she'd been laid and bent over the d'hakka saddle was the height of discomfort after the hours they'd been riding, and a few specific muscles were cramped or straining.

She was also terrified.

If she'd been alone, she could have handled this situation on her own and held her head high. Faced her own fate.

But Lysander . . . he'd been the one to kill Red Heron. He was in more danger than she was. She couldn't let them hurt him. But what could she do? Her mind ran in circles like a dog who'd trapped a branch-runner in a tree.

Time to change the subject before Lysander called her on it.

I'm worried about Onyx, she blurted in his direction, which was above her as the line of d'hakka followed the one carried her downward. At least, by now, she wasn't worried about rolling off the d'hakka's back anymore. Her captors had secured her well against the unsettling movements.

If you can call him in at the right time and place, he can kill all of them, Lysander thought.

Or he could be killed! Aish. *We'll figure this out without violence. The Darkwood have quite the legitimate reason to be upset, okay?*

All she felt in response was an ethereal grumble.

"Why do your people call you a witch?"

Brooke jolted at the voice of the young man in the half-skull mask, who held the d'hakka's six reins and sat in front of her curled and bound form. He hadn't said anything since they'd left the Gnarled Wood.

"You don't seem like a witch." He turned to glance down at her out of the corner of the skull's eye socket, long feathers bouncing from its top. "Are you?"

Brooke swallowed to wet her throat. "I am not a witch. A political enemy gave me that name as an insult." The mother of Ulysses had invented The Jade Witch to smear Brooke for daring to compete against her son, when they'd both yearned for the title of Chief in the same election cycle.

Ulysses . . . He might now hold her life in his hands, if he had any idea the predicament she was currently in. Would he send the azure masks to extract her?

"It seems to have stuck," the young man said. "Why? Do you meddle with dark forces?"

"No! It's because I can speak and listen with my mind. The Katrosi only have a few who practice aether, so my ability is unnerving to people."

"Oh." He adjusted in the saddle, and his voice sounded as if he'd relaxed. "That's not a dark power. My father has that aether as well. This is why he's called Raven Eye."

The d'hakka jostled them down another layer of branches as his words sank in. "Your father is King Raven Eye? You are one of the princes?"

"We are all princes," he said.

There were twelve riders in this group. Twelve princes!

Brooke remembered then that the Darkwood had many queens. One from each of their powerful families. Like marriage alliances within their own tribe.

"What is your name?" she asked.

"Shade Tree," he said. "You may laugh. But I am not ashamed."

Confused, Brooke considered her words. "I'm not laughing. Why would I?"

He scratched the back of his neck, but the black body paint somehow didn't come off on his hand. "The Darkwood need no shade. But outsiders speak of it as a precious thing."

Brooke considered the implications. Why was he speaking so freely with her after spending the entire ride in silence? Did he feel some connection with her, because they both had derogatory names? No, that made little sense . . .

"Why were you given that name?" she dared to ask.

"Because as a child, I shared instead of fought with other children." Shade Tree leaned back and to the side as his d'hakka rounded the circumference of a massive trunk. "They said I would not become a warrior. They always make the weakest prince an ambassador." He manipulated the reins with obvious skill that was lost on Brooke. "But I am not the weakest."

She listened and considered. Then dared to ask an even more dangerous question. "You don't seem upset with me that your brother is dead."

"Half-brother," Shade Tree said immediately. "I may not be the oldest or the strongest, but I inherited my father's wisdom. And my wisdom says that Red Heron's wild selfishness finally caught up with him. We heard some Katrosi whispering of this as well when we were in Jadenvive. Is this true?"

Surprised again, Brooke didn't know how to respond. So instead, she prayed. *Aeo, let the king be as understanding as his son!*

"Yes," she said slowly. "He attacked me, and I called out for help, and one of my guards killed him."

Shade Tree made a noise like a snake's rattle. "Before the wedding ceremony? Disgrace."

Brooke adjusted to ease a pang in her ribs. She wondered if that behavior would have been acceptable to the Darkwood *after* the wedding. Thank the skies she never had to find out.

"My father will make justice," Shade Tree said.

Justice. Justice, he said, sounding somewhat reasonable, but with her as his captive. Bound hand and foot and lashed onto a spider-scorpion's back.

Unnerved and with her tired heart pounding too fast, imagination running swiftly to every terrible possibility, Brooke decided to change the subject. "How did you find us?"

"Word of a living dragon carries swiftly on the wind." Shade Tree looked down at her again, his black gaze analyzing. "Surely you didn't think you could evade us. You wanted to ally with us because you recognize the Darkwood tribe's prowess, yes?"

She didn't want to admit it. But he'd answered her questions truthfully.

What's he saying? Lysander's thought-voice was practically steaming with anger. *Is he threatening you?*

No, Brooke said. *I just learned that these men are all princes. How many queens does the Darkwood king have now?*

Last time I checked, five.

Brooke noticed Shade Tree was watching her, waiting for a response. *It seems not all the princes think alike. And I suspect there might be some competition between the brothers. We might not be in as much trouble as we thought.*

Lysander's voice came through with a bit more calm. *Good. But don't let your guard down.*

"It's true," Brooke admitted to Shade Tree. "The Tribal Alliance needs the Darkwood."

"Well, you might never have it again," Shade Tree said over the beating of distant drums. "We have arrived."

Brooke craned her neck to catch a glimpse of fires through the leaves. As they stopped descending and began moving forward, the drum beat grew louder. Trees had been felled into massive stumps, which had been carved out and topped with roofs and punctured with windows. The largest stump had been flattened, where dozens of people gathered.

The d'hakka carrying Lysander overtook Shade Tree's d'hakka with disturbing speed. Its rider held a hooked sword above his head and yelled, "We return victorious!"

The cheers of the crowd, the wind instruments that joined the drums, and jubilation that turned the trunk into a dance floor dashed Brooke's fledgeling hope.

But the twelve mounted d'hakka didn't stop—they only circled the crowd as the princes whooped, then continued on.

A sick feeling sank into Brooke's gut and lodged there like a carcass rotting beneath the surface of a pond. "Where are you taking us?"

"The prison," Shade Tree answered, "where you will wait until my father is ready to pass judgment."

39

SOUSUKE

Sousuke couldn't remember being so happy since he was a child, before he'd realized what he was.

Would Vylia still want him if he told her the truth of who he really was, and everything he had done?

His elation crashed back down to reality like Vylia's flows of water crashing down from the surface.

She must have seen it in his face. "What's wrong?" Her waters quieted.

"I'm not what you think I am," Sousuke murmured. Admitting it all would be agonizing, but he couldn't live in the shadows any longer, no matter what came of it. "I'm not even human."

Vylia's blue gaze intensified as she studied him. She was so small in his arms. So fragile.

He wanted her more than ever in that moment, right before she would reject him. Not to control or consume her, but to cherish. He couldn't trust any other man to treat her properly. But he couldn't be protective of a love that wasn't his to keep.

It felt like someone had reached into his chest and clenched a fist around his heart. Because if he told her the truth, he would lose her, and it could put his people in danger. But was she dangerous anymore? Had she ever been?

Zeph . . . the emperor . . . was their mutual enemy now.

Vylia touched his chin and gently turned his face to hers. "What are you, then?"

Sousuke swallowed hard. "I am the spawn of a devil," he forced out. "My father is pure evil. And, many generations ago . . ." He closed his eyes, unable to meet her gaze any longer. "I am descended from Lillian and Felix as well."

He felt Vylia tense. "Then . . . you truly are one of the Lotusfall. A *ko'yeth*."

It was his turn to be surprised. His eyes flew open. "I think I forgot how much I've already told you."

"Yes, you told me a lot when you thought you were going to die in Sekoiako. I nearly expired from the anxiety." She gave him a disciplinary look that reminded him of his mother. "But I already knew more than you thought I did. The Lotusfall are the sharpest thorn in my father's side. An eternal enemy of the empire, it seems. Great effort has been put forth into studying you. Trying to extract your weaknesses."

Of course. He should have known.

"It was never my mission to harm you, Your Hi—Vy. Only to observe within the palace. And to discern if the rumors about you were true."

Vylia's dark brows lifted. "Rumors?"

"That you weren't like your father. That you were compassionate. And that you weren't groomed for leadership and tyranny like your older brother," Sousuke said. "To determine if you'd make an empress whom we could support."

"I'll never be empress!" Vylia scoffed. "Did the Lotusfall intend to murder my father and brother?"

Sousuke glanced back up the stairs, hoping for Ryon, Kira, and Tekkyn to provide him an escape from this conversation. But he'd have to have it eventually regardless.

"I'm afraid I have some grim news," he said in a low tone. "Your father was already murdered years ago."

Vylia stared blankly. "I saw him just before we boarded the ship for the Sea of Bones."

"My father murdered both of your parents when you were about eight years old," Sousuke said as gently as he knew how, but knowing he was about as soft as a chunk of shale. "The man you call 'father' now is actually my father. A *trai'yeth* called Zeph. He took your father's form and stole the throne." He felt a chill from the drenching Vylia had given him and the cool temperature beneath the earth. "And I can't believe we didn't realize it."

"The eyes," Vylia muttered.

"What?"

"My father's eyes," she repeated as her own eyes misted with tears. "I always knew he was different after my mother died. I just thought he was overcome with grief. But his eyes . . . They changed color, and sometimes his pupils looked . . . wrong. Very strange." She swiped at her lashes that were beaded with water. "Once, when I was very young, I snuck into his chambers. His eyes looked red with no pupils at all. Like a demon. I was so frightened I couldn't breathe. Thank the tails he didn't see me."

Sousuke listened, unmoving, even though his arms were beginning to burn. "I'm so sorry," he whispered.

"Do you think he would have killed me and my brother too, if we knew?" Vylia met his gaze with mutual sorrow. "Is he Lotusfall . . . ?"

"No," Sousuke growled. "Zeph attacked my mother. He is my true father's worst enemy." Could he trust her enough to tell her names? Yes. "Tameru is my true father. The *trai'yeth* who raised me and forged me into a man. The leader of the Lotusfall, alongside my mother, Rhu Hana. But please never tell anyone."

"I won't," Vylia said. "You said you are *ko'yeth,* not second generation *trai'yeth,* so you must have some human blood . . . ?"

"Yes. There are humans among the Lotusfall and my ancestors on my mother's side." Sousuke glanced over his shoulder up the staircase, but the only things descending were spilling water and rays of light. "But I have more elemental blood than most. So I owe you an apology. Because I should have had the power to use my element and save us when Sa'alu besieged us in the carriage." His throat felt tight, but he pressed on. "But my element is from Zeph: Terruth. And I was so ashamed of it—I hated it so much and lived in defiance of it. I had locked it away so deeply that I didn't even consider using it at that time, and I'd drained myself of syn, so I had little ability to use it in an emergency. Like a fool. So everything that's happened since then is my fault, because I could have stopped it. I'm so sorry." He bowed his head and closed his eyes. "I beg your forgiveness, but I understand if you—"

"You didn't do this." Vylia's hand rested lightly on his cheek. "I forgive you if that's what you want, but this is not your fault. Look at me."

Reluctantly, he met her gaze.

"Zeph didn't create the Terruth element. And he didn't create you. Evil cannot create anything. You were created by Aeo and given that power."

Sousuke felt his ears flush. But the oaths he'd just made, to keep her safe . . . He *was* Zeph's heir now.

Shame smothered him. He couldn't tell her.

"Don't argue with me."

Sousuke jerked back. "I didn't—"

"You were arguing without words," Vylia snipped. "You are responsible only for what you do, not for anything your father has done. Only you can choose what kind of person you become. And you have become a very good one."

This woman. This naïve, snooty, enrapturing young woman in his arms.

Sousuke shook his head and clicked his tongue. "It sounds like your opinion of me hasn't changed. Unwise."

"Rude!" Vylia harrumphed. "Obviously I will have to get to know you better. But so far, your manners are your greatest detriment."

Sousuke carefully let Vylia's legs down on his lap to free his right arm. "I have many other detriments. Like the oath I made to serve the emperor when I entered the imperial military. Not knowing it was Zeph."

Vylia gave a little gasp. "Do you have enough elemental blood to be subject to the Three Fractures? Surely you can't actually die of a broken heart or a broken oath!"

Sousuke pinched the bridge of his nose. "Hope not. Not keen on testing it out."

Vylia wore an enormous frown and her brows knitted together. "Does Zeph even realize it, though? And would he take advant—"

Something crashed down from above, eliciting a cry from Vylia. Sousuke looked and realized it was a body that had fallen down through the hole and landed atop the pile of bones. He shielded Vylia from the gruesome spectacle and the few that followed.

"May I set you down? I need to concentrate to bury them. And I should probably stop this flooding." The water level had already risen to the step his feet were on.

Vylia nodded and braced herself, bravely facing the pain he saw on her face as he carefully set her on higher steps. "You can stop the flooding?"

"I can try." Sousuke lifted his voice and yelled, "Bring my pack down, please!"

The tone of the responding "Oh!" made him chuckle—they must have thought he was either a dragon or naked down here. He wouldn't mention that he'd stolen some clothing from one of the recently deceased.

Sousuke closed his eyes and reached out with his senses. He could feel the earth in every direction except . . . That one. He could barely make out a stone doorway in the darkness.

"What's wrong?" Vylia asked.

"I can't sense any stone there, and yet I can see it. It's like it doesn't exist."

"Lillian must have crafted her vault from that metal that's immune to the Terruth element due to its organic nature. What was it called . . . ?" Vylia snapped her fingers. "Ironwood!"

Sousuke glanced at her sidelong. "You sure know a lot."

She shrugged. "Not much else to do but scour the library when you're trapped in a palace your whole life."

Sousuke returned his focus to the earth. Punctured deep holes into the cavern floor, draining the water. Then he slowly pushed the earth downward beneath the pit, sending the decaying pile further into the depths. Raising his arms, he summoned earth up and around, creating a burial mound as respectfully as he could.

"Rest in peace," Vylia said quietly behind him.

"Whoa!" came Tekkyn's voice from above. "What in Alani? Were you causin' those tremors? As if these stairs weren't a deathtrap already!"

"I'll dry them as we go down," Ryon said, his hand stretched out toward the top steps.

"Hold a moment," Sousuke called. "Let me try and stop the flooding." He pushed up against the upper edges of the pit, forming a ring around the circle except for where the stairs were. The waterfall reduced to trickles.

"Incredible," Vylia breathed. "What other tricks do you have lying around?"

Sousuke smirked over his shoulder. "How do you feel about dragons?"

40

BROOKE

The Darkwood seat of power didn't look anything like the courtroom in Jadenvive. Instead of strong walls and tall doors, this was open air on every side, with the strength displayed in the stump as its foundation. Instead of the chairs fashioned by Katrosi artisans, rows of seating had been carved into the wood of the stump itself, as if the onlookers also had a fundamental role to play in the dealings of justice. And instead of a judge and jury, only King Raven Eye sat before them on a high seat.

"Brooke of House Stillwind of Jadenvive," the king's voice boomed. "You are accused of breaking your marriage alliance with the Darkwood by marrying another. You may now speak in your defense."

Brooke was thankful for her political training, which helped to keep her face straight as she stared up at the king's muscled physique, accented by black body paint and crown adorned with feathers. Though not as dramatically painted or feathered as the princes, he was somehow more intimidating. And larger.

You've got this, Lysander thought-spoke to her.

She glanced at him with appreciation as he stood next to her, with both of their bound wrists tied to a hitching post like a saddled xavi.

"Your Highness," Brooke said in her loudest voice. "I deeply regret what has transpired. I was faithful to Red Heron until he attacked me. I called out for help, and my guards retaliated with deadly force—"

Outcries of rage erupted from the crowd, but the king silenced them with a slight movement of his hand. "You could have married another of my sons after Heron's death," he said, "and honored our agreement."

Brooke bowed her head. "Unfortunately, soon after, I learned that I had been removed as chief. Thus my position, which was favorable to you for a marriage alliance, was lost. This is why I chose to marry another. I apologize for not communicating with you, and I mean no disrespect. My most desperate hope is that I have not damaged relations between our two peoples. But I humbly accept any judgment to atone for my actions."

Over my dead body, Lysander thought.

Steady, Brooke said. *Respect.*

Lysander somehow sent a sound like a defiant snort through her mind.

King Raven Eye stroked his long, dark beard. "Lysander of Quin'Zamar, firstborn of King Brynn. You are accused of murder. You may now speak in your defense."

"Quin'Alor," Lysander said.

The king stared at him in silence.

He said Quin'Zamar, right? His lips looked like 'Zamar.'

Brooke cringed. *Sander!*

"Your son was drunkenly assaulting her. I—"

The crowd roared again, even louder. Raven Eye silenced them again.

Lysander didn't hide his agitation with creased brows and clenched fists. "I was her guard. She screamed for help. I helped her by ending him."

Hisses like a brood of snakes sounded from the people. Lysander raised his voice and continued. "I did my job by protecting her. And I don't regret it."

The hisses became a roar.

"Silence," the king said, and even as Brooke wondered how anyone had heard him, the crowd quieted.

He motioned to a guard on Brooke's left. "Untie her and bring her before me."

"Don't touch her!" Lysander snarled and yanked against his restraints.

Lysander, please! Brooke sent her aether with more force than usual. *Peace!*

He growled but stilled as the guard untied her wrists from the hitching post and guided her toward the seat of power.

Brooke's pulse pounded faster than the never-ending drumbeat in the distance. She watched each stair as she ascended and stopped before the king, keeping her gaze low. Fires of incense smoldered on either side, smelling of tree sap and amber crystals that flickered within the flames.

"Look at me, Katrosi."

Brooke met his black gaze.

"Do you know why I am called Raven Eye?"

"Because you know thought-speak, just as I do."

The king rested his elbow on the chair, and his chin on his fist. "Are you willing?"

"Yes." Brooke closed her eyes and took a deep breath. How many times would she have to relive that most desecrating, horrifying event? And in such a raw, humiliating way to men she barely knew, who had no right to her innermost thoughts and feelings.

But she'd do it again for Lysander, who seemed determined to achieve the worst possible punishment for himself.

Brooke looked up at the king, and his eyes seemed to spiral outward toward her and suck her into an inky abyss. She showed him everything, not withholding one sliver of the terror or disgust or rage woven through her memories.

Then, mercifully, Raven Eye retreated from her mind, and her awareness returned to the physical plane.

"I apologize for my son's disgraceful behavior," the king murmured, his gaze unfocused as he stared beyond her. "Beloved wives are never to be treated in this way."

A few gasps were heard from the onlookers. Then, perfect silence, aside from the drums and distant bird calls.

"However, Heron's crime was not punishable by death." The king gestured at Lysander. "Bring him."

Brooke's muscles stiffened, and walking required full concentration as the guard returned her to the hitching post and brought Lysander before Raven Eye.

She barely breathed as the men stared at each other for a minute that dragged on for eternity. *Aeo, hear my prayer. Let not this king's justice, but your justice be done. Help us!*

Finally, the Darkwood king blinked and relaxed, and Lysander shook his head and shuddered.

"Red Heron poisoned this man." Raven Eye's voice was louder now, and deeper. "Out of jealousy, and to prevent him from coming to Brooke's aid." He spat into the fire, causing a sizzle. "Gods forgive me for siring such an entitled disgrace. The heavens show mercy on us, that Red Heron will never inherit my throne."

Brooke felt like she could breathe again as the crowd broke into confused whispers. "Attempted murder is punishable by death. Red Heron's blood is on his own hands." Raven Eye pointed at a young man in the crowd. "Let this be a lesson to you, Running Deer. You are now my heir."

The prince bowed low and smiled at the cheers among the people.

The king turned his attention back to the outsiders. "Brooke and Lysander. You are pardoned of all crimes. This trial is concluded."

Brooke felt her hands shake as they were unbound. Lysander took her in a firm embrace and held tight. She squeezed her eyes shut and whispered prayers of praise and gratitude.

"You are free to leave, or stay as honored guests." The king's voice was much closer now.

Brooke turned to find that he'd descended and approached them. She bowed. "Thank you, Your Highness. I—"

"Am I to be removed as queen mother because my son was murdered?"

Brooke turned toward the scratchy voice. A short woman dressed in dark robes glared up at the king.

"Yes, effective immediately." Raven Eye lifted his jaw toward a woman in a white dress among the princes and raised his voice. "Queen White Cloud! You did a much better job raising our sons, my love. You are to be commended. And you now have the title of Queen Mother."

"Savage," the short woman muttered.

"This is your final warning." The king glared at her. "One more report, and I will have you exiled. Do you hear me?"

"Quite clearly, my king." She turned to Lysander and abruptly smiled. "The Slain Prince." She reached a finger toward him. "May I touch you?"

"No," Lysander said flatly.

"Very well," the woman said as the king gave her a pointed sidelong glance, then turned to his people and their pressing questions.

"Regardless . . ." The woman didn't lower her finger, but used it to trace Lysander's form, as if she were drawing him into the air. "I can see my work in you has completed." She grew a yellowing grin. "Quite nicely."

Unnerved, Brooke took a step back and between the woman and Lysander. "Who are you?" she asked. She'd seen Queen Hidden Xavi before, but this shriveled husk of a woman looked nothing like the former glorious queen. Had she ruined herself with drink?

With a disappointed purse of her lips, the woman broke her admiring gaze on Lysander and focused on Brooke. "I am the first love of the King, the first of his queens, and mother of his firstborn. Tell me, why do your people call you The Jade Witch?"

Brooke jerked back at the random question. "I . . . suppose people fear my aether gift. It was created as a political weapon against me during an election, and I chose not to fight it in order to strike fear into my enemies."

"Ha!" Hidden Xavi's laugh sounded more like a scoff. "No witch uses the powers of light. You must have no true witches among your people." Her eyes picked Brooke apart from head to toe and clearly found her lacking. "Weak."

Still reeling from the change in conversation, and feeling emotional whiplash from dread to relief to confusion, Brooke simply asked, "What is a true witch, then?"

That yellow smile appeared again. "I think you know, dear girl." She turned to leave.

"Wait, please," Brooke called. "What did you mean about your work in him being completed?"

Hidden Xavi turned back, bent and whispering. "Curses are my breath, suffering my bread, tears my drink. I speak with the dark ones, and they heed."

Brooke took a step back and bumped into Lysander. "I have never had any business with you, witch, nor would I ever," he said.

The former queen cackled. "Be grateful that I am satisfied in the completion of your suffering, slave. My three curses upon you and your loved ones have already been fulfilled."

Brooke's hand itched for her spear. Not only did her eyes and ears tell her there was something wrong about this creature, but something deep in her spirit urged her to either run or fight.

"What curses?" Brooke demanded.

The witch glanced toward the king, who had been swept away by his people, then lurched forward until she was uncomfortably close. "Many years ago, I had a premonition that my son would be murdered. I placed three curses on his killer: that his first lover would be slaughtered, that his firstborn would be lost and orphaned, and that he would never hear words of true love spoken." She smiled wide. "I see they have all manifested beautifully. And because your suffering is satisfying to me, I will allow you to live."

Brooke listened with disquiet, then watched Lysander's pale face drain of color. "That's not true; they can't all have been completed." His voice betrayed his mortification. "I've never fathered a child."

The witch threw her head back and laughed.

Brooke's stomach sank inside her as if it had turned to stone. She knew about Lysander's first love, Selene, whom Zamara had slain while pressuring Lysander to abdicate the Emberhawk throne. And not hearing words of true love . . . what a cruel interpretation and implementation. But it didn't make any sense.

"How could you have . . ." Brooke struggled with her phrasing. "It was Zamara who took his hearing and his first love, not you. Curses aren't real."

"What an amusing, ignorant fool you are," the witch said. "Tell me, my daughter-in-law who was not to be: how did your grandfather die?"

41

KIRALAU

Kira watched her husband dry the last step with warmth from his outstretched hand, no less fascinated than when he'd dried the first, though more impatient. She could finally see the door to the vault. The false godess's vault, filled with ancient treasures. Or perhaps just traps and lies.

"Sa'alu . . . he's really dead, right? You made sure?" Kira whispered to Ryon, as if the ghosts might eavesdrop. She felt uncomfortable asking such a morbid question. But the closure felt too good to be true.

"Double sure," Ryon said in a low tone as he dried the next step.

"Triple sure," Tekkyn said.

Kira could scarcely believe it. They'd done it! And with minimal damage! "How's your leg on these steps?"

"Fine." Though Tekkyn was behind Kira, she could hear a grimace in his voice. "Just need to get it treated proper before too long. I bet I could get a dozen infections from that swamp water."

Kira never wanted to see another infection again. "Let's not spend long here."

"Just long enough to satisfy curiosity," Tekkyn said.

"Are you okay with that, *balemba?*" Ryon asked as he continued his work.

Kira squinted, trying to get a clearer view of the bottom of the pit through the darkness. "We shouldn't push our luck. I'm just so relieved." She leaned closer to his back, matching his height as he was one step lower. "That really put everything into perspective. I'm sorry for acting like a brat recently."

"You were right to be worried. It was a dangerous mission." Ryon smirked at her over his shoulder. "But I've had worse."

Kira's heart fluttered, and she clutched the strange glowing thing that Ryon said was filled with Phoeran energy—Felix had called it a battery—to her chest. "Not anymore!"

Ryon chuckled as he took a step down. "Yes, ma'am."

"Yeesh, Frizz. What happened to my lil' sis with the adventurous spirit? The one we couldn't keep from runnin' off into the Gnarled Wood." Tekkyn hopped down, skipping several steps and squishing mud beneath his boots. "Marriage ruin you already?"

Kira stopped short and straightened indignantly. "I haven't lost my sense of fun. I just don't want to do anything stupid."

"Wouldn't it be stupid to come all the way here and not take a peek inside?" Tekkyn smirked up at her with a raised brow.

Kira pursed her lips. "There could be booby traps." The device she hugged to her chest could give its energy to any number of horrific ancient contraptions.

"Hmm." Tekkyn rubbed his beard. "If only we had a master trapper in this group . . ."

Kira's tight lips pulled into a grin. Well, when he put it that way . . .

"Don't worry, *balemba,*" Ryon said with a reassuring smile. "If we can figure out a way in, and if you want to go in, we'll just be careful, yeah?"

Kira released her tension in a breath and nodded as they reached the wet earth below. She nearly slipped as she passed Sousuke with his unsettling eyes, with Vylia at his side. For some reason, they were both drenched, and they stood very close to each other.

The princess smiled with a tired but loving expression. "Thank you for coming after me, Kiralau. I cannot express how grateful I am."

Kira moved the battery to her side to free one hand to clutch Vylia's with the other. "I'm so glad you're safe."

Vylia nodded with tears brimming. "The creator is very good to us."

Indeed he was, Kira thought. After all her worries, here they all were, together and safe. Albeit exhausted and hungry and desperately in need of shelter and hygiene. Necessities easily obtained in Ashena. Perhaps they could stay and rest for a few days before returning home.

Home. Whether that would be Odae's ranch, or Quin'Alor, or their new land on the border, Kira flooded with excitement at the good work ahead of them. Making a home together with the man she loved. She couldn't imagine anything more fulfilling than that new adventure.

"Give me a moment to change." Sousuke had taken his pack from Ryon, and with an unsettling shifting of earth, stepped into a small room that suddenly emerged in the side of the cavern and closed behind him.

Kira stared speechless, then looked at Vylia, who swooned after him, looking like a smitten girl half her age.

"Yup, there's another slot here." Tekkyn was standing before the stone door in the darkness. He reached an open hand out toward the battery in Kira's grip. She hurried to oblige.

Tekkyn placed the battery into a nook that Kira couldn't see with a *shunk*. Bluish white lights sprang to life all over the door, decorating it with an incomplete pattern lost to the ages. Five circles were illuminated: one in the center and four surrounding like a diamond. Two of the surrounding four had been severely damaged, and quite recently by the clean look of the stone.

Kira breathed in awe. The unnatural lights reminded her of the luminescent mushrooms of the root tunnels between Jadenvive. How had someone crafted these? Perhaps ancient schematics existed somewhere that she could read obsessively by candles at midnight. Her mother couldn't scold her for that anymore.

"It's damaged," Vylia observed. "Surely Lillian was trying to get in." Suddenly her face drained of color. "Where is Lillian's stone?"

"In my pocket," Kira said, "subdued by glass-gold."

Vylia visibly relaxed. She nodded, then brightened as Sousuke appeared at her side, wearing his own clothes and equipment once again, along with that eerie spirit blade's sheath that hung from his belt.

"We don't have to do anything else," Ryon said. "Felix only wanted us to get the dreamcatcher to prevent Lillian from getting it. And she can't get it now, yeah?"

"Yeah," Kira agreed with satisfaction. They'd defeated Lillian and her ilk, avenged Lee, saved Vylia, and acquired the stolen aether stone. Resounding success, and without any critical injuries. Time to claim victory and return home.

Insatiably curious about this surreal technology, Kira stepped closer to the door and ran her fingers along the lines of light.

"But we don't have the fourth cypher," Sousuke said. "We could go to Ashena or My'Eyah and search for my father and sister. They might be on their way here with it."

"It might be too damaged regardless," Vylia said. "That one's just an empty hole. Was Lillian trying to erode it away to force the door open?"

"Must have been water pressure alone," Sousuke said. "I can't even sense this ironwood."

Tekkyn stepped up beside Kira. "Worth a shot, anyhow. Hand me one of them key things."

Ryon dug in his pack and offered small chests to both Tekkyn and Kira. Then he stepped forward with his open palm. "Which one goes where?" He pointed at symbols above the two undamaged outer circles, and the center one.

"It's the Ancient language." Vylia pointed to the battery. "That says, 'generosity.' The center circle says, 'love.' The top one has a meaning like 'attraction' or 'feeling' and the other says, 'freedom.' The other two are too damaged to read."

Kira looked at the symbol on Ryon's palm. It didn't match any of the markings on the wall—perhaps it matched one that had been eroded. But the chest she held must have been "feeling" while Tekkyn's looked like "freedom."

"Doesn't sound like true love to me," Kira muttered as she went up on tiptoes to put her cypher chest next to its symbol.

The strange lights nearby turned green.

Kira gasped and jerked her hand away, then hesitantly back again. The light returned to blue, then faded into aquamarine, and finally green again.

Tekkyn followed suit and was rewarded with the same effect.

Ryon placed his hand by one of the damaged circles—the one that

Lillian had apparently hollowed out. Nothing happened.

He tried the other one.

All of the lights turned green and the cavern quivered. They all stumbled back as the door rumbled and sank into the earth, opening to welcome them.

Elation and trepidation clashed inside Kira as everything stilled. No one moved.

The room beyond was bright enough to make her squint. Clean, carved pillars stretching from smooth floor to tall ceiling. Walls adorned with faded paintings and the most smooth, realistic sculptures of sirens Kira had ever seen. Scandalous sirens. Kira ensured Ryon's gaze didn't linger on them.

Tekkyn stepped forward to enter.

Kira grabbed his arm. "Wait! It could be dangerous." She felt stupid saying it. What lay beyond looked more like a palace ballroom than a dungeon.

"I didn't hear Felix have thoughts about anything dangerous," Sousuke said. "But there are puzzles, mazes, riddles—things like that."

"Legend holds that it was a sort of proving ground for Lillian's priestesses before Felix stole the cyphers." Vylia pointed to a large inscription on the back wall. "I'm not certain, but I believe that says something to the effect of, 'Only the most loyal—or dedicated?—will prevail.'"

"We should go to Ashena and rest," Kira said. "I know what Dad would say: the nest of a tyrant can hold nothing good."

"What about somethin' that could help us win the war?" Tekkyn stepped inside.

Kira bit her lip and looked at Ryon. He shrugged. "Your decision, *balemba.*"

She watched Tekkyn stride forward into the vault. Nothing touched him except the bright glow, highlighting his algae-encrusted pants and other muck he must have intentionally slathered himself with for camouflage in the bog.

Nothing jumped out at him. The door didn't slam shut behind him. No spikes or flying bolts or sliding floors or anything else Kira's imagination conjured.

Tekkyn made it to the other side of the room and stopped, resting his hands on his hips before the next door.

Kira couldn't deny her curiosity. And Tekkyn was right: surely there would be something useful inside. They'd come all this way . . . If she didn't discover what was inside, she'd regret and wonder for the rest of her life.

She hesitantly stepped inside. And the others followed.

"Six colors," Tekkyn mused aloud as he pointed to gemstones of different colors on the wall above the distant door that curved into the ceiling. "But ain't there one missin' if it's supposed to be a rainbow? There should be seven, right?"

Kira hurried to join him, her footsteps clacking and muddying the wavelike pattern in the floor. "Indigo. It's missing."

"There's no doorknob," Tekkyn observed.

"It says, 'beauty.'" Vylia held her back and winced. "The first puzzle already?"

No way could Kira reach high enough to touch those gems. Nor were there any sort of ladder or stairs in this room.

"Look." Ryon was turned around toward the entrance, staring at a white beam of light from an emitter over the vault door, high overhead. He pointed, drawing his finger along the beam until it hit the gems on the far side of the room. "Maybe we need to refract it somehow. Look for a piece of glass."

Giddy with the thrill of adventure, Kira searched the room for any kind of glass or gem they could use. But they found nothing.

"What if *we* are supposed to be the glass?" Kira wondered. "Can you use Phoera to refract the light? Like your sky paint?"

Ryon's silver brows lifted. "Well . . . maybe. But Malaano priestesses wouldn't have had Phoera."

"This vault was built when Felix was Lillian's mate," Vylia said. "It's worth a try."

Ryon grunted, took a deep breath, and studied the beam's trajectory. Finally satisfied with the correct position to orient himself, he sat down cross-legged and stared up at the beam.

Kira bounced on her toes as she waited. And waited. And watched different colors of light slowly dance across the walls.

Orange slowly split into red and yellow. Indigo split into blue and violet. But as soon as Ryon had the correct colors on one side of the spectrum aligned with their gems, he'd lose his focus on the opposite colors.

After several minutes, the beam returned to white. Ryon breathed as if he'd been running. "I don't think . . . a single person can do the whole spectrum alone. Warm colors and cool colors are different kinds of energy. Maybe if Lysander were here."

"You can do it!" Kira said. "Your sky paint had many colors."

"Yeah, but they didn't all have to be controlled and put in specific places at the same time," Ryon grumbled.

Kira wrapped her arms around his shoulders and kissed his temple. "I believe in you."

Ryon rolled his eyes but grinned. "If I can't figure this out soon, I'm going to Ashena to find some steak."

Tekkyn snorted. "No good beef in these swamp lands."

"Any meat will do," Ryon growled as he looked back up at the beams.

The colors began splaying outward again, swaying like an aurora.

Kira sat down and tucked her hands under her legs to prevent her nervous energy from disrupting her husband. She watched the lights dance and tried to force herself to relax.

She noticed Sousuke looking back at the entrance. He was too still. Too rigid, even for a soldier. Kira followed his gaze.

A pair of glowing red eyes watched them through the open door.

Kira's blood ran cold.

A loud grating noise sounded from the opposite side of the room, and Kira whirled to see the closed door slide upward. Another room was illuminated beyond.

Tick tick tick tick thunk. The door fell down a few inches from the top and stopped. *Tick tick tick—*

"A timer? It's gonna lock us in." Tekkyn backed up. "No, thanks."

"Go," Sousuke said. "Everyone in."

Kira looked back, searching for the red eyes. They were gone.

Tick tick tick tick thunk.

Vylia ran through the slowly closing door. Kira swayed after her, refusing to take her eyes off the entrance again. She *knew* she'd seen them.

"What is it?" Ryon asked.

"In?" Kira blurted. "D-do you mean out?"

Tick tick tick tick thunk.

"In!" Sousuke shouted.

Kira turned and ran after Vylia. Tekkyn and Ryon followed, with Sousuke taking up the rear of the group.

The new room was far less decorated, with only symbols in a hexagonal pattern across the floor, except for a plain section on which they stood. Another door stood open on the far side.

THUNK. The door behind them slammed shut.

Dread blanketed Kira. Why had they entered this death trap in the first place? They should have gone to Ashena!

But would the red eyes have followed them there, too?

"What was that?" Kira asked, fear making her voice quiver.

Sousuke met her gaze with silent solidarity. "Zeph."

"The one who nearly killed you?" Ryon made that sound more like a statement than a question.

Sousuke nodded, his face drawn. "Those red eyes were his, watching us from the entrance."

"What? Is this Zeph a demon or something?" Tekkyn huffed.

"Worse," Sousuke said.

"You said Zeph is a Terruthian elemental?" Vylia said. "We're underground—he can crush us!"

"No." Sousuke knocked on the door that had slammed shut behind them. "Now we're surrounded by ironwood. Organic stone—we can't manipulate or even sense it. So we're safe now."

Tekkyn scratched the back of his head and flicked a patch of algae away. "Well, now we're trapped in here. With limited food and water. Is it a patient demon?"

"We can continue and open the treasure chamber." Sousuke gestured toward the distant open doorway. "Then we'll have something to offer him."

"Can he be negotiated with?" Ryon asked in a deep and quiet voice.

"Yes, he will negotiate with me. He's already made an oath to me that he will never let any harm befall Vylia," Sousuke said.

Kira watched Sousuke with suspicion. What on Alani had he offered to make that deal?

In that moment, she realized how little she knew Sousuke. She sidled up next to Ryon and gripped the hilt of her d'hakka stinger dagger. "So you chose to trap us in here rather than to face him or make a break for it?"

"There is no running from him, and no survival if we face him," Sousuke said with a dark shadow across his face. "Look, I don't like it, either. But by the time I sensed him, it was already too late. At least this way, we can get the treasure and make a deal with him. It's the only way I've survived."

Kira rubbed her thumb into her dagger and snorted. "I don't make deals with devils."

Sousuke's gaze sharpened, but something else passed behind his green eyes. Something sorrowful, perhaps? Regret?

"He is more powerful than you comprehend," Sousuke said. "Tread carefully and let me do the talking. We will avoid hostilities with him at all costs. Trust me, and we might possibly survive."

"*Aish.*" Ryon put his arm around Kira, interrupting her torrent of negative emotions directed at Sousuke. At herself. At this entire situation. "Well then, let's find this treasure. Not much choice now." He gave her a hopeful smile that melted a fraction of her anxiety. "I hope whatever's in this stupid vault is worth my headache."

42

VYLIA

Vylia knew nothing about Zeph aside from what she'd been told, but the looks on Sousuke and Kira's faces told her much more. She'd never seen Sousuke look frightened at all before. Seeing his eyes go wide and the sweat beading his forehead . . . It shook her.

But Sousuke had said Zeph wouldn't harm her. She didn't know what to think about that. The elemental who'd murdered her parents, *protecting* her? She didn't want that. Not at all. Especially if no one else was safe.

"What is all this?" Tekkyn gestured at the symbols on the floor. One looked like sugar cane or bamboo, another like a fish with circles next to it, and yet another like some kind of fruit. Dozens of illustrations carved into stone, each on its own hexagon as large as a watermelon.

Ryon nudged a clam symbol with his foot, and it immediately plummeted downward. Kira grabbed him and pulled him back, though he clearly hadn't put his weight on it.

"These are all kinds of foods and crops," Vylia realized. "Foraging, hunting, farming, fishing . . . medicinal herbs and luxuries, too. The fruits of Malaan Island."

Ryon chuckled and kissed Kira's forehead as he escaped her grasp and returned to the first row of hexagons. "I guess they need to go in a certain order."

Kira looked as petrified as Sousuke did. Vylia decided to avoid eye contact with her, lest she lose her own nerve.

She studied the symbols. That one could mean fish eggs. That one was obviously a coconut. What was that one supposed to be? Oh, but that one must be dewflower. And honey vine!

"They're in order of their harvest season," Vylia mused aloud. "First harvest of the year would be . . ." She pointed to the fish with three dots beside it. "Tuna roe. They mate and lay their eggs in massive bunches in the coastal coral in the first month."

Tekkyn stepped toward it, but Sousuke caught his arm. "Let me. I'm less likely to die if something goes wrong."

That didn't make Vylia feel any better. "What's that supposed to mean?"

Sousuke paused before the symbol and looked down at her. "I can heal myself by transforming. And wings might prove useful."

She blinked at him. "What can you transform into?"

He seemed uncomfortable. "At the moment, a bird, a hound, or a wyvern."

Why had he said that like a menu she could order from? "A dragon?" Vylia exclaimed, astonished.

Sousuke's green eyes studied her reaction as if searching for approval or disappointment. "Do you remember the wyvern that Ryon and Kira flew in on?"

Vylia's jaw dropped open. Surely not . . . Is that what he'd meant by a dragon trick up his sleeve? She thought he'd been joking again! She wasn't used to him making jokes.

He wasn't kidding about not being human.

"I was the dragon. You saved me from Lillian when she was drowning me," Sousuke continued. "But when she conjured that massive wave toward you, I caught you and we both fell through the membrane, breaking it, and so we fell into the pit." Sousuke glanced at his feet. "I guess my scales weren't a very soft landing, though . . ."

Suddenly everything made sense, and Vylia felt silly for not assembling the pieces before. She thought she'd had another fadeleaf dream. But now the truth was stranger.

Tekkyn sidestepped around Sousuke and stomped on the fish tile.

It remained solid.

"Which one's next?" Tekkyn asked.

Vylia shook her head as if to clear it and moved to examine her options on the second row of the hexagon pattern. "Umm . . . I don't recognize that one . . . I'm not sure. And I think that's the legendary clearnettle, but it hasn't been found for a century."

"I—" Kira's voice faltered. She cleared her throat and tried again. "I brought some scrolls from the library. Maybe one of them could help." She flipped her pack to the ground, pulled out a scroll, and unfurled a wet, inky mess. Her eyes went as wide as the second moon.

Tekkyn nudged another one with his boot. It dropped with a resounding clang.

"Don't do that!" Kira squawked.

"Try that one." Vylia pointed to a flower that looked like a lotus.

Sousuke tapped Tekkyn on the shoulder, who begrudgingly gave up his position in front. Sousuke stepped on the lotus, and it remained solid.

Feeling quite proud of herself and the trivia from palace histories she'd once thought useless, Vylia successfully guessed the next several rows, from starspice to purple root to chortlegrain.

"Is that supposed to be slippery elm?" Kira called from her position in the growing line behind Sousuke and Vylia that marked the pattern of seasonal harvest. "That's not unique to Malaan Island. We've got a couple of those at the ranch!"

"It seems Lillian wanted to take credit for all of the harvests, regardless," Vylia contemplated. "She was said to have brought the rains consistently, ensuring bountiful harvests year after year, and warding away dangerous storms. It's one of the reasons why Malaan grew into such a powerful empire: the ideal fertility of the land supported a massive population." She turned back to Kira behind her. "Are you certain Lillian is subdued?" She just had to ask again. To confirm.

Kira patted one of her pockets. "Yes. I secured glass-gold to the Malo stone. Otherwise she would have definitely killed us back there."

Vylia nodded and focused on the next line. They were almost to the other side, and with only a few holes in the floor. Cassava, seablossom, pineapple, and java bean, and they were close enough to the next open door for Sousuke to jump and skip the last row. He held out a hand to Vylia with the slightest grin that melted her heart.

She jumped and he caught her, though the aid was unnecessary. "Well done, Your Vyness."

She scrunched up her nose and smiled at him, not minding the closeness at all.

Although the dragon thing was odd. She'd need to see a demonstration, later.

"Good job, Princess." Tekkyn was already in the next room. "Now what in the skies is this?"

The smaller room had a closed door on the opposite side. Other than that, there were no markings or decorations at all. Each wall, the floor, and ceiling were completely smooth, flat, and one solid beige color.

It felt . . . unnatural.

"There are markings above the door," Ryon said from the ledge beside the final row of hex symbols. "Looks like . . . 'holiness'? No, 'divinity'? *Aish,* this woman is full of herself."

Kira cringed. "Don't call her a woman. We don't claim her. Call her 'creature' or somethin'."

Vylia chuckled and nodded. She hoped the false goddess could hear them. Lillian must be throwing a tantrum inside her ethereal prison.

Holiness . . . Hmm. What made Lillian holy? Nothing, of course. But this vault seemed to have been designed as an act of worship, and a testing ground to prove her most loyal followers.

Water. Water must be purified until deemed holy. Or at least, that's what the priestesses taught. They would cleanse water in so many different ways—steaming, filtering, crystal vials. Then, maybe . . .

Vylia closed her eyes and reached out with her senses. A reservoir of water sat at knee-height, on the other side of the wall to her left.

Lillian really must be hindered. She'd been blocking Vylia's power for so long that sensing the Malo element again was as refreshing as a gentle song.

Vylia pointed to where she could sense, but not see, the water beyond the wall. "There's something . . ." She called out to the water, and it resonated with her, lifting at her command. Flowed through a pipe that led upward. No, not a pipe. A bumpy pathway . . . an intricate carving through the ironwood. She felt miniature trees, city walls, tiny little houses and a market square. "It's a puzzle inside the walls."

"Huh?" Tekkyn grunted.

"Quiet," Sousuke whispered.

Vylia brought the water further into the carved city. Then through the riverbed that ran under the floor beneath their feet. Up through the jungle, then in the miniature flowing stratus clouds above the ceiling. She marveled at the craftsmanship. How long had this masterwork taken to carve? And to think, no one would ever see it.

But no matter where she led the water, nothing seemed to happen within the vault. The tiny landscape, in its intricate scale, was vast. Where was she supposed to . . . ?

Holiness. Vylia suddenly knew.

She led the water back toward the city, which she now recognized as Maqua, but from ancient times. But the land features were the same. The palace in the same location. The mountains unmoved. And atop them, intersecting the palace, was Lillian's most holy location: the spring, pool, and cascade of Beresai Falls.

The water Vylia led to the representation of the pool trickled down, down, past the floor beneath their feet.

Click.

The door opened to an expansive chamber filled with treasure.

Vylia could scarcely believe her eyes, though they must have been bulging. Her father's treasury—no, Zeph's treasury that he stole from her murdered father—was larger, but filled with more tangible assets such as syn and gold, gems and priceless artwork. This room was filled with the strangest oddities Vylia would scarcely have recognized as valuable.

To their right were two rows of display cases, each holding a single feather upright. To the left, a trident, a quiver full of arrows, a buckler, a beaded necklace, a kris dagger, a pair of shoes, and more weaponry and armor. Straight ahead looked like a junk sale at the market. A vase, a carving of a fierce creature she'd never seen before, a tall sculpture made of seashells, a circle of twigs with a web of threads crisscrossing the center, an oil lamp, a cauldron, a stringed instrument of some kind, a bowl of powder, a waterskin, and was that a birdhouse? Several items were made from angular metal, glass, or both—their function or purpose, Vylia could only guess.

The group wordlessly branched out, exploring the room with whispers of curiosity. As Vylia wondered how dust had not accumulated, she found an enormous bowl filled with silver balls of various sizes. Syn, she assumed—the only item in here that made any sense. Each ball was stamped with a lotus symbol, and their sizes were uniform, from the size of a tree nut to a few so large Vylia was certain she couldn't lift.

Click.

Vylia searched for the origination of the sound, but couldn't find it in the echoing space.

"Oops," Tekkyn said.

"What was that?" Kira demanded.

"Stepped on somethin'. What'd it do?"

They all searched, but could find no change in the room. When Vylia heard no ominous clicking timers or any imminent threats caving in around them, after a few minutes of fruitless searching, she breathed easily again.

Vylia did her best to quiet her disappointment. She had wondered if Lillian had stashed away some aquamarine or jade or pearls. Or at least jasper, topaz, or carnelian . . . Where was all the beauty that Lillian boasted of in the first room with the trial of colorful lights?

"Is this it?" Kira asked, breaking Vylia's internal pouting as she lifted the circle of twigs and threads. "I don't know what the dreamcatcher is supposed to look like, but using the process of elimination . . ."

"Indeed, it is," came a new voice from the doorway.

Vylia whirled and realized what that click had done: the doorway was now open.

A man with red eyes stood behind them with a smirk. The murderer she'd known as father.

43

SOUSUKE

"Ah, finally, something exciting!" Zeph clapped his hands together. "Thank you for opening this for me. I've been curious as to what's inside for a millennia."

Sousuke stepped forward despite his instinct to do the opposite. His training caused his mind to race through their options. But Zeph was standing in the room's only exit.

"We did it on Felix's behalf, not yours," Sousuke said. "What did you do with him?"

"I didn't *kill* him, if that's what you're implying. I'm not as evil as you think I am."

Sousuke glared. "Then what have you done?"

"Now's not the time for such boring chatter." Zeph strode inside and a trail of floating stones followed him. He stopped in front of a display case that held a black, white, and red feather. "Oh, look! Angel feathers from the Serran Wars. Incredible." A stone behind Zeph flattened into a thin disc and lopped the top off of the display case with a screeching crash. Zeph reached in and moved to do the same to the next. "Oooh! This one's from Rigel, the Angel of Death."

Sousuke rounded on him as the door cleared, and Vylia moved to remain behind his back. "Take what you want," Sousuke said. "We're only here for the dreamcatcher."

Zeph's gaze landed on Ryon, who held the dreamcatcher in one hand and a sword in the other. "Now, that's the most valuable thing in this place. Not to you, but to me. Do you know why?"

"It's yours if you let us all leave unharmed," Sousuke said.

"I don't think so," Ryon said.

Sousuke cringed. He gave Ryon a hand signal to stand down, then realized Ryon might have no idea what that Malaano military signal meant. Or maybe he didn't care.

"Such loyalty from Felix's vessel. I'll admit to jealousy." Zeph's stones continued destroying display cases around them as he spoke, and he strode from one to the next, plundering their treasures. "Felix doesn't have any need of the dreamcatcher anymore. You see, the bound aether allows us *trai'yeth* the ability to behold the sage gift. Otherwise, we cannot interact with aether. But you humans can simply find a living sage and receive your fortune."

"You can have everything else in the vault," Ryon said. He handed the dreamcatcher to Kira behind him, sheathed his sword, and drew his bow. "But this is ours."

Sousuke's pulse fluttered. Ryon had no idea what he was negotiating with. Hadn't he seen how mangled Zeph had left him in the cornfield?

Zeph frowned. "Sousuke, retrieve it for me."

Sousuke stared at him in confusion. Did Zeph really think he could order him around? He was delusional.

Something stirred deep in the pit of his stomach. Like nausea. No, like a tightening in his chest. No, he couldn't breathe . . . Dizziness and malaise swayed him. It was the most uncomfortable, ugly wave of sickness he'd ever felt, and it came out of nowhere.

What . . . ?

Zeph was observing him as if he were a pinned insect in one of the display cases. "Sousuke, serve the emperor by retrieving the dreamcatcher and bringing it to me."

It hit him again, strong as the tide. Then he remembered: he'd felt this once before. When he'd woken up in the aether-healer Nariellyn's room in Jadenvive, after Brooke had pulled him from the long sleep. He'd realized that the emperor wanted his daughter dead, and decided to keep his oath to protect her anyway. It was the same feeling then, but this was twice as forceful.

Maybe because the oath he'd made to the emperor upon joining the military had conflicted with his oath to protect Vylia at that time. Now, the command to serve was unadulterated.

Then, was this what a broken oath felt like?

Dread joined the sickening concoction in Sousuke's gut. He stumbled on nothing, somehow, and caught himself. He felt Vylia's hand on his back.

"You are not the true emperor." Sousuke hated the way his voice sounded. He straightened his back and stood tall.

Zeph grew a too-wide smile. "Ah, but I was when you swore into the Imperial Guard. Now, serve." He pointed at Ryon, who had handed the dreamcatcher to Kira. He now had an arrow nocked and aimed at Zeph's chest.

Sousuke gritted his teeth. "I will never serve you."

It hit him like a charging bull to the ribs. He couldn't breathe. His vision swam.

Tekkyn advanced, sword drawn.

Sousuke put his arm out to stop him. "Let me handle this!"

Tekkyn halted and flourished his sword, his eyes glinting blue.

Sousuke called to the collection of syn orbs in the center of the room with his outstretched hand. Slowly they obeyed, floating toward him, then dissolved into silver dust and absorbed into his palm.

Power surged through his veins, deafening the nausea. He called for more.

"You can defy an oath and remain standing? Fascinating. Let's try another." Zeph rolled dice that appeared out of nowhere on one of his flattened stones that floated in mid-air. "Come and stand at my side as my heir."

Absolutely not. He'd made that oath hoping to be the inheritor of Zeph's treasures so the Lotusfall could take advantage of them, not to be his ally.

His internal defiance morphed into a poison that locked his muscles, froze his lungs, stole his vision. He didn't realize he was on his knees until he'd already fallen.

"Sousuke!"

Vylia, behind him. Distantly, he felt her grip on his shoulder.

No, he couldn't let this dominate him. She needed him!

"The power of mortal blood on display." Zeph applauded. "I was right to diversify the blood of my heir, wasn't I? Humans can deceive and rebel without consequence. But how far will your mortality stretch in order to save you?" He put a hand to his mouth in a false gasp. "Oh, dear. You haven't wed this lovely maiden yet, either, have you? Did you fulfill that oath while I was gone? Or do you have no intention of honoring that oath, either?"

Sousuke fell into a suffocating inky blackness. Distantly, he felt himself collapse and hit the floor.

The woman he loved screamed his name. She was above him now, over the well of his tunnel vision. So far away.

Until she slapped him, and everything became clear again.

"You made an oath to marry me, Guard Rhu?" Vylia's eyes sparked with azure fire. He couldn't tell if it was a good fire or a bad fire. Maybe both?

Sousuke searched and found his voice. "So he would . . . spare you. I'm sorry . . ." He sounded horrible. Like he was choking.

Chaos broke out around him. Objects flying, people screaming.

What was happening? Ryon? Tekkyn!

They were fighting.

Falling.

44

KIRALAU

Kira cried out as her brother charged the red-eyed creature, brandishing his sword.

Zeph was killing Sousuke somehow. Obviously Sousuke's negotiations had failed. He couldn't protect them—he couldn't even protect himself.

But Zeph wasn't just a lesser elemental easily slain. What other powers did he have that he was exacting over Sousuke?

And he was standing too close to the room's only exit to grant an easy escape.

In front of her, Ryon raised his bow and aimed. Kira drew her blue dagger and dashed around him, gunning for Zeph's core.

Tekkyn couldn't plunge his sword into Zeph's chest fast enough. Just before he reached him, one of the floating stones Zeph had brought in with him disappeared—no, it *blurred*. Into Tekkyn. And out his back in a spray of blood.

It continued in an arc toward Ryon, who truly did vanish.

Then Ryon reappeared, sprawled across the floor, his bow clattering down beside him. His arrow plinked against the far wall.

Kira tripped and caught herself, recovering halfway to where she'd last commanded her feet to carry her: directly in front of Zeph.

"Do you want to die, too? I don't like to kill women." Soulless scarlet orbs peered down at her. "But if you insist . . ."

Kira's muscles locked up. She tore her eyes from the monster and looked down at her brother at her feet. There was a hole in his chest.

Her breath failed. She dropped her dagger and collapsed at his side.

What should she do? Stop the bleeding. Stop the . . . How?

Tekkyn lifted a large hand and gripped her shaking wrist. He was staring at something beyond her. "Ryon . . ."

Little minnow . . .

Numbly, Kira pushed up on rubbery legs and followed Tekkyn's gaze to the heap that was Ryon.

There was more blood around him. Spilling beneath him like a dropped skin of wine.

Kira's heart seized. The room swayed as she staggered toward her husband.

Ryon stared at Tekkyn, his face ashen. His chest moved, but his breathing didn't sound right. Blood emerged from his lips and slipped down his cheek.

"No!" Kira cried, crashing down at his side and pressing her hands against the wound in his chest.

The wound over his heart.

"I've got you," Kira choked as blood seeped up through her fingers and stained his leathers. "Hang on!"

I can save him if you become my vessel.

Ryon's jittering gaze focused on her. Lost their focus. His lenses had fallen off somewhere.

His lips moved, but no sound came out.

Kira's vision blurred with tears. "Hold on. Don't go. Don't leave me!" What should she do? What *could* she do? "Help!" she screamed.

You must release me now or he will die. Only I can save him.

Ryon reached up and gripped her bloody fingers. His grip tightened. Then weakened.

His gaze went to the ceiling. His labored attempts at breathing slowed. And stopped.

He fell still.

The blood no longer flowed.

45

SOUSUKE

Vylia took up the only clear part of Sousuke's vision. Cradled his face in her hands. "Stay with me."

He was so dizzy. Disoriented. His allies were fighting. Losing. But what could he do? His body was like sludge.

Aeo, help us!

"It's okay," Vylia said. "This is one oath you can keep. There's no one I'd rather marry."

Sousuke tried to focus on her, but her words were nonsense. "You don't even . . . know me." He was falling. Back down the well.

He wasn't the only one on the ground anymore. Shattered glass everywhere.

"I know enough! What do you want, Sousuke?" Vylia was crying now. She shook him. "Do you want me or not?"

"Foolish boy," another voice said. "Just get up and save yourself."

In the corner of his vision, Zeph had the dreamcatcher. What had he done? Bleed him!

Sousuke wasn't in the treasure room anymore. He was in a void. He couldn't breathe.

He reached out for more syn. But where was it? There! He sensed it, urged it toward him, and prayed simultaneously. Just a little more . . . Would he lose his mind? He was already gone.

They were done for. But he would resist until his soul was removed from this realm.

Vylia slapped him again, and the blurry room warbled back into his vision. "Listen to me, soldier! Will you marry me?"

He struggled to stay with her. "Not like this . . . Not under duress," Sousuke fought against his lungs. They had solidified into stone. "Not . . . because of *him*—"

"It's not because of him!" Vylia yelled. "I've favored you for months—years! I choose you! I chose you already! Since before we set sail from Ceemalao. Do you hear me?"

He heard her. But it couldn't be true. "You're just saying that . . . to . . ."

Vylia's tear splashed against his cheek. "Would you rather die than marry me?" Her voice was woven with several different shades of hurt.

No . . . of course not. But it was too good to be true. He wasn't worthy of a princess. Their culture was very clear-cut. The royal House Rhu wasn't even real—it was a façade for the Lotusfall. He had no right to ask for her hand.

But she'd asked for his.

He'd known for years that Vylia looked at him differently. He'd just ignored it, knowing that if anyone found out he was a Lotusfall "traitor," he'd be executed immediately. Vylia had no idea how impossible her youthful infatuation was.

But was it an infatuation if it hadn't stopped for years?

It *was* real. Her eyes told him so. And everything was different now.

He would marry her. And he would be the luckiest man alive. If they lived.

"If you . . . insist," Sousuke said.

Many kinds of relief lighted upon him, and he gulped in a colossal breath. His vision returned to behold Vylia's relieved and joyful face.

She kissed his forehead as he caught his breath, and he revived.

"Amazing the amount of oaths you can defy and still draw breath," Zeph said in a sour tone. "Though it seems your limit is two."

Reality smashed back into Sousuke, ruining his amorphous bliss. He pulled away from Vylia and grasped for whatever was tangible. It still felt like a mule-bear was sitting on his chest. But he could see.

He wished he couldn't.

Tekkyn lay on the floor, unmoving. Ryon also lay nearby, Kira wailing over him.

Blood. So much blood.

"My patience has run out," Zeph said. "Come and stand at my side or die with them."

Sousuke enraged, rolling over and pushing Vylia back, away from the devil. He hauled himself, crawling, to Zeph's side. Feeling another release of a vise around his lungs, his strength returned, and he pushed up to his feet.

"Very good." Zeph's smile grew wide. "Feel better?"

"Much. Now, please save my friends." It took every shred of restraint to remain in control of white-hot anger.

Zeph clicked his tongue. "They attacked me first. And I'm no healer."

"You've been alive longer than any other *trai'yeth*, right? You must know of a way."

Complimenting Zeph tasted like rot on his tongue. But he had to try. Kira's wailing tore at his soul. Vylia moved to Tekkyn with an expression of horror.

"Hmm." Zeph tapped his fingers on his chin. "There is one item in my cache in Malaan. But it's entirely too far away to save them in time. That one may already be dead."

Was that the same cache where Zeph might have stashed Felix, if he truly hadn't killed him? "Tell me, please," Sousuke said. "I already swore an oath to keep your secrets."

Zeph snorted. "And you've just displayed that you can defy oaths and live to brag about it."

Sousuke scrambled for a response, feeling every hair standing on end due to his close proximity to this monster. "I *was* dying. Just not instantly," he said. "Tell me. I am your heir. The family you wanted. Your inheritance. I'm standing at your side, aren't I?"

Zeph *tsked* yet seemed pleased. "Always full of demands. No respect. You'll have to work on that." He watched Tekkyn cough up blood as if he were examining a slug writhing in salt. "Go to the Whistling Night and order a silver wolf on the rocks from Big Jym."

Sousuke blinked. The same tavern one used to contact the Lotusfall, when one ordered a different drink—a fire in the sky?

Zeph's smile elongated as he studied Sousuke's face. "That's right. I know your secrets. How do you think I got to your mother? Be thankful I've showed mercy and haven't obliterated the Lotusfall from within. Yet." His eyes narrowed over his smile. "You are the weapon with which I will finish Tameru. He was a fool to let you live."

Sousuke called an orb of syn. Formed it into a spike.

And stabbed Zeph in his core.

Zeph didn't move. His smile froze, and his red gaze drilled into Sousuke.

The flat surface with the dice atop it floated closer. The dice lifted and dropped. Rolled.

Sousuke thrust the spike in further. Twisted it. He must have hit the core!

"Thank you for the donation," Zeph said. The syn spike dissolved and melted into his chest, sealing up the wound with silver.

Sousuke stumbled back. His hand went for the sword sheath on his belt. But it wasn't his own sword—it was Division, which hadn't killed him, and certainly wouldn't kill Zeph, either.

He reached out for the earth. But they were surrounded by ironwood. And the floating pieces of stone Zeph had brought with him were under his control.

"You have defied me for the last time." Zeph raised his hand, and something clanged against the ceiling. A crack splintered across the ironwood above them. It split again. And again.

"Prove your strength worthy of all my efforts and generosity. Or die, so I can make a new heir of less belligerent stock."

A column of earth crashed through the ceiling, striking Sousuke with shards of ironwood. But he stopped the encroaching stone above. Compacted it into a spear. If *trai'yeth* couldn't be killed with syn, he would try everything else.

Light and water poured down from the hole above. Where was Zeph? Blood dripped into Sousuke's eye, smearing his vision with silvery red.

CRACK. The lights in the vault winked out.

Vylia screamed. Sousuke whirled in her direction and raised the spear, searching for Zeph's chest.

Zeph reappeared in the sunbeam from above, holding Vylia like a shield in front of him. She shouted something indecipherable as chunks of ironwood fell and crashed into the floor, smashing the remaining display cases into fragments of flying light.

Zeph and Vylia shot up through the hole to the surface, a disc of stone beneath their feet. More discs hauled treasures from below up behind them, followed by a stream of syn orbs.

Sousuke rushed to follow, but stopped at a cry from Kira. Tekkyn, Ryon, Kira—they would all die down here. But Vylia—Zeph had sworn an oath not to harm her.

The earth quaked, and the ceiling collapsed.

Sousuke couldn't stop the ironwood debris, but he planted his feet in a wide stance and caught the earth crashing down above them. All of it.

It kept coming down. Slowly. He couldn't lift it. Too much. Way too much . . . It would crush them in slow motion.

Sousuke commanded the rest of the syn that Zeph still pulled, ripping control away, now that he was closer. Silver orbs collided and melted into him. One . . . three . . . seven. As many as he could take without losing his grip on the earth above.

His muscles would tear at the strain. His bones couldn't hold this much weight.

Unless they were made of metal.

Syn imbued him. More power than he'd ever felt before.

The mass of earth halted. Reversed . . . floated upward. At an agonizingly slow pace.

Water poured down from the surface. Flooding around his ankles. His shins.

Tekkyn and Ryon, lying on the ground—they would drown before Sousuke could lift the earth above them.

But he couldn't lift the crumbling mass all the way up to the surface. Even with dangerous levels of syn, even with all of his strength . . . his consciousness began to fade under the strain.

He wanted to pray, but words escaped him. Despair pooled even faster than the rising waters. He knew it, deep in his soul: even if he were strong enough, he couldn't save Ryon or Tekkyn. Their fates were already sealed. This vault would be their tomb.

46

VYLIA

Vylia kicked and clawed until Zeph released her. She landed in the bog waters, which cascaded down into a messy, shuddering chunk of earth and stone that roiled below them like a living cylinder.

Zeph must have cut a circle above the vault's treasure chamber, destabilizing it to tumble down and crush the ironwood below. Curse him!

She couldn't see through the hole Zeph had brought them up through. But she could *feel* it. And the rising waters below.

Vylia closed her eyes. Remembered her training—the technique she'd used to find Uma in the ocean during her final wavesinger trial aboard their ship on the Sea of Bones.

She sensed many objects within the water. Rocks, debris, ruined treasures. Human bodies. Two of them, their shapes unmoving within the flood.

Vylia chose one and commanded the waters to fold around it. Lift it. And draw it up through the hole in the earth.

She opened her eyes. A man's body floated in a bubble of water suspended before her. She directed it to the ground beside her and set him down gently on his back.

It was Tekkyn, broken and bleeding. He coughed up water and gasped shallow, ragged breaths. Then shot her a look of pained gratitude.

"Ryon," he managed.

Vylia sent her water back down into the dark. Refocused. Found Kira clutching Ryon to her chest, holding his head above the waters. Could she hold them both at once? It wouldn't be safe, and the hole could collapse at any moment.

The mass of earth was lifting—taller than she was, now. It lurched to the side and began dumping itself into the bog.

Yes! Sousuke was doing it!

But she could sense that the waters were past Sousuke's knees now. Rising too quickly.

Vylia urged the current to gently tug Ryon away from Kira. She clung to him even tighter. *Kira, let him go!*

The earth kept rising. Too slowly.

Vylia stood and assumed the wavesinger's stance. Concentrated, then sent a wave of water up through the hole, widening it and splashing a treasure-laden mess into the bog. Then another. And another.

The water she brought up joined its whole and cascaded down in an endless pour.

Vylia fought against panic. She could stop new water from flowing down, but then she wouldn't be able to bring anyone else up. She couldn't do both!

She felt the water level below, up to Sousuke's chest now. Ryon was underwater. Kira took her last breath as she clung to her husband, before it swallowed her.

Vylia clutched the waters around Ryon and Kira and willed them upward. Through the trembling earth. They crashed down next to Tekkyn in a heap.

"Impressive," Zeph murmured behind her. "Perhaps this will all work out nicely after all."

Kira hissed and charged at Zeph like a wild animal.

Vylia swept Kira aside with a wave of water before Zeph could end her, too.

Exhaustion lapped at her. She wasn't a *trai'yeth* or *ko'yeth.* She was just a human elementalist. And she was pushing her limit.

"He's proven himself!" Vylia yelled at Zeph. "Look at this! Isn't it enough for you? Help him!"

"He's got plenty of syn now." Zeph lifted up on his toes as he watched the earth roil and rise.

Vylia struggled to catch her breath. "He can't breathe underwater!"

"Then will you help him with that, daughter?" Zeph tilted his head at her. "You are quite skilled yourself. And it seems you've taken a liking to him." He flashed white teeth. "I regret not seeing the value in you before. You are more than a pawn."

"Is that your way of apologizing for trying to have me murdered, like my parents?" Vylia turned her back on him and searched the waters for Sousuke. "He will never submit to you, nor will I. If you can't see that by now, you're an imbecile."

"Such little faith, my dear." Zeph stepped between Vylia and the rising earth, towering over her. "You are the key to breaking him. And we have only just begun."

Vylia clenched her eyes shut. Tried to ignore him. Where was Sousuke? There!

Floating. Drifting. Unmoving.

The earth stopped its controlled fall into the bog. It collapsed back down into the vault in a torrential heap. The opening was no more.

Vylia roared, and the waters roared with her. Up in a stream through the muddy debris, like a fountain from the deeps. She grasped for Sousuke's form and willed him upward through the current.

She didn't have enough strength for a soft landing. Sousuke's body splashed down into the bog.

Vylia sloshed over and hauled him up onto a patch of land with the help of a surge of water.

Sousuke rolled to his side and hacked up liquid. His eyes flitted open to behold her, radiating a green so intense he no longer looked human.

He pulled a knife from his belt and cut into his forearm. Silver blood oozed out and poured into the mud, turning the bog into a shimmering, congealing mess.

Vylia's stomach flipped. "Why—"

Sousuke slumped, and the knife dropped from his hand.

Vylia bent over him and checked his pulse. She found a beat that matched its time with the silver pumping from the severed veins in his arm.

Her heart squeezed. What should she do? Bind the wound?

She remembered what Sousuke had told her about how dangerous syn was in the Sekoiako village. He must be draining his syn to preserve his sanity.

But how much blood could he afford to lose?

A low, mournful wail sounded behind Vylia. Surely that gut-wrenching noise hadn't come from Kira.

47

KIRALAU

Ryon was gone.

Kira's heart cracked and shattered into a thousand pieces.

I can save them, little minnow.

Kira put her hand over the wound in his chest again. Shook him again. Breathed into him again. Screamed his name again.

But he was gone.

I can bring him back to life. And I can save the other one before he dies.

Pain. The pain in her soul was a hundred times worse than anything she'd felt physically. And compounded—she'd only barely begun to heal from losing Lee.

But I can only bring one back from the dead, so you must act quickly.

"Liar!" Kira snarled at Lillian's tiny whisper. "Only the creator has that power!"

Indeed! It is the creator's power. Deep magic left over from the making of the world, in one of the gardens of creation. I know where one of them is—hidden deep beneath the ocean, not too far from here. Release me, and become my vessel, and I will resurrect him.

Sobs wracked her. She couldn't.

But she also couldn't lose Ryon.

Vylia asked me to save Sousuke, and I did. Look how powerful and invincible he is now.

"You lie," Kira whimpered. "If you had that power, for only one person, you would save it for yourself."

I am desperate, Lillian said. *You have bested me and killed my men.*

Hindered my power. My chosen vessel rejected me. And now, what will you do with me?

Kira hugged Ryon tightly and gritted her teeth. "We will make it so no one will ever find you again! Now leave me alone!"

I know. So that is why I offer you this: my greatest power, which we can take from the creator to bring back your love. And there is a healing power here, in one of my relics, that I can use on your brother. I am your only chance to save them both.

Kira nuzzled into Ryon's shoulder. But his arms didn't lovingly shelter her. He felt cold.

She wailed, her throat raw and voice failing.

Why had the creator allowed this to happen? What had Ryon and Tekkyn done to deserve this? What had *she* done to deserve this?

He'd abandoned them.

Or was the creator even real at all?

Lillian was real. She was here, now, offering life. What did the creator offer?

He couldn't be good. This wasn't good. They'd done everything they were supposed to. Everything right. And this was the reward?

Was she really supposed to let her new husband and last brother die, when a second chance was within her grasp?

The deep magic was the creator's power. If he wouldn't give it, then Kira would take it herself.

She withdrew the keystone from its pouch on her hip. Stared into its cloudy facets.

She didn't know how to use aether. But she focused and concentrated on the aether stone with all her will.

And it vanished.

Light surged through her, like living mist in a hurricane. Bright and churning and eager.

It filled her. Lifted her.

"No!" Vylia cried from the mud beneath her. Out of reach.

Yes, good. Now, quickly, discard the glass-gold and absorb the Malo stone as well.

She felt so powerful. Powerful enough to do *anything.* Perhaps she could save them herself.

But she had no idea how to. What if she directed this storm onto Tekkyn to heal him, and it hastened his death instead?

And she didn't know where the garden of creation was.

Quickly, while I can still save them both. Your brother is dying.

Kira reached into her other pouch and withdrew the opal. Unwrapped the bandana. Dropped the Valinorian brooch into the swampy water below.

"Kira, *no!*"

A wave of water ballooned up from the bog, mounting up and surging toward Kira. Out of the corner of her eye, she saw Vylia directed it with her arms.

The wave stopped before it could touch Kira and fell harmlessly back into the bog with a splash.

I won't let her touch you. Nothing will ever hurt you again.

Kira raised the opal. Its many tangled colors flashed as if in anticipation or excitement.

"Swear you will save them both," she whispered.

I swear it.

Kira willed her newfound power into the Malo stone.

Energy flashed like lightning, blinding Kira as it invaded her. Crawled through her veins and infected her heart. Kindled there, then reached out, turning every fiber of her being.

Then it burst outward, knocking Kira back to splash in the mud.

Dazed, Kira righted herself and looked down. Mud sloughed off of her, somehow not quite sticking to her clothing.

And she was *glowing.*

"Incredible," Lillian breathed. But her voice wasn't in Kira's mind any longer. It was right in front of her.

A snow-white fox with seven tails, much larger than what a fox should be, turned its breathtaking face toward her. Its eyes swam with a dozen colors, just as the Malo stone had. Its eyes were twin water opals with no pupils.

"Well done, my beloved."

Kira couldn't breathe, couldn't speak. She watched the kitsune survey the area, then focus on a glimmer in the mud near Zeph, who bent over Sousuke's barely moving form. Pure water lifted from the bog, extracting itself from mud and algae, and carried Lillian toward them.

Vylia slid into her path, her arms outstretched. Before she could speak, a blast of water knocked Vylia off her feet and tossed her far away to splash down in the distance. Lillian sped after her.

"Stop!" Kira screamed. "Don't hurt her!"

Lillian stopped. Turned.

Kira's blood chilled under the ethereal stare. "P-please don't hurt her."

Lillian remained still apart from her flicking tails. "As you wish." She turned back toward the glimmer in the mud. Clear water bubbled upward, lifting a crystal needle that floated in mid-air toward her. Then she turned to Tekkyn.

Kira stumbled over to watch the white fox hover over Tekkyn on a disc of swirling water, not dirtying her paws on mud or blood.

"Listen with your mind," Lillian said. "No need to strain yourself to speak, my child."

Tekkyn's breathing was shallow and uneven. He blinked at the surreal thing above him, and as Kira anxiously waited, finally, he nodded. "I . . . will."

Lillian smiled and sank the needle into the wound on his chest. Kira watched in a combination of horror and amazement as flesh knit itself together around a small crystalline protrusion.

Tekkyn breathed deep and blinked, his expression clearing from agony to astonishment, to relief, to exhaustion.

Kira leaned closer. "Tekkyn?"

He flashed her a weak grin. "Thanks, Frizz. That . . . was pretty wild."

Kira embraced him, clinging tightly while avoiding the needle. Tears burned her eyes, and she looked up at Lillian with blurred vision. "Thank you. Now Ryon."

Lillian's ears folded back on her head, and she dipped her head, then moved toward Zeph once again.

"My Empress!" Zeph called. He stood with open arms and bowed low.

"My plan to release you has come to fruition, it seems."

Lillian floated more slowly, examining him in her colorful gaze. "I heard the priestesses say it was the emperor's order to remove my mirror from Felix's glass-gold prison. I thank you for this. However, you took no direct action in ensuring my return."

"I thought it best to send you with Vylia, whom I was certain would be your chosen vessel, to allow you to woo her at your own pace." Zeph slowly returned to standing with a smirk. "You know my love for games of chance. Eternal life is so boring without dice to decide the fates, yes? I bet on you, knowing you'd find a way, my lady."

Kira gave Tekkyn's arm a squeeze before moving back to Ryon's still form, close enough now to see Lillian bare the slightest hint of white fangs. "You said you had to save them quickly!" Kira cried.

"Do you possess any water forms?" Lillian asked Zeph. "I require something swift."

Zeph huffed a laugh. "I have a sample of every animal form you could ever desire. Even your favorite extinct leviathan. I have never died."

"It's extinct?" Lillian frowned. "Give me its remains."

Zeph tilted his head. "I can't. It's in my core. But I'll happily give you a ride."

Lillian didn't respond. Not even her tails moved as the colors in her eyes swirled in thought.

"How long did you sit on my throne and let me fester in prison?"

Zeph's eyes grew wide. He sank into a crouch as earth exploded upward between them, sending water everywhere in a white fury.

Then he turned and ran.

Water rose higher from every side. So high that Kira couldn't tell what Zeph was transforming into, nor see its top through the glare of refracted sunlight. So much water that the level of mud sloshed lower, draining the swamp.

It crashed back down faster than Kira could blink.

Frigid wind and a boom of sound hit her like a bull. She curled over Ryon as the wind subsided and water rained down on them.

She dared to look back up.

The water raining down was silver. The entire bog was silver.

Lillian lifted her nose, and a sphere of water lifted in tandem, swirling with hundreds of remains—bones, scales, horns, claws, feathers, fur. She opened her mouth and swallowed it all.

She sat still as Kira looked on in terror. What had she unleashed?

This was a monster, now matter how angelic it looked. She'd killed Zeph like it was nothing. But she'd lied about saving Ryon. She was a demon!

"Fear not, my dear." Lillian grinned. "Everything is all right now."

Her foxlike face morphed, growing fangs and scales and horns. So many horns. Claws. A single tail like a dragon's, but longer. So much longer.

She grew until she blotted out the sun. The largest creature Kira had ever beheld. As large as Navarro's city square. She'd only ever seen illustrations.

A leviathan.

Water raised up all around her. Lifted Kira, Ryon, and Tekkyn, then relics and silvery powder from all around them. Lillian opened her enormous mouth and enclosed them.

Kira refused to let go of Ryon as they settled on an enormous reptilian tongue. Fangs taller than Lysander closed all around them a prison bars.

She squeezed her eyes shut and prepared to be swallowed and digested.

Melodic laughter flitted through her mind. *Do not worry, little one. I will save him as I promised. Now, find the dreamcatcher and hold onto it for me, please. Ensure it is not damaged. I will make haste to the garden in the depths.*

Kira couldn't see anything as the teeth closed, shutting out the light. But she'd had a glimpse of the ancient relics that surrounded them moments before. She felt across the slimy tongue and found the bent twigs bound with what looked like a spider's web beside her.

She clutched it to her chest, lay down beside Ryon, and wept.

What have I done?

Light warped and bled out before her, but what she saw wasn't the inside of a leviathan's mouth. It was a forest . . . No, a house in a forest. No, a homestead.

Ryon. He was older and bearded. But that was unmistakably her husband's smile.

A child. She looked just like Kira, with Granny's eyes. Then another—a boy who resembled Lee with wild hair, but silver like Ryon's. And another girl who looked like Aegwyn.

They jumped and rolled in a pile of yellow and orange leaves, wrestling and laughing. The trees—she knew those trees. Cherry and jomoco and summerfruit in rows, with joyberries growing beneath their shade in a beautiful orchard.

The trees died. Walls of stone were there instead, weathered but standing together as a mighty fortress. Her vision shifted. Some kind of small castle, or perhaps a stronghold or shrine, on the hill overlooking the waterfall. Within it, the keystone. On a pedestal, surrounded by thick glass.

Buildings crumbled. New trees grew. New buildings rose. Now it looked like some sort of school, with students scurrying around with arms full of books. A fountain with the statue of a woman erected in its center, water flowing from her hands.

The woman looked like . . . Kira.

Felix was there. He looked like a man, but with the same shade of green in his eyes. Somehow, Kira knew it was him.

He looked at her.

The vision shattered.

Kira gulped in foul-smelling air, returning abruptly to the leviathan's mouth. She blinked but saw only darkness. Felt Ryon's cold hand beside her.

What was that? Lillian's voice demanded. *Did you use the dreamcatcher?*

"I . . ." Kira's voice sounded hollow between the rows of fangs. Had that been a vision of the future? Then, did that mean . . . Ryon really would live? And they would have their homestead together? And a family?

So then, Lillian must be able to keep her promise to revive him. Somehow.

Tears welled up in Kira once again, but this time, they were tears of relief. She pressed her eyelids shut, willing herself to emblazon every detail of that joyful vision to permanent memory.

"I'm sorry," Kira said. "I didn't mean to."

It's all right, minnow. You are still imbued with the keystone. It must have activated it. Lillian's sigh echoed through her head. *My foolish mistake. A great loss, but . . . perhaps I can find a living sage.*

Her voice turned gentle. *What's most important is that we are together now. I will return your love to life, and you will never want for anything for the rest of your days, my beloved.* Kira felt Lillian's favor press upon her mind like the first cool breeze of autumn. *We will return to my palace in Maqua and reclaim my empire as one.*

48

FELIX

The sun didn't rise wherever Felix was.

He felt like his bones would crumble without the sun. He felt so weak. Weak and . . . mortal.

He'd always been able to make his own light. With any vibrance and color and type of energy that he pleased. But now Phoera had abandoned him. He couldn't even sense it.

Felix pressed his nose into the bars all around him. Solid strands of glass-gold woven like a net, too close together for even a rat to squeeze through. Or a nightjar.

Zeph had thought of everything.

Surely he wouldn't just leave his plaything alone in the dark for so long. Felix was beginning to think Zeph was dead.

Aeo! What good am I to your people if I'm trapped here forever?

Perhaps this was penance. He deserved an eternity in darkness for all of his crimes. Sousuke didn't know the majority of it. Only what had made it out in public and written in the history scrolls.

His heart squeezed at the thought of the half-mortal boy. *His* boy. Sousuke was so much more like Felix than Zeph. He may have the body of a Terruthian, but his blood was as fiery as any Phoeran.

He was just like Felix before he'd fallen. Corrupted by power. Crowned himself as his own god, and Lillian his goddess.

No. Sousuke was stronger. Defiant against evil, even his own evil. Especially his own.

Aeo, please be with him.

Curse that boy for reawakening his desire for family. The walls Felix had built around his solitary heart had been impenetrable for centuries. Now his suffering would be multiplied as he sat here and rotted.

Alone.

How long would his sanity last?

But what good would Felix be if he were free without his element, anyway? He was nothing but a fox. A dark fox with a mind and the ability to speak.

And enough memories to haunt him for eternity.

THE STORY CONTINUES
IN THE KATROSI REVOLUTION BOOK 4: ELDERSOUL

ACKNOWLEDGMENTS

Hoo boy, it was a long wait for this book! To all of my readers who hung in there and encouraged me along the way, thank you.

To Angela, who made me realize this wasn't the final book—it needed to be whacked in half and released as two different books . . . you were right. Hopefully the ending, which was originally intended to be the mid-point of a single conclusionary story, won't result in book burning. I'm so sorry y'all waited so long only for me to deliver a brutal cliffhanger. Trust me. The darkest night comes before the dawn.

Angela, your friendship means so much to me. I can't thank you enough for everything you've done for me and with me over the years. We're in cahoots.

To my husband, for your evergreen support and unconditional love, for your listening ear and solutions to all of my creative puzzles, thank you!

To my firstborn, for all of your creative ideas and patience with your wild mama, thank you. Your joy and humor are invigorating. And to our new little one who listens and Riverdances at 5AM. You are a miracle, and you are evidence of the God who defied science to knit you together and give our family new life.

To the Christian speculative writing community, for never letting me feel alone.

To my beta readers: RJ, for your lively passion, and for always making me laugh and pushing me to be a better writer; Mackenzie, for your bubbling joy and beautifully honest perspective and encouragement; Kimberly, for your priceless wisdom and always helpful critiques; and Desirae, for your eyes that are even sharper than your blade. Thank you so much for your time and input. I cherish all of your thoughts, and I couldn't do it without y'all!

To my editor, Sarah, for all of your expertise, kindness, and patience with me during this pregnancy. I'm so grateful for you, sister.

To my family and friends, for your abundant encouragement, even when (and especially when) my confidence fails.

And to the God of lands above and below. Thank you for holding my heart and creating with me. Holy, holy, holy is the Lord God Almighty, who was and is and is to come. With all creation I sing praise to the King of Kings. You are my everything, and I adore you.

AUTHOR BIOGRAPHY

Award-winning sci-fi/fantasy author Jamie Foley loves strategy games and homesteading. She's terrified of red wasps and uses them for lightsaber training. When she's not working as the typesetter for Enclave Publishing or The Christian Writers Institute, or being a suspicious monarch at Fayette Press, she's probably drawing maps to Cair Paravel. Her husband is her manly muse and amateur theologian. They live between the Texas Hill Country and the family cattle ranch, where their hyperactive spawnlings and wolfpack roam.

Get a free short story when you sign up for Jamie's email newsletter at www. jamiefoley.com/newsletter. You'll get behind-the-scenes goodies, giveaways, and exclusive opportunities like first dibs at joining Jamie's beta team, ARC review crew, and cover reveal ninja squad.

@jamiesfoley
www.jamiefoley.com

If you enjoy *The Katrosi Revolution*,
you'll probably love these other clean fantasy series:

A **DRAGON** BY
ANY OTHER NAME

THE
STONES OF TERRENE

CAPTIVE & CROWNED

This time, beauty is the beast. And she wants prince charming dead.

Welcome to Terrene— where dragons exist, the past haunts, and magic is no myth. Welcome aboard the Sapphire.

The half-dragon King of Torva needs a queen, but the human bride he has captured may prove to be more trouble than she's worth.